RIORDAN'S REVENGE

BODY COUNT - BOOK 3

Jolie Vines

WWW.JOLIEVINES.COM

Editing by Emmy Ellis at Studio ENP.

Proofreading by Lori Parks and Patricia Brown.

Cover design - Natasha Snow https://natashasnow.com/

Alternate skull cover design: Qamber Designs Media.

Cover photography by Wander Aguair.

Cover model: Kirin S.

Formatting by Cleo Moran / Devoted Pages Designs.

Claim your man, wild girl.

BODY COUNT

JOLIE VINES

READER NOTE

Dear reader,

Here we go with part three of our wild ride of a dark romance murder mystery! We get another complete romance plus all the answers. This story brings an epic end to the Body Count series.

Not read the previous two yet? Jump back and start with Arran's Obsession.

The secret code

Throughout the three books, there's a sneaky extra clue to the killer. Want to work it out? Flip the page to find out how.

The audiobooks

Love to listen? The audiobooks are multi-cast with Allie Rose, Shane East, Lucas Webley, and Zara Hampton-Brown.

Everyone ready? Let's get dirty with Riordan and Cassie.

Love, Jolie

THE SECRET CODE

Ready to work out your clue?

In each Body Count book, one character will give another a four-digit code. Find all three of the codes then turn them into words using your phone's alphanumeric keypad.

You may wish to read on until you've found the code in this book then return to this page.

The codes are in order of the series (code one is in Arran's Obsession, code two is Connor's Claim, code three is in Riordan's Revenge). The numbers are in order.

As an example, if the code was 439, the 4 could be G, H, or I. So to get the answer, which for this example is 'HEY', you have to work through the possible combinations.

Find the codes then use the keypad to get sleuthing.

If you need an extra clue, it's two words that fit the following format:

_ _ _ _ _ _ _ ' _   _ _ _ _

Need the answer? It's at the very end of the acknowledgements.

Happy clue-solving!

TRIGGER WARNINGS

Many of the warnings from Arran's Obsession still apply. (may contain spoilers):

Kidnap

Serial killer

Death and murder

Injury

Spanking and edging

Teetering on the edge of a cliff

Restraints used in sex

Tracking (both hero and heroine)

Depiction of torture

Somnophilia

Morally grey heroine

Graphic violence against women (attempted murder)

Depiction of rape (off screen, brief, not heroine)

BLURB

I was a walking red flag, but that skeleton-masked man was mine.

I always knew I was different—my obsession with catching Deadwater's murderer with my Skeleton Girls Detective Agency, my hunger to hunt predators with my steel sharp and my manicure perfect.

And now, my dangerous instalove for the skeleton crew's new recruit.

Riordan, with his tousled dark hair and striking green eyes, would be wise to run far from me. But it was infatuation at first sight, and there's nothing I won't do to keep him close. Even if it means risking everything.

Yet love isn't simple for someone like me. If Riordan dared to love me back, the scars of my past could surface, and in the chaos, I might become his greatest threat. Until then, I'm ready to help him take down his enemies, to share his battle and make Riordan's revenge my own.

But the murderer still haunts the city, and whatever happiness we find together is under threat.

How can I keep us both safe when the next name on the killer's list is mine?

***

Riordan's Revenge is the final installment of the *Body Count* dark romance, murder mystery series that shot to #1 on Amazon in the US and Canada and has become an international bestseller. The Skeleton Girls Detective Agency's guessing game concludes in this thrilling finale of the trilogy.

PLAYLIST

Girls Like You by The Naked and Famous
Cola by Camelphat and Elderbrook
Midnight City by M83
Judith by A Perfect Circle

Closer by Nine Inch Nails
i like the way you kiss me by Artemas
I Can Fix Him (No Really I Can) by Taylor Swift
Come Through by Rui + Voluptuöus

On Your Knees by Ex-Habit
Rush by Dutch Melrose & benny mayne
Take Me Back to Eden by Sleep Token
The Death of Peace of Mind by Bad Omens

Songlist curated by Jolie Vines Reader Group on
Facebook. You deliciously sultry people.

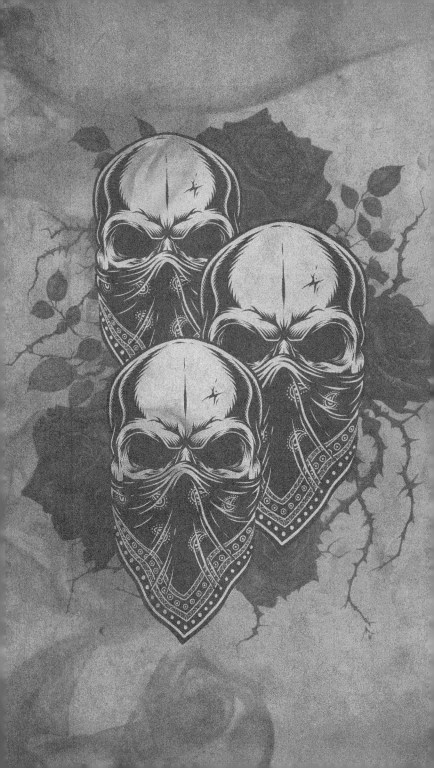

1

Riordan

The furious thrum of wheels on the road beneath my captor's car mirrored the beat of my heart. In the darkness of the back seat, I lay paralysed, conscious but unable to move, whatever drug I'd been dosed with in full effect.

The plush leather under my cheek told me the vehicle was high-end. The pace said I was being delivered somewhere with urgency.

Focusing, I willed my eyes to open. My fingers to twitch. *Nothing.*

Anger flashed inside me like lightning.

I'd joined the skeleton crew knowing what I was getting myself into, and now I was in the hands of a rival gang without the control of my body to fight back.

I'd expected to die from my career change, but not yet.

Trapped with my thoughts, I fought for logic. If they'd wanted me dead, I wouldn't have been kidnapped to be locked up and used as collateral.

Except that didn't make sense.

I wasn't important enough in the chain of command of Arran's crew. I was a new recruit, not trusted to do anything beyond security and grunt work. Realisation dawned, and I groaned inwardly. No, for fuck's sake, I was wrong. This was about my sister. Genevieve was Arran's girlfriend, so torturing her brother made perfect sense.

Through me, they could control her.

Which meant I was in for a world of pain.

The car slowed, my driver silent as we turned off a fast road, possibly a motorway, and entered a twisting country lane. I had no clue how long we'd been travelling, but it felt like hours, which either put us in the Midlands of England if we'd gone south, or north to the Highlands of Scotland. I couldn't call it.

After a while, the car slowed and idled, and the driver rattled something and a clink outside followed. A remote gate, I guessed. We passed through, and the car swept around another road. At last, the smooth running sound changed to gravel. A car park.

This should've been my chance. As a prisoner, my opportunities for escape were in moments of transit when they took me from one place to another. I was almost certain that I wasn't handcuffed, which meant they trusted in the drug.

My breathing quickened, and I tried to force my body to wake. It didn't respond. I fucking yelled in silent frustration.

If I couldn't will my limbs to move, I'd be caged. Tortured, perhaps. Maybe they'd kill me if they couldn't get what they wanted from Arran.

We came to a halt, and the engine cut out, silence settling with ominous tension. I listened hard to clue myself in to where I was. Then a mutter from the driver flipped my world upside down again.

"Oh fuck de fuck. I've really done it this time."

Christ. I exhaled in a rush of relief. I knew that voice. *Cassie.* What the absolute fuck?

She popped the door, and another voice came from outside. A woman's, though I couldn't make out anything in her greeting to Cassie except her accent. She was Scottish, too, which gave me a further clue to the direction we'd taken. Her tone was soft. Gentle. As if she knew Cassie. Abruptly, the vibe changed.

"Is that a body?" the other woman gasped.

Cassie's voice held a strange tension. "I need help getting him into the house."

"Sin's on his way down," her friend replied. "Oh, he's here."

Another set of footsteps crunched the gravel, and a male voice entered the chat, rumbling an affectionate greeting to Cassie before his attention came to me. "Is he dead?"

"No, just knocked out."

"Who hurt him?"

I strained to listen. Try as I might, I couldn't remember the moments before I'd been attacked. I'd been at work at the warehouse but after that I drew a blank. If I'd been rushed, I couldn't recall the hit.

Cassie's reply socked me in the gut.

"I did."

A pause followed. Her male friend choked. "What the fuck, Cass? Who is he?"

"His name's Riordan."

"Which tells me nothing. Is he dangerous? Why the fuck didn't ye cuff him?"

"I'll explain everything. Can ye bring him inside? Be gentle with him. He's important to me."

Her friend grumbled a complaint but came to my door, the cool night air brushing over me where two meaty hands pulled my lifeless body into a fireman's lift.

"Heavy fucker," the man complained.

I swung under his rolling gait, then we reached a building, and my eyelids cracked open enough for me to witness the stone steps he climbed turn into a marble-floored entrance.

I stared, trying to work out where the hell I'd been taken. Somewhere fancy. My narrow glimpse reminded me of the stately homes my mother would take us to for family days out. Centuries-old stonework and echoing rooms. Elaborately framed doorways and oil paintings on the walls.

My captor, because I was an idiot to think anything less, jogged upstairs with me, my head bouncing off his broad back, then we entered a room and I was set down on a sofa. By luck, my eyes stayed open enough so I could take in the three people with me. The woman, braided hair, perhaps in her mid-thirties, snapped on lamps then settled into an armchair, her gaze on a pacing Cassie who was still in the same sequined black dress as last night. Then to the huge Scotsman who'd carried me. I was a big man, but he was a beast, not that I could've swung for him if I tried.

The woman reached for the man's hand, and they swapped a worried look. They centred on Cassie, though this attention gave me nothing on who they might be.

My working theory? For all Cassie had pretended to be Arran's friend, she was something else. Working for a rival, probably. Which was entirely fucked up because

I knew he cared about her. I'd got entirely the wrong impression as well.

From the first moment of seeing Cassie, I'd wanted her. Attraction had smacked me down, enough for me to realise I'd needed to push her away. I'd faked a sex act with another woman to deter her interest and cut off mine.

Thank fuck I'd never kissed her. The regret hit a strange void inside me.

The big guy caught her wrist as she passed and slowed her pacing. "Sit, Cassiopeia. Tell us what the fuck is going on."

She eyed him but dutifully dropped into a seat.

Then she stared at her hands.

The woman tried this time, her tone gentle. "Ye never mentioned a boyfriend. Is that what he is?"

"He's... It's hard to explain."

"Is he a member of Arran's crew?" she pressed.

At Cassie's tiny nod, the man swore then abruptly left the room.

Cassie watched him go. "He isn't my boyfriend, not exactly, but he is mine."

Hers? My heart thumped out of time.

"You're going to have to walk me through that," the woman said.

Cassie sighed. "He has green eyes."

"Do we think that's a good enough reason to kidnap someone?"

Crumpling down in the chair, Cassie ground her fists into her cheekbones. "Fine, no, it isn't. But I also knew he was mine from the first time I saw him. Isn't that how ye felt with Da?"

Da, as in Dad?

They were her parents?

There was a passing resemblance to the huge man—black hair and blue eyes—but not to the woman. She was short, like Cassie, but that was where the similarities ended. In her face shape and mannerisms, there was nothing of Cassie, nor did she seem old enough to be her mother, but that didn't mean much.

A rush of memories hit me. Cassie and I had shared a meal in her room at the warehouse after I'd hunted her down to challenge her on why she'd been tinkering with my bike. I'd caught her putting a tracking device on it, and at the time, I'd laughed it off. I'd reasoned away why she might be doing it. Arran or Shade keeping tabs on me, most likely. I'd challenged her, and she'd shared her dinner with me. I'd been fucking charmed by her cute conversation.

A conversation in which she'd told me her mother was dead. Funny that, as the dead appeared to have risen.

The scale of Cassiopeia Archer's lies grew.

The door clicked, and her father returned with a roll of silver tape in his hands. He knelt beside me and tugged my hands free then drew out a length of tape with a rush of tearing adhesive.

Cassie's eyes widened. "Is that necessary?"

Her father gave a gruff, "Aye, it is."

Her mother raised a hand. "I just want to get a few things straightened out. This man, Riordan, is that right? You're calling him yours. Does he share the sentiment?"

No, I fucking didn't.

Cassie gave a sorrowful shake of her head.

"And he's unconscious because?"

"I knocked him out a little bit."

Her mother took a steadying breath. "I see. Do ye understand he might be upset when he wakes?"

With a sound of frustration, Cassie nodded again. Her mother inclined her head at the big guy, and he taped my wrists together, taking care to be thorough. Then he moved to my ankles, securing those as well over my jeans.

I focused on breathing. On the furious race of my heart.

Then Cassie spoke again. "I know what you're saying. But I also want ye to think back on how ye began. Or Camden and Breeze. He bought her in an auction. None of ye had conventional starts to your relationships. I took him because I wanted him but also because it was necessary. I'll make it good. Riordan is mine. Whether he knows it yet or not."

I knew the fucking opposite. She was insane for what she'd done.

None of that explained the strange emotion that leapt in my chest at her claim. She'd said *mine*. The word found an empty part of my soul and made a nest there.

In that conversation in her room, she'd asked me didn't everyone want to be wanted? It had stuck with me. I'd thought about it way too often.

Cassie, too. Every inch of her.

I was a fool.

I wasn't hers, and who knew how far she'd go if she'd been willing to do this. The moment the drug wore off, I'd fight for my life to get out of here.

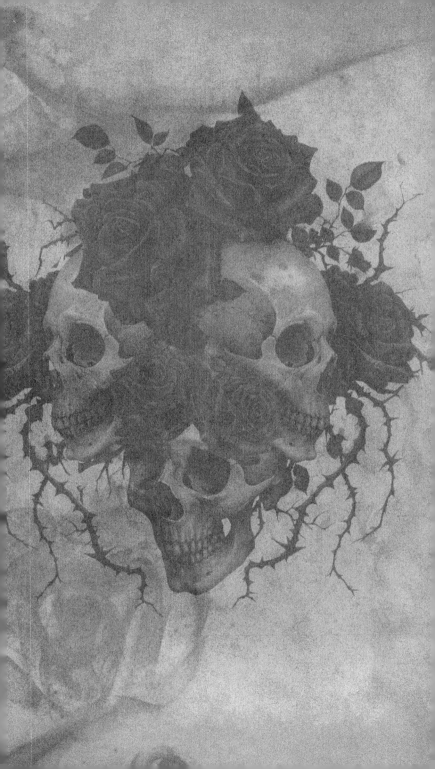

2

Cassie

Sin stared then huffed a strangled laugh. Lottie brushed her hands over her lap.

"Well," she started.

The apartment door burst open, and a small, dark-haired missile of a boy dashed inside. "Cassie!" He threw himself at me.

I caught Magnus, Sin and Lottie's youngest, in a hug. "Oh no! It's a Mag attack."

In his superhero jammies, the six-year-old knelt on my lap and put both hands to my cheeks, commanding my attention. "You've been gone for ages."

"Did ye miss me?"

He stuck out his tongue, then his gaze slid to the constrained Riordan. Coming back to me, he cocked his head, and I braced myself for an awkward question over why I had a stranger tied up on my couch.

"Can ye drive me to school?"

Ah, man, kids. "Not today, but I'll be here when ye get home."

The boy pouted.

Sin muttered about the time then collected his son from my lap. Magnus yelled in protest, so Lottie took over and carried him out, a look returning my way to say our conversation wasn't done.

Left alone with me, Sin held his gaze on mine. "We have to get the kids ready. Do I need to be worried? Any more than I already am, I mean."

He didn't specify about what, but it wasn't necessary. I'd turned up with a body at the crack of dawn and with no good explanation beyond my wild claim. He needed to know if I was running from something.

Slowly, I inclined my head, fear tightening my belly.

He gave a short nod. "Bad timing. Or maybe good. The older kids are at camp, and nearly everyone else is away."

My four brothers, their wives, and a whole army of kids lived in our mansion. It was good that they weren't here.

A yawn overtook me. "Can you activate security then we'll talk later? I need to call Arran because of what I did." I flicked my fingers at a still slumbering Riordan. "But first I need sleep. Give me a few hours?"

"I can't protect ye if I don't know the full story."

"Why do ye think I brought him?"

Sin muttered about hot-headed women then left me to lock my door.

For a moment, I drooped against the frame. It was after seven, and the first tendrils of daylight filtered into my apartment. An apartment which held what would be a very pissed-off Riordan once he woke. Maybe it was better that Sin had trussed him up with tape. That way, he wouldn't be able to escape until he'd heard me out.

With a sigh, I kicked off my shoes and shucked my jacket. Then I knelt next to Riordan on the sofa and examined his biker boots. I'd seen him take them off once previously and figured out the buckles, dropping both to the floor with heavy thuds, the tape just out of the way.

"I'm sorry if I scared ye," I said as I worked. Being busy with my hands meant I didn't have to meet his eye. "I don't know if you can hear me, but I promise no harm will come to ye. Not from me and not from my family. You're completely safe here. I don't know how long you'll be unconscious for, and I don't want to ring Shade to ask. Not until I've spoken to Arran, and I'll wait until you're awake to do that." Another yawn overtook me, and exhaustion threatened my consciousness. "I'll explain everything soon."

Climbing onto the sofa, I curled around his feet like a kitten. Then I let sleep claim me, secure in the knowledge I'd managed to get us both to safety.

Even if Riordan had no idea from what.

A few hours later, I woke, sensing someone's focus burning into me.

I blinked and found Riordan's furious eyes trained on mine.

"Oh, hi. Awake?" I stretched out my limbs and unfurled myself.

He didn't answer, instead, slowly wriggling upright on

the sofa cushions. His movements were slow and clumsy, and guilt oozed cold in my veins.

"I don't know if you heard anything I said earlier," I began.

"I heard."

His gruff voice was music to my ears. His brown hair fell in his eyes, and I resisted the urge to reach out and brush it aside. With his cut jawline and protective-German-Shepherd energy, Riordan was too pretty. Which was a huge part of the problem I had with the man.

Well, aside from kidnapping him.

I needed to make a better impression. Spreading out my hands, I gestured around us. "Welcome to my home. It's called the Great House, and we're in the Cairngorms National Park. I live here with my family."

"You told me your mother was dead and your father a people trafficker." Riordan took in the room, probably looking for exits if he had any sense.

"All that's true."

"Then the two people in here earlier were figments of my imagination."

It took me a second to work out what he meant. "Oh, no. That's Sin and Lottie. My brother and his wife. They raised me from the age of six, and I call them my parents sometimes. They have their own kids, though."

Riordan finally brought his attention back to me, hostility in his hard gaze and mistrust as deep as Deadwater's river. "What am I doing here?"

I pulled a face. "I needed to leave the warehouse in a hurry and I got scared. No excuse, but I wanted to take ye with me."

His eyes widened. "So you just did? You drugged me."

"I know, and I'm really sorry. I'll never do it again. I can be impulsive, and it seemed like a good idea at the time."

He gave a snarl of incredulity. "Are you kidding? How the hell did you even get me out of the building? Scratch that, why am I here? What's going to happen to me?"

"You're here because you're mine. I can't explain any better than that, but I will call Arran so he knows where ye are. There's something else I need to tell everyone as well. Let me get Sin and Lottie back first so I don't need to repeat myself."

I found my phone in my pocket and sent a text. In under a minute, my brother thumped on my door, and I let him in.

"No Lottie?"

He glowered at Riordan but answered me. "Should be along in a minute. She's feeling under the weather."

Internally, I fist-pumped. My sister-in-law had paused in having babies once Magnus was born so she could go to university and get a midwife's degree. The minute she graduated, I knew the two of them would get on with baby number five.

Now probably wasn't the time to celebrate.

"Your boy's awake, then." Sin gave a head tilt to Riordan.

He got an equally dark glare in return.

I ushered my brother to a seat then video called Arran, keeping the screen on me.

He picked up. "Cassie. Finally returning my calls. Is there a reason Manny spotted you on the CCTV smuggling one of my crew out of the building?"

I'd known Arran since I was a child and considered him family. A relationship which now needed mending after I'd thoroughly abused his hospitality.

My confidence wobbled.

With my gaze down, I launched into my story. "Last night, I had to leave the warehouse in a rush. Shade left his knockout kit in your office, and I borrowed it."

On the screen, Arran narrowed his eyes. "How did you get into my office?"

I rummaged in my bag and produced a set of keys. Jangled them. "Ye gave us these, remember?"

We were investors in Arran's warehouse, myself included.

A muscle ticked in his jaw. "What was Will doing with you?"

Will was the security guard I'd paid to carry Riordan. "Dude took a bribe before I even finished the sentence. He also sneaks off duty to vape and leaves the back door unguarded. You need to kick his arse to the kerb. I've done ye a favour in exposing him."

Arran just stared. I pressed on.

"That's confession number one. The second is a bit more complicated."

I panned the camera around, showing him the man on my sofa.

"You knocked out my new recruit using the stolen drugs then bribed my guard to kidnap him?"

Why was everyone so hung up on that? "Yes, but he's awake now."

"Right," he drawled. "Is he okay?"

"Unharmed, though fucking confused," Riordan reported back.

Sin spoke up. "Arran, tell me about your employee."

"Thought I spotted you there, Sinclair. Any clue what's happening?"

"None. Tell me what I need to know."

Arran grumbled but answered. "Riordan's Gen's brother. Works hard. What are you asking?"

"Cassie claimed him. Need to know if he's good enough."

"She claimed him?"

Riordan's lips parted. A wash of panic chilled me, and I held up a hand. The last thing I wanted was to scare him off. I'd called him mine, but if everyone else did, too, it could be a bit much.

"There's a reason I acted like an insane person. Something else I need to tell everyone that might help explain my actions." From my pocket, I pulled a white piece of paper. "This showed up in my room last night."

I put it on my lap and sent a photo to Arran, then passed it to my brother.

Arran squinted at his phone. "What am I looking at?"

My heart beat erratically. Sometimes, I did thoughtless things. Like driving too fast because I was hurt and angry. Or moving three hours south to live above a brothel because of the need to find myself. Drugging and kidnapping a man was definitely up there with my best.

Then again, it had been a long time since anyone had threatened my life.

"A message from Deadwater's serial killer telling me I'm next."

3

Riordan

*O*n what was probably the strangest day of my life, several facts formed from one short conversation.

First, that both Arran and Sin, Cassie's brother/father, had accepted her so-called claiming of me with barely a blink of an eye.

Second, that I'd heard rumours of Shade, the skeleton crew's enforcer, doing the same with Everly and everyone taking it as fact.

Third, that the moment Cassie informed us of the threat against her, my focus shifted from my own concerns to hers.

What the hell was up with that?

"Read me the note," I demanded.

Cassie's cheeks pinkened. She took the piece of paper back from her brother, who leapt up to stalk to the window, and read it. "Meet me on the river path at five. I need to get you alone." Her gaze rose to mine. "It's signed with your name."

Shock stole another portion of my anger. "I didn't write that."

"I know. That's the reason I ran. And why I took ye with me."

She peeked at me with such an expression of regret and something closing in on fear that my stomach clenched.

Her brother gestured between us. "Catch me up. I'm missing the connection to that being a threat."

Arran obliged. "You're aware that Alisha, a key member of my crew, was murdered. She was the fourth woman killed in Deadwater in the space of a few months, and the murderer lured her away by use of a note. It claimed to be from Convict, who she had an emotional connection to. The last time any of us saw her was with a smile on her face at the prospect of meeting up with him."

Sin swore. Both his meaty hands were bunched into fists. Mine were, too, I realised, held in front of me with my wrists taped.

He snarled a question. "Where's that note now? Is it the same handwriting?"

Cassie replied, "Alisha told one of the dancers about it, but Dixie never saw the note herself, so she told me. It hasn't been found. Either way, I wasn't taking any chances. I knew what it was and I took action."

Her brother growled out something about how he'd end anyone who threatened his family, then questioned Arran on all that was happening to find the killer.

The media storm, the hapless police, the dead ends of suspects they'd looked at.

I watched Cassie, my emotions at war with themselves but concern winning, despite my better judgement. What she'd done to me was unforgivable, but I could maybe understand it. She'd been threatened. The cute-as-fuck

Scottish lass with her abundant black curls and curious mind had received a death threat. Dread added to my concern. Once, I'd nicknamed her wild girl. Better wild than dead.

Her gaze lifted and locked on to mine.

A zap of electricity hit at the eye contact. I slow blinked to reject it.

She gave me a lopsided, rueful smile. "I really am sorry. I'll cut that tape now. I forgot it was there."

Her brother paused his discussion with Arran. "Not yet."

Cassie raised an eyebrow at him.

"I'll show him how to free himself in case it happens again. If he's a target in the same way ye are, it could prove useful."

A target? The drug Cassie had used on me was still affecting my brain, and my memories were cloudy. I'd struggled to remember the previous evening, but it resolved in a quick succession of scenes. I'd been working as security in the brothel. Moniqua, who I'd once slept with, though I had no memory of the night, had come to me and asked for my help. She'd told me something that was just on the edge of my brain. Christ, what was it?

My pulse quickened. A rival gang had approached her. She'd been afraid. It was important, but why?

Her words returned. I sat forward.

"Bronson is using sedatives."

Everyone went quiet.

"Explain," Arran ordered.

I closed my eyes to focus in on what I knew. "Last night, a woman came to me and told me that Red from the Four Milers is trying to get her to work in his strip club. He put pressure on Moniqua, but she refused. She then told me his second-in-command uses sedatives on women, and Red threatened to send him after her next. She said she was scared."

A crash came down the line, and I imagined Arran slamming his fist on his desk.

"The killer used sedatives on some of his victims. It was in the post-mortem results," he said, presumably for Sin's benefit.

I knew that, but how?

I returned my gaze to Cassie, more memories creeping back. I'd tried to put her off me by pretending to be into Moniqua. Then, guilt-ridden, I'd gone to her room to look for her. She had a detective's wall of the killings, including that clue written on a sheet of paper pinned up against a map of Deadwater, string linking the sites the murder victims had been found. I'd read it right before her injection knocked me out. She must have been lying in wait, maybe thinking I was the killer.

Fuck, what a mess.

Voices sounded at the other end of the phone, Shade's tones adding to Arran's. He'd summoned his enforcer. Then silence followed as if Arran had muted the call.

Cassie's brother reached out a long arm to cup her shoulder in a show of reassurance. Distracted, and still staring at the note, she squeezed his fingers.

For some reason, that gesture socked me in the gut.

So fucking typical of me to be floored by a father figure providing comfort.

The leader of the skeleton crew came back on the line. "That was valuable intelligence, Riordan. After Alisha's death, we've been unable to bring the action I'd planned against Red and his people. Not with camera crews outside and reporters blaming the brothel for attracting a predator to the city. This is exactly what we needed to act."

"What are you going to do?" I asked.

"We'll let you know when it's over." Movement and voices crowded his on the open line. Arran was leaping to work, using the information I'd given him.

I struggled forward, life returning to my limbs. "I want to be a part of it. I'll come back."

"No. Stay and guard Cassie. Whoever wrote that note was using you to get to her. I need you to keep her safe, yourself, too."

Safe with the woman who'd abducted me? What a fucking joke. I tried again. "How am I supposed to do that? I've got no transport. No weapon. Nothing beyond the clothes on my back."

"Noted. Leave that with me." Arran spoke again to whoever was in his office then hung up.

Cassie's brother grabbed her hand and tugged her from the room, addressing her in low and urgent tones. Her one-word answers were far more muted.

Her brother returned alone.

He took the opposite seat to mine. "I need to know your intentions towards my sister."

"She fucking kidnapped me. My intentions are to get the hell away from her."

"You're not going to do that. Arran ordered ye to stay, and I'm reinforcing that. Not for his sake, but for Cassie's. Tomorrow, my wife and I will be leaving in the morning and staying away overnight. The rest of my family are elsewhere, and we've made arrangements for the three kids who aren't at camp to stay with friends. I'm going to pull Struan back, that's our older brother, but I can't be sure when he'll arrive. The one thing I am certain of is Cassie will not be left alone."

I worked through his problem. I shouldn't give a fuck, but I couldn't help myself. "You leaving here means Cassie would be unprotected. Tell me why I should care."

His gaze shifted over me like he was sizing me up. My biceps under my skeleton crew black t-shirt. My frame. I sat taller as if I needed to prove my worth.

"Because she's Cassie," he replied simply. "Arran said you're a hard worker. Can ye fight?"

A scowl formed on my lips. "I spent the past seven years working construction then one month in a gang. Unless you count the times I had to knock back my drunken stepfather, no, I have no experience of fighting beyond taking care of myself. But that's beside the point."

He palmed his chin, thinking. "Struan can help with that. Cassie's good with a blade and is a decent shot, but at close range, her size and strength are a disadvantage."

"For fuck's sake. You're talking about a woman who drugged me to bring me here. Why does no one else think what she did is messed up?"

"We do. We also respect her choices."

"I'm not hers to choose. I'm also not her fucking boyfriend and I have no interest in staying here to play bodyguard."

He leaned forward so his forearms were on his knees, and his expression morphed to something dark and deadly. I'd seen the same shift in his sister when she'd tortured a man in the warehouse's basement. Then, I'd been unexpectedly turned on. Her brother bringing that same energy chilled me.

"A killer threatened my sister by pretending to be ye. I get your concerns, but that's pride talking. Get over it. There is no other priority than her safety. Do ye hear me? Let's make one thing clear. Hurt her, or allow her to be hurt, and I'll end ye."

I gave a slow nod in reply. Anything else would be risking my neck.

Cassie's unique form of crazy obviously ran in the family.

"Glad we understand each other. If it's your ego you're worried about, our brother Jamieson's girl had to spring him from prison. My lass left her island to hunt me down. Sometimes, women make the show of strength, so fucking deal with it. Now, sit up straight and raise your hands above your head. Get your elbows close together so there's tension on the tape, then you're going to bring your hands down quickly so your elbows go either side of your ribs."

Sin acted out slashing his wrists down and breaking them apart. "One swift action and it'll shred right through that. Good practice if it happens to ye again."

Incredulous, I followed orders and got into position, enough strength returned to my muscles to comply.

It didn't feel like this would work, but I had to get free. I needed to take a piss. To work out how to get out of here. To call...

Would anyone be worried about me?

Genevieve would hear from Arran that I was away from the warehouse. She'd tell Everly, my other sister, who now knew that we shared a father, a secret I'd carried for years. Neither of them would be alarmed. They were friends with Cassie, the three women thick as thieves. It would probably amuse them to hear what she did.

Shades of embarrassment threatened my mood further. I'd been captured by a five-foot-nothing lass, but only because she'd been able to knock me out. I wasn't in any real danger from her.

But she was. Someone had threatened her.

"Fucking hell," I growled out. Then with a savage downwards slash of my hands, broke the tape that held me.

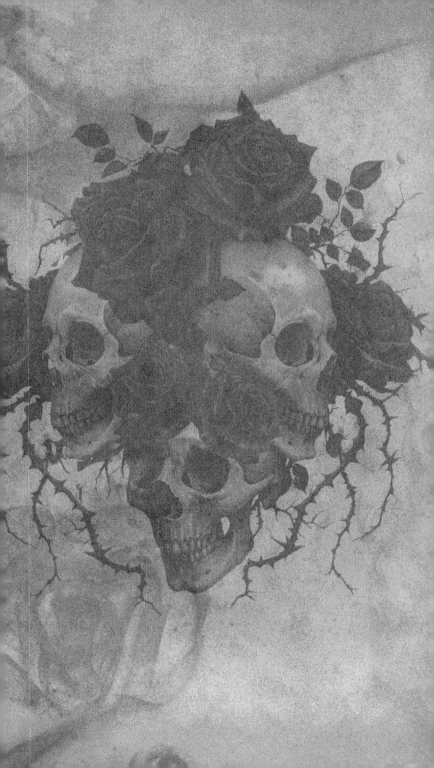

4

Cassie

*L*ottie's quiet guidance made the backdrop for us preparing dinner. She loved to cook, I just liked being close to her. We were both happy.

After I'd slept the morning away, and our family meeting had ended, the kids had returned from school. I'd received hugs and heard their stories, all while keeping an eye out for Riordan as Sin took him around our property, giving him a tour of the security features.

The gate. The perimeter fencing. The one place where a footpath led through a broken wall, cameras all over it to capture anyone using the intended easy access point. Our little trap for any trespassers.

On their drive out to the far reaches of our estate, I'd held my breath. There was nothing stopping him from doing a runner. To be honest, I wouldn't blame him. That didn't change the urgency which had directed my act of stealing him away, or the need for him to come back.

My heart had restarted when they returned to the house, and the two of them were now sequestered away in the great hall.

"Cassie, are ye listening?"

I blinked and focused on Lottie's concerned face. Then I hung my head. "No. Sorry. I was away with the fairies."

Patient indulgence tugged at her lips. She dusted her fingers on her cute floral apron and joined me at the tall stools on the breakfast island. She claimed my hands in hers.

"Repeat after me. We do not kidnap people we like."

I rolled my eyes but dutifully repeated the words.

Lottie inclined her head. "The best way to share our feelings is to talk about them."

Again, I copied her.

"Good. Now let's combine those."

I tried it out. "Kidnapping is the best way to show a man you love him."

Her mouth fell open. I grinned at the reaction, nothing so fun as shocking my family.

Behind me, someone cleared their throat.

Oh *fuck*.

Wincing, I turned around. Riordan leaned on the kitchen doorframe, tall, dark, delicious, and with an expression telling me he'd heard exactly what I'd said. Goddamn it.

"Cassie. Your brother tells me you can access the house camera feeds on your phone. Do they work?"

I collected my phone from the counter, unlocked it, and opened the app with our alert system and camera views. Then I held it up for him to see.

He prowled closer to check and gave a short nod of acknowledgement.

"Want me to put it on your phone?" I offered.

"Don't go giving access to just anyone. That's hardly safe," he chided.

"You're not just anyone."

Riordan's serious gaze held mine for a beat, and he poked his tongue into his cheek. "Right. I forgot that for a moment of insanity. Silly me."

He stalked away. I collapsed onto the work surface and buried my face in my hands.

"Seriously, is that how he heard the first I love you?"

Lottie rubbed my back. "Don't worry. He'll know it was a joke." A pause followed, and her tone changed. "It was a joke, right?"

"I don't know. Probably? It is if I'm to believe Elsa from *Frozen* who says I can't marry a man I just met." From my pit of misery, I only lifted my head when the silence became too great to bear.

Lottie examined me for several seconds. "Should I be concerned?"

"About my mental health? Ye tell me."

"There's been some big events in your life recently, and it would be understandable if they'd rattled ye, even without that threat. It could be a good idea to go over the write-ups from your sessions with Doctor Hillier."

As a teenager, I'd seen a therapist who'd helped me handle the overwhelming feelings that plagued me every day. She'd told me I had post-traumatic stress disorder alongside attachment issues. I had techniques to manage my triggers and low points, but facing that shite felt like such a drag.

I groaned and pulled a face. "Ye steal one man and everyone thinks you're crazy."

"I never said that. What I mean is your tough time at college led to the abandonment of your studies, followed by a fair amount of soul-searching over what to do with your life. Then there was the living at Arran's warehouse."

"It's no mystery why I was there," I grumbled.

"Because of your ma. I know. Ye wanted to understand what her life had been like to clue in to what yours could be. Just remember, you're your own person, and a strong one at that. Ye have choices she never did."

I pondered this, watching Lottie potter around with the last of the dinner prep. "Even though I've never found anyone who met her, I bet it's safe to say she never kidnapped a man."

The returning smile was soft. "I think you're probably right. I wish we didn't have to go tomorrow, but it can't be helped. When we're back, we can have a long talk."

Lottie had a hospital appointment in Edinburgh and was also suffering motion sickness, so didn't want to do the long drive twice in one day. I hadn't pressed for more details, knowing she'd share when ready. But yeah, definitely preggo.

"Promise me you'll go over those therapy notes?"

I jumped up, hugged her, and gave her my yes, then returned to my sous chef duties.

With dinner plated up, I hollered for the family to come in. Sin and Lottie's two younger kids, Daphne and Magnus, plus Wren, Camden and Breeze's dainty little daughter, were the only three home. Their older siblings and cousins were spending the week at school camp, and all the younger kids were away with their parents.

It still made for a noisy meal, and I slid glances at a silent Riordan who ate his chicken like he was starved but made no effort to talk. No matter. We took some getting used to, and this was an easy way into our family dynamic.

When we were done, Sin took on clean-up duties, refusing Riordan's offer of help. Lottie directed the children into the great hall so they could run around and burn off their instant energy boost, heavy autumn rain preventing them from doing so outside.

It left me and Riordan alone, with Sin the other end of the kitchen, clattering pans. My captive stood as if to leave.

"I need to ring your sisters."

He stalled. "Why?"

"So I can explain what I did?"

His forehead lined. "Is that necessary?"

"Girl code. I stole their brother. They should hear it from me, if Arran hasn't spilled already."

To my surprise, instead of a snarl, he uttered a bark of a laugh and dropped back down to his seat. "This will be good. Before you do that, I need to know how long I have to stay."

I shrugged. "With me? Forever. In this house, maybe a couple of days?"

At the end of the kitchen, Sin swung open the door of the utility room and disappeared inside.

Riordan watched him go then returned his gaze to me. "How can you say things like that?"

My breathing quickened. This was an opportunity to explain myself. To make him understand the shock I'd got on first sight of him, down on the floor of the warehouse's nightclub when he'd been in the middle of a fight to protect Genevieve.

Riordan had stormed the warehouse, assuming his sister was in danger. Jamieson, the youngest of my brothers, had been the one to finally restrain him. I'd been dancing on a pillar and had remained there, admiring his protective instinct and the way his t-shirt rode up his taut stomach in the scrap. The happiest feeling had filled me at the realisation of what I wanted him to be. The big *mine* statement my brain had made.

Instant, complete, and forever.

But I couldn't find the words.

The moment passed, and Riordan gave up the attempt. "You think it will only take Arran a matter of days to wrap up whatever he is doing?"

"It's a targeted hit. He's going after Bronson. With just a few key players, maybe even just him and Shade, they can take that arsehole down."

He squinted at me. "How do you know that?"

"I don't for sure, but that's exactly what I'd do if this was my plan." I rubbed my hands together, the summary of this far easier to construct than any of my own feelings. "Arran has evidence now that links into what we already knew about the killer, giving Bronson the metaphorical smoking gun. He leapt to action, which tells me he already suspected the man and this was the final puzzle piece. He's not going to wait around."

"What kind of man is Bronson?"

"An arrogant fuck, and nowhere near as protected as Red, the leader of the gang. Your sister came face to face with him when she strayed into their territory. He's a frontline kind of man, therefore easier to grab. Red will be pissed off, but Arran's evidence will stay his hand because he doesn't want the murders to continue either. It's bad for business. Besides, he can't bring a war in the same way that Arran can't—there's too much press attention. Too many cops on the street. It would be begging for trouble."

Riordan settled his chin on his hands, that gaze turning curious. "What happens once Bronson's taken?"

He was listening to me. Actually listening. A fizz of energy sparkled through me at his attention.

"Methods," I made inverted commas in the air with my fingers, "will be used to get the truth out of him. But it's possible he's our man. None of our other suspects could have killed all the women. We kept hitting blanks and alibis. Bronson wasn't even on the list, only Red, so that was an oversight, which I'm kicking myself about. The first course of action in interrogating him will be to work out his motive. It should be fun."

Riordan folded his arms and sat back. "Shame you won't get to see."

I blinked. "Of course I will. I'll be there with bells on."

"In the room with a killer? One who threatened your life?"

I could've laughed. If he thought me intimidated, he was wrong. "Aren't ye sweet, worrying about me? I come from a family of criminals. I've been waiting to make my first kill in the name of protecting something I care about. Which in this scenario is the warehouse and all the women who work there. Fuck that guy for killing Alisha. Fuck him for killing Cherry, Natasha, and Amelia. Don't ye think it poetic that a woman will end his miserable life?"

Riordan only stared.

With a grim smile, I lifted my phone. "Now to make my confession."

At Riordan's sigh, I dialled my Skeleton Girls Detective Agency chat group to add Genevieve and Everly to a call, their two concerned faces appearing almost instantly on my screen. Genevieve's blonde hair contrasted Everly's brunette that matched Riordan's chocolate shades.

"I have something to tell ye both."

I didn't hide my mistakes. Being open and honest was important to me for more reasons than I could list, but right before I could give up my crime, Riordan reached out and claimed my phone from my hand.

His determined expression quickened my pulse. My stomach flipped at the touch of his fingers to mine. I held my breath in anticipation of whatever he was about to say.

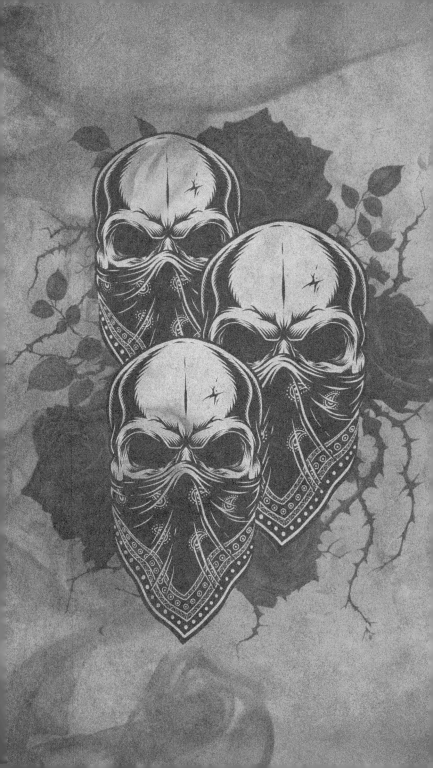

5

Riordan

Genevieve's eyes widened as she took me in. "Arran said you'd gone somewhere with Cassie."

Cassie rounded the table to my side, kneeling on the bench next to me. "I took him."

I had no idea of my motivation, maybe it was pride taking the wheel, but I wasn't about to be a victim. "I'm here as Cassie's bodyguard," I amended. "Are you both okay? Tell me you're safe."

The two women confirmed that they were and that the warehouse was on lockdown with all crew pulled back until some event had taken place. Arran and Shade were keeping their information close. I didn't doubt Cassie's guess at their actions, though.

Gen's gaze shifted across the screen. "Is it true that you got a letter, Cassie?"

My tiny, crazy captor paled then reached for her pocket, extracting the killer's note. I'd only seen it from across the room earlier and stared at it like it could give up any further clues. Block capitals in a black ink. Plain paper, unlined. Nothing further that gave me any insight into its source.

Yet some motherfucker had written that in my name in order to trap Cassie.

My sisters listened to her explanation and puzzled over the message and the implied threat.

Everly pressed her fingertips to her lips, her shock obvious. "The killer tried to lure you out by pretending to be Riordan? Thank God you didn't go. But how did they get in your room? Whoever it was had access to that floor to deliver it. Has anyone pulled CCTV?"

Cassie gave a dramatic sigh. "There won't be any. This is terrible to confess, but I've been messing with Arran. To stop him keeping an eye on me, I disabled the camera in the hall. I can't believe I was such an idiot."

Both cooed over her, trying to make her feel better. I raised a wry eyebrow.

She noticed. Cringed.

Eventually, she got off the call with a final comment from Everly about sending her something for their shared hobby, whatever that was.

Cassie peeked at me. "Why did ye jump in like that? I was ready to take the blame."

"If you'd asked me to come here with you, I would've." A simple truth but honest. Staying for tonight was also my decision, no matter Arran's order or her brother's strong-arming.

She hung her head. "Oh. If it counts for anything, I'm really sorry for what I did. Not for ye being here with me, but for scaring ye."

"In the car, I couldn't see you so had no idea who was driving. I thought another gang had taken me. It was right after I'd put two and two together on Bronson."

Her eyes flew to mine. "God. I made such a mess of it.

If I promise to make it up to ye, can ye forgive me?"

"Don't bother. I'm only staying because you'd be vulnerable if I left. I won't let you die on my watch, but that's it."

Her shoulders slumped.

Why the hell did that make me feel like the bad guy?

One of her little nieces, a copy-paste of Cassie, ran in and commanded her attention. Cassie took her hand and exited the room, barely looking at me. But someone else was. I lifted my chin to her brother across the kitchen, waiting for his condemnation. Sinclair stomped over, two open beer bottles in his hand. He held one out.

I took it. "Is it drugged?"

He snorted. "Not my style. If I wanted ye unconscious, I wouldn't need anything but my hands. The beer's non-alcoholic, though, as you're on duty this evening." Resting a hip against the island that separated the long family dinner table from the rest of the kitchen, Cassie's brother pointed his bottle at me. "Once we're gone early tomorrow, you'll be here alone with Cassie."

I swigged the cool beer, noncommittal, though I'd already decided to stay. Then a random question formed. "Did Lottie really make the first move on you?" It seemed so unlikely. I'd taken a quick measure of her over dinner and found her quiet and calm. Nothing like his and Cassie's bolder nature.

No smile broached his lips. "I didn't tell ye that to warm ye to my sister. I'm naw her fucking fluffer. As far as I'm concerned, you're an unknown quantity and therefore have a mountain to climb to prove you're good enough. What I need now is a walk-through of what ye learned today so I can feel better about naw being here. Give me

Cassie's main vulnerabilities."

A pop quiz. Great.

Despite my annoyance, I listed what I'd already identified. "The size of the house is a problem. More entry points than can be easily defended. If more than one person attacks, that's an issue."

Sinclair drank his beer. "Every door and window has sensors which alert if it's open or broken. There would be no element of surprise, and the exact entry point would be known."

"And if that system's offline?"

"It won't be."

I pressed my lips together, no choice but to believe him as he wasn't going to share how everything worked.

"Fire would be my next concern. You pointed out the sprinkler system, but again, if that's down, or if the smoke's coming from a non-extinguishable source, that's a problem. If we can't breathe, we have to run."

"Has your target been known to use tactics like this?"

I considered his question. "No. He's drugged women and abducted them but always in a low-key way, from what I can tell."

"What evidence supports that?"

I thought back to what I knew and pieced it together, really paying attention to the murders, thanks to what I'd read on Cassie's detective wall. "Cherry, the first woman he killed, worked the churchyard steps across the street from where I used to live. Anyone could lurk in the dark graveyard surrounding the church. He hid then killed her where he caught her. Natasha Reid was drugged, suggesting he needed to abduct her to somewhere quiet to do the deed. With the third woman, Amelia Martin, he broke into her temporary home, telling me he'd watched the place as she was house-sitting. It makes sense now as we know the Four Milers were targeting the mayor and that was next door. With Alisha, he got her to come to him. All of that tells me his tactics are subtle and with the intention to stay out of sight."

Not the smash and grab I'd described with a raid or flames. He'd sneak in and kill without a fanfare.

Sinclair watched me. "Then tell me again Cassie's vulnerabilities."

There was only one conclusion I could reach. "Being alone."

He tipped his head in what looked like satisfaction at my thought process matching his. I got a small burst of pride.

It was short-lived. The hulking man pinned me with a dark stare.

"Are ye the killer?"

My jaw dropped. "Of course I'm fucking not."

His savage regard continued. "I'd do anything for my family. Take, maim, kill. I wouldn't hesitate. Arran tells me ye fronted up to him to protect your sister. That true?"

Annoyed, I inclined my head in agreement.

"Then understand that whatever lengths you'd be prepared to go to, I would go tenfold. Any of Cassie's family would. She's been through a lot in her life and deserves only good things. Lock that warning into your head as ye keep her safe. Tell me again how you'll manage it."

He tapped the table to mark his point.

Two competing emotions battled inside me. I wanted

to tell him to go fuck himself for his attitude. I also respected him for doing all the things I would for Gen or Everly, though on steroids.

I worked my jaw. "I'd feel a whole lot more comfortable if we had someone watching the outside. Two or three people who could take on an intruder while I play bodyguard. You're asking for vulnerabilities, that's the greatest one. I'd stand between her and a blade, same as I would for any woman whether she deserves it or not, but if I'm taken down, she's on her own."

"Good thing Arran's sending crew members and I've got friends flying over to help. Like I said, you're an unknown quantity. I wouldn't trust ye as far as I could throw ye."

He gave me a smirk then strode away.

A few hours later, Cassie was sequestered away in Sinclair and Lottie's apartment, putting their kids to bed while I remained in the hallway, waiting her out.

Pissed off, I glowered at the house. My first impressions of it being a stately home were accurate. It was a goddamn mansion, with a dramatic staircase that swept up from the wide entrance hall to the floor where the family each seemed to have their own apartment. The kitchens downstairs were big enough for a team of people to work in, which they probably did hundreds of years ago, and every inch of my surroundings was marble, stone, or carved wood, and littered with antiques.

I hadn't paid enough attention to Cassie's rooms when I'd been in there, only looking for an opportunity to leave. Now I was staying, I'd get a second chance.

Adjusting my position from my lean on the wall, I admitted a fact to myself.

It wasn't just safety features I wanted to see. Her home would give me clues to the woman herself. The pictures on her walls. The items she surrounded herself with. I'd done the same in her room at Arran's warehouse, taking in a rack of short and sparkly dresses and the plentiful stash of makeup—at odds with the killer edge I knew her to have.

I didn't understand her.

No, that wasn't exactly right.

I couldn't trust my gut, which told me she wasn't dangerous to me. I couldn't believe my instincts which sat up and begged for more when she called me hers.

I needed Cassie to prove me wrong so when this was over, I could walk away from her without regret.

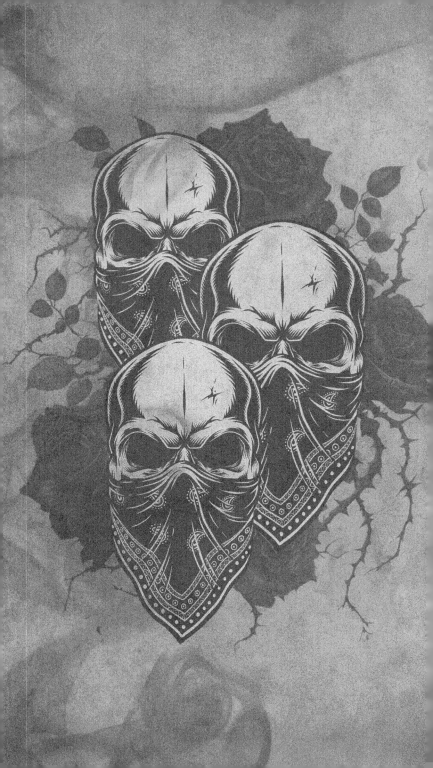

6

Riordan

In Cassie's apartment, she closed and locked the door with a side-eye peek at me. Silence fell around us.

"Well, this is more awkward than I was anticipating."

I moved to the window. Peered out into the dusk. "What exactly were you expecting?"

"Oh no, I'm not sharing that."

Her cheeks pinkened, but she gestured around the big room. "This is my living space, obviously. Those doors at the end are to a hall. First on the right is a kitchen. There's a huge fridge which is mostly just filled with drinks, though I had a thing for fancy ice cubes for a while so the freezer's stocked, and then on the other side, there's double doors to my bedroom. The bathroom's down there as well. Make yourself at home. Take a nap, if ye want."

I propped up the wall, folding my arms. "I work nights and have had more than enough rest."

"Right. Courtesy of moi."

I twisted my lips. "Besides, who knows what you'll do to me in my sleep. Actually, for all I know you could just dope me again if you get bored."

Her jaw dropped in pretty shock. "I steal one tiny needle and suddenly I'm the queen of sedation."

"What did you do with the rest of Shade's kit?"

"I never took it. After I found the note, I ran downstairs to Arran's office to borrow a gun, discovered Shade's little leather pouch, stole one dose then returned back upstairs. Ye were in my doorway and scared the life out of me."

My view of events shifted. "You thought I was the killer? That's why you took me down?"

"No. I knew it was ye. I shot out half the contents of the needle so I didn't kill ye, and the rest is history."

She could've lied. That alternate reality was a damn sight more acceptable than the truth, and more importantly, forgivable. But Cassie was unapologetically honest.

She bounced on her heels. "If you don't need rest, want to watch a hockey match with me? I've got some work to do, but the matches are fun. The dudes really go for it with their fights."

"We're not friends. This isn't a hangout."

Cassie puffed out her cheeks and gave a rueful smile, giving up on persuading me. Pottering around the room, she collected a folder of paperwork and her tablet then settled on the couch. She switched on the TV and found a hockey channel, the sound on low, and got to work with a notepad, drawing up some kind of action list while referring to her paperwork and what looked like emails on her tablet.

I prowled the room.

If there really was a team of people arriving tomorrow, as her brother informed me, I could leave. Which meant there was only tonight for me to take my reading of

Cassiopeia Archer.

Like the rest of the mansion, the structure of her big living room was high ceilings and crown moulding to within an inch of its life. It was a corner apartment, one floor up. The right-hand wall held three huge windows, the central of which opened onto a balcony, while the other exterior wall hosted a curved bay.

The view from each was concealed by heavy velvet curtains that ran ceiling to floor. They were a moody, stormy grey which made a plain backdrop along with the white plaster walls and the plush rug atop polished wooden floorboards. Even the sofa was linen-coloured, warmer where the pools of lamplight met. Here and there, gold accents brought the subtle hint of extreme wealth.

Time and time again, my eye was drawn back to Cassie. Her glossy black curls, her patterned playsuit, the boldness of her sea-blue eyes whenever she peeked at me.

She was a flare of colour in the calm surroundings. Unmissable.

I forced my attention off her.

The wall behind us, that held the exit to the hall, was heavily decorated with bookshelves and endless picture frames. Kids and adults smiled back, her family, clearly. Many were taken here in the mansion they owned. Some elsewhere in Scottish locations. Mountains, pine forests.

It told me how much she cared about her kin.

Back home, in the flat Gen and I had shared with her father, he'd kept photos of loved ones. I'd never made that list. I wasn't sure anyone had a picture of me on display anymore.

I drifted over to Cassie's books, unable to pull myself out of the comparisons. We'd never had a bookshelf. I'd never even had my own bedroom, sleeping on the sofa after our mother died and Gen's dad was forced to take us in, and interest curled in my gut over the legacy of books Cassie had kept, presumably starting from when she was small.

A series of adventure stories featuring kids on a boat. Graphic novels with cute anime-style characters. Romance novels with skulls and daggers on the covers. Or half-naked men.

I'd always figured people kept bookshelves to show off collections of classics, like Austen or Brontë. Books you were forced to read at school. Not Cassie.

Interspersed between the different series were Funko Pop! characters, I guessed from the books, or maybe her favourite shows.

None of it screamed crazy. It all felt normal.

Until my gaze settled on an ornament at the end of the row. Next to a thick tome was a polished, bleached skull. The top of the cranium was hollowed out, and items were stuffed inside. A university identity pass. A ticket stub to see a band. Between the skull's teeth was a piece of paper with the words 'FAILS'. What. The. Fuck?

"Come on!"

I spun around at Cassie's yell. She knelt on the sofa, a hand out in outrage. Her gaze slid my way.

"Sorry. That was a bad tackle. Check out the replay."

I curled my lip at the screen. "I don't know anything about the game." Hockey for me had been played on a muddy field in winter with sticks and a ball.

"Me neither. I'm just watching for the hot guys and yelling because everyone else is."

She beamed, and something tightened in my chest.

So much, I didn't turn back to my morbid find. This attraction made no sense. I'd wanted Cassie from the first second I saw her. She was pretty. More than a little dangerous. I wanted to scoop her up and hold her. Even after she'd drugged me.

I had to be as fucked in the head as her skull ornament.

And I was still staring. She tilted her head in question, her interest in the sport lost, and her focus fully on me. It quickened my breathing. Sent my blood south.

Her ringtone blared out, breaking the moment and releasing me from its grip. Cassie fumbled her phone and swiped to answer, cutting off the music that was the theme tune to a police procedural TV show.

"Skeleton Girls Detective Agency, Cassiopeia speaking, how can I help?"

Everly's laugh came over the line. "I like that greeting. Genevieve and I want to talk about exactly that."

"Ooh, I'm so down."

"Have you got the note to hand?"

She jumped up. "I left it in my bedroom when I got changed. One sec."

Cassie trotted away, still chatting with my sisters. I moved over to the sofa, intending to mute the TV for her. But as I reached for the control, my gaze fell on her notepad.

I'm not obsessed with him. It's hyperfixation, she'd written.

I swallowed and skipped my gaze off it, unintentionally focusing on her paperwork instead. At the top of each scattered page was the name and office address of a therapist, and there were notes beneath which Cassie had annotated.

She'd been working through this? And had reached a conclusion about me?

No way would I read those, but I was an asshole for jumping back to her notepad list to see what else she'd decided.

I'm probably just sex-starved.

At some point, it will be over. I just have to ride it out.

Do nothing permanent.

Don't hurt him.

The strange sensation in me expanded. She was trying to fix herself and the impulses that had led to her actions towards me. And I was even more fucked up for the hit of disappointment that her obsession wasn't real.

She returned, and I dropped the remote and resumed propping up the wall. Cassie's gaze drifted over me as she talked with the women.

Everly's gentle voice came over the line. "What I don't get is why the note is signed in Riordan's name."

Genevieve answered. "Alisha's note was signed off by Convict, who she'd had some kind of relationship with previously. Maybe a one-night stand, but it was enough to draw her in. Why would they think the same would work on you, Cassie? Why Riordan?"

Cassie's dark eyebrows furrowed. "That's easy. Because I have a thing for your brother."

I palmed my forehead.

Genevieve choked. "Since when? And how would anyone know?"

"I told Dixie, and she said she'd inform all the other women so no one made a play for him. That wasn't fair of me, though. It's all one-sided."

"Does he know?" my sister spluttered.

Still focusing on the phone, Cassie jacked her thumb at me. "If he didn't before, he does now."

"He's listening?"

She winced. "My bad. Shocking video call etiquette. I should have mentioned he's here on security duty, though he's mostly ignoring me."

For fuck's sake. I left my post and rounded the sofa to sit next to her, then raised a hand for my sisters.

"No comment from the bodyguard," I told them both.

Cassie snickered and huddled in closer, her shoulder brushing mine. Her pretty scent surrounded me, and need surged at the light touch. Her bare skin to mine, just below the sleeve of my black skeleton crew t-shirt. Soft and smooth to bulky and hard. There was no reason it should take effort to keep a neutral expression, yet there I was, inching away, gritting my jaw, and forcing my attention to stay on the screen.

Genevieve peered at me. "I called Dad earlier and asked him to pack a bag for you, since you're staying away. Want to guess what he told me?"

"I can imagine."

"Should we talk in private?"

Cassie already knew about that shitshow. Everly and I were brand-new to being siblings, and it was better for both of us to share our lives if we were ever going to make up for lost time.

"No need," I said. "He kicked me out."

Genevieve clasped her hands to her mouth. "That isn't what he said. He claimed you left after a fight. He kicked you out? God. Why didn't you tell me?"

Because I'd been hurting. Because I hadn't wanted her to lose faith in the single parent she had left. A man who was a terrible person in most other ways but whose one saving grace was that he loved her. Almost as much as he hated me, the cuckoo in his nest. Another man's child he'd been forced to tolerate.

I heaved a sigh. "What good would it have done? I only stayed in that flat because you were there. Now you live in the warehouse with Arran, I can look for someplace else."

Her gaze flickered with acceptance. "I found your car in the warehouse's car park. There's a tarp over the back seats. All your stuff's in there, isn't it?"

I shrugged, accidentally touching Cassie again. "I haven't found anywhere yet. It doesn't matter. I'm pulling long hours, so paying for a room somewhere would be a waste of money when I'm out most of the time. I shower and do laundry in the club. I sleep in my car. It's fine for now."

Genevieve sighed then groused about me keeping everything inside.

Everly shook her head. "I can't help feeling this is my fault. You told me we shared a father only because you were trying to protect me from an abduction attempt. You can't say it's a coincidence that your stepdad kicks you out straight after."

"It's not a coincidence," I conceded. "I challenged him and brought an end to the pretence of our relationship. It had to happen at some point."

Everly asked Genevieve something about her dad, and I exhaled, sitting with my thoughts for a moment. My biological father, Everly's dad, was far worse than the stand-in who I'd believed had fathered me right up until my mother had made her confession. Days before she died.

The mayor of Deadwater might have produced two children in Everly and me, but that was the only good thing the man had ever contributed to the world. The more I learned about him the angrier I got. He was corrupt. Abusive. The unknown bane of my life. He'd rejected my pregnant mother and told her to get rid of me.

Maybe being raised by a parent who never wanted me was the lesser of two evils.

Hurt added to my upset, unwanted but real.

The mayor was the reason I'd pushed Cassie away. I planned to get my own back on him, which had consequences. Falling in love with someone was out of the question when I'd very likely end up dead.

A hitch of Cassie's breath pulled my attention back to the moment. She held the phone in front of us then tapped something that switched us from being the small in-image picture to taking up the whole screen. Then she leaned in closer and took a screenshot. I stared at it. Her amused pout and my more serious expression. Her dark curls brushing up against my shorter brown hair. Something unidentifiable in both of our expressions.

"Couldn't resist," she whispered. To herself, she added, "That one's going straight in the spank bank."

My sisters were still talking. I twisted to stare at Cassie.

The pink on her cheeks returned, and she gave an embarrassed little shrug. "What? We look good together."

I didn't deny it.

Her grin shifted to something devilish. It sent another rush of desire straight through me. The image of her gazing at a picture of me and sliding her hands down her body. Holy fuck.

"Oops. Should've asked permission. If ye don't like it, tell me to delete it."

I clenched my fists and didn't say a single goddamned word.

Throughout the dark hours, Cassie switched the hockey for a telenovela she claimed was crack-level addictive. She curled up on the sofa under a blanket, her bright-eyed gaze half on me.

I guarded her. Stayed alert.

"If I doze off, feel free to check the cameras on my phone. My PIN is two-two-six-three."

"I won't use it." Still, I committed that number to memory.

By the time morning came and her brother thumped on the door to tell us the cavalry had arrived, I was on the edge of my nerves, waiting for something to happen. Yet it hadn't.

We exited to the echoing marble hall downstairs, and Cassie hugged her family goodbye. Sinclair took me aside for one last word.

"Something occurred to me in the night. My guess is Cass came here for your sake, not hers. She likes being part of the drama. Lives for it. Right now, she'll be thinking about the action happening in Deadwater. She might try to go back. I'm counting on ye, Riordan Jones, to keep her safe."

With a meaningful look and a hard smack on the shoulder, he walked away, hailing the skeleton crew that had just arrived with rumbles of tyres on gravel.

He was wrong about Cassie.

He was also wrong about me. Now she was covered, I was free to go.

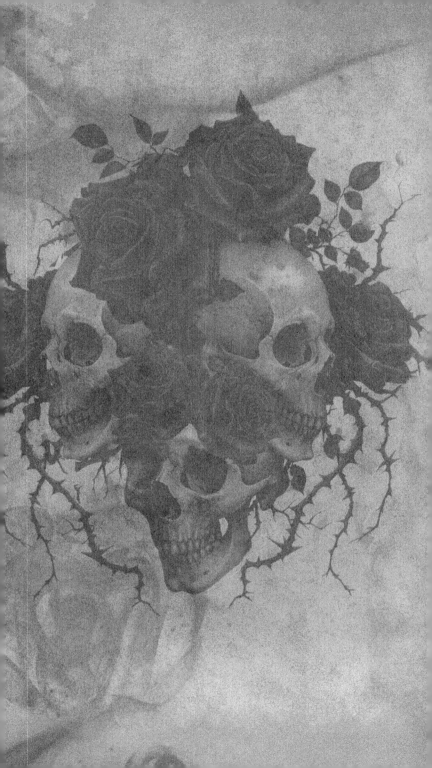

7

Cassie

*H*e was going to leave.

I wouldn't blame him either, and I shouldn't have a problem with it. Last night, I'd gone through hours and hours of therapy notes. The conclusion I'd reached was a logical one, and an exact scenario my therapist had modelled out. She'd described how I might meet someone at a point when my defences were low. That I'd fall hard and convince myself I was in love at first sight.

That it would be a reaction, not a reality.

Sullenly, I stared out the mansion's front door, the damp breeze ghosting over my skin. My therapy notes told me whatever I thought I felt for Riordan was temporary. It would leave me as quickly as it had arrived, so starting a relationship on those terms was sketchy and unfair.

Next to me, Riordan waited, his hair mussed from guarding me all night and his broad shoulders stretching out the skeleton crew t-shirt I badly needed to steal so I could wear it to bed once he'd gone.

How could it be fake, the butterflies in my stomach when his green-eyed gaze came to me, or the fizz of attraction at how his muscles moved under his shirt?

"Just a hyperfixation." My mumbled words were lost to the hails of the men getting out of the cars.

Behind one was a trailer with Riordan's bike strapped onto it. He spotted it. Smiled.

"Can I ask a question?" I blurted.

Halfway to taking a step, he wheeled around. "No, I'm not taking you on my bike."

I poked out my tongue. "It wasn't that."

Though now it was everything I wanted.

He tilted his head. "Then what? We need to talk to your protection detail."

My confidence faltered. What did I want? Originally, it was simply him. I wanted to place my palms flat on his chest and gaze up at him. I wanted him to pick me up so I could curl my legs around his waist and our faces would be at the same height. I wanted soft kisses and hard... Other things.

Directly in my eyeline, he'd ordered his ex-girlfriend, who'd never really been a girlfriend and was more like a ghoul, to her knees. I hadn't stuck around to watch her blow him. The jealousy had been too great. She'd preened, joyful at being allowed to touch him.

I wanted the right to do the same.

If that was the answer to making my feelings go away, I needed more time to frame the question.

"It's delicate," I managed.

"Then we'll deal with the crew first then get to real talk later."

He strode to the door, fist-bumping one skeleton crew member then giving a nod of greeting to another, all while not straying far away from me. Cool. That worked for me.

Under the cover of the porch, I joined him and hugged hello to Mick and punched Lonnie in the arm, turning to the last man with surprise. "Tyler, what are ye doing here?"

Arran's bear of a team leader gave me a chin lift. Tyler was the tough, outdoorsman, ultra-capable type. The kind of guy who could defuse a bomb then use the cables to rewire his boat.

"Cass. Daniels pulled me in to run this show."

He shoved his fingers into his dark-blond hair, and I tilted my head, working out why the heck an intercept guy had been put on bodyguard duties. Tyler operated undercover in remote corners of the country and over in Europe, shutting down trafficking rings. Often by force. I'd only ever met him a few times, but he was an important part of Arran's crew. A deadly and effective killer but gentle with the women he saved.

"He wants ye in Deadwater," I concluded slowly.

A meaningful glance was my answer. It told me to hush.

I shut my mouth. In a heartbeat, I'd worked it out. After Bronson was in our clutches, Arran still meant to take down the Four Milers. He needed Tyler there to handle the trafficking routes that brought women into their strip club which we knew also fronted a brothel. Not one where the women had any choice over being there.

I also had my own level of interest in Tyler. There was information I needed and had never been able to obtain, and had often thought that Tyler would be a good person to do some digging. I'd planned to ask Arran for his contact details, and oh look, he'd just walked straight into my house.

I sensed someone staring at me and peered up at Riordan. He glanced from me to Tyler, his jaw tight. I jumped to make the introduction.

"Riordan, this is Tyler. One of Arran's most trusted. Tyler, Riordan's a new recruit."

Tyler reached out a big hand for a shake then jacked his thumb at his car. "Brought your bike. I was careful with her."

"Appreciate that," Riordan grumbled back.

He stomped away over the gravel in the direction of the trailer, and I stared after him. Something had pissed him off, but unlike Arran's strategy, I was at a loss to work this one out.

A short while later, with Riordan's bike safely offloaded, two other men arrived, the thud of rotor blades having us all gaze skywards. Max and Maddock McRae both worked for the mountain rescue service and had flown over by helicopter from where they lived elsewhere in the Cairngorm mountains.

Riordan's face was a picture.

Max was tight with my older brother, Struan, who was also due to return home as soon as he could. My whole family had been messaging me, but I'd played down my worries. I was covered. Six men and little ol' me. It was safer for my relatives to stay away.

The other fact was this would all be over soon. The minute Arran had Bronson, the killer would be off the streets. I'd be able to rest easy. While contributing to the torture of the misogynistic prick.

"Everyone in the great hall," Tyler ordered. He palmed my shoulder then handed over a rucksack. "Daniels' missus told me to give that to you. Most of it's for your boy."

He gestured to a silent Riordan who now had on his collarless leather jacket that must've been returned with his bike. Guilt panged in me. This morning, I'd thrown on a hoodie and leather boots, the corridors chilly now autumn was here. I should've raided one of my brothers' wardrobes for something his size.

Then again, I was pretty certain he wouldn't have taken it.

The great hall of our house had been rebuilt after Jamieson had burned the place down, and we'd redesigned it to be a useable space for the family. There was kids' play equipment, a big oak table, and even a bar.

I plonked down in a seat and hugged my knees, listening to Tyler work through a plan. He had the camera and alert feed running as he spoke, arranged with each man to have access, then moved on to comms. A schedule. Exactly what they'd do if someone entered the estate or even the building.

All listened carefully, nodding when needed. Soon, Tyler was done. He dispatched Max and Maddock to one side of the house and Mick and Lonnie to the other. They'd stay close rather than head out onto our expansive estate. If the killer was coming for me, he had to get past them and into the house first.

Tyler centred his attention on us. "From what Arran tells me, Riordan is acting as close protection, correct?"

Riordan folded his arms and didn't immediately answer. By any reasonable measure, he was free to go.

Panic clutched at me with tiny, sharp nails. I leapt up and mangled my fingers together, turning to the man I'd called mine. "Can we talk for a minute?"

He followed me outside into the entrance hall.

I spoke before he could. "I know you're thinking about leaving. Please don't."

"Because you'll be down one highly efficient guard?"

I toed the floor. "Sure."

His dark eyebrows merged. "I call bullshit."

"What? It's one of my reasons."

"Say something had happened after you'd knocked me out, if Bronson had followed your car and run you off the road. How would I have protected you?"

Well, fuck. "You would have wanted to?"

He gave me a look. It wasn't hatred. It brought a smile to my face.

I couldn't contain a little hop. "You're right. It was thoughtless and impulsive and you'll let me make it up to ye. I did some research last night that helped me work out that my feelings for ye probably aren't real. I figured I'm responding to the attraction alone and making it more."

Something flared in his eyes.

I hitched my breath, fascinated. "You're attracted to me, too, right?"

The interest sank into a moody glower. In his hand was a water bottle from a pack someone had brought to the table. He popped the cap and took a drink.

"Is that yes?" I summoned every nerve I possessed. "Because I had an idea. To say I'm sorry, how about an apology blow job?"

Riordan choked and spun away, coughing and sputtering.

"What? Ye let Moniqua and ye don't even like her. I don't know how and want to learn."

Tyler exited the great hall. "I'm doing my best not to listen, but the open door is doing nothing to conceal your voices." He stalked between us then paused to touch a finger to my shoulder. He made a hissing sound. "On fire, kid."

To Riordan, he added, "You'd better be good to her or a whole army of protective big brothers are ready and waiting to roll in on you."

He walked away, whistling.

Wincing hard, I shot Riordan an apologetic glance then pounced after Tyler. "Before ye go, there's something I wanted to ask."

"Hell no. I don't want to hear." He took off down the corridor.

I chased him. "Get your mind out of the gutter. It's about something else. A woman I need tracking down."

Tyler stopped. Swung around. The fright left him, and professional seriousness with a deadly edge replaced it. "Is she in trouble?"

I peered back. Riordan was far enough away not to hear me, but I still pitched my voice low. "She's dead now, so not anymore. It's my mother I've been trying to hunt down. More specifically, anyone who knew her."

"She was a sex worker."

Not a question, but I indicated yes.

"Text me what you know. But get upstairs first and hole up in the safety of your rooms." The blond bear gave me a wolfish grin. "Have fun."

I padded back to Riordan who'd recovered himself

but refused to meet my eye. He followed me upstairs, and with every step I climbed, the more my body warmed. My offer had been a serious one. Banging him could solve multiple problems, my obsession being only one of them.

At the end of the hall, we reached my door. I took the key from my pocket and slid it into the lock, sensing Riordan close behind me. So much that if I just tipped my head back, it would hit his chest.

Momentarily, I shut my eyes, caught up in the tension of how near he was. Then his hand enclosed mine. Helped me turn the key in the lock.

A touch of his skin quickened my pulse.

Riordan swung the door inwards, and I stepped into the apartment. Cautious hope added to the mix of potent need bubbling inside me, and I spun around, walking backwards as he prowled through the space with me, heading for my bedroom.

Inside, the backs of my legs hit my bed, and I sat with a rapid exhale. Nervous. Thrilled. Needing the dark-haired man to lead the way.

From the entryway, with one hand to the frame and the other the door, Riordan looked me over. Then his gaze took in the four corners of the room.

This was it. He'd advance on me. Kiss me. Breathless, I parted my knees to give him space.

Riordan's dark gaze returned to me. "Try to get some rest."

What?

He ducked out and closed me in. By the time I'd jumped up and followed, he was at the hall exit, the big gold key in his hand.

"See how you like being the prisoner, wild girl."

With a smirk, the arsehole slammed the door. A click of the lock followed.

"Hey!" I ran at the door. Thumped it with my fist. "No blow job for ye."

A dark laugh came from the other side.

"Guess I'm going to have to get busy by myself," I snarled back.

"I'll be right out here. I won't leave you," Riordan called.

I hoped to hell he was telling the truth.

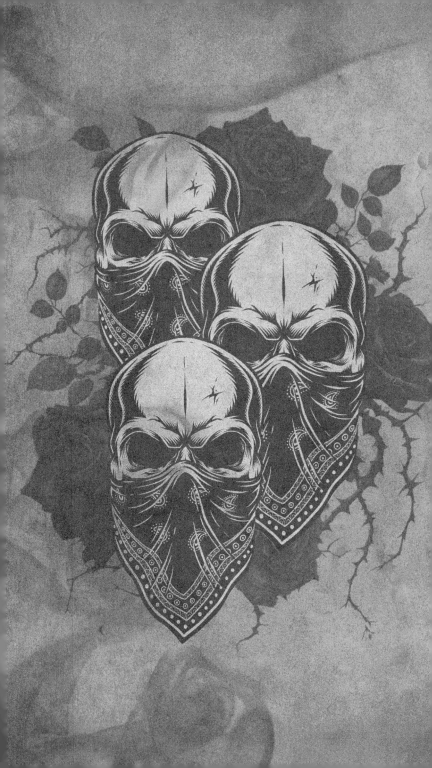

8

Riordan

Outside in the cold, I slid down the wall to park my backside on the floor. Cassie's apartment was the safest place for her, just as out here was safest for me.

My dick disagreed.

That motherfucker had been alert and raring to go from the moment she made her offer. *A lie.* From before that, as well. Accepting her was the only thing on my mind.

I'd order her to strip for me. Piece by piece. Her hoodie, her dress. She'd unclasp her bra, and I'd die a thousand deaths at the sight of her tits.

I palmed my face and hid my eyes, needing this to play out, even if only in my head.

Next, she'd remove the remainder of her clothing aside from a tiny pair of knickers. A shocking red pair, knowing her. I'd tell her to keep those on.

I'd never had a lap dance, but I'd seen countless while working in Divine. I'd seen far worse in the brothel, but if I let my mind go there with Cassie in the frame, I'd come in my fucking jeans.

She'd straddle me. Tip up my chin to kiss my cheek while commanding me to keep my hands on the back of the sofa. From her comment about wanting to learn, I guessed she had limited experience, which gave me the strangest sense of...what? Duty? Care? Red-hot fucking need?

Either way, she'd learn fast. Or I'd embarrass myself at the first touch. One or the other.

She'd want me naked, because this wouldn't be a one-way show. She'd take from me as much as I was getting from her. I'd let her remove my shirt. Enjoy her hands sliding over my body. She'd make some quip about strong muscles.

Her touch alone made me hard. God only knew how I'd feel at her fingers reaching my waistband.

I groaned under my breath and repositioned myself on the floor.

From inside the room, Cassie made a sound.

I paused, one hand to the cool floor to jump up. The noise came again. Wait, it wasn't her, but someone else's feminine tones. A male voice joined in.

"I've come to fix your bedroom light. Wouldn't want you alone in the dark, mama."

"I'm so glad you came so fast."

"Not what most of the ladies say. They want me to take it slow."

She was watching porn.

Holy fuck.

The man continued speaking. "Like my toolbelt?"

A thud followed, presumably him taking it off. Cassie

uttered a gleeful laugh. I pictured her rubbing her hands together and thumped the door with my fist.

She giggled again. "We could be doing this right now, just saying. The difference is that I can act on my problem solo. You're stuck out there having to listen."

With a grumble that was fifty percent desperation, I closed my eyes, unable to move away but equally unable to go join her.

The backtrack of cheesy dialogue and sultry music continued, with the porn star guy commenting that he had to strip to his underwear so he didn't get the woman's quilt dirty while he fixed her overhead light. Then he groaned in shock as she crept up on him and tugged down his shorts to reveal his dick.

"I'm holding a live wire. I can't let go. Mama, you're killing me here. This isn't part of the service." The tone changed. "Yeah, that's all for you. I was hard when you answered the door in that shirt with your nipples poking through. Right then I knew you were a dirty girl."

Cassie was probably taking notes on the sex act. I strained to hear any sound that wasn't the film. At last, the guy ordered the woman to let him come on her face and not in her mouth.

I expected another joke. A line about how Cassie was watching carefully. Instead, I picked up a small sigh that was all her.

But of pleasure? Frustration?

I gritted my teeth and let my imagination fill in the gap. She was touching herself for sure. Damning need zapped through my veins, so much, my balls tightened without even a single jerk of my dick.

I breathed through my nose.

Was she naked? Did she have a toy to play with or just her fingers? In my head, all options played out. She'd be shy but enthusiastic. Willing. So goddamned beautiful on her knees.

My dick thickened all the more.

Abruptly, the porn show cut out. I took a sharp inhale, hopelessly turned on.

"You done?" I demanded through the door.

No reply came. No further noises followed.

I waited and waited, my blood still running hot, but Cassie wasn't answering me now. After long minutes, I picked up the faint sound of breathing, as if she'd taken a nap after her hard work.

For fuck's sake.

I was charged up still, desperate and on the edge, though I wasn't going to touch myself. Not only for the sake of being out in the corridor but because it didn't feel right. I wanted her on me. Under me. With me.

That electricity in my veins shifted to something else. No matter how badly I was attracted to Cassie—a need that apparently refused to die no matter what she did—I had good reason not to go there.

The longer I sat in the cold corridor, the darker my thoughts became.

Anger ate away at me. A bitterness that I'd never felt in my life, not even when I'd realised the reason Genevieve's dad hated me. Adam Walker had never been kind to me in his whole life, not when I was a kid and not when I'd returned to live with him as a teenager. Yet he'd kept up the façade of being my parent, at least on paper, and presumably for the rest of the family's sake.

When I'd finally confronted him, he'd laughed in my

face.

It hurt to think about. Not his rejection but the child version of me wanting his approval and having no hope of getting it. He'd fawned over Gen, and I'd watched from the sidelines. Mum had doubled down. I realised now that she'd done everything she could to give me what I needed, and I'd loved her with my whole heart. I missed her so badly I was almost proud of Adam for hunting down and ending the life of the gangster who killed her.

Almost. I was in a gang now. That revenge could've been mine.

Yet over all of this was a worse consideration. The true source of my twisted hate.

The mayor. For all Adam had done, he'd never wished me dead. Mayor Makepeace had happily thrown that in my face along with the jibe from his partner in crime, Piers, that he'd only ever wanted a son to be proud of. Implying that could never be me.

A chill crept in around me.

The mayor had been equally vicious to his daughter. Everly was a sweetheart. Gentle, helpful, and softly spoken. He'd given her over to a man who would've abused her.

Yet it was whatever he'd done to my mother that killed me. She was openness and truth, but he'd forced silence and fear. I wished I'd had time to ask for more details, but history spoke for itself.

Revenge was a cure for a bitter heart. Mine was broken. There was no chance of fixing it if I was to go head-to-head with the mayor, and I couldn't live with the knowledge of what he'd done.

Someone needed to bring him down, and that person

was me.

I didn't know how, but a month ago, I hadn't been in a gang with access to dangerous men and weapons. I only wished I'd had more time to learn.

The morning crept on. A storm rolled in and darkened the windows at the end of the hall. Rain spattered the panes.

I kept to my post. Read the updates from Tyler and the team. Watched the cameras which I'd now accepted access to. Nothing happened to make me worry. Or to distract me from my spiralling thoughts.

Eventually, I clambered up. I needed a quick bathroom break but wasn't willing to open the door to Cassie again. The cameras showed me Tyler was in the entrance hall at the bottom of the staircase, so I tried the doors across the hall. The first two were locked, but the third gave me what I was looking for. I did my business, splashed my face with water, then stomped back to my post.

Cassie's door was wide open.

My heart lurched. I flew forward and stuck my head in her living room. "Cassie?" I bellowed.

A click from behind had me spin around. Cassie was at the far end of the corridor. She'd changed. Spiked heels—the source of the click—and a floaty red dress with long sleeves but an ultrashort hem.

I stared at her, my heart racing. "How did you get out?"

"I have a spare key, obvs."

Astonishment flashed along the path of my upset. The whole time, she'd let me believe I had the upper hand. Yet for all the long hours I'd spent out here, she'd been able to leave.

My chest rose and fell on a heavy breath. None of my

mood had left me. Being outsmarted by Cassie yet again was the nail in my coffin of control.

"Back inside," I growled.

"Nah, don't think I will." Holding my gaze, she stepped backwards.

I took a pace in her direction.

Cassie turned and fled.

For fuck's sake. I bolted after her, my heavy biker boots thudding and echoing on the floor. At the grand staircase, she fled down in a rapid staccato beat of those damn high heels. I put on a burst of speed with an arm out to catch her. Her hair ghosted over my fingers, just beyond my grasp. There was no one else in sight in the entrance hall now, and Cassie reached the marble floor and spun around, still moving away and with the most infuriating smirk on her face.

"I worked out why they called it a rampant rabbit—"

With a snarl, I grabbed her. Then I crowded her to a pillar. "Stop talking."

She peeked up. "Why?"

"You're driving me insane."

Cassie hesitated for a beat then wound her arms around my taut neck. She jumped into my arms. I had no choice but to catch her.

And hold her.

Surprise chased away some of my pain. In my arms, she was warm, a slight weight that felt good. Somehow not strange. She crossed her ankles behind the small of my back, her dress riding high around her waist so the only thing keeping her decent was me.

Fucking hell.

"What are you doing?" I managed.

Her reply was a whisper. Her lips so close to mine. "The first time I saw ye was in your fight on Divide's floor. Ye were savage. Ready with your fists and so determined. Know what I wanted in that moment? For ye to hold me, just like this. But that isn't why I leapt into your arms. You're upset about something. I can feel it pouring off ye. I also knew there was no way I was going to get under your skin without a chase. You might not be ready to kiss me, but don't tell me you're not in need of this, too."

She tucked her head into the crook of my shoulder.

Goddamned hugged me.

I was frozen. Furious.

Her heat defrosted me until, glacier-slow, I sank into the hug. It was impossible to resist. My head came down next to hers, those curls of hers a soft pillow. My grip on her tightened then settled to a close hold. The pillar supported us both.

When was the last time anyone hugged me for the sake of comfort?

Though I'd relaxed, my heart thundered.

It was all I could hear, the race of my blood in my ears. Then Cassie's breathing took over. Her steady inhales and exhales. A hitch as I squeezed her closer.

Those bare legs of hers were stretched wide around my middle, and I shifted my hands to make sure her dress covered her. Which meant I was cupping her ass. She made another soft sound.

I inched back to see her face. Her pretty eyes were hazy. Her pink tongue moistened her lips. Too fucking tempting.

I forced out words in a growl. "If you run like that

again, I'll tie you down."

"Didn't figure ye for kinky, but I'm game."

Lightning crackled between us.

Someone cleared their throat.

I whipped around to find Tyler at the end of the corridor.

"Lunch is up. I messaged you both but I can see you're occupied."

Fuck. I was on the clock, working for the skeleton crew while allowing myself to get entirely distracted.

In pain, confused, *hard*, I set Cassie on her feet, ignoring her huff of frustration.

Hugging her, or allowing her to hug me, had been yet another mistake. No matter how good it had felt.

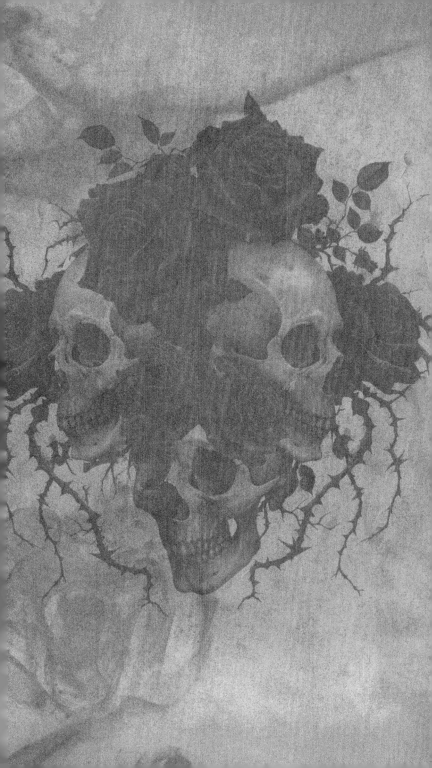

9

Cassie

"Ty," I commanded the attention of the bear. "Talk murder to me."

The intercept guy's blond eyebrows dove together, and he delivered a plate of sandwiches to the table. "Don't shorten my name. I don't like it."

"Ye call me Cass."

"You're affectionate and cute. I'm very much not. Besides, no one uses your real name."

I pointed at Riordan who'd grabbed a sandwich and chowed down like he'd been starved. "He does. He full-names me when he's grumpy with me."

Riordan pointedly ignored my tease. He'd fired questions at Tyler about whether there had been anyone seen nearby but had otherwise remained silent.

Tyler sighed. "Anyway, by murder, I assume you mean the Deadwater killings?"

"Bingo. I want your insight. I formed a detective club to solve the mystery and want to sense check what we know."

"Of course you do." He twisted his lips, his gaze

am playing catch-up, but when I heard about the first death, I figured it had the feel of either an obsessed man, a random act of aggression, or an initiation."

I cocked my head. "Cherry had clients but none we can pinpoint as being obsessed. We also know it wasn't random because of the three who came after, but what do you mean initiation?"

"Gangs and other secretive organisations often use a binding act to recruit new members, particularly to an inner circle. Some kind of proof the as-yet untrusted person isn't there to betray them and that they're a good fit."

"Such as by creating a mutual secret both have to keep."

He pointed a ham roll at me. "Exactly. Killing a defenceless sex worker in a graveyard fits the MO. Easy pickings, but jailtime for the perpetrator if the person they're trying to impress squeals."

My mind sped. "The first person we suspected was a man named Don who was a low-ranking member of the Four Milers. It makes sense that he would want to climb up the pecking order. But he was found dead in his burned-out car down the hill from where Cherry was killed."

"Maybe he did it then sped off to report in and lost control? Then afterwards, you have a copycat." Tyler took a large bite of his food.

I toyed with mine, gazing into the middle distance. "Or the Milers are recruiting several people and each had to do the same thing." As explanations went, it didn't feel strong, but a good detective was willing to consider anything.

"The Milers?" Tyler scoffed. "Don't make the mistake of being casual with that fucking drugs gang. They would never be so with you."

"What if Don isn't dead?" Riordan suddenly said.

"Couldn't they identify the body?" Tyler asked him.

"His cousin, by marriage, so not genetically, was the only relative he had, so they weren't able to DNA test the remains. Nor could she identify the lump of charcoal that was left of him. I took her to talk to the police and pathologist myself."

Insidious envy crawled through me yet again at Moniqua's friendship with Riordan. A hit so hard I couldn't reply.

"Have there been any sightings?" Tyler asked.

Riordan raised a shoulder. "None. It's just bothering me that it's a box left unticked."

Tyler palmed his jaw but moved on. "The multiple-recruitment theory doesn't necessarily stack up either. Killing as an entry requirement probably wouldn't be mandated for anything but the top tier. Convict got accepted by drug dealing for them."

There was an interesting note in his voice when he said his crewmember's name. A hesitation, like it carried weight. Convict was a double agent, working for the Four Milers in order to win back the trust of Arran and Shade. For some unknown reason, Tyler was interested in him as well. I packed away that intrigue for now.

Tyler asked Riordan about his initiation into Arran's gang—something I knew hadn't really happened yet—and I took up my phone to send my thoughts on the conversation to my Skeleton Girls Detective Agency group.

Instant replies came in.

> **Genevieve:** Super ooh! New theories for the list.

> **Everly:** Interesting, but it doesn't do anything to support B as a culprit.

She was right. I tapped back a reply.

> **Cassie:** Only as a mastermind. Any update on his capture?

> **Genevieve:** We're not allowed to talk about it, even over encrypted chat.

> **Cassie:** Rolling my eyes at Arran but okay. He's probably right.

> **Genevieve:** I also haven't seen him in a day so literally have nothing to say.

I snorted a laugh.

> **Everly:** We miss you. Is everything okay there?

If I'd hugged anyone but their brother, I probably

would've launched into my feelings on that, along with a blow-by-blow of how I'd tormented him through the door, but I had a strange rush of protectiveness over the man. Even with them.

Cassie: I'm good. Stay safe.

Both ordered me the same, and I set down my phone, testing Tyler's theory against Bronson's possible motive. He was already high up in command. Did he want the top spot and therefore had been building a case to prove he'd earned it before overthrowing Red? Or could he be secretly recruiting killer members to help him seize control?

All questions to put to him when we had him in our grasp.

At the end of the table, Riordan, already done with a second loaded sandwich, sat back and regarded me. There was an interesting expression in his eyes. "I remembered something from two nights ago."

I curled my legs under myself to face him. "Shoot."

"Moniqua came to find me in the brothel."

My lip formed a sneer. "Ugh. The ghoul."

Tyler swung his gaze between us. "Why is Moniqua a ghoul?"

"She haunts Riordan."

Tyler clucked his tongue with clear judgement. "And you let her blow you?"

At Riordan's scowl, I cracked up. Tyler really had overheard everything I'd said in the hall.

Riordan ignored the tease. "She mentioned someone

told her Alisha and I had been shut away in a room together."

"Was she jealous?" I would've been, and I'd liked Alisha.

"I don't think so, and that isn't my point. What if someone was angry at Alisha for being with another man? They could've killed her for that."

Tyler inclined his head, apparently in agreement.

"Got Moniqua's number?" I asked. "I'll ask her who was gossiping."

Riordan watched me for a beat then found his phone and handed it over, unlocked, and with a call list on the screen. I braced myself for how he'd saved Moniqua. If it was under a cute tag, like *Moni* or *Sidechick*, I'd throw up.

But there was nothing with her name or anything resembling it. *Gen, Ev, Arran, Shade.* A few numbers without names.

He gestured at it. "Her number ends six-one. She told me that in the conversation where she asked for my help because the Four Milers had threatened her."

Had to resist being the mean girl. "She was scared?"

"So she said."

"I could find her a job in the warehouse? I'll need to do the rotas soon so can fit her in."

"I suggested that. She turned her nose up."

"Probably because she wanted big strong Riordan to step up and protect her. Maybe letting ye fall on her mouth a few times, too."

Tyler choked on a laugh. Riordan's glower deepened.

After the conversation he'd just recalled, he'd let her sink to her knees and undo his jeans. Right in the middle of a brothel where people had sex all around me all day, that one act had threatened my very soul.

It had taken everything in me not to storm over and drag her out by her dyed-black hair. I'd walked away. A few hours later, when he came to find me, I'd kidnapped him.

Wow, that was as messed up as the telenovelas I adored.

Gritting my teeth, I held my thumb over her phone number. "If she's really freaked out, she'll take the offer."

"Wait," Riordan said.

I lifted my gaze to his. My cheeks burned.

He slid that dark gaze to Tyler.

The bear took the hint and jumped up. "Need to make a call. I won't be far away. Don't leave this room."

At his exit, Riordan sat back. "You're jealous of Moniqua. Why?"

Because her lips had been around his dick. Because she touched what was mine. I pouted and glared back. "What difference does it make?"

"I want to know."

"So ye can tease me? Nice."

The tormenting glimmer in his eyes didn't cease. "Maybe I'll give you a detailed description of what she felt like to make you run from me again."

My breathing stuttered. Oh God. That had no right to be so hot, yet the antagonism sent flames of heat through me.

Riordan had teeth. I liked it when he snarled.

A dismissive huff was all the answer I could give, and I stabbed Moniqua's number with my finger. She answered immediately.

"Riordan." Her voice was breathy down the line. Vomit.

"No, it's Cassie from the warehouse. I'm just borrowing his phone."

Silence met my words, then, "Uh, hi, Cassie. Is he okay?"

"He's fine. I wanted to ask ye something." I framed the question about Alisha.

She sighed. "I've been thinking about that, too, since she was found dead shortly after, but it was only one of the girls who said it. She was just gossiping."

"Who?"

"Dixie? She's really sweet. One of the few people who've been nice to me there."

Dixie wasn't a suspect. She was a dancer, a sex worker, and also my friend. About as capable of murder as Lottie. We'd drawn another blank. With fading energy, I moved on to make Moniqua the job offer.

"Stripping and sex work in the brothel aren't for anyone to take up casually. Ye can go behind the bar, or there's a cleaning crew that always needs people. It isn't glamorous but it'll keep ye safe."

She hummed. "Can I think about it? It's really kind of you to offer. I don't mean to be ungrateful, it's just not where I pictured myself, you know?"

Aye, because she'd pictured herself under Riordan.

I told her she could message back whenever then got off the call, stabbing the screen with more violence than was necessary. I hadn't wanted Moniqua to be reasonable. It would've been way more fun if she'd been a bitch to me.

I would've had an outlet for my twisted mood.

Tossing Riordan back his phone, I stomped to the door and called out, "Tyler? Ye can come back."

He was right outside and followed me in. Gestured at Riordan. "I've got something for you. Arran sent it."

From his waistband, he produced a gun. More specifically, a Glock 17. A nine millimetre, self-loading, boring-as-fuck pistol, commonly used by the police. I knew that because I still had the matching one I'd stolen from Arran's office when I'd taken the sedative needle.

Riordan accepted it. Turned it over.

"There are other weapons in the house," Tyler was saying, "but those belong to Struan, Cassie's older brother, and I wouldn't touch anything belonging to that madman without permission. Right, Cassie?"

I faked a smile.

Struan had given me shooting lessons in a range in the woods when I'd been eight years old. Even after we'd stopped being on the run and our enemies had been handled, he'd been convinced we were still in danger. Sin felt the same, but Struan was the driving force behind all our security measures. Even now, he never relaxed.

None of that interested me now.

I watched Riordan, mixed up in too many feelings at once.

My obsession wasn't going away, no matter how much I tried to convince myself it wasn't real. No matter that he flaunted Moniqua to torment me.

All it did was show me he cared. And filled my head full of wild and wayward thoughts on what I'd do to keep him.

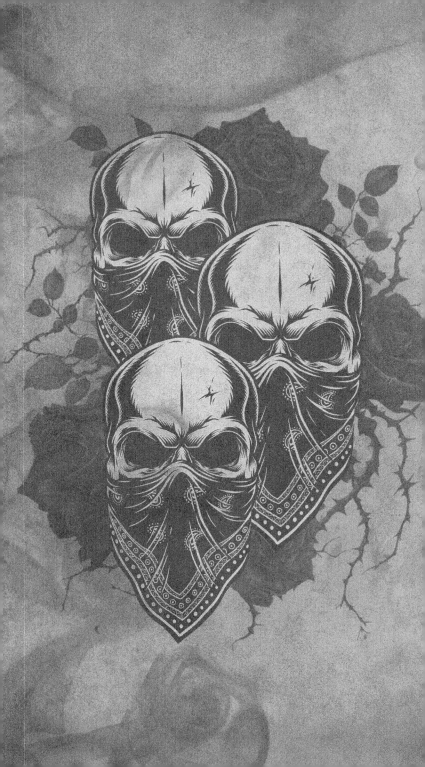

10

Riordan

"Ever shot anyone?" Tyler asked.

I gripped the gun. It was heavier than I expected. A good fit for my hand. I'd seen Arran handle a weapon in his office but figured they mostly used knives. One sniff of a gun in the city and the cops would descend en masse. Actual gun use was furtive and rare. More of a threat than a reality. Apparently, the same didn't apply out here in the wilds of Scotland.

"No," I admitted.

"Ever used a gun at all?"

My jaw clenched.

His eyes widened in recognition of my apparent failure. Annoyance rushed through me. The emotion was short-lived.

Simultaneously, all of our phones alerted.

I recognised the tone. It warned of someone at the perimeter. Tyler leapt up and snatched out his phone. I scrambled to Cassie, energy punching through my muscles in anticipation of a threat.

"Front gate," she identified.

Over Cassie's shoulder, I watched the alert screen. On the camera view, a car idled, a man behind the wheel in the dark, rainy afternoon. Despite the clear picture, I didn't recognise him, though he definitely wasn't Bronson.

Cassie stared at the intruder. "Oh God."

My heart thumped harder. "Who is it, a Four Miler?"

The gates slid open.

She lifted her gaze. "Nope. Worse. My brother's home. From the snarling he's doing at having to override our lockdown, Struan's furious."

Minutes later, we were out in the marble-floored entryway, facing off with an obviously dangerous man.

Cassie squeaked in happiness and flew at him, and he caught her in a one-armed hug, tucking her in at his side while never taking his gaze off me.

"Struan, meet Riordan." Tyler leaned on the now-closed front door.

I nodded to Cassie's brother. Undeniably her relative from the black hair and blue eyes, but also from the general air of menace that clung to them both.

Aged perhaps around thirty, Struan drew a harsh focus over my frame, nothing in his expression of a warm welcome. He was an inch or two shorter than me, but worlds apart in degrees of toughness, with an unnerving stare and a curled lip that told me he didn't like what he saw.

Adrenaline coursed through me as if I was facing a threat. If he could read the thoughts I'd been having about his sister, this guy would tear me a new one.

Then Cassie pushed up on her toes and whispered something in his ear.

His eyebrows dove together, and he slashed his attention her way. "What are ye talking about?"

"Exactly what I said."

I stared. What the fuck had she told him? I needed to know. If she'd said I was hers, she was keeping up that claim. I didn't give a fuck if it was just to save my life.

Tyler spoke instead. "Riordan is Arran's new recruit."

"How new?"

"A month," I answered for myself.

Incredulity flashed over his vision, then Struan jacked his thumb at the double doors that led to their great hall. "In there."

Tyler strolled over and joined me, throwing an arm across my shoulders to guide me where I'd been sent.

Behind, Cassie asked her brother where he'd been.

His answer was a low rumble. "Theadora's working on a case. I took Selene to stay with Scar and Burn, otherwise I would've been here sooner. Wulf's at camp with his cousins."

Who the hell were Scar and Burn? I guessed the other names were his wife and kids.

Inside the hall, Cassie bounced to the bar and took a high stool, turning it to face the room before she climbed on. "Did you see Max outside? He's been part of my guard, but I heard the helicopter go then return, so I wasn't sure if he's still here."

"He isn't. We spoke on the phone. He and Maddock took a shift then two more crew members relieved them."

Though he was providing answers, Cassie's brother was still focused on me. He lifted his chin. "So, ye want to be a gangster. Can ye fight?"

I held in a sigh. "I'm a construction worker turned club security. I can fight if I have to." Shit, I'd left the gun Arran sent me on the kitchen table. Couldn't admit that now.

Struan didn't appear convinced. "Yet you're the one locked away with my sister. What the fuck was Arran thinking not training ye?"

He unzipped his black jacket and tossed it to the floor. Then he toed off his boots.

In front of him, there was a soft play area for kids. Foam blocks, a ball pit, and various scattered toys. Struan dragged the ball pit away and booted the rest to the sides, clearing the space to reveal a padded floor surface about the size of a boxing ring.

My pulse skipped. I stood taller, recognising what he was doing and anticipating pain. For fuck's sake. I was going to cop a pounding. I was younger than the man preparing to fight me, but I lacked technique. Experience.

This was going to hurt.

It wouldn't help me to complain about how I'd been brought here, nor did I want to. I'd changed my perspective on it and had chosen to remain.

There was no way I'd allow him to make me look weak in front of Cassie.

As he worked, Struan spoke. "Riordan Jones, twenty-five, six-three, drives a Ducati Diavel, fucking nice bike. Stolen, I imagine, but your 2006 Range Rover's a piece of shit held together with Sellotape and prayers. No criminal record, which tells me you're a sneaky fucker or adept at dodging, considering you're linked to two gangs."

"You have me dead to rights. Almost. The bike I rebuilt from a wreck, and I've no links to the Four Milers."

"Ye took a job for them."

"Which I never carried out and only for a good reason."

"Which was?"

"None of your business, stranger." I was an idiot, provoking him.

Even Cassie wasn't interrupting his show and tell.

Done with his task, Struan stood on the far side of the area. He rolled his shoulders then beckoned to Tyler, though his attention was still on me. "As welcomes to the family go, I'm naw sure you're going to enjoy this, but it's essential for me to know Cassie's protected. Be warned, I willnae go easy on ye when it's your turn in the ring. Tyler, come at me. Jones, watch and learn."

The intercept guy stripped his shoes, socks, and jacket, and took a position opposite Struan.

Both men dropped into a fighter's pose. This wasn't a beatdown. It was an education. Something I needed. That Arran had suggested but we'd never got around to.

As much as I wanted this, another objective rang true. Maybe a few hits to the head would fix my insanity for the girl with the dark curls who couldn't take her eyes off me.

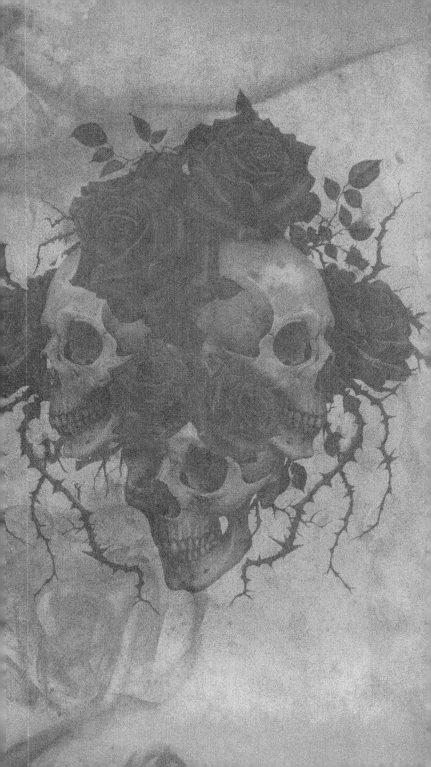

11

Cassie

*A*fter one particularly brutal throwdown, Tyler lay flat out on the mat and groaned.

Struan wiped sweat from his brow and pointed at Riordan. "You're up."

I shot forward on my stool, nearly tipping it over. "If ye hurt him, I'll—"

"Don't finish that sentence, Cass."

"Don't tell me what to do. He's important to me. You'll respect that."

Riordan moved into position, shooting a quick look my way. Tension filled the room, and he centred on Struan. Ready to prove himself to my overprotective arsehole of a brother.

Likewise, Struan wasn't going to let my objection slide. He lifted his chin at his new opponent. "So I know everything about ye, but what do ye know about Cassie?"

"This a test?"

"Aye, motherfucker, so answer fast. What's her surname?"

"Archer."

"What does she drive?"

"A scarlet red Audi."

I fist-pumped subtly. That was the car I'd taken into the city. Go him for noticing what I'd stolen him in.

Struan continued. "Model?"

"I don't fucking know. Not a car guy."

"Yeah figures. When's her birthday?"

Riordan stalled, and I squinted at him, wondering why. He knew the answer. I'd confided it in an odd moment of sharing we'd done in my room on the cam girls' floor. Then his gaze slid from mine to Tyler's. *Right*. He didn't want to overstep.

Damn my heart.

"Ye can say," I told him.

"She doesn't know for certain."

Struan watched him. "Fine. Then ye aren't just a walk-in. What are Cassie's strengths?"

"She's persuasive. Dangerous with a knife. Her mind is wild."

My heart fluttered again at the praise in Riordan's answer, but I knew what was coming next.

Struan's lips formed a flat line. His gaze cut to me. "And your main weakness, Cassie?"

"My size," I grumped. I had a list to pick from but got his point.

Riordan scowled, his face only in half profile to me now. "She can't help that. Why point it out?"

Struan prowled the mat. "Because I don't sugarcoat shite. No matter how much she trains or how her brain is streets ahead of the rest of us, she will never have an equal chance to fight off a man who gets his hands on her. Not without a lucky shot to his head or a knife to his gut. It's not a slight on the fact she's a girl. Women have strengths we lesser mortals can only dream of. It's a fact because I want her to stay alive. It's one we recognise because that's the tactic a lot of men will stoop to. They'll use violence to force her to do what they want, or worse. I won't pretend for the sake of her ego." He tossed me an uncommon grin. "As big as that fucker already is."

I pulled a face.

"So Cassie needs trusted people around her—"

"Cassie's the queen, and I'm her loyal subject," Riordan finished. "Got it."

Struan scoffed. "If you're in her bed, you're a lot more than that."

"Not going to warn me off?"

I stared, hooked on the antagonism. Riordan had no reason to stand up for me. We weren't anything. Not on his half. I was still fighting my own battle of mine/not mine. My brother had obviously riled him.

"Far be it from me to comment on who my sister chooses to fuck," Struan snarled back. "But I'm happy to demonstrate how much you've pissed me off."

Riordan cracked his neck. "We just going to stand here comparing dick sizes or have you got something bigger to show me?"

My brother concealed a flash of amusement. Without a word, I understood its meaning. *Heh. Maybe I like him after all.*

He centred on Riordan.

Then brought the pain.

For as long as I could remember, my brothers had fought, sparring against each other and Arran, too, when he came around. I'd taken the lessons to heart at a young age. By a quirk of fate, five street kids had changed from urchins to wealthy. We owned a mansion. Had investments for days. None of my nieces or nephews would ever worry about where the next meal was coming from. None would ever be homeless.

Yet that still didn't afford us peace of mind.

Money talked. The threat of violence silenced.

All four of my brothers could walk into any room and command the attention of everyone there. Even Camden, who was peace-loving but whose scarred face gave him a brutal appearance. I would never be awarded the same respect just by existing, certainly not by the opposite sex. But that also gave me the opportunity to be more subtle. Piers hadn't feared me until I sliced into his dick.

I hoped his nightmares were of my smile and my blade.

Struan worked Riordan through a series of classic steps. How to throw down someone running at you. How to get them into a headlock. How to break their arm.

Both men stripped their shirts. I nearly died at the reveal of Riordan's taut, muscular body. I already knew he had inkwork on his arms, but it was across his back, too.

I wanted to taste every damn line. I needed him closer to explore it all.

More, I watched in wonder at the pretence he was putting on for no reason I could understand. Maybe learning to fight was important to him, but I wasn't. Stepping up to my family made no sense.

As fast as Riordan learned, gaining my brother's

approval with sparse but meaningful guidance as Struan didn't waste words, the bruises stacked up, too. At one rough landing, I shot from my seat, convinced he'd broken his neck.

"Sit the fuck down, Cass," Struan snapped.

I did, though my heart hammered.

Riordan climbed up, breathing hard and dripping sweat. He wiped the blood from his nose, then returned to his position. "Again."

If my crush on him was ever going to fade, today was not that day.

A while on, Struan called time and clapped Riordan on the back, muttering something I couldn't hear. Then he strode away, calling out to Tyler that he'd take point.

"Are ye done?" I yelled at his retreating back.

"For now. Go back upstairs," Struan ordered.

Riordan snatched up his discarded shirt and prowled out of the hall. I scampered to keep up.

We returned to my rooms.

Inside, I locked the door then leaned against it, my fingers fluttering at my chest.

Riordan tossed his shirt to the rug. I trailed my gaze over him and down the dusting of hair that led beneath his waistband.

Then I clocked the welts and red bruises, some already dark. Guilt swallowed me whole.

"Are ye okay?"

"Why, want to kiss me better?"

I stared, shocked at the sass. He'd flirted back. Ho-lee shite.

Yet there was no humour in his savage expression. If anything, his mood seemed darker than ever.

"I need a shower."

"What's mine is yours." I directed him to my bedroom.

Riordan kept close behind and snatched up the rucksack his sister had sent but which had stayed abandoned by my couch when he'd locked me in.

In my bedroom, I eyed my bed but stepped into the en suite, flipping on the light then the shower. Water thundered down in the spacious stall, the gold-flecked tiles gleaming.

From the cupboard, I pulled out two towels then draped them over the rail. Then I turned back to Riordan, huge, in my space, his mouth luscious. I should leave. This was my cue.

I didn't.

"Why did ye play along with my brother's questions? Would've been easier for ye to say we weren't a couple."

His glower remained in place. "I was facing a beating either way. Better for him to assume he had to leave the scraps for you."

I laughed under my breath. Stepping closer, I traced my gaze over his bruised cheek. My fingers shook. "That wasn't it."

"Then maybe I just needed to get back behind closed doors with you. You ran from me. I should punish you."

My insides tightened.

God, yes. To whatever he had in mind. The steam from the shower rose. I heaved in a breath of humid air, my dress clinging to me.

"I liked watching ye fight."

"Enjoyed seeing me bleed?"

I raised my finger to his cut lip. It came away red.

Both of us stared at my fingertip. I took it to my mouth and sucked, tasting his blood on my tongue.

With a sound of anger, Riordan captured my wrist. His other hand snatched my waist to tug me against him. Coarse jeans to slick silk. Rigid muscles to soft flesh.

I parted my lips in shock. At exactly the same second, he kissed me.

Hard.

All restraint fell away. It was a desperate, bruising kiss. Nothing like I'd imagined but so much better.

For weeks, I'd lain in bed and pictured him doing this. His touch wandering my body. His limbs tangled with mine. Our first kiss. My first kiss ever. In my head, I'd pictured it being gentle and just a smidge more romantic. In reality, he gave me something entirely different and probably better suited.

A claiming.

His lips forced mine wider, and I moaned at the touch of his tongue. The copper of his blood. He tasted masculine. Startlingly unfamiliar. *Mine.*

It was all I could do to hold on and try to follow his lead.

He tore his mouth away, breathing hard. "You drive me fucking crazy, Cassiopeia Archer."

I couldn't find the words to tell him it was the same for me.

But I found others. "The problem with ye telling me not to run again is the fact I know you'll chase me."

The water thundered down behind him.

He snarled a laugh. "Put your damn wrists out in front of you."

I could've obeyed him, but where was the fun in that? Holding his gaze, I reached for the hem that flirted with my thighs and then stripped my dress. Moist air coated my hot skin.

Riordan's focus slipped down to the lingerie I'd picked out earlier with him in mind, after I'd made myself come to a dirty movie while I'd imagined him listening. A matching set with a lacy red balcony bra. It pushed my boobs up in a scandalous fashion and revealed the circular surfer tattoo at my ribs.

His nostrils flared, and he marched to the bathroom door. For a horrible moment, I thought he was going to kick me out. But no. My black satin dressing gown hung on a hook. He whipped the belt off it and prowled back over, brandishing the rope.

"Wrists."

This time, I obediently offered them up.

He bound them together efficiently, then grabbed a towel from the rail and tossed it to the floor. "Kneel."

Slowly, I lowered to my knees, my head in line with the bulge in his jeans. A moment of panic washed over me. I didn't know how to do this. Any of it. And I couldn't use my hands either. I needed him to lead me through it. "You'll have to tell me what to do. I don't want to be bad at this."

Riordan's lip curled. Still holding the other end of the cord, he strung it over the towel rail on the wall behind me, then pulled. It lifted my arms above my head.

I squeaked in shock and found my balance, the cord holding me up as he tied a knot.

Riordan backed away. He cupped his bulge, anger still in every move. "You want this? Watch how you make me feel."

Holding my gaze, he removed his shoes and socks, then undid his jeans and yanked them down, stepping out of both them and his black boxer shorts in one go. My heart thumped wildly at the sight of a fully naked Riordan, and I soaked in every inch of his flesh.

Mainly the significant inches between his legs.

His dick stood tall. It was big. Bigger than I'd guessed with a thick vein running the length. He was hard as a rock. Difficult to imagine fitting it in anywhere.

He stepped under the spray and tipped his head back so the water soaked his hair and slid down his form, darkening his ink.

Then he took his dick in his hand and held it, his heated gaze all over my breasts in my sexy bra. He stroked himself from root to tip, his mouth open in obvious pleasure.

I growled and tugged on the rope. "Let me go."

"No. Watch what you can't have."

Pushing up on my heels, I tried to get my fingers to the knot. It was a weird angle. No matter how I wrenched at it, I couldn't get it loose.

Fury descended.

I made a strangled sound of frustration and tried to stand. If I could get a good enough angle, I'd pull the damn rail off the wall. But I twisted and dropped, hanging from my wrists for a second before I righted myself.

A dark laugh came from Riordan, and I spun back around to scowl at him.

"That's it, fight. Show me what you'd be like if I tied you up in a bed," he goaded.

In his hand, his dick pulsed. I breathed hard, losing my momentum to stop struggling and stare. He was enjoying me being like this. I hated it. Badly, I wanted to join him. Touch him.

Which was exactly why he'd stopped me.

Damn him. Gritting my teeth, I regained my control, crouched on my spiked heels with my hands above my head. If he thought I was going to do what he expected, I'd make him think again.

I was inexperienced for sure, but he'd never make me docile.

With my gaze held on him, I opened my knees. He already had full sight of my breasts, but I wanted to test how far this went.

Riordan's smirk dropped. As did his gaze, his focus landing straight between my legs. My core pulsed.

He swore and squeezed his dick.

I wondered how I appeared to him. Tied up, angry, my curls no doubt wild in the humid air, my body on display in my red lingerie. Could he see that I was wet?

Slowly, I rocked my hips.

He groaned and smacked his hand to the wall of the shower, his broad chest inflating with a heavy breath.

The hand gripping his dick worked faster. The movement nearly hypnotised me, but I didn't give up my part in our strange and dirty stare-off. I rolled my body again, taking my action of trying to escape and turning it into a sultry show. I might never have been naked in front of a man but I'd seen the ladies at the club work the poles and perform stripteases.

Every move was slowed down. Purposeful.

Sex just minus the contact.

I was limited without the use of my hands, but I imagined Riordan being underneath me. Then acted out fucking him so he could almost feel it.

Under the shower spray, he slid his fist up and down in jerky motions. His gaze remained glued to the space between my thighs, and quickly, his actions concentrated on the end of his dick.

I moaned, the sound slipping from me. Electricity slid over my skin. I needed to be touched. To have him cross the room and kiss me again then use those clever fingers on me. Never in my life had I wanted anything more. And there wasn't a single thing I could do about it. *Infuriating.*

Then he tipped back his head and stopped moving, his mouth open in a silent groan. In his hand, he came. Ropes of cum spilled against the glass, rinsed away by the water, more coming.

I whimpered at the sight. It felt like a gift to witness.

It felt like a waste.

My body cried out for him, but he turned his back and put his head down, washing away the evidence and not looking at me anymore, fuelling my annoyance once again.

He'd wanted me enough to come while staring at me. He'd tied me up so neither of us could take it further.

Mine for a moment then not. The whiplash hurt way more than it should.

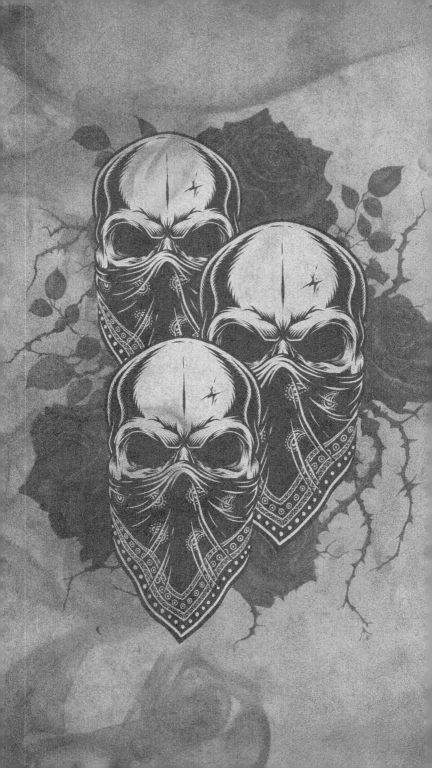

12

Riordan

Shame dogged my actions in finishing up in the shower. I rinsed down the wall then smacked the button to kill the water. Stepping out, I snagged a towel and wrapped it around my waist then took my fingers to the knot constraining Cassie.

Never in my life had I wanted to tie up a woman.

She was so fucking pretty like this.

The second the rope was loose, Cassie yanked it free then burst up to standing. She shoved me with both hands, barely rocking me, then passed me to peer into the mirror. "What did I tell ye about my hair and humidity?"

In quick, clearly annoyed actions, she snagged a bottle of hair product and sprayed her curls, glowering at my reflection in the mirror.

Vaguely, I recalled the time I'd busted her putting the tracker on my bike. I'd tugged her hood down to identify her, and she'd jerked it right back up, saying something about her curls and the rain.

"You're angry at that?"

"Get out, Riordan."

I backed away, hunting down my bag in her bedroom where I'd dropped it. Inside, Genevieve had packed me a selection of clothes—she still had the spare key to my car—and I pulled on joggers and a fresh crew t-shirt.

Tiredness hung over me. If Struan's lesson had worn me out, his sister's provocation nearly ended me.

At the bottom of my rucksack was a small, wrapped bundle with a tag reading Cassie's name.

I returned to the bathroom door and knocked.

She swung it open, still in only her fucking sexy lingerie, her body a sight I'd dream about for years.

"What?"

Words escaped me. Heat swallowed me whole.

In the shower, I thought I'd taken my fill of her. I'd let the crackling energy between us crest. I'd orgasmed staring at her pussy and pictured being inside her while she rode me. Or bending her over in the stall and losing all control.

Yet one minute on and I was raring to go again. My dick thickened, and my mouth dried.

Helplessly, I held up the packet.

Cassie squinted at it then took it from me and breezed past. "I'm going to get dressed. Or maybe first lie on my bed and copy what ye did. So leave me alone."

Holy fuck. I backed to the wall, hands behind my back. Her bed was wide. Far too big for her alone.

"I want to watch."

Her lip curled in a pretty snarl. "No."

"Why not? You already tormented me earlier when I was outside in the hall."

"Ye turned my first kiss into the most frustrating

experience, so excuse me if I don't want a repeat."

"Your first kiss?"

"Aye, jackass, so leave me alone."

Something tightened in my chest. I'd guessed that she was inexperienced, but not that much. Fucking hell. I'd attacked her. Tied her up.

"I didn't know." A step took me closer.

"Well, now ye do." She folded her arms, not meeting my gaze.

The challenge had left her. She'd never backed down from me in the past. Dropping my hand, I puzzled at her, confused and insanely horny again. More, I wanted to make amends.

"I owe you three kisses for how rough I was." With my pulse racing, I took a step. "The first I'm giving you now. The others will come later."

She peeked at me through her eyelashes.

I approached the bed. Tipped up her face and gave her a second to react then brushed my lips over hers. If circumstances had been different, I'd have kissed her like this for our first time. A peck. A slow return.

Another, teasing her lips to meld to mine.

Cassie whimpered. The sound shot desperation through me in a drugging wave that I fought to manage. She followed my lead, rising on her knees to meet me better. A promise to come with me to where I led. I tilted my head. Parted her lips with mine then pulled away.

Over a heavy breath, I told her, "One."

Then I left her to slam the door after me.

Holed up in her living room, I adjusted my junk and strained to listen for any sound.

Music started. 'Rush' by Dutch Melrose and benny mayne.

I sighed and checked myself. There was a reason I'd tied her up, beyond the fact it was the sexiest thing I'd ever imagined. The pull to her was insane. A full-force draw I temporarily couldn't ignore. Restraining her hands had stopped her from touching me, an event which would have had me lose my mind completely. Yet a simple fact remained. I couldn't get involved with her. It wasn't fair and it wasn't safe. For either of us.

She was right to kick me out. It was what I deserved.

I exhaled and slumped on the sofa cushions. Thank fuck for logic. I just had to follow that path.

After a while, the music cut out, and Cassie emerged from her room, her movements brisk and her attention on her phone. She took the opposite end of the couch from me, some kind of material in one hand and her phone in the other.

"I'm talking to your sisters. Say hi."

She turned the camera on me. Onscreen, Gen and Everly peered out. Both held the same piece of cloth and string Cassie did.

Genevieve squinted at the phone. "Is that a black eye?"

I rubbed my face. My whole body ached now the adrenaline had worn off. "Cassie has a mean right hook. What are you all doing?"

Everly held up her hands. "We're learning embroidery. I need a hobby so am exploring options. Cassie and Genevieve are supporting me. This is a sampler, and it contains all the different stitches we need to practice. If we do it together, it'll be fun."

'Fun' sounded dubious, and Cassie sewing was a far

sight stranger than seeing her with a blade or any other weapon. I eyed her. She pouted back at me then set the phone down on the coffee table, propped up on its side so we were both in shot.

Threading her needle, Genevieve scrunched up her nose. "While we work on the first, what is that, a straight stitch? Surely I can't fuck this up. Anyway, while I try, I want to tell you both about the march that's happening in Deadwater this weekend."

"What kind of march?" I asked.

"For women's right to safety on the streets. There's been protests in town and outside of the warehouse."

Cassie jerked forward. "They're protesting *us*? I knew from Arran the reporters had said we were to blame, but people believe them?"

Gen nodded. "Apparently. There's been some shitty gossip videos made over how the strip club attracted the killer. The proof being that Natasha's body was left outside and Alisha was an employee."

Cassie stabbed her sampler, drawing through the baby-blue cotton. "That's bullshit."

"Horrible," Everly agreed.

Gen clucked her tongue, her focus on the needle she was still trying to load with thread. "It's also good. In an unexpected twist, those same social media warriors patrolling outside in search of clout are protecting us."

I nodded. "Makes sense. Red can do even less to attack the skeleton crew with such a big audience."

Cassie gave a small smile of approval. Coming from the queen of gang strategy, I got a glimmer of pride.

Gen continued, "Exactly. Soon, we'll bring an end to this. Until then, we can wait behind a shield of morally outraged keyboard warriors."

That word replayed in my mind. "Soon?" I repeated. As in Bronson was almost caught? It meant we could go back.

"Soon." My sister poured meaning into the word.

I ducked out of the conversation, reclining and thinking about the strange mission I was on, not voluntarily at first but by choice now. When it was over, I'd be back to life in the warehouse. I'd see Cassie around, but she wouldn't be next to me all the time.

An odd surge of emotion curled in me. It felt suspiciously like regret.

Distracting myself with my phone, I flipped through the cameras, then messaged Tyler to check in.

> **Tyler:** All is quiet. I'm going to grab some sleep. I suggest you do, too.

To the tune of Cassie cursing her stitches, then to a telenovela she put on the TV as background noise, I let unconsciousness drag me under. It happened quickly. I'd been on high alert and couldn't remember the last time I'd closed my eyes, but the orgasm took the edge off enough to allow me to relax.

The blackness was a welcome and warm escape.

My dreams didn't play ball. In them, I was running from danger, my heart racing so fast it felt like it could explode. A black car chased me, screeching through traffic and herding me down alleys and side streets in Deadwater's suburbs. Doors slammed. First Gen's father then my ex-boss appeared in entryways and rejected my need for sanctuary.

I ran out the end of the street to find my way blocked by a churning river. The water boiled, frothing grey and white.

In my hands, I held something small. A little life. Maybe a bird or a kitten. All I knew was that it was precious and I had to protect it.

A bullet whistled past my ear.

From the car's window, the mayor leaned out. He taunted me with a cruel smile and words I couldn't understand. He held a comically large handgun like something from a Western. Then he fired again.

The bullet lodged in my chest. It punched me back into the water.

The river closed over my head, freezing cold, cutting off my air, and I sank down, clutching my precious creature like my faltering heartbeat could save it. I tried to fight. To swim. My body didn't respond.

There was nothing for us but to drown and die.

With a gasp, I woke, frozen still but with my pulse racing. It took several seconds to realise I could breathe easily. And to recognise the warmth of the woman curled against me.

Cassie had crept close while I slept, as she'd done when I'd been knocked out. Except this time, my arm was tucked around her frame, and our hands were entwined and linked at her chest.

My heart skipped a beat.

I didn't know how long I'd been asleep, but maybe she'd seen my nightmare. Turned off the TV, forgiven me for the shower incident, and decided I needed comfort.

All I knew was that contact. Her heat spread down my arm, doing the same thing as last time she'd touched me like this—battling the cold inside me and giving me something better. My breathing sounded loud in my ears. Adrenaline from the nightmare or maybe the fight still ghosted through me.

I couldn't move. Not to withdraw my hand and not to bring her closer, though it felt like the most natural thing in the world to lift her onto my chest and kiss her awake.

In the darkness, I was hers and she was mine.

For a minute, I'd pretend.

Cassie stretched against my body, her bare toes drawing down my leg and her ass too close to my groin for comfort. She turned so we were facing each other.

"Everything's okay. It was just a nightmare. Ye shuddered with it then relaxed, but it came back so I cuddled up. Ye are so nice to sleep with. I've never done it with anyone else."

I asked a question that had plagued me, easy to say in my half-awake state. "Why did you proposition me?"

"Seem to recall ye were the one with his dick in his hand in my bathroom."

I heaved in a breath. "Before that."

Cassie's blue eyes focused on me. "They say do the thing that scares ye."

"Seriously."

"I am being serious. I live by that. It helps me every day."

"What scares you, wild girl?"

For a moment, she just watched me, then her throat bobbed. "Everything. I think I'm broken like that. I get nightmares, too."

"What about?"

"I lie awake at night and think that my family's gone. As a kid, it was even worse. I had to ask Sin and Lottie for my own rooms so I could move out of theirs."

"How would that help?"

"I didn't want to disturb them by repeatedly checking on them in the night, particularly when they had their babies."

She'd done it to help them, not herself.

Cassie continued, "I'm scared of heights so I put myself in perilous situations to deal with it. I refuse to be afraid of men like Piers so—"

"You took a knife to his dick."

Her lips curved into a dangerous smile. "Exactly. Then I kidnapped the guy I wanted because I was scared for us both."

"Wanted, as in past tense?"

Her smile faded. "That's the real reason behind my offer. I know it isn't real so forcing it would make it go away."

My fucked-up heart wished it was real. That odd sense of jealousy I'd been struck down by when she'd chatted so easily with Tyler, fucking Ty, as she'd called him, wouldn't stop burning inside me. Memories of her tied hands and her lithe body flexing against the constraint of the rope hit like bombs. In that moment in the gathered dusk, burrowed in together on her sofa, desperation nearly stole my breath.

Wanting her was as real to me as breathing. Nothing had changed.

"I'm sorry I tied you up," I finally managed.

Unaware of my pain, Cassie sighed. "Don't be. Can I ask ye something? Before I go further down that why-ye rabbit hole of an explanation." At my chin lift, she continued. "I think I know the answer to this, but have ye killed anyone yet?"

"Of course I haven't."

"At some point, if ye stay working for Arran, you'll have to. You'll want to. I already know you've accepted the place for what it is. Your sister went through the same mindset shift, with a bit of coaching from me."

I hesitated, because I'd thought about it but dismissed it. Arran had his enforcer in Shade. He didn't need another. "I don't think I'd kill someone without extreme circumstances. How would I be sure that person really deserved it?"

She held up a finger then a second and third, counting them off. "If they try to kill ye. If they hurt someone ye care about. If they commit a crime so awful the world deserves the peace of them being gone. Easy."

The man in my dream deserved to die. For killing me. For taking the life I was trying to protect. "That's got to be a tiny amount of people," I muttered.

"Wrong. Shade has a revolving door of men to dispatch. They just keep on coming."

I watched her, poised to frame the question but almost unwilling to ask. "Who does he kill?"

"Rapists. Paedophiles. Men released from jail and allowed back in the community. He watches them until he's sure they aren't reformed then disappears them for the good of everyone else."

As much as I thought I'd understood Arran's crew,

new pieces of the puzzle kept being revealed.

Cassie wasn't done. Something gleamed in her eyes. "They're the tip of the iceberg. There's nearly seventy thousand adults on the sex offenders register in the UK. Over ten times that who are deemed by the cops an active risk to kids. Nearly a million actual or potential paedophiles. A *million*. Then there's far, far more who are a risk to women—the police estimate around four million men."

Her lip curled. "Maths was never my strong point, but there's sixty-eight million people in this country. Twenty-six million of those are adult male. Which means one in every seven men is a serious predator or an abuser. Fifteen percent. Even if a tiny portion of those predators are women, ye can't make those odds much better. Swing a bat around any public place and chances are you'll hit at least a few of them."

Fucking hell. "I had no idea."

"Right? Because the focus is always on the women and how many suffer. It needs to be on the problem. The perpetrators. Abusers aren't rare. They're common. Think about the men ye know. Most people won't associate with the worst types, but how many would laugh off a friend sharing porn containing an obviously underage girl? Or ignore them referring to a passing woman as a bitch or a slut? Or turn a blind eye to a drunk buddy acting like a predator in a nightclub? I see it and I know that there's a decent chance one among them is hiding a darkness and that they're the one-in-seven. That's why I want to be part of Arran's crew. The closer I get to the problem, the more I want to be a part of battling it. I want to avenge those women and kids."

Emotion flared inside me. Deep and fierce heat that

had kindled with seeing her take on Piers. She'd been fearless. From her explanation, that had just been the start of her mission.

"You want to deal with them in the same way Shade does."

She pretended to polish her sparkly nails. Gold, too. Her accent colour, it seemed.

"A worthy goal, no? Which brings me to my point. I consider myself a good judge of character. I saw ye step up to protect your sister. Since then, I learned all you've done to support her and keep her safe. Ye did the same for Everly and went up against Shade who's scary as fuck to the average person. Is it any wonder my mind took a little jaunt to wanting to ride ye like a cowboy? I found the one good man and decided to keep him."

Sinking my eyes shut, I dropped my head back to the cushion, overwhelmed. Hard again. Luckily, I was lying at an angle she couldn't feel. Her ruthless edge, her certainty over her calling, it was all so deeply attractive to me. Almost as much as when she'd claimed me.

My words formed of their own volition. "Back to the proposition. Would you ask Tyler the same question?"

"Oh my God, are ye jealous? Please say yes."

I said nothing.

Instead, my mind shifted to my goal. My dream. The predator I wanted off the streets. It aligned with Cassie's calling, and suddenly, I wanted to impress her. Explain myself and everything that needed to be said.

Except I'd told no one about this. Not a single soul. And opening my mouth was a risk I shouldn't take.

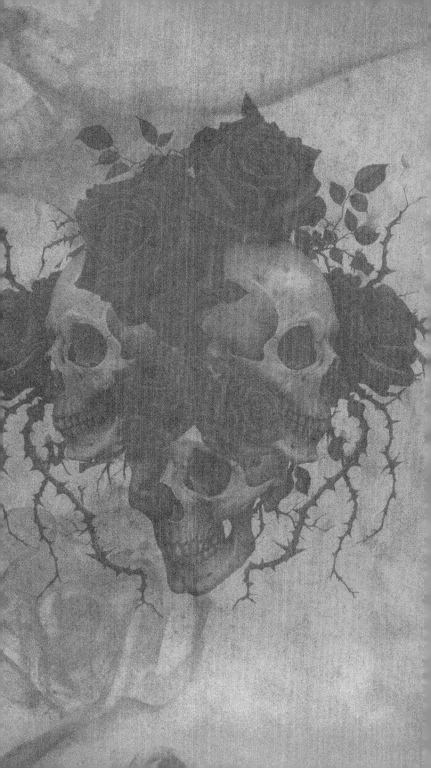

13

Cassie

Riordan sat up, shifting away from me. "Talk to me about your predator elimination plan. How will you identify them?"

Reluctantly, I gave him some space. "Shade uses a list that the cops give him. Those are people who already committed the worst crimes. I was thinking about throwing my net wider. Get access to the list of predators who live in the community, so aren't just jail releases like Shade gets his hands on. Maybe offer an anonymous tip-off form where people can report concerns. They can give as much detail as possible with any evidence and I'll do the rest."

"What exactly?"

"Investigate them. Provoke them, probably. Take them in and hurt them if I need to. Then if the claim is real, bye-bye baddie."

He went quiet for another long while. Then his stomach growled.

Shite. I should've fed him. I picked up my phone and tapped out a message to Tyler, asking for someone to bring us up something. Assuming all was still secure, we could've gone down, but I wasn't willing to give up the strange pocket of closeness we'd found.

I'd watched him sleep. Got so distracted when he flinched from his nightmare that I'd missed my telenovela, resisting until I let myself curl up against him.

Nothing had ever felt better.

My phone buzzed, and I dragged my gaze back to it.

"Tyler's going to bring us dinner," I said.

Riordan exhaled then reached for the remote, handing it to me. "Put on that show you've been watching. I fell asleep at a cliffhanger, and it's been bugging me."

Heh. I cued up the TV. "Knew ye were watching it as much as I was."

"I'm a prisoner. We don't have much to do in jail."

I cracked up. "Says the guy who locked me in here then tied me up."

He groaned and adjusted his position on the couch, the lamplight falling over him and softening his hard edges. Darkness had fallen again, but we'd never opened my curtains, it being safer to have no way of anyone seeing in. With only the lamp on behind me, it made for another cosy night.

In any other circumstance, romantic.

The telenovela started with a recap, but I dismissed it. Then I paused. "Did ye miss anything? I can run that again."

"Alexia is having an affair with a guy in the next town over. Her husband is a pilot for an aid organisation and is away a lot, but is due home. She regrets her cheating and wants to be a family again with their three kids.

The cliffhanger was her showing up to tell the lover whose name I didn't catch that it's over. She wants him to promise never to reveal what they did for the sake of her marriage."

"Jeez. Ye really are enjoying it. The lover's name is Eduardo."

"That's it."

His gaze met mine. Something hot crackled between us. All that cuddling in our sleep and this was what did me in.

My chest constricted, and it took a long minute until I was able to focus on the screen and the montage of sex and dates the two lovers had been on.

In her lover's doorway, Alexia trembled and rang the bell.

Eduardo answered. "Baby? What are you doing here? You've never come to my house before."

"I needed to do this in person. We said a month and our time is up. It's over. I'm married, Eduardo. I need you to promise never to contact me again."

Eduardo gave a cry of pain and thumped the wall.

He rattled a framed photo that Alexia stared at and the camera zoomed in on as if it was scandalous. Two men, arms around each other in clear familiarity. The lover and another, older guy.

"Who's in the picture?" Riordan asked.

"It's her husband. A younger version. Check the identi-moustache."

"That's Dirk? In Eduardo's house? How do they know each other?"

I smiled as Alexia shrieked the same question.

"What is this? How do you know this man?"

Eduardo frowned, drawing in two oddly perfect eyebrows. "That's my father."

"Plot twist!" I took a shocked breath.

He laughed under his breath. "The woman clearly has a type."

"Derek is my father, but we were estranged for most of my life," Eduardo revealed. "He works out of the country, so we've only met a few times. I'll get to see him again when he returns home soon. Why?"

Alexia slid to the floor, digging her fingers into her perfectly styled hair as she whispered to herself. "One month. I ruined my life for one month of him, and it's cost me everything." Then she froze and lifted her gaze. "What do you mean 'Derek'? That isn't his name."

Adverts rolled at a break in the show.

A scenario played out in my head, distracting me so I forgot to skip to the next part of the episode. In the telenovela, they'd given their affair a time limit. All the fun but with an expiry date. That brought drama, but only because the scriptwriters had tricks up their sleeves.

I was the author of my own life. I knew what I wanted, and that had narrowed in on two major points. The role I wanted at the warehouse. And Riordan. I wanted him more than I wanted air in my lungs and blood in my veins.

On the coffee table was my stack of papers, my closed notebook on top. Annoyance rippled along the path of my certainty. That summary I'd written told me this wasn't real. My therapy suggested Riordan was an obsession that would burn out. I hated the idea I could hurt him if this ever got off the ground.

Riordan made a sound of frustration and grabbed the

remote, stabbing to pause the TV.

"Aren't we continuing?" Weakly, I pointed at the screen.

"No."

I rolled my head on the cushion to stare at him. Words stuck in my mouth.

He worked his jaw. "Tell me you're not obsessed with me."

Oh fuck. He'd been thinking about it, too. I swallowed. "I am, but what I feel is fake."

"Describe it."

"What?"

"Exactly what you feel for me."

"Hell no."

The opposite of fear. The source of all things sweet.

I went to leap up from the sofa. Riordan grabbed me by the waist and hooked me back. I landed next to him with wide-eyed alarm, then braced a hand to his broad chest.

Every small touch was shocking. Every push-and-pull interaction somehow vital.

Slowly I withdrew my hand.

Riordan made a sound of pain and dug his fingers into his hair. "Then I'll talk instead. No matter what, I can't be anything to you. Not long term. It can't happen."

"Why?"

"I won't live that long."

My stomach tightened. "Are ye sick?"

"No, but there's someone I intend to get revenge on which will mean I'll likely end up dead or in jail."

He... My brain instantly offered the solution. "The mayor."

Of course. Of course he'd want that man dead after everything he'd done.

Riordan exhaled in a gust. "How is it you can read me like that? No hesitation."

I shrugged. Like it wasn't obvious. "Tell me why."

"Arran took me into his crew at the moment I was realising I had no purpose in my life anymore. After my mother died, I worked and supported Gen. I kept our lives ticking over. But she's found her own path now, and I have the chance to take my own. I'm not cut out to be a gangster. I don't give a fuck about territory and reputation, and in the back of your car, I realised how easily my life could be over the minute someone decided to make it so. One person ruling over the city already wants me dead. He tried to give his daughter to a rapist piece of shit. The sister I should've been raised with. There is nothing good about that man, and the world will be a better place with him out of it."

"So you'll be the one to take him down."

Abruptly, he leapt up and stalked to peer from the curtains out into the dark.

I pursed my lips. "You're skeleton crew. They'll help."

He dropped the material and scoffed. "They won't. Shade would've killed the mayor a long time ago if Arran didn't need him. Arran talks about the balance of power in the city and how it works for his objectives. He keeps his business running smoothly because of who he can bribe and who steers the ship. The mayor's at the centre of that. As much as I respect Arran, I can't tell him what I intend to do because he has reason to stop me."

I couldn't contradict him. He was right, at least in part.

Riordan returned, stopping a few feet away. It might as well have been miles. "It's a death wish. I'll take my revenge but it will be on my own, and I'll be acting against the leader of my crew. I don't fear the mayor. Not him or anyone he cons into protecting him. But if he doesn't kill me, Arran will."

The world spun around me.

Fuck, no. Fuck no with fucking bells on it.

Riordan was not going to throw his life away for Mayor Makepeace. Whether or not my obsession was real, I was a ride or die kind of girl. I was Team Rio all the way, even if just as a friend.

Ugh, that word sucked.

I'd also learned a huge amount about this man in the space of one short conversation. He was still grieving. I didn't know how many years ago his mother had died, but Genevieve had been a teenager. Maybe a decade? His ma confided in him a terrible secret which he couldn't share with anyone. Not even after she died. He'd been trapped in needing to keep a roof over his sister's head, all while reeling over what he'd found out.

The man they were living with wasn't his da. He never had been, in anything more than the most basic pretence. Riordan had been left with more questions than answers, and it was like looking in the mirror.

I was hung up over my mother. I'd also wanted my father dead, but that was a done deal. He'd been in the ground a long time.

Sitting up on my knees, I stared Riordan down. "You're right that Arran doesn't want the mayor gone yet, but he'd never hurt ye."

"He's ruthless."

I snorted. "He's also in love with your sister. Ye could do anything, and he'd stand by and watch."

"Shade has every reason to kill the mayor. He is a borderline psychopath, and though he's in love with Everly, he hasn't yet done the deed, even knowing what she suffered. That's because Arran refuses to allow it. If I go in, they'll stop me. If I persist, Arran can't just stand by. He might not be the one to take a blade to my throat, but he has fifty men who would happily solve the problem for him."

For a moment, I hesitated. I couldn't deny the truth in that. I didn't think it likely, but also it wasn't impossible.

Slowly, I trailed my gaze up Riordan's throat to the curve of his jaw. He hadn't shaved, his shower time being used for other things, and scruff darkened his face, taking him from boy next door to potential murderer.

I liked it.

He watched me. Leaned in then rocked back.

I had no idea what I was doing, but I couldn't let him be hurt. I'd also never wanted anything more than to take the pressure between us and break it.

He owed me two more kisses. I wanted more.

"What if we make a deal?" I asked.

"What kind of deal?"

"The game Arran operates in his basement ties couples together for thirty days. That's based on the amount of time it takes to do two things: To form a habit and to create an emotional bond. That's why he keeps the winning couples together. Orders them to have sex every day."

With an inscrutable expression, he waited on me to continue.

"Give me something like that. Ten days."

"To do what?"

"Help ye get your revenge on the mayor."

His nostrils flared. "Not exactly what I was hoping you'd say."

"And," I interrupted, "we belong to each other for that time. We do anything we like. Be on call for the other and take everything we need."

A hot rush of desire had me digging my hands into the cushion, wishing he was under me. The core of my body directly over his hardness. Desperation added to my swirling emotions.

His hands formed fists. "There are so many reasons why that isn't a good idea. I've told you mine. You have your own."

"Because I'm obsessed? From what my therapist taught me, everything I'm feeling will go away if I indulge it. It's the denial which is driving me insane. That's the reason I'm the way I am. I want to possess ye. When I do, it'll stop. Ten days will be enough without risking ye getting hurt."

His gaze searched mine. "I won't fall in love with you, wild girl. I can't."

My heart hurt. "And I'll fall out of love with ye."

Some part of me was about to break. I wasn't sure what. All I knew was this moment and how locked in I was with Riordan.

A thump rocked the door.

Riordan whirled around then swore and relaxed again

when my brother identified himself.

"I've brought food. Open the fuck up," Struan grumbled.

Riordan strode to answer. I was stuck in hope.

Riordan's revenge was so simple yet shot through with difficulties. That was fine. I was skilled with cutting through the noise and taking action. Yet there was conflict in it for me, too. In murdering the mayor of Deadwater, I'd be acting against the wishes of Arran and his crew, damaging the trust I was earning in the place I wanted to call my second home. All for the sake of a man I'd temporarily decided was mine.

What I couldn't be sure about was which side of the issue I'd regret.

My musings were cut short as the door swung open. And my brother pulled a gun on Riordan.

14

Riordan

*S*truan stalked into the apartment, a tray in one hand and a gun in the other. His gaze took in the corners of the room then me. "Cosy in here."

I held my ground.

The door clicked closed, and the dangerous man set down the food and lifted his chin to his sister. "Eat."

The barrel remained trained on me.

"We got a problem here?" I asked.

Cassie's voice followed mine. "Um, Struan? Why are ye aiming at Riordan?"

I didn't take my attention off him. No one had ever pulled a gun on me before, but this almost certainly wouldn't be the last time.

Tension strung out between us.

Cassie reached down the side of the sofa and returned upright. In her hand, she held a gun of her own. "Bang, bang. Stop it."

A beat passed, and Struan shrugged then flipped the weapon in his hand and held it out to me. "Ye left this downstairs, so Tyler informs me. Why?"

I curled my lip, not taking it, and also not liking the fact I had to admit another fault. "Carrying a gun and working out how the fuck to fire it would be a waste of time. I'm better off without it. Or I was."

Cassie's brother sighed. Dropped his arm. "Ye can't shoot? I'm going to brain Arran. What did he do, recruit ye then leave ye to fend for yourself?"

"His friend died," I countered. Arran was grieving.

"Aye, that's no excuse for dropping the ball with the person protecting Cassie."

From the sofa, Cassie stowed her weapon like nothing had happened and snagged a chicken drumstick. "In Arran's defence, he didn't know I'd claimed Riordan until I kidnapped him. But I'm inclined to agree."

Struan grumbled and dropped into an armchair, setting the gun down on the table. My heart restarted, and I had half a mind to snatch it up and see how he liked being on the other end of the barrel. The psycho would probably enjoy it.

"Once you've eaten, we'll move on to lesson two. Shooting and disarming. Really should've been able to flip control just then. I gave ye every chance." He folded his arms and rested back then switched his gaze to Cassie. "Bullshit that Sin and Lottie have to stay another night."

She ducked her head and shrank in on herself, all her bluster gone in an instant. "I don't like it either. I just wish they were home and everything was okay."

Cautiously, I took a seat next to her then helped myself to some of the food. Bottles of ice-cold water beaded on the tray, and I downed half of one before attacking the chicken. It had a barbecue marinade, plus there were hot, salted chips in a bowl. I needed food badly, yet as much as I concentrated on consuming calories, I couldn't help noticing Cassie's change in attitude.

What had her brother said? That Sin and Lottie were staying away? Cassie worried about them, she'd told me it had been a problem when she was a child, and I'd bet any money that hadn't gone away. This would stress her out even more.

When the meal was done, we left the apartment, Struan going ahead with my gun casually lodged in his waistband. I shrugged on my leather jacket. Beside me, a quiet Cassie had already donned a thick hoodie. It had cat ears on the hood that she'd tugged up over her curls.

Cute as fuck, yet she wasn't smiling.

I nudged her. "Everything will be okay with your folks."

She shot me a surprised look. "I know. I was going to tell you about Lottie and Sin, but they only just messaged when I started talking to your sisters. There wasn't time to process it, and it's only a delay in their appointment, so no news. Also, sorry about my brother and the gun. He makes points in dramatic ways."

"Runs in the family," I grouched.

Cassie snickered and bumped her shoulder to my arm.

It was just an acknowledgement, but it felt like the most natural thing in the world to throw my arm around her as we walked along.

I resisted.

She'd offered me a deal I'd barely started to get my head around. Both parts of it demanded my attention. With her strategic mind, revenge on the mayor could be so much easier. It might even save my skin. She had resources. An army of dangerous relatives like some kind of Mafia princess.

But it was the second part of the offer that tripped me up.

"Ye still haven't given me an answer," she said, low.

We passed the top of the staircase, continuing on down the corridor. Ahead, her brother took a corner, disappearing out of sight. In a patch of darkness, I stopped Cassie. Rounded on her.

"Two," I said.

She tilted her head. "Two?"

I pressed my mouth to hers. With a squeak of surprise, she stilled, then kissed me back.

Head rush.

Hot blood.

Muscles taut to stop from grabbing her too roughly.

I meant to be brief, but the way she met me and moved with me flipped a switch in my brain that sent me back for more. I tugged her closer. Stifled a groan at another perfect press.

My heart thumped out of time.

Breaking away, I kissed below her ear then whispered, "Whatever I'm facing, why does it feel like the biggest danger is you?"

She twisted her lips in breathless amusement but didn't reply.

Around the corner, Struan waited at the top of another broad hallway. I peered into the gloom. Down one side, moonlight filtered through windows in silver slices, and the other side was decorated with portraits.

Heavy wooden frames containing oil paintings, the glimmer of gold around the edges proclaiming their age and importance.

"What is this?" I asked.

"Your training ground." Struan took the gun to a side table then pulled something from his pocket. Bullets, from the heavy thud of the box and the clink of metal.

What the fuck? I dove my eyebrows together. "Enjoy bullet holes in your antiques?"

Her brother uttered a laugh, and Cassie curled her arm through mine, leading me down the corridor. I followed her gentle pressure, the easy contact almost familiar yet still startling.

"A little bit of history," she said. "All the people in these portraits are our ancestors. Our father, who if ye recall was one of the worst people to have ever breathed, was so proud of his family history that he bred us kids in order to preserve it. But he had a second part to his plan. He chose sex workers to bear his children then left us to be raised in poverty. His reasoning was to toughen us up so none of us would ever take wealth and luxury for granted. Right at the point he was ready to claim one of us, we were kidnapped by someone else, but that's another story."

We stopped by a side table. On it was a white vase with blue painted flowers.

Cassie picked it up and held it out. "Throw it."

I hesitated. It appeared old. Probably valuable. The type of object you edged around so you didn't jog the table it sat on.

She rolled her eyes then reared back and launched the vase down the corridor. It hit the floorboards and shattered, pieces skidding away into the gloom.

From behind, her brother laughed under his breath.

Cassie took hold of my arm again and continued strolling. "The problem was, McInver, that's his name, didn't anticipate how much we'd hate everything he stood for. He assumed whichever of us he picked as his heir, which was Sin by the way, would fall at his feet with gratitude and keep his memory and family traditions alive. My sister-in-law researched that history, and there's nothing pleasant about it. Our ancestors got rich mostly from hurting other people. So these arseholes," she drifted a hand over the nearest painting on the wall, "don't deserve your respect. But they do deserve your bullets."

Nearer the end of the hall, I picked out something new in one of the portraits. Holes.

"You use them as target practice?" I asked.

Cassie beamed and squeezed my arm. "On occasion. We usually shoot into a sandbank on the estate, but this does just as well when I can't go outside. Pick who you'd like to ventilate."

My mouth fell open in silent humour. Striding to the wall, I lifted down a painting of some old guy in a white wig. Pieces of the destroyed vase crunched under my feet, and I followed Cassie's direction, staggering slightly as the fucker weighed a ton, and propped his artwork up on a table at the end of the space.

We returned to Struan.

"Who'd he pick?" he asked.

"I think a great-grandfather four times removed. Another Sinclair McInver."

"Nice choice."

He handed me the gun. It was heavier than before. Loaded.

"Pretend he's someone ye hate and put a bullet between his eyes."

I hefted it. Exhaled. "You want me to shoot into the dark?"

"Think some fucker coming after my sister is going to wait until ye have good lighting?"

He had a point. It shouldn't have been so easy to raise the gun, yet no caution or nerves troubled me. The man in the painting became the mayor, and I was on the riverbank with a chance not to fall.

"Do I need to take off the safety?"

"It doesnae have one. It'll only fire if ye squeeze the trigger. Put the pad of your index finger to that then use the gun's sights to line up your target. Straight arm, slow your breathing."

I did, but peered back to make sure Struan and Cassie were well behind me.

Struan tilted his head. "What are ye waiting for?"

Fucking hell.

With my sights on the distant painting, I squeezed the trigger. A jolt and a crack and the bullet tore from the gun, just like in my dream except I was the one behind the weapon.

It hit something far down the corridor, right as I was recoiling from the shock. Spinning around, I set the gun carefully down on the table then shook out my hand. Cassie danced over.

"Let's see how ye did losing your bullet virginity."

The three of us jogged down and took in the portrait with a hole a few inches wide of the man's head. If this had been a real person, I would've missed. My shoulders sank.

To my surprise, Struan clapped me on the back. "Ye did well. None of us hit the picture the first time. Now I'll show ye how to avoid pulling left when ye shoot."

The lesson continued. He talked me through how to load and unload and which way the bullets went in the cartridge. How to check if there was one already in the chamber. How not to hesitate if I was in a fight and the other person was armed.

Struan's gaze went purposefully to his sister. "If her attacker is aiming, he plans to kill. Don't second-guess someone else's deadly intentions. Rely on your own."

After Cassie's startling police statistics, my view of the world was already shifting.

I took the lesson to heart.

Two shots later, I hit the bull's-eye.

Pride flushed warm through me. I put my finger to the hole in the middle of the McInver grandfather's forehead.

Struan whistled. "Nice. Perhaps we'll all despise ye a little less if ye keep working this hard."

I snorted. "Glad to impress you."

"Let's not go crazy now."

At the end of the corridor, Tyler approached. My urge to celebrate with Cassie thinned with the way he regarded her.

"Something wrong?" she asked him.

"That favour you asked, I need to talk to you about it."

Cassie gazed up at him wide-eyed then nodded. "Follow me."

She directed Tyler into a room off the gallery, leaving the door ajar. I stared after them. What the hell did he need to talk to her about that no one else could hear? Thoughts battered me. I'd asked her if she planned to offer Tyler the same thing she had me.

What if he took her up on it?

I scowled and kept my gaze on the narrow slice I had into the room. Cassie perched on the table, her hands white-knuckling the wood either side of her.

Tyler leaned in and spoke low to her, their faces close.

My grip on the gun tightened.

Then he stepped back, and Cassie leapt to her feet and fucking hugged him.

I lurched. Struan grabbed my arm and neatly took the gun from me.

He regarded me dryly. "Don't kill Tyler for looking at Cassie wrong. Or any other ally, for that matter. If they touch her against her will, that's another matter, but if you're not sure, use your fists to make your point. Save your bullets for those who deserve them."

My phone buzzed, a similar sound coming from Struan and from inside the room.

The alert system.

My heart pounded. I straightened and reached to check my screen. "The gun," I demanded.

Struan returned it to me, his wry amusement gone as fast as it had arrived.

Someone had breached the gates.

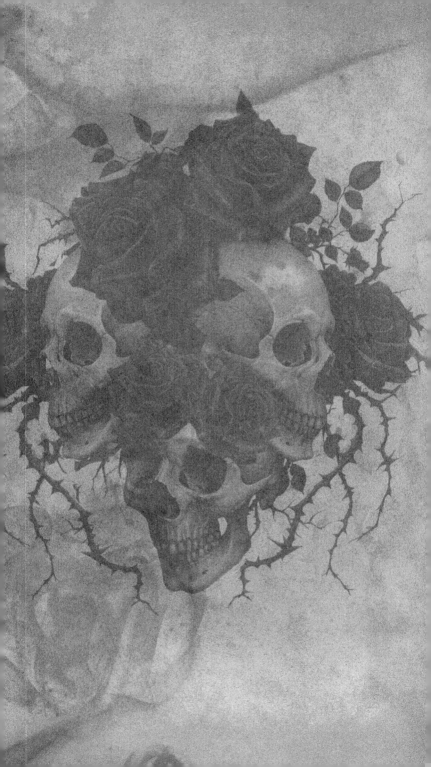

15

Cassie

*S*truan was the first to make the identification. He squinted at his phone then sighed. "Stand down."

Tyler jerked his head up, midway through instructing the others hidden around the place to move to positions of intercept. "Who?"

"Jamieson."

I grinned. Not that I'd been scared, but I'd wanted Riordan to meet the youngest of my brothers again.

The single other time they'd encountered each other had also been my first sight of Riordan. I'd fallen immediately in love. The same could not be said for him and Jamieson.

Tyler eyed me. "Don't suppose it would help any to ask you to wait in your room?"

"Are ye crazy? Let's go say hi."

The four of us made for the stairs that led to the entrance hall. Tyler held me back so the others could descend first.

I watched Riordan alongside my brother. His leather jacket was open over a skeleton crew t-shirt, his gaze attentive, his body loose as if ready to fight. Similar in many ways to Struan though lacking the same surety. Struan could handle anything that came at him. Riordan was only just learning how. He was willing, though. And capable.

Happiness filled me. We were both at the start of a journey. We could learn together.

At the bottom of the steps, our intercept man left me with a mutter, morphing into the shadows.

Riordan replaced him at my side. He leaned against a pillar, bringing himself closer to my height. "What did fucking Tyler want when he took you into that room?"

"There's that jealousy again. Love that for me."

He didn't reply.

I touched his chest and drew an imaginary line to mine. Then scrubbed it out. "Last I checked, ye hadn't answered my question. There's nothing going on here. We are distinctly not fucking."

From nearer the front door, Struan griped, "In hearing range." Then after a pause, "But good to know."

A thud followed from outside. "Open up, motherfuckers."

Struan unbolted the door, and a spark of amber light fell the other side as Jamieson appeared in the frame, pitch-black night behind him and his lighter in his hand. My heart lurched. I loved all my family. Struan was dark energy and ready to bring pain without losing sleep over what he had to do. Sin was the father figure, powerful, supportive, and ready to judge with his fists. Camden was our measure, a checkpoint and a balance. If he was willing to go there, the cause was just.

But Jamieson was most like me. A little bit wilder.

Emotionally led. Inclined to do daft things on the flip of a coin. Or in his case, a flick of his lighter wheel.

Jamieson's shadow advanced.

Struan swore at him. "Why the fuck didn't ye let us know it was ye?"

Tyler choked. "You didn't either."

Struan glowered. Jamieson gave a low laugh.

"I come with news." He eyed the man at my side. Stalled. More sparks flared. "Riordan fuckin' Jones. Last I saw ye, Shade had ye locked in a cell. Next thing I know, you're all over my family's group chat."

Riordan shrugged. "Seem to remember knocking you on your ass as part of that encounter."

Jamieson prowled closer. "Yet here ye are, fucking my sister."

"Not fucking," Struan intoned.

Riordan palmed his face.

They really needed to mind their own business.

I scowled at them both. "Get your nose out of my love life and tell us the news."

Jamieson secured the door and ushered us into the kitchen where he raided the fridge, answering between piling up food.

"As of an hour ago, Arran and Shade captured Bronson Lesk. They've got him at a safe house, and tomorrow afternoon, they're going to announce it."

God.

Everyone spoke at once, asking questions and demanding to know how Jamieson knew.

"You were there?" Tyler asked.

"Naw, but I heard it go down. Arran called me while he was on a stakeout."

Jamieson's gaze slid to Riordan. Purposefully, I moved to stand in front of him, showing my ownership and the fact that yes, I wanted him here.

My brother twisted his lips but continued. "Next thing I knew, shite went down. I heard it all because there was no time to hang up. Arran and Shade were able to take the arrogant bastard entirely unseen. It was fucking poetry."

"Red doesn't know?" Tyler again.

"Arran will tell him personally. He wants to give evidence as part of that call."

My fingers twitched, my mind distancing to the warehouse's basement. To torture methods and a furious, bloodied Bronson. "They'll work on him right away, then."

Jamieson tilted his head at me. "Why, feel like you're missing out in your random side quest of living at the warehouse?"

Tearing into a pack of sandwich meat, he swapped a glance with Struan.

It boiled my blood.

"Yes," I snapped. "Though it isn't random. I'm working there."

Jamieson rolled his eyes. "So give it up already."

I scoffed. "Try telling me what to do again once you've got your head out of your arse."

His smile died. "To be clear, the skeleton crew took out the Four Milers' second-in-command tonight. A violent serial murderer."

"One who's been targeting women and who I'm going to enjoy cutting pieces off of."

His gaze darkened. "They will hurt him before they kill him. There will be retaliation. Ye need to stay far away from Deadwater."

"The fuck I do."

Jamieson slammed the fridge. "This isn't a game, Cass. Ye don't have to prove anything to anyone. It's Arran's war that he doesn't need help winning."

"Yet he was on the phone to your dumb arse. Tell me he wasn't asking for your help."

Jamieson faltered.

Fuck. I was right.

Struan shifted in front of me and moved Jamieson away, blocking my view of him. He spoke low to our brother, the arsehole.

I sensed Tyler's gaze on me.

The intercept guy scratched his chin. "He has a point. Deadwater will be a battleground."

"Are ye staying away?" I poked my tongue into my cheek. "Will the brothel close? Will Everly and Genevieve be sequestered away in the countryside like obedient little women?"

He didn't reply.

My brothers turned back.

Jamieson took a long breath. "All I'm saying is with your track record, you're due to lose interest in the place anyway. Why go back when it's at its most dangerous?"

Damn. An arrow to the heart. I knew I was flaky, but that hurt.

Struan took over. "Meant to tell ye earlier, Thea wants to talk to ye about Project Audrey. She could use your help."

The pain curled inside me and intensified. Jamieson warned me off, Tyler backed him, and now Struan was sliding in a safe alternative, like any of them had the right to.

Yeah, fuck all of them.

Without another word, I turned on my heel and stormed away. Upset zinged in my veins. For the first time in my life, I'd found a calling. I loved the warehouse and all it stood for. The gang war was just one aspect of that and necessary to return balance to the city. More importantly, Bronson being taken off the streets meant the world was safer for women. That was the point.

Bootsteps followed me, drumming up the stairs.

"Are ye going to try to control me, too?" I asked Riordan.

"Wouldn't dream of it, kidnapper."

I deflated. "Oh, yeah. Sorry."

We turned the corner.

He spoke again. "Why do you think your brother will be helping Arran?"

"Jamieson burns things down. He's good at it. He destroyed Arran's family home, on Arran's request, of course. The two of them razed it to the ground and sent that house of horrors to the gods. He also turned the hostel where we'd been held prisoners to cinders. This place got a bit of a scorching as well at one point. Luckily while our father was alive to know about it."

"Your other brother referenced two people called Scar and Burn. I take it the latter is Jamieson?"

I managed a nod, though my mind was in Deadwater.

At my room, I unlocked the door. Riordan closed us in

and waited for me to continue.

I paced. "Like with calling in Tyler whose specialism is trafficking, and who will no doubt be shutting down the Four Milers' women-abducting routes, if Arran wants Jamieson, he intends to cause damage."

Riordan watched me. "He's going to burn down the Four Milers' buildings."

"Exactly."

It was so much bigger than taking a predator off the streets. While my brothers were celebrating Bronson's imminent demise, I saw a different side. Jamieson wasn't wrong. Arran was bringing a war. It would be dangerous to associate with him.

"Then there's you, facing your fear head-on with a plan to take revenge on Bronson for everything he did to those women."

I lifted my gaze to Riordan. "It has to be me. Or at least I need to play a part. I was next on his list. Even despite that, a woman ending his life is divine justice, and your sisters won't want the honours."

For a long moment, he held the eye contact. I didn't know what he saw, but I knew the effect it had on me. The spark of electricity in my chest. How he quickened my breathing and made me feel like I was about to run for my life.

Riordan claimed he wasn't going to try to control me, but I had an overflow of invested men who would do anything to protect me. I loved my family, but they needed to back the hell off. Whatever Riordan said next would either kill or cure me.

"Then we'd better pack up and go."

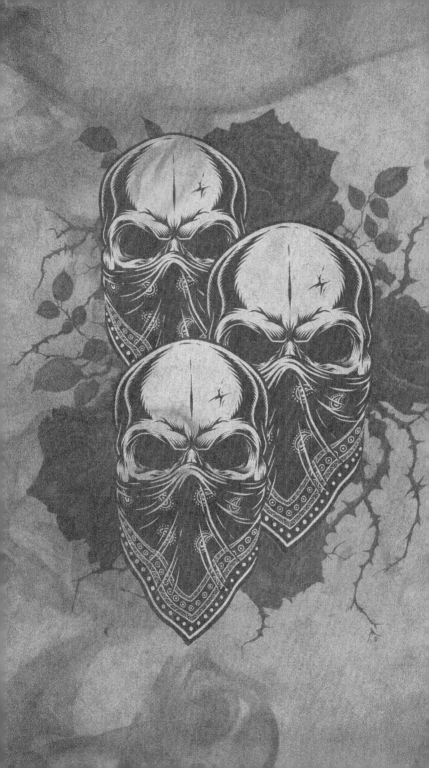

16

Riordan

Cassie stared at me, her lips apart and desire right there in her eyes. Then she briefly shuttered them. "Thank fuck ye said that."

"You expected different?"

"Maybe I just couldn't see a way to get my third soft kiss if I was mad at ye, too."

Heat swarmed me.

I pointed at the back of the couch. "Sit there."

"Yes, boss."

Dutifully, she perched on the sofa back. I moved in on her. Parted her knees to get closer and dropped my mouth to her waiting one. We started slow, Cassie anticipating me. She'd learned the way I kissed her and was giving it back. An angle to her head, our faces meeting perfectly, closed eyes and soft, shared breaths.

Lightly, her fingers ghosted up my side. Fire trailed in their wake. I stifled a groan of need. Without breaking the kiss, I captured her wrists and held them behind her back.

It changed her posture so her chest was out and her shoulders back. Heat drowned me. It would be so easy to tie her up like this then strip her and fuck her. The natural next step and the path our energy was leading us to.

Had to stop. With a growl, I kissed her once more but lightly and shifted back.

No part of me liked my actions.

"Three," she breathed, counting for me because I'd lost the ability.

"We should go."

"We should spend a week just doing more of that."

I wanted nothing but what she described. I held my gaze on her, on a knife's edge of going back in for more.

Cassie pressed her fingertips to her mouth. "There's something else I need to do first. It's regarding what Tyler told me."

At whatever expression I'd taken on, she grinned. "It's not what you're thinking. I asked him to help me find someone, and he found that information."

I considered that. What felt like forever ago, in her room in the warehouse, Cassie had confided that she'd never known her mother and that she was an orphan. She didn't even know her birthday because the woman had concealed it. The weight of Tyler's information had to be heavy on her. It was a fucking relief to me, though for a very different reason.

"Your mother?"

She huffed out a breath. "Stop mind reading me."

"You started it. So, he found someone who knew her?"

Cassie nodded. "A woman who used to work with her and who lives in Aberdeen. I need to see her."

I checked my phone for the time. It was after midnight. Aberdeen was a couple of hours' drive east. Deadwater was over three hours south. It made a much longer trip, but a possible one.

"Then we'll go there first. We need to be back at the warehouse and locked in when Arran makes his call to Red. I don't care how many protesters are outside, it's going to be dangerous as fuck in Deadwater. Not just for you but for everyone. We go now or we don't go."

The lamplight danced in her eyes. "Don't tempt me with a good time."

Packing took under a minute. I retrieved my bike helmet and backpack, shoving the gun under the possessions my sister had sent. Cassie collected a few things from her room and changed into warmer clothes, zipping herself into a jacket.

We stole out of the apartment like thieves.

From elsewhere in the house, voices sounded, and instead of taking the main staircase, she directed me to another corridor and down a narrow set of steps that led to a back door.

"Worried about seeing your brothers?" I asked.

"More worried about what I'll say to Jamieson if he tries to manage me again."

"Will he stop you?"

"I'd like to see him try."

Outside, a cool and dry night greeted us, with no sign of any remaining skeleton crew, presumably Tyler having sent them home, nor was there a helicopter anywhere in sight. It really was over. The siege had lifted.

Across the car park, we reached the red Audi. Cassie gave a growl of anger and kicked the nearest wheel. Flat. I circled the vehicle. All four of them.

One guess who had done that.

She turned on her heel and marched to a low building that edged the car park. Throwing open a door, she hit the lights and revealed a row of expensive vehicles. I recognised a Rolls-Royce, and the others were clearly high-end and well-maintained. Cassie bypassed them to a lockbox on the wall.

It was empty.

"Let me guess, that should contain keys."

Mutely, she nodded.

My pulse quickened. I'd never done this before but instantly had the answer. I held out my helmet. "Unless they've vandalised my bike as well, get ready for a crash course in riding pillion."

Cassie lifted her gaze from the garage floor. Amusement replaced the frustration in her features. "Weird way to propose, but I accept."

"What?"

"Ye know that putting me on the back of your bike is as good as an offer of marriage?"

I folded my arms. "No, it isn't."

She sauntered past, collecting my helmet as she went. "I'm not fussed about the type of ring ye buy me, but be aware that I'm telling everyone our news. Shall we go?"

Glowering, I stalked after her.

After my bike had been delivered, I'd moved it to the side of the house. It was where I'd left it, and a quick examination told me it was untouched. Perhaps Jamieson hadn't seen it, or knew messing with my property would be a step too far.

I stood in front of her and took the helmet. "I'm going

to tighten it so it fits your head."

She grumbled about it flattening her hair but let me touch her. Carefully, I eased it onto her head, tucking her soft curls under.

"Won't ye be in danger not having one?"

"I haven't come off a bike since I was learning to ride at sixteen. The greater risk is once we head south and hit up the motorway and then the cities. If we're seen, I'll be pulled over, and as we're both armed, that's a shitshow in the making."

"Wait, if ye don't mind a stop on the way, I'll get us another."

"Whatever works. It'll beat getting stopped by the cops." I reached for her bag, stuffing it into my half-empty one.

Cassie shrugged it on then tapped out something on her phone. "Hey, fiancé, I'm going to need your phone number so I can give ye the addresses we're heading to."

I pursed my lips but recited the digits. Cassie saved it then drop-called me so I had hers. Then she held up a pausing finger. Turning, she backed up against my chest and activated her camera, taking a shot.

"What? I need one for your profile. There. Now I've sent it to ye as well. Our first engaged couple's shot."

I rolled my eyes. "You're incorrigible."

"I'll take that as a compliment."

A door opened somewhere in the mansion, and a shout followed. "Cassie?"

Her smile fell. "Mind if we just leave? I'm seriously not in the mood."

"Fuck, okay. Step over the bike to get on."

Cassie peeked at it. "I'm too short. I'll never get my leg over."

"Then climb on me, little backpack." I crouched and tapped my shoulder.

Her eyes danced. "Too cute, Rio."

I barely had time to process the nickname when she clung to my back, wrapping her arms and legs around me, her weight so slight as I climbed on the Ducati. Cassie dropped into her seat. I reached back to set her boots on the pegs.

Then I snapped her visor closed and revved the engine.

At last, it was time to leave.

We circled the mansion and spat gravel, not looking back. Cassie whooped, letting go of me to make a hand gesture I couldn't see. Yeah, fuck her brother.

A few miles down the road, I stopped to extract my phone and set up navigation. The first address Cassie had sent me was only a thirty-minute drive away, but I had the unfortunate bad habit of seeing arrival estimates as a challenge.

We zipped through dark countryside, the roads completely empty and perfect for biking. We had a full moon, my bright headlight, and elation guiding us. Wind rushed me, cooling my blood but doing nothing for my building energy. Particularly at the feel of Cassie so close. Her tight arms. Her hands. Her thighs.

After what felt like no time at all, the route took us past a loch and through a pair of tall stone gateposts, the road continuing over a bridge and to a castle. We hooked right, circling the ancient building. Cassie directed me to a set of steps that scaled the outside of the castle wall.

I killed the engine. "Who the hell lives here?"

Scotland was littered with castles, but I'd never met anyone who owned one.

A man jogged down the stairs, a black helmet in his hands.

"Him," Cassie said helpfully.

A second on, and I recognised the red-headed thirty-something as one of the people who'd flown into protect Cassie. A mountain rescue man, as I recalled.

"Hey, Max, sorry for the midnight request," she chirped.

"Nae bother. I worked late tonight anyway. Good to hear it's all over." He lifted the helmet. "Did my best regarding cute. Luckily Lia had the same idea once. We had it stashed in the flat."

Cassie removed my helmet and accepted the new one, gleeful at the decoration. It had two black cat ears. I flicked them to make sure they were road safe. Fixed ones would break her neck if she came off and they caught the road. These were flimsy, though. Not dangerous. I slid it onto her, getting a buzz at her blue-eyed gaze holding mine for a beat.

She was too fucking adorable.

I liked this. Liked the instinctual way she held me as I rode.

"You a biker?" I forced my attention back to Max.

"Aye, but I'm a da, too, so I don't get out so often. Where are ye two heading in the middle of the night?"

"Somewhere," Cassie answered.

"Be sure to stay safe in that somewhere."

"Thanks, Max. See ye."

She tapped my back, a clear signal that we weren't hanging around. I gave Max a fist bump, tugged my helmet on, then biked out of there.

The empty roads weaved through the Cairngorms National Park. I took it steady at first, just enjoying being out and not wanting to let loose for Cassie's sake. But she rode so perfectly with me, banking out with me at corners, and even shifting her hands from my body to the engine block when I had to brake.

When we hit a straight coming down a foothill, a wide-open road ahead of us, I squeezed her hands, linked across my middle.

Hold on to me.

She hugged me harder.

I let rip with the throttle. My bike was built for this, and the Ducati flew. Fresh air, moonlight, good tarmac, and Cassie's laugh was music to my ears. From all the hours I put in at work, I hadn't taken a long ride in months. For the first time in forever, I got a burst of freedom so strong, it staggered me.

We passed a ski centre and came down off the snow roads, on the Highland tourist route. In a matter of months, the road could be icy and risky on a bike, but in the middle of autumn, it was perfect.

I could almost forgive Cassie the kidnap attempt so that I experienced this.

My body had constructed a different argument altogether. Worse when her fingers slid under my jacket to link over my t-shirt, nestling warm against my skin. I wanted her. Desperately, I wanted to stop in some dark lay-by, perch her on the bike, and kiss her stupid. I wanted to mess with her. Strip her by the side of the road. Brand the image in my mind of her body draped over my bike.

But I didn't forget our destination.

Nor the way I guessed she was feeling at what was coming up.

A couple of hours in, we hit the outskirts of Aberdeen. The closer we got, and the more urban our surroundings with streetlights and city roads, the more rigid Cassie became. When we arrived at Union Road, she squeezed my shoulders, and I cruised to a halt.

"There it is. That building above the pizza place."

With the engine off, I helped her down then stretched out my body, scanning our surroundings. Duncan House was our target. An unremarkable block of flats above a row of shops and in between others on the city centre street. A man sloped up to the door panel and pressed a buzzer.

Adrenaline sparked inside me.

Cassie tapped my helmet. "Keep this on."

"You're not doing the same?" She'd already removed hers.

"Might need it as a non-lethal weapon."

She collected something from inside my backpack, then tightened it on her shoulders. A crackling sound came as the man's buzz was answered, and I jumped forward to catch the slow-moving door before it fell closed behind him.

We entered to a plain staircase.

Cassie consulted her phone briefly then jogged up to the third floor. The same man waited outside a flat.

He slanted a look at us, focusing on me over Cassie's head. In my leather jacket and black helmet with the visor up, I knew how I appeared, and leaned into the intimidation until he took a step backwards.

"That's the flat we want," Cassie whispered.

The door opened, and a woman in her dressing gown appeared in the frame.

Cassie launched forward. The woman gasped and recoiled, closing the door. Cassie was already there, and my hand landed beside hers to force it open.

To the waiting man, I jacked my thumb. "Fuck off."

We hadn't had time to discuss a gameplan, but we didn't need one. We were in.

The sex worker, as I assumed she was, fled down the short hall in her flat. "Colin! Wake up."

Cassie and I burst into the living room to the woman shaking awake a skinny man on the couch.

In the light from an uncovered lamp and a silent, flickering TV, he jerked up, eyes red but immediately trained on us. "The fuck's going on?"

From a pocket, Cassie extracted a handful of notes. Fluttered them.

Instantly, Colin switched his gaze to the money. She threw it at him. "Get out. We won't hurt her. Call the cops and the opposite will be true."

Without a second glance, Colin snatched up the cash from the filthy carpet and fled. I'd been ready to use my fists, but cash talked just as loud.

Cassie's target was probably in her early forties and as thin as her betraying boyfriend. She clutched her dressing gown closed at her chest and backed to the wall, her bobbed blonde hair swinging. "Whatever ye heard, they're lying."

For a long moment, Cassie watched her. "Do ye recognise me?"

"Don't know ye from Adam. If ye leave, I'll forget I ever saw ye."

"Take another look, DeeDee."

At Cassie's tone, or maybe the use of her name, the woman lost some of her panic. "No one calls me that anymore. Who are ye?"

"Someone's daughter. It's important that ye tell me her name."

DeeDee's gaze turned cautious then curious. Her eyes flared wider with recognition. "No. It cannae be."

"Who do I remind ye of?" Cassie pressed.

"A ghost, sweetheart."

"Did the ghost have a name?"

Slowly, DeeDee nodded. "Cassandra Archer. But surely not. No way."

My stomach tightened. Tyler's information had been right.

Cassie sagged. Automatically, I crept a hand to her shoulder to support her. Her fingers touched mine, then she regained control.

From her inside pocket, she collected another bundle of cash. Then she perched on the sofa Colin had vacated. "I said I wouldn't hurt ye and I won't. I'll also pay for your time and replace the money you would've made from the john we just scared off. In exchange, you'll tell me every detail ye recall about Cassandra. Now."

DeeDee sang like a bird. Hesitantly at first, and a little better after I removed my helmet. She shared details of a woman she'd known twenty years ago. Cassie's mother.

They'd worked side by side as teenagers new to the sex trade, and had been friends.

"I was there the day she found out she was pregnant." DeeDee finished rolling a joint on the beer-can-strewn coffee table. She sparked it up. "I guess that was with ye."

Cassie pressed her lips together. "Ye don't have to pretend it was a happy moment. I know who my father is. Or was."

DeeDee pushed her hair behind her ear. "We all knew your da. He used to send cars for girls, and the drivers would have money to buy dresses. Everyone went to him once."

Implying they didn't a second time.

The woman spoke on, describing her own encounter with McInver. How he liked his women to put on a show with each other. I concealed a cringe at the image of the lecherous old scrote.

"Was Cassandra a favourite of his?" Cassie asked.

"I don't know about that, but she was willing to go back for more. She had goals none of the rest of us did. Ambitions."

Cassie's breath hitched. She leaned in. This was important to her.

DeeDee held out the joint in offer and shrugged at our refusal. "Waste of time if ye ask me. All ambition buys around here is time in the big house or a quicker death. Your ma wanted to run her own brothel. She lined up a few of the girls to work for her. Seventeen, and she acted like she could take on the world. Then she got knocked up. Even with a belly out to here she could scare the shite out of some arsewipe who wouldn't pay for a trick. I'd see her march up to cars and give them an earful. Fearless. Then she had ye. I remember the day like it was yesterday."

I took the seat next to Cassie. Her hand crept out to twine around my wrist.

Her fingers shook.

"Do you remember the day of the week?" I asked.

"Sunday, right at the end of the month. Cassandra's mother was Catholic, and she joked that ye were her gift from God. She hid ye, though. Social services were sniffing around. Guess they got her bairn in the end, if she didnae raise ye. I always wondered what happened to her."

Cassie sat back, silent and seemingly stunned.

"You didn't keep in touch," I asked in an attempt to fill in a gap.

"Naw. She vanished one day. She always had an eye out for danger, either from the social or her da. I figured she'd ran from one of them."

Cassie sucked in a breath. "Did she ever say who her parents were?"

DeeDee's gaze narrowed, then she sat back. "Don't go barking up that tree. It isnae worth your bother."

"Why, are they bad news?"

"Once upon a time, they were the worst kind of bad news, but most of them are dead or serving at His Majesty's pleasure in Barlinnie."

A notorious Scottish jail.

"They were gangsters," I confirmed.

She nodded. "Ever heard of the Spring Hill gang? Your grandfather ran it. Made money from protection, lending money, and dealing. That kind of thing. At age fifteen, Cassandra was told she was getting married. That's why she ran."

"Mafia," Cassie breathed.

"Aye. Leave well enough alone. Ye still have an uncle or two living the life so better stay off their radar." DeeDee checked her phone. "I have a client downstairs. Is this going to take longer?"

Cassie stood. "No. Here. The money I promised. Thank ye for telling me about her."

DeeDee snatched the cash and disappeared it inside her dressing gown. "Anytime, sweetheart. Come back if ye want more."

Cassie hesitated then bent to the coffee table to collect a pen. On a receipt, she wrote something. "If ye remember anything else, anything important, can ye call me?"

DeeDee's expression shifted. "She doesnae live around here anymore. I won't see her to tell ye."

"Ye won't see her at all. She died a long time ago."

The sex worker blinked. "Well, shite. She deserved better."

We left, and I spotted Colin in a doorway across the road, lurking, and at least not calling the police. Though I guessed that didn't happen much around here.

Cassie strode to the bike and took her helmet, which I'd carried, and shoved it on. Now obviously wasn't the time for talking. Even if I had words to say, I wasn't sure she wanted to listen.

Besides, I'd realised something she wouldn't want to hear. Like her brothers, I had the urge to wrap her up in cotton wool. Lock her away safe where the world couldn't touch her. If I told her it, she'd probably knee me in the balls.

Cassie raised her gaze to me.

Broke my heart with the weariness in her features.

"Take me home."

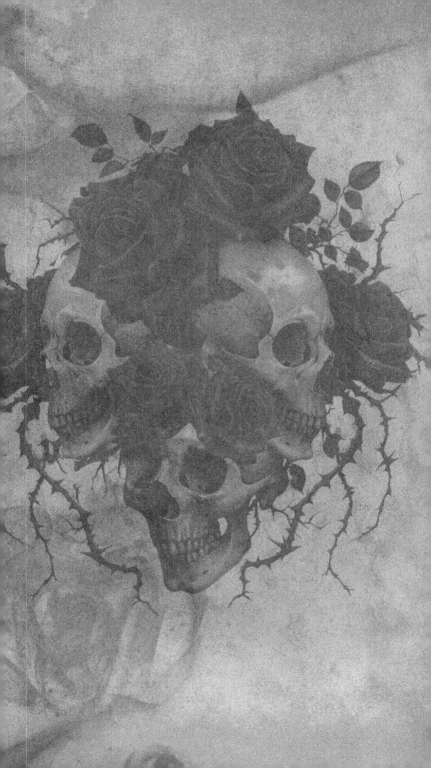

17

Cassie

Riordan sped us into the night, heading south, and my brain raced over thoughts and feelings just as fast.

The engine roared. I wanted to scream.

Out of Aberdeen, we reached a junction, and I sucked in a breath, suddenly realising where we were. Tapping Riordan's arm, I gestured for him to take the road to the left. The sea road. A slower route down the east coast of Scotland but one which held a place that was precious to me.

I wanted to at least drive past it. To somehow help crest the strange feelings brewing in me.

Without pause, Riordan signalled where I'd directed and drove us on, past the sign for the Stonehaven and Dunnottar Castle, then Catterline Bay. Even through my borrowed helmet, the salty tang of the sea made it to my nose, and emotion continued to rock me.

As if sensing my weird state, Riordan drove more slowly.

Then I saw it.

Almost hidden by overgrowth, the switchback led

down the low cliff. I stiffened and pointed, and my fiancé, because I was running with that, turned the bike almost three-sixty to take it. We cruised down the potholed road, bumping over ruts then crunching rocks at the bottom. He stopped, engine off, a hand already waiting to help me down.

In zombie fashion, I stumbled, my boots sinking into the loose gravel of the beach.

Silence greeted me. Nothing but the hushed pull of the waves.

It had been years since I'd come here. Not one thing had changed. Not the house to our left with the glassed-in porch and the shed full of surfboards. Not the exact arrangement of rocks in the silvered, calm sea. Yanking off my helmet, I set it down and paced to the water's edge. It rushed up to greet me. Like it knew me. Like it was welcoming me back.

Riordan approached, scrubbing over his flattened hair. "What is this place?"

"Nowhere, really. It was home for a few days when we were on the run."

He watched me for a beat then sat in the gravel. "This after the hostel Jamieson burned down?"

He was piecing together my history. I kind of loved that he cared.

"Aye. But that was back on Torlum."

"Where you were kidnapped to? Tell me about it."

It was better than trying to get to grips with what I'd learned about my mother. Staring out at the dark horizon, I considered my own past. "None of us knew each other growing up, apart from Sin and Jamieson who had seen each other in passing. We didn't know we were related until one by one, me and my brothers were kidnapped and taken to Torlum. It's a remote, desolate island in the Hebrides. The locals were told our presence was a young offenders rehabilitation type deal, but really, we were picked up because we were McInver's kids and he was dying. Someone else wanted his inheritance, and as we had no idea who we were, hiding us away meant the executors of his will would never find us. I was six years old when they took me."

"Holy fuck."

"Right? Except for me, for the first time, I had a family. I had four big brothers and their girlfriends. From nothing to everything, and every single one of them gave a fuck about me. It was in that house over there that I realised I wanted Sin and Lottie as my parents. That I loved them. We swam in this bay." I choked on a thick throat. "We weren't even here that long before the homeowner discovered us trespassing and called the cops. It's just always been in my mind as the real starting point of my life."

"What happened when the police came?"

I hung my head. "They took me. I had to go back into foster care. I didn't see my family again until Arran's father kidnapped me as a hostage. It was the end of us being on the run because he got what was coming to him."

"Arran killed him?"

"He wanted to, and so did I. There were too many cops there. That man is rotting in jail now, but not before he murdered Arran's mother, Audrey."

Something registered in Riordan's gaze. "Project Audrey. Your brother mentioned that to you. What did he mean?"

"It's a service Thea runs. She's Struan's wife and a

social worker. We help women who are at risk of losing their kids to social services because their lives are fucked up. They get referred to Thea's team, then helped with legal matters and housing. Whatever they need. It's very worthy. We named it after Audrey because Arran's warehouse is the front of the business. Many of them come via that route after being trafficked. Thea wants me to work for her."

He wrinkled his nose. Without a word, I read his thoughts.

"Yes, it's worthy as hell. Yes, I'd be bored out of my mind. It's not for me, as much as my family would apparently prefer that to the path I'm taking. I get it. They've seen me pick up and drop obsessions like no one's business. They saw me quit uni and take an apparent wild card job at Arran's warehouse so obviously they're expecting me to quit that, too. Did ye see the skull on my bookshelf containing the souvenirs of my failed obsessions? I can't really blame Jamieson for acting the way he did."

Stooping, I picked up a pebble and flung it at the water. For a few minutes, neither of us spoke. I got lost in memories. Riordan just watched me.

Finally, I returned to the events of this evening and the dots that were now connected.

"All these years, I wondered about my piece of history that came before this place. Before my real family was formed. All that time and my mother's friend was just a couple of hours away. We searched records. We asked people who Arran encountered, women who worked for him. Nothing."

"The information DeeDee gave, the fact you were born on a Sunday, does that give you a date of birth?"

It did. God. "The thirtieth of October."

"Ten days away."

"More importantly, it gives me something real about her. Up to this point, other than her name, all I knew was that she'd sold her body to McInver. She had ambition. I can follow that."

"The ambition, right? Not selling yourself."

Caught in too many competing emotions, I hauled in a breath. "When I was new to the warehouse, I talked to some of the women about what it would be like to work there. On my back."

"Theoretically?"

"No."

Riordan stared, his features almost hidden now that the moon was setting. "You said that in the club on the night of the game, but I convinced myself you were joking. Why the fuck would you want that?"

All of a sudden, I needed to provoke him. I needed him to jump up and grab me, because I was reeling and had to fix my energy on something. For whatever reason, with him, I'd never been able to make the first move. For all my big talk, touching him scared the life out of me, yet it was everything I desperately wanted.

I took a step in his direction. "I asked that question because I wanted to know what it would be like to work in the brothel. To prove to myself that sex was just transactional."

To feel closer to the mother I never knew.

Shoving his hand into the pebbles, he rose to standing. "You were going to sell your virginity?"

Fury poured off him.

My breath quickened. *Yes, more of this.* Eagerly, I

nodded.

Riordan released a pained sound then turned and stomped back up the beach. My heart fell. He was leaving?

My panic was short-lived.

At his bike, he snagged the rucksack I'd left there and rooted through. A few seconds later, he came back down with something in his hand and marched straight up to me.

He thrust his wallet against my chest. "Sell me your first time."

I rocked back and fingered the leather. Something hot flashed through me, burning up on the challenge. I needed more.

"Ye can't afford me."

"The fuck I can't. At least if I paid, I'd have some pretence at control."

Pulling back my hand, I threw the damn wallet as far as I could into the water. It landed with a plop and disappeared beneath a wave.

In outrage, Riordan watched it fall then came back to me. With barely a pause, he snatched hold of my biceps and tugged me against him.

His mouth took mine in a brutal kiss.

He devoured me, no softness in the move. It should have been made of anger, but all I tasted was passionate need. Desperation. An undeniable connection that exploded as he slanted his mouth over mine and opened my lips for his tongue.

I clawed to get closer. Frustrated by his height, I pushed on his shoulders, and Riordan dropped down on the sloped gravel, taking me with him so I was straddling him. He lay back; I plastered myself to his body, his arms tight around me, one spearing into my hair to control my head. He'd redone our first kiss with hearts and flowers. Soft touches and care.

That wasn't my style at all.

I needed him like this. On the edge of anger and crazy. His fingertips digging in. His need burning bright. It's how I felt for him all the time.

Our thighs moved against each other's.

My fingers twisted in his waistband.

With a groan, Riordan rolled us, protecting my head from the damp pebbles with that big hand of his, and settling into the cradle of my hips. I arched into him, his hard dick meeting the juncture of my thighs through too many clothes. Then he grabbed my wrists and held them together, stopping me from touching him.

He kissed my throat, driving his nose up my jaw before lightly biting it. "You make me insane. You're too wild for me. All I want to do right now is tie you up as punishment for even having those thoughts."

Breathing hard, I gazed up at his darkened features. "Deal."

His gaze searched mine. "What?"

"I'll add that to the offer. Ten nights of belonging to each other. We sleep together. Eat together. And when we have sex, you can tie me up. Either way, I'm calling ye my fiancé when we get back to Deadwater. Take it or leave it."

I held the eye contact, my heart speeding along so fast I thought it might shatter. It almost did when he finally spoke.

"Deal."

18

Riordan

Climbing off Cassie, I popped the button of my jeans, unzipping my boots next then stripping my lower half aside from my boxers. My jacket followed them in a pile.

On her elbows in the pebbles, she licked her lips.

I controlled a curl of heat. "Don't look at me like that, wild girl. I'm not taking your virginity on a cold beach."

"Striptease says otherwise?"

By way of an answer, I turned and strode to the waterline then entered the sea. Freezing water licked my ankles and calves. I muttered a curse and explored the seabed with my hands. Thick seaweed brushed me. Fucking hell.

"Little to the left," Cassie called from the shore.

I followed the direction.

"Now a little deeper."

My dick pulsed, unhappy with me for stopping the show, even if it was the right thing to do. Then the water closed over my knees and my balls shrivelled.

"Oh, yeah, baby. Right there," she crowed.

I shot her an evil glare but my toe touched something square-edged. I plunged my hand in and pulled out the ruined wallet.

Cassie beamed as I trudged back in. "Told ye so."

I shook it at her, and she squealed and scampered away.

From a distance, she smirked at me.

Shaking off the seawater, I dried myself as best I could then dressed again, putting a hand out to Cassie so we could return to the bike. She gazed at my extended fingers then clutched them.

"We're holding hands. You're ridiculously sweet."

"And somehow not only in a relationship for ten days but also engaged."

She shrugged, skipping at my side. "Ye won't regret it. I'll learn to give good head."

At my sound of anguish, she laughed. "By the way, ye have really nice legs. Perfectly shaped and strong."

"Get on the bike, Cassiopeia."

"Oh no. I've made ye grumpy. But only my first name has been deployed. Have to work harder to get the whole shebang."

Back on the coast road, Cassie tucked herself against my back and cuddled down, trusting me to drive us the long trip back to Deadwater.

We were halfway when dawn stretched its light across the sky. It turned fully pale by the time we were creeping into the city's outer limits.

Deadwater was split across Scotland and England, cut in half by a wide, tidal river. The city centre was on the English side with suburbs on the Scottish part. We bypassed them and hit the bridge which took us into town then down the harbour road to the warehouse.

We'd been away for days, and I'd left in traumatic circumstances.

Yet somehow, I couldn't regret any of it. All I knew was the mischievous, bright soul who clung to my back so I could carry her off the bike. She stayed hugging me for a moment then jumped down, her gaze taking in the building.

Everything looked the same. The tall, red-bricked structure had a cobbled street leading to the front and the car park set down a level at the back. My sister had warned of protesters, and there was evidence of some kind of activity at the front, but we didn't linger to take it in.

I wanted Cassie safely inside. As far as we knew, Arran hadn't yet revealed his kidnap of Bronson, but that didn't mean the rival gang was unaware. Even now, they could be lying in wait. Taking either one of us would be a prize that could compromise the skeleton crew's position.

At the back door, Cassie entered a code.

The panel turned red, the door remaining locked.

She repeated it with the same effect then growled and thumped the glass. "Open up."

A figure in a skeleton crew t-shirt appeared the other side. He hesitated.

"Jed? For fuck's sake."

A pause followed, then the door clicked and swung inwards. Cassie marched through, and I followed.

"When did the code change?" she demanded.

"You'll have to ask the boss that," Jed replied.

I'd met most of the crew, but this guy only once. All I knew about him was that he was Scottish.

He slid a glance over me. "Going to need to frisk ye both for weapons."

I lifted my chin. "I'll save you the trouble. There's two guns in the backpack, both owned by the crew. We also both work here."

The man shrugged. "That may be so, but ye haven't been here for the past few days. Things have changed."

"What other than the code is different?"

He eyed me. "Not sure I can tell ye that."

"Can ye let us in?"

Jed glanced at the inner door to the hall. It formed an airlock in case of emergencies, so I knew it would be locked, too. And Jed wasn't budging.

"Okay, well, you're clearly after the prize of sending me insane." Cassie raised her phone. Dialled someone. It connected. "Shade, can ye come down to the back door for a second?"

Jed's eyebrows shot up into his hairline.

Cassie hung up and folded her arms, her toe tapping.

A minute passed, then footsteps sounded on the stairs and Shade shoved through the door. His piercing gaze shot over us all, his typical pissed-off expression installed.

"What's the problem?"

Cassie pointed a finger between us. "We're back. Apparently we need to know the protocol to come back inside. I'm annoyed and just want to go to bed so I called ye."

Shade gave a world-weary sigh and palmed his

tattooed throat. "Jed, check the fucking list next time. They're both on it."

"They're armed," Jed hissed.

Shade pursed his lips. "Good. Cassie, Riordan, follow me."

He led us past the basement entrance and up the steps to the ground floor, taking the corridors through to the management office. Inside the room, he rested back on the big desk and adjusted the bright lamp so it wasn't blinding us.

"I assumed you'd be back today. Jamieson filled ye in, then?"

Cassie nodded. "Bronson's in the skeleton crew's slammer. I want a piece of him. Or several. I'm thinking of starting a trophy cabinet, and he'll be so pretty as a piece on my shelf."

Something glimmered in Shade's eyes. Maybe the promise of blood.

Cassie examined her nails. "I'll stay back at first, if ye like, but I'm serious. I want to be in the room."

The gang enforcer chewed on her request for several seconds. If he said no, she'd be gutted, but I didn't think that was going to happen. Shade and Cassie had a kind of mentor/protégé relationship going on, from what I could tell. He'd let her take on Piers Roache as Everly's champion. More, if Bronson was the killer, he'd threatened Cassie directly. She had a right.

He inclined his head. "We'll have a strict game plan, discussed in advance."

Cassie's eyes flared. "I'll follow your lead. Have ye already started?"

"No. He's out cold until tonight. Arran will delay telling

Red until after we've made a first attempt. The whole plan is being set back as there's no sign they know he's gone."

"Good. I need sleep and to talk to my ladies first. We need to girl-detective what questions to ask."

Shade adjusted his position, a hand coming up to stifle a yawn. "Ev will be glad you're back. She missed ye." His attention settled on me. "What's your story? Here voluntarily?"

I bristled at the jibe. There was no love lost between me and Arran's second-in-command, or at least there hadn't been when we met. I'd gone after him for kidnapping Everly. The arsehole had damaged my bike. But Everly was dating him now. If they were serious, he'd be in my life because she was. The sister I barely knew. Since then, he'd offered to pay for the bike repairs, though I'd already made them, scratches to my bodywork the only remaining injury.

I thought our position towards each other had changed. His attitude towards me had shifted slightly. Softened was the wrong word, but he'd been less hostile. He'd even offered advice.

Holding his gaze, I tipped my head at the woman across the office. "I'm formally telling you I've claimed Cassie."

"Funny, I thought it was the other way around." He slanted his eyes at her. "By the way, if ye ever touch my drugs again, I'll—"

Annoyance shot through me. "Don't finish that threat."

He lifted his eyebrows. I was begging for trouble. Twice, I'd gone up against him. Still, I would never let him talk to Cassie like that.

Shade held my gaze. "Noted. And I'm naw saying you're whipped. Just need to know you're here because ye want to be."

"Leave my fiancé alone, and I'll do the same with your drugs," Cassie chided.

Shade's mouth fell open. "Fiancé?"

Christ alive. I dropped my glare on her. "Cassie, come here."

Dutifully, she trotted over. "Yes?"

"Tell him we're together by my decision."

She peeked up. "It's true. Oh, and because we made a deal."

Alarm chased my other emotions. She couldn't tell Shade about my plans. If it got back to Arran—

Happily, she smiled at the enforcer. "Riordan and I are going to be fucking over the mayor. I'm not sure how yet, but think death by a thousand cuts and it'll be along those lines. We cool?"

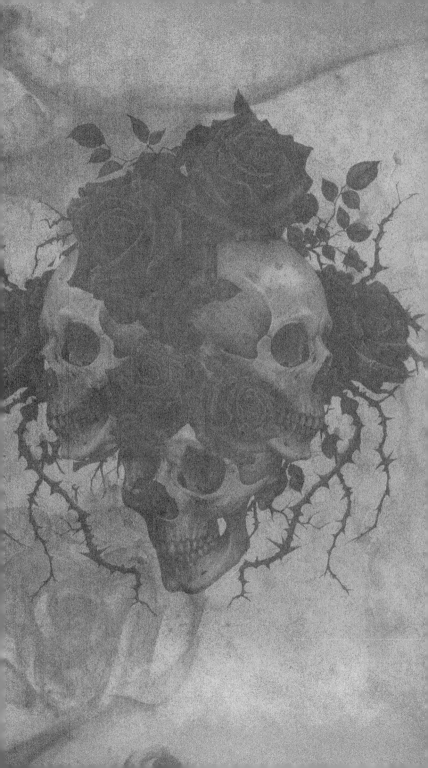

19

Cassie

*S*hade stilled. At the same second, Riordan fisted my shirt at my lower back and held it, something very telling in his hidden grip.

I'd pissed him off.

Good.

Riordan's problem was that he was a lone wolf. Not by choice. He was alone in the world with few who cared about him. Obviously Genevieve did, and maybe Everly, but beyond them he had no tribe. I could give that to him. Help him see that people were ready and willing to help if he was prepared to trust.

More importantly, this way, he wouldn't die in the process of getting his revenge.

I wasn't wrong.

Shade looked between us. Something in his gaze told me he was weighing up Riordan's claim above his own, just as I'd anticipated. The mayor had hurt Everly. But Riordan was the man's son. His neglected, overlooked child. For all Shade wanted the right to avenge the woman he loved, he operated on an honour code. All the men here did.

Some kind of decision resolved, and he tapped the table, moving to the door. "Do what ye like, but keep it subtle and don't kill the fucker. Not yet. Talk to me if ye need help."

He directed us outside. "Share any results, aye?"

Shade strode away. I breathed out and squinted up at Riordan. My stomach tightened at his scowl. Other parts of me did, too.

"On a scale of one to nuclear explosion, how unhappy are ye with me right now?" I asked.

Riordan swung around and stalked away. At the lift, he stabbed in the code to open the door then propelled me inside, his touch light but his intention anything but.

I skittered along, excited at his mood swing.

I liked him grumpy. It was very possibly my favourite side of him because it helped him break out of his restraints. He let his passions lead where he otherwise wouldn't go.

When he stabbed the button for the fifth floor, I smiled more, because that passion was directing him to the bedroom I'd secured here.

My pulse picked up, my skin coming alive with anticipation. I was wet for him. Ready for everything. This was day one of our official time together, and I didn't want to waste a second.

On the cam girls' floor, we fast walked to the end of the corridor. I unlocked the door and let us in, cursing myself for not having done more to make the place comfortable. It had been a functional little nest for me, holding my clothes on a rail and my detective map on the wall. I'd do better for the rest of our time.

I tossed my coat to the corner. Turned to face him. "I know you're angry that I told Shade our plan."

"My plan. Told to you in confidence."

I settled on the bed, rested back on my elbows, and regarded him. "It was Arran ye didn't want to know, and this is ours now. I own it, too. I get that ye dislike Shade, but I trust him and I know he'll have our back. You've made the claim on the mayor, and it's greater than his. He won't stop ye, but we can do the decent thing and clue him in. We can let him help."

He stalked closer.

I readied myself for whatever was coming my way. "Ye also laid claim to me. Which was hot as fuck, by the way."

Riordan set a hand down on the mattress beside me and bent so his face was right over mine. He forced me back to lying, his muscles taut. At the same second, his other hand went to the button of my jeans. I couldn't read his expression. All I could do was follow his prompts. Lifting my arse, I let him strip me, my pulse quickening when he did the same to my top half, leaving me in just my bra and knickers.

It should've been sexy, but something was off in his clinical method. His touch didn't linger. His gaze clung to me then jerked away.

A muscle ticked in his clenched jaw. "Get up the bed."

I scooted to the pillows. My heart raced like his bike's engine. He could do anything to me right now and I would let him.

Riordan knelt over me, still in his leather jacket. He gazed down at my breasts then stole one hand under my back, unclasping my bra. He swallowed and pulled it free from my arms, capturing both wrists as he came up.

In rapture, I stretched out my arms above my head, hooked on everything he was doing. I'd been almost naked in my bathroom in front of him. This was a step on. Something was going to happen.

I wanted him to look at me. To see me and want me.

From his tented jeans, he was already there.

Riordan dragged his gaze from my body to my outstretched hands. He placed them against the wrought-iron headboard, a fancy design used as a backdrop by the women who filmed themselves in front of cameras. I held them there, closing my eyes for a beat to let the sense of overwhelm wash over me.

This was it. Even though I'd pissed him off, it was still happening.

He was going to fuck me, and I was going to love it.

Movement at my hands had me springing my eyes open. Riordan tied off my bra. It was tangled around my wrists then secured to the headboard.

For fuck's sake. He'd tied me up again. Fine. Maybe I deserved that.

I struggled against the constraint, trying not to get annoyed.

He tested the knot then sat back. "Remind me of the rules for our time together."

His voice was a gravel pit.

I growled. "Ten days and nights. We sleep together, eat together, revenge together, and have sex every day. You're mine and I'm yours."

"That's what you want, for me to fuck you now? Take the virginity you were ready to throw away."

Wriggling my shoulders, I managed a nod.

He held my gaze then stripped his jacket, tossed it to the floor, and climbed off me. His skeleton crew t-shirt went next, giving me hard muscles and inkwork to stare at. Then the rest of his clothes followed, one by one in a slow, deliberate tease. His boxers were last, and he shoved those down, his rigid, thick dick swinging up.

Holy hell. Naked Riordan was a sight I'd never get over, but it was his dick that caught and held my attention. That was going to be inside me. I swallowed. My pussy pulsed in anticipation.

Riordan grasped my knee and crawled onto the bed, settling between my legs. For a moment, the cold exterior he'd assumed shook. Real emotion flashed in his eyes. Desperate need and a dozen others I couldn't name.

He masked it. Drove his fingers up my thigh until he reached my underwear.

"Sure you want this?"

"Please."

He hooked it aside then palmed his dick and took it to the juncture of my legs, running it up and down my soaking wet centre, his gaze avid but his chest rising and falling. Confusion broke over me. I'd expected to be kissed. To be built up. For us to play first and full sex to be a natural end to it.

Then again, I'd made him angry.

Holding my gaze, Riordan lifted my backside and at the same time, thrust inside me.

Fuck. I opened my mouth on a gasp, jerking to loosen my hands so I could take them to where he speared into me. But I couldn't free myself. He'd tied me up too well.

With another jerk of his hips, he embedded himself deeper, then again and again until his body was flush against mine. That huge dick was inside me.

Cold panic mixed with strange pleasure.

I throbbed. Desire spread out from every place he touched me inside.

God, this was better than my vibrator.

Riordan lowered his face to mine, his jaw so tight it might crack. "I won't let it be said that I don't keep my word. But hear me now. If you want to keep this deal, you'll never again make a decision for me. Ask me. Consult me. Involve me. Never, ever go over my head. Obey that, and maybe we can do this again."

With a groan of pain, he pulled out of me and righted my underwear, tugging the quilt over my almost naked form. In angry moves, he got off the bed and dressed again.

Then he went to the door.

Finally, my brain re-engaged. I bucked against the constraint. "Don't ye dare leave me like this."

He curled his lip. "Enjoy missing Bronson's moment in the sun."

With that, he killed the overhead light and locked me in.

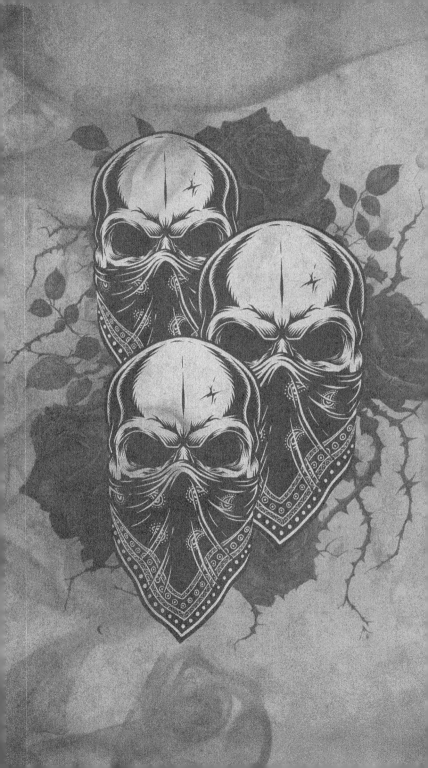

20

Riordan

Silent, I prowled into Cassie's room, careful not to wake her. After I'd tied her up, she'd cursed me through the walls for a good while then had apparently fallen asleep. Whatever I'd been feeling, guilt argued loudest in my head.

I'd taken a walk. Cooled down.

Slunk back to her like I couldn't stay away.

In the dark, I climbed onto the bed and untied her, then cuddled the infuriating lass. She didn't stir. In minutes, I let exhaustion pull me under.

A kick to my shin woke me.

Blinking, I trained my gaze on a furious Cassie.

"So you're back."

I shrugged. "We're supposed to sleep together."

"Untie me, jackass."

"I did that hours ago. Your arms are literally wrapped around me, koala girl." Reaching, I activated my phone's torch, shining it on the wall to give us light.

She squinted, flexing her hands behind my neck. Pink

stole over her cheeks. "What time is it?"

"Not time for Shade to be missing you yet."

"I hate ye."

A flicker of unease passed through me. "Don't say that."

Her pout faded. "Fine. Maybe I don't."

"Even though I was rough with you." For her first time, I should've been reverent. Careful.

"Gentle is boring. Doesn't mean I've forgiven ye though."

"Ye told Lottie that you loved me."

Cassie groaned. "Knew that would come back to bite me in the arse."

"Is it true?"

"Yes."

Something broken shifted inside me, warmth spilling over shattered edges, soothing and stormy at the same time. It felt like repairing damage. It felt fucking wonderful.

"Describe it."

"What? No. It's embarrassing."

"I want to know how it feels before it goes away."

Cassie flexed against me. Not for the first time since I'd got in bed with her, I was very aware of how naked we were, both of us just in our underwear.

Her body drove me insane. Last night, I'd been inside her. It was for seconds, but that connection had meant the world for that short time. An unbeatable sense of closeness, even in anger.

As if she read my mind, Cassie ran a hand down to her

underwear. Stripped it. "I'll talk if ye put it in me again."

God-fucking-damn her mouth. I kicked my shorts off and rolled her to her back.

"You're not tying me up this time," she warned.

"Fine."

I settled against her. With her black curls spread across the white pillow, Cassie gazed at me wide-eyed.

"You're so fucking beautiful." I dropped my mouth onto hers.

Instantly, she melded to me. We'd gone from savage kisses to gentle ones then back again. This one, I slowed down. Slicked her tongue with mine then broke away to travel down her body.

"Talk." I tasted the skin of her chest then kissed her breast, ending up at her nipple. "Does this feel good?"

She moaned and dug into my hair. "Y-yes."

"Then tell me how you love me or I'll stop."

I panted, my lips losing suction until I only hovered. I latched on again when she started talking.

"I fell in love with ye instantly when I saw ye in Divide. I watched ye for less than a minute and knew. It stopped every other thought process and shouted loudly in my busy brain."

I hummed, moving to the other breast. Perfectly shaped and mine to toy with. "Keep going."

Cassie breathed, her head tipping back. "I said that I wanted ye but I don't think anyone heard. I made my claim out loud."

I came off her to admire my work, her nipples wet and hard. "Why?"

"Everyone needed to know. It's like marriage vows. It

has to be public or it isn't real."

I grumbled, though my interest spiked. "Then what? How did it actually feel?"

I explored her belly with my lips. Widened her thighs with gentle pressure.

"Kiss me there and I'll tell ye exactly what it's like."

Holding her gaze, I laid my lips on her clit, opening her with my thumbs.

Cassie moaned and dropped her head onto the pillow, her eyes closing. "It felt like nothing else. Wonderful. Warm. Happy."

I reached for another greedy squeeze of her breast.

"Nothing's changed since then," she confessed.

I drew my hand back down and trailed it over her centre. She was so wet for me and so responsive. Every touch had her shivering or surging against me. I was dying to be inside her. Against the bed, my dick thickened. But we had time yet.

I kissed her between the legs again, flicking her with my tongue. Cassie squirmed and pushed into my touch, her lips parted in desire.

"Tell me you're still in love with me. Not just casual love but being completely in love. If that's what you feel, I want to hear it."

"Then fuck me. If ye don't, I'll die."

Hot urgency claimed me. I'd planned to toy with her for longer, but the need to be inside her was far more powerful. Coming back up her body, I positioned myself at her entrance. Then I just gazed at her. I needed a second. I wanted to mark the moment. It felt vital.

Cassie grasped my hip and lifted her ass, pushing me

inside her.

We gave up twin sounds of pleasure.

Whatever words I'd had vanished. All I knew was the tight fit. The need to get her screaming. Rising over her, I caught her gaze with mine.

Purposefully, I drew out then fucked back in. Under me, she went still. I'd taken her virginity already, and I knew she used sex toys, but this would all be new. It felt like that for me as well. The red flush on her cheeks extended to her chest, and I trailed my gaze down further to where we were joined.

A mistake.

The image of my dick spreading open her pussy would never leave me. It branded into my brain. It also made me want to come harder than ever before.

"Talk," I growled and rolled my hips, going in deeper.

Cassie writhed then bucked to meet me. "It's like walking around in a dream. Soft and safe. Ye scare me—oh fuck, that feels good—but I know you'd never hurt me. The love makes that so certain. I'd do anything for ye. Go anywhere. Change anything."

Such a dangerous statement.

I worked harder, jacking my hips and filling her over and over. Cassie drove her heels into the bed.

All words faded while we discovered how we fitted together. She squeezed every inch of my dick. I wanted to be gentle and slow but quickly found a rhythm that had us both panting.

Joyful, I banded my arms around her and rolled so she was on top, but I kept the control. Kept fucking her while our mouths met.

She broke the kiss. "Roll us again, I like your weight on me."

I did, a hand to her ass to help me drive in deeper, slower. Cassie took it. Moaned at the angle. Louder when I brushed over her clit with my thumb.

"Keep doing that and you'll make me come."

"This?" I kept the pressure and position exact.

Badly, I wanted this to work for her. I'd pushed her last night with how I'd walked out. An apology orgasm would go some way to repairing the damage.

"I want those words when you come," I ordered.

She clutched at me.

Then around my dick, she pulsed. "I'm utterly, heartbreakingly, happily in love with ye, Rio."

Rio.

My orgasm slammed into me, taking me by surprise. She was already coming, and the sensation was like nothing I'd ever felt. I groaned, filling her up, coming inside her though I hadn't intended to. Warmth and happiness joined deep satisfaction.

Then I dropped down on her chest, breathing hard and with a mind empty of all but her. Dizzy, I lay heavily on her. She let me.

"Forgive me," I finally said. I needed her to say she did.

Cassie sifted her fingers through my hair. I sensed her smile in her words.

"Grovel."

"I'm sorry. I shouldn't have treated you that way. You deserve better, and I'll learn from it. You're so fucking incredible. I'm at your feet, begging you."

Her happy laugh stopped my words.

"Forgiven. I love ye, remember?"
Until she stopped, I'd never forget.

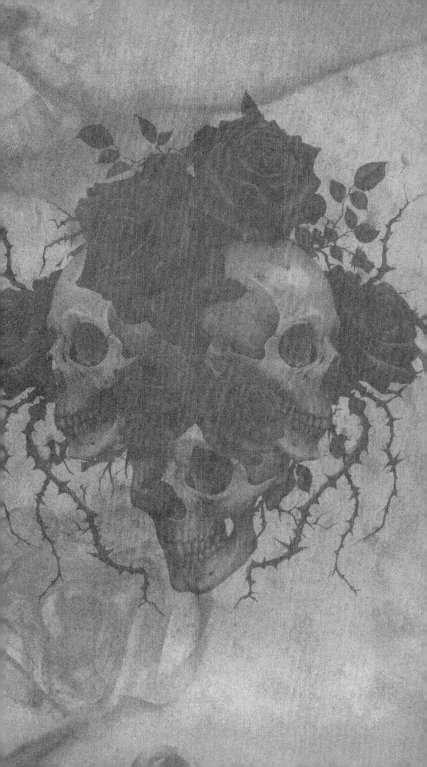

21

Cassie

I bounded down the stairs, Riordan's fingers entwined in mine. "So, sex with me, did ye like it?"

His grip tightened. "What sort of question is that?"

"One ye should answer way quicker."

"Then yeah. Holy fuck, yeah."

I preened. "I'll get better, but that's good to know."

"You don't need to change a thing."

"Oh, I intend to learn tricks from any of the women here who are willing to teach me. After I've hung out with Bad Boy B, I need to finally get the staff rotas done or Everly's events aren't going to get off the ground. I'll also start planning out our revenge plot. It's going to be a busy night, but I'll have details to run past ye later." I peeked at him. "No decisions made on your behalf."

With his free hand, Riordan mimed his brain exploding. "It should not be so attractive to think of you making a man bleed then carrying on your daily admin."

A grin stole over my face. "Then I get to come home to ye. That's the best part."

Reaching a landing, Riordan stopped up. "Still in love with me?"

"Holy fuck, yeah." I copied his words.

He groaned. Drove his fingers into my hair and laid his lips on mine. I was two steps higher so a perfect height to meet him. My belly fluttered with butterflies, an explosion of happy little wings beating lust through me. The kiss turned heavy in a heartbeat. I clawed him closer then looped my arms around his neck at the same second he picked me up, winding my legs about his waist.

Our mouths fused, a scorching hot kiss taking over every thought. This, I was quickly getting addicted to. His big body. His devotion to kissing the hell out of me.

Something clanked in the stairwell above us.

Neither of us stopped.

Riordan walked me backwards and opened a door in the wall behind me, and I blinked my eyes open to find him shutting us into a supply cupboard.

Darkness surrounded us.

Turning us, Riordan hit a shelving unit, something rattling and falling over that I didn't care enough to wonder at.

"Are we going to have sex in here?" I asked.

He kissed my cheek. "I just need to hear you say it again before the night gets busy."

My heart squeezed, tenderness boosting my certainty. "I'm in love with ye, Riordan."

He made a gruff sound then hugged me. "Call me Rio when we're alone."

"Rio. Rio, Rio, Rio. Why do I get the impression that's a privilege?"

"No one else calls me it, aside from my family occasionally, and this is very different to that. I like it on your lips."

His tone changed. I inched back and found his mouth with mine. Coaxed another kiss from him in the dark. For this evening, I'd chosen a cute, black playsuit with black boots, both of which would hide the blood if I got spattered. The wide-legged shorts made easy access now for Riordan to feel up my thighs.

We'd had sex under an hour ago. I still wanted more. I hadn't minded being a virgin. Not once I realised I'd been waiting for the right man to lose it to. Now I had him, I didn't want to waste a minute of our time.

His tongue tangled with mine, and my insides clenched. I drew my hands between us to his waistband, fumbling to open his jeans. Riordan let me, notching his forehead to my temple at the first caress of my hand to his dick. I palmed him and gave him a stroke, his strong arms holding me away from his body so there was space. This was the first time he'd let me touch him, and I thrilled at the exploration of something new and fascinating. In a romance book I'd read, I'd heard it described as velvet over steel, and that was close. What that didn't convey was the uncontrollable joy at how his grip tightened on me when I got something right in how I touched him.

My breathing came harder. I wanted more.

"Put me down," I ordered. "I'm going to try this with my mouth."

He shivered. "We don't have time to play, and when we do that, I'll need to reciprocate. A lot."

I pouted, but he was right. Shade had summoned me with a thirty-minute warning, and I'd taken most of that time over my makeup. I had to be downstairs in ten or risk missing out.

Riordan nudged my face to receive his kiss again. "I'll fuck you hard and fast. Will that do?"

Thank the gods. "For now."

He supported me with one hand and wrenched my shorts and underwear to one side, taking a moment to feel me up. "Do you hurt from earlier?"

"A little. Don't ye dare stop."

"You're so wet. Some of that is from me. I don't know how I'm going to deal with you walking round wearing my cum all night."

Fresh heat struck me down, and I moaned, kissing him again until he stopped teasing and lowered me onto his dick. His thick length speared into me. I gasped, and Riordan made a masculine sound of pleasure that was louder again. With his hands on my thighs, he lifted me up and down him.

I adored the way he filled me. My body gave way to his, and it was the most perfectly intense feeling because of his size. My sensation of helplessness made the pleasure a thousand times greater. I could do nothing but hold on. Later, I intended to spend a lot of time getting to know his dick. I wanted him in my hands. Between my lips. I needed to know how he tasted.

I also suspected I was going to get addicted to him fucking me very fast. Riordan worked in and out of me, delighting my pleasure zones and stretching me good. He adjusted his hold on me to bring his hand to my face, gripping my jaw so he could kiss me some more. While he kept the kiss slow, his hips worked faster.

Pretty quickly, I was breaking my mouth away to suck in air.

"You were made for this. Made to take my dick. You do it so well."

I whimpered at the praise and tucked my head against his broad shoulder. One final thrust, and pleasure burst through me. I clutched on to him, possibly losing consciousness for a second, as next I knew, Riordan had crashed us into the shelving unit and was slamming into me. More things fell from the shelves, clattering to the floor. If anyone was passing outside, they'd have no doubts what was going on in our dark little hideaway.

Dizzy, I held on for dear life.

Then I remembered my magic words.

Putting my lips to his ear, I whispered, "Hey, Rio? I'm so in love with ye."

He groaned and thrust into me a few more times, each rigid, each pushing in as far as he could go. Then he held still and came.

Fresh heat broke over me. "God. That sensation of ye pulsing inside me nearly breaks my brain."

It took him a minute to answer, a kiss preceding it. His chest inflated on heavy breaths.

"Same as when I feel you, wild girl."

His lips met mine for another long kiss, easier now we were getting acquainted. I was learning him. Maybe he was teaching me, because prior to him, I had exactly no skills.

Seemingly reluctantly, Riordan set me down then used his phone for light. In a corner of the small room, there was a box of paper towels above a sink, and he snagged some then handed them to me to clean up the cum trickling down my inner thigh.

My cheeks flamed. "Stop looking."

"Can't. I'm getting hard again at the sight."

"Rio! It's embarrassing."

"You can ask to get on your knees for me but you don't want me to see you leaking my cum? Too bad. One day, I'll lick it out of you."

"That is so fucking hot."

He crowded me. Kissed me. I let him, my resistance crumbling to nothing. Especially when he captured my hand to show me what it felt like between my thighs.

It took another minute until we broke apart.

He kissed my cheek. "Question. It's somewhat late to ask, but are you on the pill?"

"What if I said no?"

"Then I'll take responsibility. But I get the impression you've already thought this through. If you wanted a baby, you'd have one."

I chuffed amusement. "Of course I'm on contraceptives. No babies for me."

He squeezed me. "Thank fuck for that. I didn't want to give up going bare. The feel of it is unbelievable. I need a lot more of it."

"You've never gone without a condom?"

"Never. I should've told you."

"Then I took your virginity, too. Everything else before me doesn't count."

"Agreed, wild girl."

Outside, we emerged into the light, and I grinned at him. "My lipstick is on you."

He let me clean him up, his gaze sliding down to my cleavage.

My heart thumped. "I'm going to be torturing a man tonight. While thinking about what we just did in that cupboard."

"While soaked from me."

"That turns ye on," I confirmed.

Slowly, he nodded. Pressing up on my toes, I kissed his cheek, in total wonder of all things Riordan-shaped. And the love thing only expanded deeper in my chest.

Down on the entrance level, Shade emerged from Arran's office. Inside, Arran sat behind his desk with a group of men in my eyeline. Tyler, Manny, and Jamieson, others I didn't know. I glowered at my brother, and he scowled back.

Shade closed the door on them, shutting us on the outside.

I pointed my chin at the room. "War council?"

He didn't answer, instead, walking away with a gesture for us to follow.

"I wanted to talk to Gen and Everly," I called after him.

"No time. Our subject is awake."

Subject. Heh. Bronson was about to be subjected to a grilling, the likes of which I'd never been part of in the past.

We descended the steps to the rear exit of the warehouse. Another group of skeleton crew waited, all big men, all with serious scowls and lined foreheads.

"Jeez, anyone would think we were heading to a funeral," I quipped.

Seven pairs of eyes slashed to me.

I giggled. Extended my manicured hand to the door. "Shall we?"

Shade exited, the crew moving with him. Riordan held back. Tugged me in for a quick kiss, the same solemnness infecting him.

"Be careful," he grumbled.

I stalled. "You're coming with."

"Manny assigned me to the brothel tonight."

I took a quick breath. *No.* I needed him.

Shade reappeared in the door. "What's the delay?"

"Riordan stays with me."

"Need him to hold your hand?"

"Yes! At all times, preferably, if I don't need it to wield a blade. You'd better understand emotional literacy if you're going to keep Everly."

The enforcer raised an eyebrow.

Riordan grumbled. "Bronson targeted Cassie. I need to know why. If she was random or selected. I want to hear it from his lips."

Shade gave us another appraising look then shrugged. "Tell Manny I've reassigned ye. Now get in the fucking car. Ye ride with me."

Outside, rain darkened the evening, falling in fine threads across the yellow streetlights.

I settled into the back of a matte black warehouse 4X4 Shade had chosen over his own ride. Riordan slid in the other side, tapping out the message he needed to send. I summoned my thoughts.

I'd expected to have longer to prepare. At least time to grab a snack. Ah well, it was probably better done on an empty stomach when I was hangry, and at least I'd already spent time at home researching one or two things.

Shade pulled out of the car park and spoke. "Now

we're out of any potential earshot, I'll prepare ye for the different approaches we can take to getting information out of Bronson and the start I've made."

"Ye mean torture techniques?"

He took a corner, other skeleton crew cars ahead and behind. "Exactly."

My stomach fluttered. "So, my mind goes first to psychologically terrorising him in order to disorientate—a pitch-black room, sensory deprivation. Fuck with his head over where he is and how long he's been there. Ye could also have used pain as a teacher, leaning into physical intimidation, but Bronson is a seasoned gangster. Chances of him squealing over an electric shock or two are small, so that would be saved for when it's meaningful. Emotional leverage would be limited—he's single, an only child, and has no kids that anyone knows of, plus with him over fifty, his parents are either dead or ancient, so he's less likely to give a shite. Bribing him won't work. He probably won't take a bargain. Drugs could help, but I think he's an addict so will be suffering withdrawal. Further drugs would react unpredictably and might kill the arsehole." I cocked my head. "I guess that's why ye had to delay the interrogation? Your knock-out drugs fucked him up?"

Shade's mouth fell open. "Fucking hell. Correct. Continue."

"Seducing him is unlikely to work, same with offering any kind of emotional connection. We don't have time for some cute little thing to tend his wounds and pretend to sell us out. Next on the list is exploiting rivalries. My money would be on that, because it's where I think he started. We tell him his gang sold him out. Red wants him gone. That kind of thing. Lastly, we break his sanity and torture him until he's exhausted. Never quit." A cold smile broke over my face. "That will be sweet."

Silence followed.

Riordan choked. "Where the hell did you learn all of that?"

"I've been researching this for a while, but when ye locked me in my room, I searched up a list of torture techniques and went through each in turn. Shade, did I miss anything? I'm right about how ye started, aren't I? He's in a stress position in a dungeon with music blasting? It's the best approach to break his hostility on waking."

"Aye, that's exactly what I've done. Jesus."

I beamed. Impressing Shade was important to me. I wanted to do what he did, and he was the key to that world. "Sorry for speed talking at ye, but the slow delivery of information I already know kills me. So we enter and silence the music then stick a spotlight on Bronson. Flip him the right way up and tell him Red refused to bargain him out so he has to answer questions to save himself. It's his only option."

"That was the approach I considered. I'm on the fence about which technique to settle on for information gathering. Any one of them could be our way in. Everyone is susceptible to one, and your assessment is good, but it's a paper exercise. Ye don't know the man. For example, in your research, did ye turn up that he came to Deadwater after serving time with a man who became the previous Four Milers' leader? They established the gang together. He loves the life."

"He's loyal," I mused.

Shade nodded. "To the Four Milers. Not to Red. He's different to my usual bodies. I don't know for sure yet that he's guilty."

"Right. The only evidence we have is the girl who told Riordan that Bronson uses sedatives."

The dark night sped by our windows. We'd taken a route back over the bridge to the Scottish side of Deadwater and out towards an industrial area of delivery warehouses and manufacturing plants, all closing down for the evening.

Shade tapped the steering wheel. "There's something else. Arran and I saw him take down one of our crew. He said that Red was out of town, and I got the impression he was hostile to his boss. This was the night Alisha died."

"Who did he take down?" My mind supplied the answer as I framed the question. "Convict, right?"

"Aye. He throttled him then somehow knocked him out. It was too dark to see."

Riordan shifted in his seat. "Is Convict still alive?"

"Unknown."

The two men swapped an expression of disquiet.

My mind raced. "I'm going to make a quick call. I'll put it on loudspeaker. Then ye can tell me how I need to behave."

To his muttering about who was running the show, I dialled my Skeleton Girls Detective Agency group with a voice call. Genevieve and Everly both answered.

I told them where I was and who with, then asked my question. "I just wanted to go over the deaths one more time so I can work out what I want to get from tonight."

Genevieve snorted. "An admission of guilt would be nice."

"He's hardly going to do that," Everly said. With measured consideration, she walked me through all the facts we knew about the murders. How each woman was discovered. What was in her post-mortem. What we knew about her background.

Cherry, Natasha, Amelia, and Alisha. They wouldn't be left unavenged.

When we were done, I hung up and let my thoughts simmer. Tyler's words surfaced.

"If Bronson is discontented with Red," I mused, "his motive could be a hostile takeover of the Four Milers with the murders his proof that he can lead them successfully."

Shade turned off the road, into the car park of an industrial building. Grey sidings. No company name on the front. "Exactly where I landed. What approach would ye take?"

The car stopped inside the wide frontage of the building.

I wrangled my fingers together.

"That we only give a fuck about Alisha. We can't tolerate the slight to the skeleton crew. He owes us for her alone, and he has an opportunity to make amends. Therefore, for him, he still has a chance to take over from Red. Behind that, we test him on the other killings. There are details we know that never made it to the press."

Shade killed the engine and twisted in his seat. "Good. Now for your behaviour in the room. I'm the lead. I do the work and I call the shots. He's my prisoner. Ye can listen in but you'll stay out of his eyeline, at least until we know why he's interested in ye. Say one fucking word, and you're gone."

I bristled, filled with energy, ready to go. "Fine."

Riordan stalled us. "I have a theory. Moniqua told me Red went to her flat to try to recruit her. What if she named you as a target? She could've acted in desperation. Given a name of someone she'd recently heard of. She didn't seem that pressed about me, but she knows who you are, and the bitchy move fits."

I chewed on that, because a similar thought had occurred to me. I'd only been on the Deadwater scene a couple of months. The people in the club knew me, but I'd had no interactions with the other gangs in the city. Not like Alisha would've done. My name on their lips made no sense, unless it was given to them.

Shade directed my thoughts. "There's only one way to find out. Let's go slice and dice Bronson."

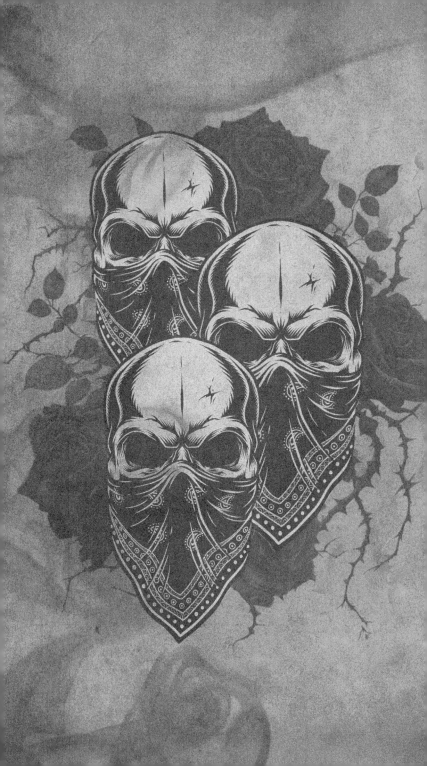

22

Riordan

Inside the cavernous, windswept space, Shade strode to the far left of the building, a set of steps leading down to a subterranean level. We followed. The wind cut out, replaced by a thudding sound—the music Cassie had guessed would be part of Bronson's psychological torture.

She'd been on the money. Scarily so.

Some of the skeleton crew who'd come with us remained upstairs while another unlocked a door at the bottom of the metal steps, revealing a domed ceiling over a wide, underground room with the feel of an air-raid shelter or a bunker. He locked us in, and my spine tingled with anticipation. Or perhaps mild panic. I wasn't claustrophobic, but the place had a bad vibe. Nothing good happened here.

The back wall of the bunker contained a reinforced door, multiple locks securing it closed. Two guards stood either side, and at a desk nearer us, monitors displayed a nightmarish view of inside that room.

Of a man, trussed up by his feet which were tied to a hook so he dangled from a metal beam. Each hand was also constrained, and outstretched so he was inverted in a swan dive pose. Over his head, a burlap sack concealed his features. It didn't hide the pain he was in.

He raised his head, his body flexing, then dropped back into the torture position.

Above him, water dripped. Not a steady flow, but an intermittent trickle, hitting his face and soaking the material covering it. That was why he kept moving. He couldn't breathe.

Horror and nausea sank through me.

This was fucked up. The whole world of gang violence scared the hell out of me, and I hated that it existed and that I was a part of it.

This wasn't my life. I didn't want it.

Then Cassie brushed by me, and my emotion evaporated. If she'd followed that note and walked out of the warehouse in search of me, he would've taken her. He would've killed her. Any pity I'd felt fled.

More, she was here and facing a man who I knew had to scare her. She'd told me how she tackled her fears head-on. It was admirable. I could take a lesson in that.

Cassie settled at a desk and reached into her bag, extracting a skeleton mask, then she tugged it over her head. It was a full-face version, concealing all but her eyes, different to the half-mask I took from my back pocket and tied on.

Then she jumped up and came to me. Pressing up on her toes, she held up a makeup palette. "You're too pretty. Let me dirty ye up a little."

I smirked and allowed her to paint out a black band across my eyes. The other skeleton crew members had done the same, though I doubted theirs was from a high-end makeup line.

Across the room, Shade consulted with the guards and spooled through some of the footage of the room. After a minute, he gestured for us to fall in.

The locks slid out. The bunker door opened. A wall of noise hit us, and we walked the strip of light piercing the entrance.

Along with the noise, a sour odour assaulted my senses.

Shade pointed to a seat against the back wall for Cassie to take. He positioned me to Bronson's right. From a table, he collected a lamp and turned it on, indicating for the door to be closed behind us.

Oh fuck.

I swallowed. Like it or not, I was an active part of this. I needed to step into my role. But another aspect was stealing over me. I fucking loved watching Cassie in her element. When she'd taken on Piers, holding a knife to his dick, cutting him, I'd been hard. It was all her, not the torture itself, and I had exactly no idea why.

Perhaps it was a good thing that Shade had forbidden her from taking part. Me popping a boner while she dripped with blood wasn't a good look.

The spotlight hit Bronson.

Then the music cut out. A horrible keening came from the prisoner. It changed tone, weakening but not stopping, as if he realised something had altered but his brain was delivering the news slowly.

"Grab that," Shade ordered me.

I twisted the metal chair he pointed to and positioned it under Bronson. Shade unclipped one hand then the other, finally lowering the chain that held our captive's legs until I could guide him into the seat.

His old-boy button-up shirt was saturated, as were his jeans, a gross stain running down them. He'd soiled himself. Fucking hell. I quickly calculated how long he'd been like this. Maybe twenty-four hours, though most of them not awake.

Shade refastened his hands and legs to the chair, and I stayed close in case Bronson lashed out. Instead, the man slumped to one side. At his spine, one of his hands shook uncontrollably.

Shining the light on his sorry form, Shade stood calmly for a second then removed Bronson's mask.

"Bronson Lesk. Confirm that ye can hear me."

A low, rasping breathing came from the prisoner, but no words.

Out of nowhere, Shade reared back and smashed his fist into Bronson's face. The chair toppled, and Bronson collapsed on the floor. I waited for a signal then heaved him upright again, morphing back into the shadows.

"One more chance or I'll put ye back on hold with the nice music."

Blood dripped from his nose, and Bronson swayed on each breath. His eyes remained closed, but his lips moved. "I hear. Everything."

Shade squared up, ready to proceed, but Bronson spoke again, his tone creepy as fuck.

"I can hear how excited you are to have me here, Connor Michaels. Bet your dick got hard every time you thought of me in your little dungeon. I know you've got some lackey assisting you instead of your boss. He wouldn't have been so gentle. Who's at the back? Soft, quick breathing. Smells good. Is that your bitch? Hey, sweetheart, come and suck an old boy's cock, won't you?

Might be my last chance." He gave a wheezing laugh.

I stiffened and darted my gaze to Cassie. Perched on her chair, she squinted at Bronson as if scrutinising him. There was no fear in her expression, only interest.

I reset my expectations. What they'd done had barely affected the man, other than to his physical form.

Shade took a few steps then turned back around. "Good for ye, keeping some of your marbles. Forgive me if I'm not impressed. You'll know why you're here, then?"

"I'm sure you're dying to tell me."

"Ye fucked with my crew. I can't let that lie."

"Ah, you're after a confession. To get it, you'll tell me how Red knows I'm here and doesn't care. Then, you'll offer me some glimmer of hope so I spill my guts. Let me save you the trouble. Whether Red gives a fuck about me or not makes no difference. If you're expecting him to come after me, guess again. He won't take the hit for my sake."

The confidence and arrogance stunned me. He was seeking to lead rather than follow.

Shade considered his words then, from the side table, picked up a tool. A handheld device with two prongs at the top. A taser, my mind supplied. I'd never seen one in real life.

"Open your eyes," he ordered Bronson.

The older man chuffed a laugh. "Make it worth my while. Tell your bitch to flop out her big tits in front of me."

Shade gritted his teeth. "You're losing your touch, old man."

"No fist to the kisser? So it isn't her," Bronson

continued. "Who, then? Not Arran's slut. Not if he's left you to it. Then that cunt Alisha met her maker." He laughed.

Cassie bounced to her feet.

Bronson cocked his head. "High heels. Surely not one of your dancers. Who else is hanging on your crew? Ah, got it. Arran's little sister. Don't tell me that teenage cunt is into this. Talk about crazy running in the family." He paused for a second. "Little girl, when I'm out of here, I'll break in your room and rape you in your bed. Bet you'll scream for me."

Ice stole through me. How fucking dare he talk about Cassie like that.

Shade made a sound of disgust and advanced on the man, but I did, too. Holding his gaze, I gestured to the taser. He handed it over then tapped his throat. *Right.*

Without hesitating, I jammed the device into Bronson's neck and pressed the button. Electricity crackled. The taser jerked in my hand, but that was nothing to the effect it had on the prisoner. He jolted then seized, his muscles holding him from the seat. He moaned. Frothed at the mouth.

I hoped it hurt like hell. Maybe it would reset his brain and get her name out of his goddamned mouth. Maybe he'd die. Better to have one less predator on the streets.

Just as I was about to stop, fingers curled around mine. With a maniacal grin, Cassie squeezed, giving him an extra burst of power.

"...eight, nine, ten."

I lifted my head to Shade's counting. He slashed his hand. We released the trigger, and I staggered to the wall, breathing hard. What the hell had I done? A single threat to Cassie and I'd been willing to kill a man. One we still needed evidence from.

Holy fuck.

Returning to her seat, Cassie linked her gaze to mine. I wasn't sure what I could see there, but fucking hell, I wanted to lay her out and strip her then fuck her over Bronson's dead body.

A weak cough dragged my attention back.

Shade folded his arms. "Shame, you're still alive. If you'll shut your fucking mouth, I'll get on with business. First, Marcus isn't supplying the Four Milers anymore. I killed him for dealing to ye. Your using his drugs fucks over my reputation."

I guessed Marcus to be the dealer of Shade's sedatives, the ones they suspected Bronson of using.

Bronson's chest rose and fell. Anger mixed with pain in his features.

Shade continued. "With Red out of town, we'll be paying a few visits to your new establishment."

"Like I give a fuck," the man spluttered.

Shade smiled. Palmed a blade. Untying Bronson's right arm, he spread his fingers. "Furthermore, for the insult to my crew and the life lost, I'm taking your trigger finger as first payment. Any more will be cut as and when ye piss me off enough. If you're alive that long."

"Wait," Bronson gasped and choked up pink spit. "I know what you want. Your man. I fucking knew Convict was a plant the minute Red brought him in. You can't hide that shit from someone like me. I've been around the block. I'll always guess your next move, and son, that was weak. Just as shite as Red's judgement. He should've listened."

Something flickered in Shade's eyes.

He lifted his gaze to Cassie, and I followed suit. She thumped her chest. Shade nodded like her meaning was obvious. The answer filtered into my mind. They were hunting for Bronson's weakness. She'd mimed bravado. No—pride. Bronson had an opinion on Convict that Red had ignored.

I barely knew anything about Convict, other than he'd been forced out of the skeleton crew the evening I came to rescue Everly from the nightclub. So he'd been a double agent.

"He's dead," Bronson finished. "There. We good? No more fake phone calls home. No more bullshit jobs. He's a corpse."

Shade recoiled in shock. With a curled lip, he sliced into Bronson's index finger. Blood dripped. The man screamed. Shade wrenched his hand down to the chair's armrest and finished the job of severing it.

He tossed the finger to the floor. "Ye killed him for no reason. We wouldn't take him back."

Bronson bucked against his ties. Blood flowed from the stump and dripped to the floor. Shade sighed then collected a med-kit, efficiently bandaging up the wound.

"Wouldn't want ye dying on me. Not when there's more I need."

Bronson flushed red. "Why in God's bitch name am I here then, Michaels? What information do you need? Need me to tell you about your mama's loose cunt?"

Shade palmed a knife and took it to Bronson's neck. He pierced his skin with the tip, blood oozing out in a trickle.

Bronson's hands trembled again.

"You're right that Red doesn't care that you're here. As far as he's concerned, you're an old man and no use to him. I heard he's already put out a call for a new second-in-command. He's replacing ye."

Bronson's composure broke. "That fucking piece of shit. He doesn't have the stones to go it alone. I'm the brains behind the Four Milers and have been for twenty years. They're mine."

"Not anymore. Word on the street is he has a first choice. Someone who proved they're as ruthless as he needs."

Shade was winding in a fishing reel with Bronson locked on to the bait. He'd gone for the man's pride. He'd hit the mark.

Lowering to capture Bronson's furious gaze, Shade smiled coldly. "I don't think ye know anything that will help me. I'm out of here. Enjoy the music while I'm interviewing the others."

"Wait! Who else did you take? They won't talk for shite. What the fuck is your game plan?"

"They already did. How do ye think I know about Red's new boy? Whether ye make it out of here or not, your role just got downgraded to lackey."

Shade tossed me the sack to put over his head again. Bronson's protests muffled but didn't stop. Not when we untied him and splayed his arms out wide. Only when he was inverted did the anger change to a moan.

The three of us left.

Anticipation curled up in me. What had we got? Shade hadn't asked any questions about the murdered women, or why Cassie had been next. If Moniqua had gone running to him with Cassie's name, we were none the wiser.

Except outside the door, with the music blaring and killing my eardrums, then muting as the bunker closed, Cassie and Shade shared a slick high five.

"Got him," she said.

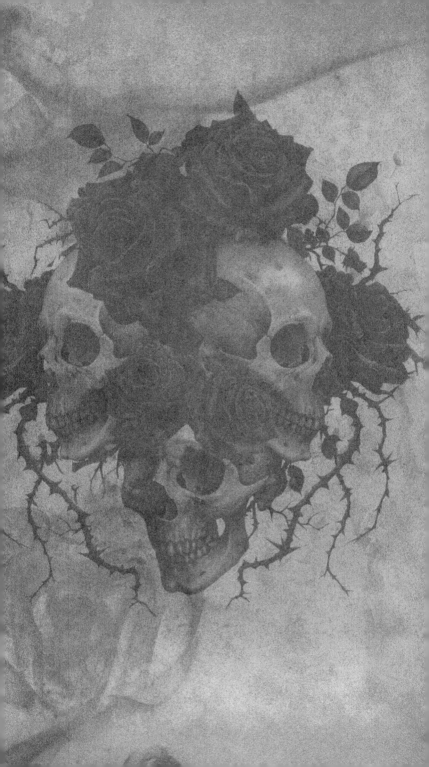

23

Cassie

Shade directed us out of the bunker and through the warehouse. In the confines of his car, he spoke again. "Cassie, summarise."

I rubbed my hands together. "He folded like a cheap chair when pressed on Red's disrespect. That plus a little pain will have him thinking up every piece of information he can bargain with."

Riordan's eyebrows dove together. "You were priming him?"

Shade nodded. "Each sentence was a test to see what he'd react to. It pissed him off that I killed his dealer, but he didn't give a fuck about Red's brothel. Then I implied to him that someone else has taken some big win to Red in order to get Bronson's job. If he's the killer, that's going to eat at his pride. I took one finger for one fallen crew member. He'll believe he can get away with losing another for Alisha. It's an incentive to live and get revenge."

"If he isn't the murderer, he'll spill whatever information he has on them as a bargaining chip," I mused. Then I checked myself. "Sorry about Convict."

Shade's eyes flashed with stark pain. "I can't think about that now."

He got us on the road.

From my bag, I took a pack of baby wipes so Riordan could clean off the eye black.

Back at the warehouse, Shade left us with a murmur about seeing Arran. I wanted to ask to be included in round two, but the guy was on a mission.

Riordan tugged me against him. "Come hang out in the brothel to do your work? That way I can keep an eye on you."

I loved that he needed me near. With a shy nod, I let him lead me upstairs. Outside the entrance, he glanced inside but stopped me.

"There's something I've been thinking about. The last time we were here, Moniqua approached me."

Ugh. I folded my arms.

"Nothing happened between us. I went to your room to tell you that."

"Definitely looked like she was on her knees with her lips in an 'O' shape."

"That was purposeful. The second you left, I stopped her."

I should've been relieved, but the opposite was true. He'd allowed her to do it, or even ordered it, to put me off. Damn.

A lick of pain curled inside me, a strange sensation that sank my mood. For days, I'd been focused on keeping Riordan. Indulging in the feelings I had for him. Enjoying kissing and all that went with it, too. But did he actually like me in reverse?

I took a step back. Confusion mixed with a rush of trying to remember him ever saying so. He enjoyed sex with me. Was that it?

"No biggie," I lied. "I need to get to work."

"Wait."

Hell, no. Particularly as I was shite at hiding emotion. Turning, I stormed into the brothel. In the centre of the floor, a client twisted his fingers into the bra strap of one of the sex workers like he was weighing her tits. Daria purred at him, her expression flickering at whatever she saw in my face. I skipped along quicker until I was behind the bar and in the office.

Riordan pursued me the whole way, storming after my flight. He braced himself against the office door so I couldn't close it on him. Then he burst past, shut us in, and collected my hands in his.

"Stop and listen. I'm sorry for what I did."

I scowled. Tried to loosen his grip. "Doesn't matter."

"Bullshit, it does. I hated it then, and it's killing me now."

This gave me pause. I stopped struggling. "Why?"

"I don't know how you've got under my skin so fast, but it was already in play then and I was trying to deny it. I pushed you away. I regret it and beg for forgiveness."

Damn. "If you're begging, shouldn't ye be on your knees?"

Riordan held my gaze then slowly, with heat replacing his worry, he knelt. He traced a finger up my leg to the hem of my shorts. "I'm sorry for hurting you. It was wrong."

I draped against the wall. "Tell me what ye think about me."

He kissed my knee. "I'm finding myself oddly crazy about you. Satisfactory enough?"

"Keep moving north and it will be."

He trailed his lips up my thigh. Took my loose shorts with him. At the crease with my leg, he hovered, his hot breath warming my skin.

God. Please. Just two inches to the left.

"Tell me you forgive me."

"Fine. I do."

"Good girl. What did I tell you I'd do if you ran from me again?"

"Chase me?"

"Punish you." Riordan pressed his lips to my underwear, right over my clit. Then he jumped up. "I have work to do."

"You're stopping?"

"Yep."

"Ye can't leave me like this," I squeaked.

The arsehole tossed me a smile that told me he could do exactly that. I watched him walk away, hot and bothered but smiling.

A familiar figure trotted down the hall from the opposite direction. In a jaunty hat, gold bikini bottoms, and a short, dark-blue, cutaway jacket which barely covered her round boobs and played peek-a-boo with her nipples like some kind of seventies porno space cadet, Dixie grinned at me. "What's got you grinning like that?"

"My boyfriend likes me."

She snickered. "Lucky girl."

I gave a dreamy sigh. "How the hell does one person

take up so much space inside me?"

"He's well hung, too? Put a ring on it. And yes, I mean his dick."

I burst out with a laugh. "I meant in my heart or soul or whatever, but that, too. Hey, Dix, got a minute? I need you to tell me the days you want to work but I also need to ask something more interesting."

"Anything for you, hun."

I exhaled and set my mind to my task, the wobble over my increasingly precious connection to Riordan over. "Give me your best ideas for petty revenge. Oh, and after, your personal favourite sex position, with detailed instructions. I need to learn."

Dixie's smile sharpened. I knew her as a sweetheart. Since I'd come here, she'd befriended me and helped me out. She was the queen of gossip but had the appearance of someone who didn't let shite bother her.

Apparently, I'd been wrong in that.

"Revenge is my favourite flavour, bestie. Grab a straw. I'm pouring."

Dixie listed half a dozen suggestions without breaking a sweat, clearly having put thought to this for her own reasons.

Delighted, I made my notes.

After we were done, and for the next few hours, she helped me work my way through the sex workers in the brothel, taking the time between clients to track down staff and even call the ones who were at home, getting their approval for the rota and help with my other questions. Pretty quickly, I'd compiled two lists.

When I was done, I hugged her then moseyed out to the main receiving room. Riordan was nowhere in sight, but that was in my favour. I had something I needed to do.

My little secret.

A surprise for him for later.

Manny was at the guard station which had a mirrored wall that looked out on the brothel's receiving room. He called another dude in to replace him then escorted me to the lift. We passed the hotel-style fourth floor, the cam girls on five, the storage area on six, then emerged into seven.

No one else came up here.

No one else's pass worked for this floor, except for mine, Arran's, and my family's. A long time ago, Arran had brought us the design of the warehouse, his pet project. We'd invested in it, a way of tying him into our family—something that was important to Jamieson. The seventh floor on his plans had been left vacant.

Jamieson had made a suggestion. I was beyond grateful for that now, despite being pissed off with my brother.

The hallway mirrored the one on the floor above, with two doors either side. I unlocked one.

Manny followed me in. "I half forgot this was here."

"It's never been used." I twirled around in the space. It was another apartment. Oak floors. Red-brick walls. Even a kitchen and bathroom, installed a few years ago but never touched.

"Until now?" Manny asked.

My belly tightened with anticipation. Here, Riordan and I could be locked away together. We could play house. Order food. Hide away from everything.

"I'm claiming it as my new home."

I moved to the arched window that gave a view of the harbour walk outside. From the hall, there was access to the fire escape and the roof. Somewhere I liked to go for fresh air and to give myself headspace. It would be a home away from home.

The views over the city were to die for.

A shadow fell over me. In the reflection of the glass, Manny was right behind me, a hulking shape around my much smaller form.

My pulse skipped. Some instinct had me freezing up.

Manny wasn't dangerous, was he?

I'd come up here alone with him, and no one else knew. No one would have a clue where I'd gone if I didn't return. What was I thinking? The chief of Arran's security team was a big man. Old enough to be my father, but stoic and strong. Quiet, but didn't they say to watch out for those?

My skin crawled. I couldn't see his expression in the reflection, but I could dive left and be on his weak side.

He moved in closer, leaning right over my shoulder.

I tensed, ready to make a break for it. I had one chance, and that meant taking him by surprise so I could reach the exit.

But the man chuckled. "Still a queue down there. I like to see it but I wonder if these people have work in the morning."

I released a breath.

Manny stepped back. "Sorry, there's me being a space invader. My wife tells me off for that. So, this place is yours?"

Fucking hell. I willed my heart to stop thumping.

"I need furniture," I told him, my voice tight. "But until it arrives, can I please bring up the bed I've been using on floor five?"

"I'll get everything sent up. Nice for Arran to have family nearby. He needs that."

Ashamed of myself, I left the flat and dove into the lift, Manny happily moving with me.

I grabbed my phone. "Speaking of Arran, I need to tell him what I'm doing."

I dialled him. He didn't pick up. Neither did Shade.

"No one's answering. Where are they?" I asked.

Manny gave an easy shrug. "Crew business."

"I don't suppose you'll tell me anything more."

"Correct. Need-to-know basis." He tapped his nose.

We exited the lift on the ground floor. Manny saw me into the strip club's dressing room then left me with the security guards there. Being back in a busy room should've helped me, but I was still rattled.

I forced my attention to the present. Manny wasn't wrong. Arran had been devastated by the loss of Alisha. He'd cared about her. He'd be cut up about Convict, too. I'd find him later for a chat.

Another hour of shift management with the staff who only stripped for their living and I had a set rota. One we'd repeat over and over, swapping individual shifts where needed and arranging overtime for the fun events Everly had planned. Manny had showed me the system where they managed the staff, and with a sense of achievement, I uploaded it, perched at a mirrored table with striptease music in the background.

A small burst of sadness accompanied my work. The

previous staff rota was Alisha's, complete with her notes, often in pink type. Overwriting it felt all kinds of wrong.

For all my efforts and my meandering thoughts, the sense of disquiet didn't lift.

My skin still crawled. Manny wasn't the culprit, so then who?

I knew the names of all the dancers around me and was in the eyeline of the security guard, but something still felt off.

A hand landed on my shoulder.

I squeaked and spun in my chair to find Arran looming over me. With my hand to my heart, I exhaled. "You scared the life out of me. Having trouble answering your phone?"

The skeleton crew leader twisted his lips in a smirk. "I've been busy. I still am, but I just wanted to say welcome back." His gaze ticked over the busy room then came back to me. "You asked me once if you could dance here. I like you managing the staff a lot more. Fuck knows I don't have the headspace to pick it up."

A darkness hung in his eyes. Arran's building of the warehouse and his mission to protect women abused by men like his father had formed a constant backdrop of my teenage years. I knew him well enough to tell when he was hurting.

"Cassie. Someone's looking for you."

I turned to find Lara nearing. In her black-and-pink club uniform, and with sparkly strands in her hair, she was a friend of Genevieve's, but not someone I'd talked much to. Clem managed her shifts as front-of-house staff.

"Who is it?" I asked.

"Oops. I didn't get a name. She said you'd want to see

her."

Well, that didn't help. "Thanks."

I came back to address Arran, but he'd gone.

Frowning, I returned to Lara. "Wait, while you're here, I'm doing the rota and wanted to check something."

Her smile lessened. "Clem manages my hours."

"I know, but I've been going around to all the dancers and other staff tonight so I might as well check your details are correct." I read out her address from the notes.

"Actually, it's wrong. I moved. I'm living in Harbour Point now." She recited the new address. An apartment on the waterfront not far up from the warehouse.

I whistled. "Nice. Did ye go in with roommates?"

She gave a short laugh but didn't answer. Something in that snagged in my brain. That address was a prime location, and the apartments shiny and new. I'd already noticed that she'd reduced to part time in the past few weeks. It didn't add up.

Equally, it wasn't my business. I returned to why she'd sought me out. "On the visitor, got a description?"

"About twenty, black hair, pretty."

My stomach tightened. There was one person I knew who fit that to a T. Moniqua. "Could you please bring her to me?"

Lara hesitated. "You don't want to go somewhere private?"

Why would she ask that? "No."

A minute later, and Moniqua followed Lara back in. Lara spoke in her ear, then Moniqua found me and approached.

"Cassie, right? Can we talk?"

My mind summoned a series of pictures starting with her on her knees in front of Riordan and ending with my hands around her scrawny throat. I produced a tight smile and gestured for her to take a seat. At the top of the room, there was enough space to speak without being heard, though I took care to make sure the guard noticed my visitor. With an elbow to the bright workstation, I leaned in. No fucking way was I waiting on her to start.

"Did ye give my name as a target to the Four Milers?"

She widened her eyes. "What? No!"

I waited. Liars had tells. The longer you gave them, the more they revealed.

"I never would. I didn't even know your name until we spoke on the phone. Plus I have nothing to do with them now my cousin's gone. When would I even have done it?"

"When Red came to your flat."

She dropped her gaze. "He wanted to recruit me as a sex worker. I'm a girls' girl. The last thing I'd do is try to get them to pick on someone else."

"Has he been back?"

"No. I think he assumed I was alone and would come running, and I am, but in the opposite direction. I swear I'm telling the truth." She shuddered. "I actually came here to ask if I could take you up on your job offer. I didn't want to call Riordan to do it. It didn't feel right if you two are together. I'll delete his number."

For fuck's sake. Her words rang true, which made it much more difficult to hate her.

Though not impossible.

I chewed on that for a moment, trying to make sense of what I knew. Bronson mentioned me at the bunker, though his rape threat felt more like him trying to get a rise out of Shade because he'd failed to do so with Everly.

If Moniqua hadn't fed him my name, then who?

Maybe I was just one of a long list of potential murder candidates.

Either way, I had to make a decision about the slumped-shouldered woman in front of me. It would be better to keep her close.

"Ye can work the bars down here," I decided. "Between Divine and Divide, we have shifts every night. Clem runs them. This side, the uniform's like Lara's, in Divide, it's a skeleton crew t-shirt and black shorts. Ye can wear a bandanna if ye like the vibe, though most of the staff don't bother. We protect our own here."

Moniqua's gaze flew to mine. "Thank you. I'm so grateful. I can't even explain."

"Then don't, and don't make me regret my decision. Go to Divine's bar now. I'll text Clem to meet ye."

She left me.

With my notepad open, I ran over the revenge ideas my colleagues had given me. Everything from minor irritations to rage-inducing acts.

Perhaps I'd save one or two for Riordan's sort-of-ex, if she crossed me.

I turned to my next list. The sex positions training the girls had given me. Several had offered demos which I fully intended to take them up on. I pulled my phone from my pocket to take a picture for Riordan.

Instead, there were missed calls from him along with several texts. With bated breath, I read through them. I'd switched my phone onto silent when talking to the staff and had forgotten to check it for a while.

Riordan: I'm taking a break for a couple of hours. Meet me in your room if you can.

Riordan: I guess you're busy. I ran into Everly and had a quick chat.

Riordan: Don't freak out, but I'm heading out for a little while. There's something I need to do.

My breathing stopped. What the hell? I scanned the final message.

Riordan: I know you can track me. Watch my location if you want, but don't you dare leave the warehouse. Let me do this thing.

Another heartbeat, and the tracker I'd glued to his bike loaded on my screen. Holy fuck. I burst from my seat and ran for the corridor as if his words had lit me on fire.

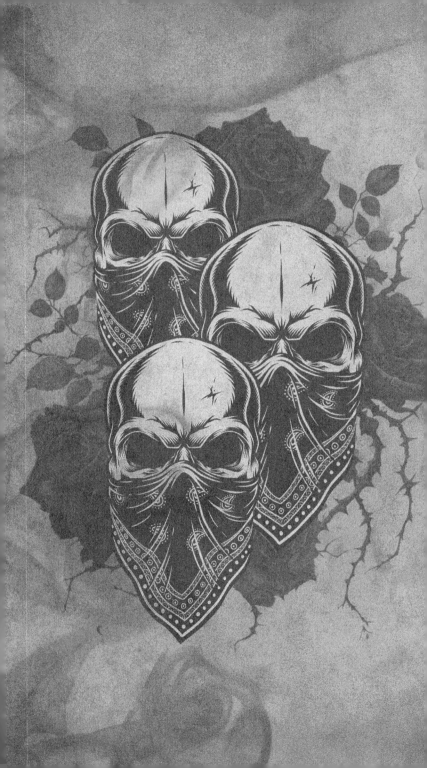

24

Riordan

My black trainers landed with silent thuds on the mansion's back patio, and I adjusted the skeleton mask down across my lower face, making sure I was covered. Before I left the warehouse, I'd made a last-minute change out of my biker boots, and though it had felt weird speeding across Deadwater without them, I'd made the right choice.

Stealth was my goal this evening.

In the shadows, I held still and gazed at the building. A new camera had been installed high on the back wall, but it was an old-fashioned kind that rotated. I counted ten seconds from one side to the other. No problem. I could get inside in less.

Burglary wasn't a skill I'd honed, but breaking and entering had been an unfortunate side-effect of living with Genevieve's dad. The old boy would go on drinking binges and lose his keys. He'd then return home and call a locksmith, insist that they replace the chamber, get inside, then fall into a dead sleep. Gen would come home and be stuck outside, unable to rouse him. The first time it happened, I was seventeen, and I'd worked out how to use my sister's hair pins to release the lock.

Odd how that skill was serving me in breaking into my bio father's house again.

The camera swung back my way, and I held my breath, counted to three, then darted across the open space. At the back door, I slid my skeleton key lock pick—an upgrade I'd acquired—into the lock. The pins clicked, and the lock gave. I ducked inside the kitchen.

All in under seven seconds.

Earlier this evening, I'd chatted with Everly, and she'd given me the lowdown on our father.

"He's a stickler for routine and obedience. He likes things just so but is frugal, so most of his trips to other cities or abroad are sponsored by others. He declares it all, though. It's too public for him to hide, so goes on his mayoral calendar."

She'd shown me it.

He was away tonight, though returning in the early hours. The opportunity had grabbed me by the balls and not let go.

"A big part of his ego is made up by the fact we're descended from royalty, though by a lord sleeping with a servant. Father ignores that point."

I'd told her I preferred it.

"You know, I do, too. But Father is so nuts about it, he had a heraldic family tree made. It's painted onto cloth and hangs in the formal living room. It's his pride and joy."

Out of the kitchen, I prowled down the darkened hall.

Everly's information had not only primed me for the mayor being out of town for at least a few more hours, but also clued me in on the fact that any security measures he would have put in place since she left would be basic. He didn't like spending money.

She'd also given me a target for my plan.

Originally, my need for revenge had taken shape in my mind as an explosive event. Life-changing. Possibly life-ending. Cassie had suggested a drip-feed plan, and I fucking loved the idea. To slowly drive him insane would be perfect.

I'd also had to get over myself and throw the first stone.

Cassie's bravery in everything she did had inspired me.

At the front of the house, the formal living room lay in darkness. Shutters had been closed over the lower half of the sash windows, but enough light from the streetlamps filtered in to show me my target.

Over the mantel was the family tree artwork. My relatives, all neatly listed. A smile curled my lips, and I pulled the flick knife I'd taken from Cassie's bedroom when I'd waited for her. Carefully, I lifted a chair and took it to the mantel, settling it without a sound on the rug.

I climbed up.

My fucking hand shook.

As a kid, I'd wanted a father's love so badly. Gen's dad hadn't given any, so I'd started to see myself as unworthy. Now I knew my biological father thought the same, that feeling could be gutting, which made no sense because I didn't respect either man. I didn't want it. I needed to prove what I really thought of them.

Steeling my nerves, I sliced down one side of the picture, the sharp blade cutting through with ease. Next, I stretched to the top of the frame and cut again, angling the blade to come down the right-hand side. With my free hand, I supported the material as it fell away, only the base of it connected now.

A *clank* came from somewhere inside the house.

I froze and listened.

No one else lived here. Everly had told me the housekeeper had quit. There was a security team who patrolled the street, but they didn't enter homes without reason.

Heavy footsteps thudded on the stairs, descending. Fuck. Whoever it was would pass right in front of the living room door.

I was a sitting duck. I couldn't move without either the chair or the painting making a sound. Nor did I have an easy route out of this room. Whoever it was, I'd have to rush them. I was good for a fight, better for Cassie's brother's extensive lesson, but that would mean abandoning my prize.

Annoyance curdled my blood.

The person finished their descent and strolled past the living room entrance, a phone raised to their ear.

My mouth fell open, recognition instant.

It was Piers Roache. What the fuck was he still doing on the scene?

Luckily, he was engaged with his call, and not with the house. His voice echoed in the hall. "No, it wasn't like that. Are you fucking listening?"

I held my breath and made a choice. I wasn't giving up my mission. Not for him. If I needed to, I'd take the fucker out.

With slow, steady actions, I lifted the painting and pierced the final edge.

"I don't give a fuck about that bitch," Piers continued on. "He still wants my money but he has less to offer. Yes, the business centre is going ahead. Without me, it couldn't happen. Makepeace rubs people up the wrong way. His daughter was the diplomat who opens doors. Stupid slut."

A clink followed, ice in a glass, which meant he was in the kitchen.

I packed away his words for dissection later and cut the last of the painting free from its frame. Then I rolled it up and folded the knife. Piers was in my path, which meant I needed another route out. If the front door was unlocked, I could make a break for it across the front garden and down to the street. I was fast. Dressed in black. With any luck, I'd make it back to my bike. If it wasn't, I'd waste time I could've used to rush Piers.

Choices.

In the formal living room's entryway, I peered out. The front door had a deadlock which gave me hope. Locked from the inside. It would open if I pulled both handles.

I squinted right, seeing nothing but the entrances to the kitchen and to the room across from it which Everly had called the mayor's Council Chamber. All heavy furniture and oak panelling. The place where deals got made and old white guys got their dicks sucked.

I'd contemplated a little graffiti scored into the Council Chamber's table as an added bonus of my visit, but now was the time to get the hell out of here.

But just as I readied to go, something appeared at the window beyond.

A small figure, peeking in.

I stopped dead.

No fucking way.

I took another glance at the skeleton staring back at me. It was the same fucking full-face mask Cassie had worn to Bronson's interrogation. My heart lurched. I didn't want to believe it. I was seconds away from freedom and getting away with my theft, but I couldn't leave.

Not if Cassie had disobeyed me and had pursued me.

Piers droned on, the arsehole moving on to another topic, though he remained in the kitchen. My other option was to exit through the Council Chamber which had French doors to the garden, though was directly in line of the camera.

The one Cassie stood right beneath.

Clenching my jaw, I jogged down the hall, the heavy painting flopping under my arm. I dove into the Council Chamber and backed against the wall, just as the kitchen door opposite creaked open.

"He'll be back any minute," Piers told his caller.

For fuck's sake. My careful—okay, spontaneous— plan was falling to pieces. If Piers entered the formal living room, he'd see the picture frame with a gaping hole in it. If he changed his mind and came in here to wait for the mayor, we'd have to brawl and I'd lose the picture.

All I had left was speed. I homed in on the French doors. There was no key in the lock, and the handle twisted noiselessly but didn't give. Fuck. Grabbing my skeleton key, I worked the lock. For every millisecond that passed, my heart beat faster. Sweat broke out on my brow, and I fumbled the key and almost dropped the painting.

Cassie appeared on the other side of the glass. I glowered at her and made a second attempt. She didn't budge. Didn't let me out of her sight. All I could see was her eyes, and the expression in them nearly ended me.

I'd scared her.

Panic had me working faster, then in a rush of fucking heaven, the lock gave.

To hell with any noise. I burst out of the door and lifted Cassie straight into my arms, wasting no time in sprinting down the patio and onto the grass. She whimpered and held me tight, clinging to my front while I put all my power into my legs to run. At the end of the garden was a newly installed fence that blocked up a gap to the neighbours' garden. Not a problem for the millionaires who lived on this road but perfect for burglars. No wonder the mayor had stumped up to fix it.

Earlier, I'd scaled it easily. Now, I had a passenger.

I manoeuvred Cassie onto my back. "Hold this. Don't drop it. And don't let go."

She clutched the painting, freeing up my hands to climb. Footsteps thumped down the garden. Something rustled in the bushes.

"Who the fuck is that?" Piers shouted. "Stop, thief."

I kept climbing, hauling us to the top then throwing a leg over. A glass shattered on the sturdy fence panel an inch from my hand, raining splinters over my arm and to the ground. I didn't look back. I ignored the sour stench of whisky that sprinkled on my skin. All I needed was for Cassie to hold on while I dropped us down the other side.

Still clinging to me, she squealed and jerked.

I twisted back. Beneath us, Piers had seized her ankle. My heart pounded, fear soaring. I gripped the fence to keep us balanced. If I let go, we'd fall.

"Get the hell off me." She kicked out at him.

Piers' expression shifted from anger to something different. In the low light, I picked out fear. He'd recognised her voice.

"You," he snarled.

"Hey, Piers, how's the dick?"

For a second, he faltered, but then recovered and bared his teeth, grappling for her other leg. "What are you holding? What did you steal?"

"I'll take your balls if ye ask nicely." She kicked again.

"I'll hurt you for what you did, and I'll take pleasure in it."

Fury broke over me. Loosening one hand, I hung from the other with a death grip and threw a punch at Piers' ugly face. He dropped his hold and fell, clutching his face. With a whimper, Cassie climbed me, clinging tighter as I righted us on the fence.

On top once again, I didn't waste time in swinging over and using my rubber soles to slide down the sheer drop then let go and fell the rest of the way, landing like a cat on a pile of loose earth. Cassie stayed in place, for once obeying orders.

A thud hit the fence. "I'll fucking end you, bitch. I'll destroy you from your mouth to your cunt and force your boyfriend to watch."

Cassie gave a dark laugh. "Not if I get there first, mushroom dick."

If Piers was trying to come after us, I wasn't waiting around to see. I turned and ran full pelt down the neighbours' garden and out along the side of the house. The need for stealth had gone. A light sprang on, and someone called out, but I kept going, all the way to my bike.

"Do you have a car?" I asked.

"Nope. Cabbed it."

A thousand furies descended over me but I didn't voice them. At the kerbside, I jammed the helmet on Cassie then revved the engine.

Without pause, I got us the fuck out of there.

Down the expensive row of houses we flew. The wind whipping across my hot face did nothing to cool my raging emotions. I had to assume Piers would call the police, which meant sticking to quieter roads the second I could and not taking the more direct route home. Likewise, if any passing lucky cop spotted me biking without a helmet, they'd pursue us.

We'd be caught red-handed.

I'd take the blame so Cassie could walk free, but breaking and entering with theft would land me jail time, particularly with the victim being who he was. I smacked the handlebars and ran a red light, too shaken up to notice until the last second.

A horn blared. I swore and banked around a corner.

Cassie giggled then trailed her finger down my back, drawing a heart.

I forced my breathing to slow and cut through the suburb, emerging into the next and doing the same until we stole down a street that led to Deadwater's town centre. If we could cross that, we'd be within easy reach of the start of the harbour walk. That route was pedestrianised, which meant no cops, at least not in cars, and I could bike down it mostly unseen. We'd be back at the warehouse in under ten minutes.

A siren wailed somewhere nearby.

Cassie squeezed me. I pulled into a side road and cruised on until we passed a junction onto the city centre.

A police car zipped past. Shit. Needed to get out of sight. Killing the engine, I wheeled the bike backwards and into a lane.

We waited in the dark, concealed in shadows. My chest rose and fell, my heart still racing.

Cassie's fingers linked under my jacket then crept beneath my t-shirt. She caressed my belly, and a poorly timed kick of lust sank through me.

I didn't stop her.

I craved her touch. The thought of her being in danger did bad things to me. It broke something in my brain.

The sirens grew louder. Another answered, coming from a different direction. I scanned the walls of the surrounding buildings, though couldn't yet see any strobing lights. It could be for us, or it could be for one of the hundred other crimes taking place in town tonight.

Cassie popped my jeans button.

I gripped her hand. "Stop."

She relaxed, so I eased my hold, training my senses once more on the night. Around us was mostly offices, all in darkness at the late hour. If I—

In a fast move, the wicked girl opened my jeans fully and plunged her hand inside. She wrapped her fingers around my semi, and fire spread through my veins, starting at her touch and blitzing through me. On reflex, I sat back to give her better access, lost to every other thought.

She stroked me. I gritted my teeth to stop from making a sound.

For a dazzling few seconds, I followed that pull. The unstoppable force of her. How she owned my need. An engine roared nearby.

Fuck, *wait*.

We could be discovered any second. A passerby coming home from a club. The cops taking a right up our road and hunting in the alleys.

I had to end this.

But she felt too good. Cassie eased her hand up and down, a dark little chuckle following when I was harder than nails in seconds.

My blood pumped faster, and I flexed my limbs, trying to keep my mind aware of more than just sex. It was a losing battle, though I noted the sirens passing then moving deeper into town.

It took an embarrassingly long time for me to take action. Reaching back, I palmed her thigh, unable to resist sliding my fingers up her bare leg and under her shorts. I should squeeze her to tell her to cut it out. My touch roamed higher.

She shivered. Oh fuck, that action threatened to end me. But we couldn't linger here. No matter how my body demanded it.

Cassie needed to learn a lesson about restraint. She couldn't always do what she wanted. For her own good, I had to teach her.

Whipping an arm back, I brought her to my lap. Just as rough, I pushed her to lie out on the engine and handlebars with her legs wide around me to expose exactly the part of her I needed to torment.

Cassie moaned into her helmet. I had half an insane mind to drag it off and kiss her senseless.

Yet that lesson was still needed.

I slid my hand under her clothes to cup her between the legs. "If you fuck around like this, you'll get us into trouble."

Another sound of pleasure.

I rubbed the heel of my hand into her clit. "Danger turns you on, doesn't it? Do you want me right now?"

She arched into the touch. I grazed my fingers into her underwear and eased one into her, my whole body thrilling at her tight heat squeezing me. Fucking hell. I didn't want to stop. An ease in and out had her bucking onto me.

I could make her come in seconds.

Pulling free nearly killed me, but I flipped up her visor, putting the finger that had been inside her into my mouth. "Tough. Now hold on and don't slide off from how slick I've made you."

Cassie glowered, her blue eyes narrowing before she slammed the visor back down and let me get her back into place.

Wheeling out of the lane, I peered into the street then gunned the engine, shooting over the junction and down the lane across from us. Deadwater had started as a medieval harbour town and still retained the twisted, narrow roads and multiple places to hide.

I knew them well. Took us along lesser-used ones and evaded any waiting cops. At the harbour, I followed the river, bumping over the cobbled boulevard, the neon pink-and-black signs of Divine and Divide soon coming into view. People ambled along, some staggering, one yelling at me to get on the road. I flipped him the bird and kept going.

Cassie resumed her torture of playing with me.

I didn't try to stop her. Soft fingertips caressed my shaft, and I glanced down to ensure I was still covered.

I drove us around the back of the warehouse, half out of my mind, parked up, then tapped my shoulder. Cassie understood, clinging on to me when I carried her off, the painting wedged between us. I turned from the building and reinstated my jeans, though I could do nothing to hide the bulge.

Once we were inside, I tugged off my bandanna and set Cassie on her feet. She removed the helmet then took the stolen goods back from me with a buoyant grin. Fucking infuriating. Without giving her the chance to speak, I wrapped my bandanna around her face, forcing it between her teeth, then tied it off behind her curls.

The joyful expression dropped to a dark scowl.

At the desk, the guard raised his eyebrows but said nothing. If he challenged me again, he'd regret it.

I propelled Cassie through the inner door. "I'm so fucking furious with you. What you did at that house was insane."

She stopped dead in the hall. I grabbed her hips and threw her over my shoulder, striding out to the central corridor and to the lift. It was waiting, and I ignored all of the gawping peanut gallery to carry her inside. When the doors closed, Cassie thumped my back with her fist. I didn't let her down.

On the fifth floor, I paced to her bedroom and threw open the door.

It was empty.

The bed gone. All her clothes missing, my rucksack, too.

All that was left was her detective wall, the map of Deadwater and connecting pieces of string still in place.

What the fuck was going on? Was she leaving? I

dropped her onto her heels again, and those furious eyes trained on me. She wrestled with her gag. I snatched her hands away to stop her removing it. If she was walking out, I didn't want to know.

Cassie pointed back to the lift then freed her hands to show me seven on her fingers.

I dove my eyebrows together. "Seventh floor?"

She nodded, then growled and bucked against me when I picked her up once more. She dropped the painting. I snatched the thing up and returned to the lift. Selecting floor seven did nothing until I held up my pass. Then, it lit up and we moved, exiting to a part of the warehouse I'd never been before. Cassie pointed at a doorway, and I held my pass over that as well.

It turned green. I entered an apartment.

Though mostly empty, there were signs of life. A door open. A line of kitchen spotlights lit. I crossed the living area to a hallway, finding myself in a bedroom.

All of our possessions were here. Not just the bed we'd used, but Cassie's clothing rail. Fucking hell, the bags from my car had been brought up as well. That could only have been my sister's doing.

Confusion dogged me for several seconds, but an explanation could wait. Pure emotion guided my next steps.

Cassie had misbehaved tonight. She'd gone beyond the pale. If I hadn't seen her first, if I'd been out of there before she arrived, she could have been *hurt*. I needed her to understand just how out of control that made me feel.

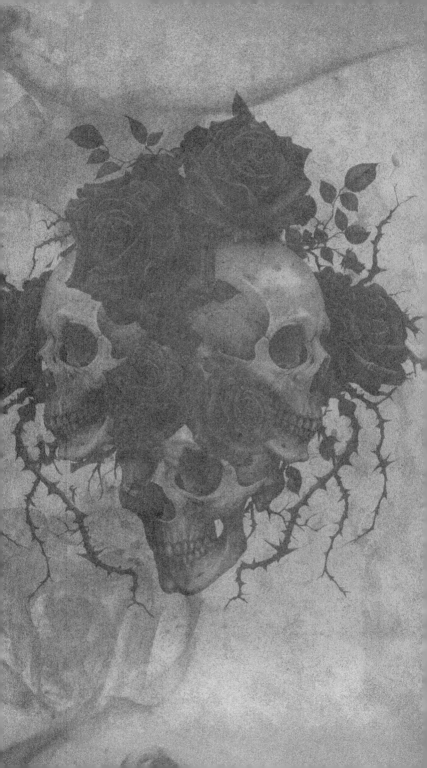

25

Cassie

Riordan tossed his stolen item to the warm oak floorboards and backed me to the bed. A thrill ran through me. With my mouth gagged, I couldn't question him about it, but now wasn't the time.

He tore off his jacket and discarded it to the floor then kicked off his shoes. The rest of his clothes followed until he was down to his boxers. I plopped onto the mattress, unable to stop staring. His body was mouthwatering, the low light showcasing his muscular form. I'd had nowhere near enough time to explore him.

He paced away from me then returned. "The one thing you have to do is to stay safe. Which means never being alone or vulnerable. My last message asked you to stay here. Yet at the very place I absolutely didn't want you to be, you were there."

Riordan raked his fingers through his hair, his distress plain in his darting move and the worried crinkle around his eyes.

He reached for me, standing me up to roughly unzip the playsuit and pull it off me. He did the same with my boots, knickers, and bra until I was naked.

I trembled with need.

"Lie out. I'm going to tie you up. You're going to let me."

Fucking hell. I wasn't sorry about going to the mayor's house. I'd been scared out of my mind for him. Plus I'd got a taxi, so it wasn't like I'd walked the streets. But it was obvious I'd scared him as well.

I didn't like that so much.

Shuffling up the bed, I settled my head on the pillow and stretched my arms up to the bedstead.

Riordan went to a bag and rifled through it. He extracted a length of blue rope, and I widened my eyes. My gag was so annoying. I wanted to ask why he had it.

At the corner of the bed, he fastened the rope around my wrist and looped it to the rail, circling to attach it to my other wrist. Then he returned to his jeans and brought out a flick knife.

My flick knife. I frowned at him, the gag preventing a full-on scowl.

Riordan severed the rope and took the other half to the bottom of the bed.

Oh no. He wouldn't dare. I kicked out at him, but he seized my ankle and neatly tied it to the post, copying it with my other while I bucked and reared. The man was frighteningly good with knots. I couldn't get free. The rope was in no way loose or too tight.

Fucking knot-Goldilocks had trussed me up well.

Stepping back, Riordan tossed the folded blade then took his time looking over my naked body. "I like it better when you can't talk back."

I growled. My gaze slid down his tall frame. I needed

him to fuck me to make this better. He swallowed then stripped his shorts, giving me the view I wanted. That hard dick pointed right at me.

He stroked it, lingering over the end with his gaze locked on the juncture of my thighs. An internal battle appeared to play out, as he climbed onto the bed and knelt between my legs.

He palmed my skin, driving up to my waist. Hot hands, calloused from his bike and from hard work. I adored his touch on me. It made me feel beautiful. He reached my breasts, at the same time, angling his dick to my core.

"I wasn't going to fuck you but I can't resist."

Riordan speared into me. I bit the gag and arched into him as much as I could manage. His hand shifted to my belly, the heel so close to grinding against my clit.

"You're so perfect. You make me feel too good."

A mind-blowing glide in and out.

Another, and I couldn't control a moan of pleasure. Riordan groaned in deep need and fucked me harder, his thighs meeting mine and jerking me up the bed. Tied up, I couldn't do anything but take him, but he was giving me exactly what I needed.

His palms slid over me, then he gripped my hips, lifting me for a series of hard hits. I bowed out my legs with the inch of play I had. Deep inside, I pulsed from where he hit my G-spot again and again.

He stilled. "Did you bring your vibrator?"

I slanted my gaze at a bag. He pulled out of me and went to it. Found the toy. Then came back to the bed and brandished it. Leaning over me, Riordan touched the vibrating tip of it to my sternum then dragged it down between my breasts, over my belly, and down to my wet centre. He passed it over my core, getting it slick, then switched it off. I tugged on my ropes. This was such a tease. I could hardly bear it.

Holding my gaze, he pushed it into me.

I groaned again and dropped my head back, my eyes closing. I wanted him. Only him. Nothing beat the feeling of him inside me. I craved it. Needed it.

With the toy in as far as it could go, Riordan released it.

My pussy pulsed.

The vibrator edged out a centimetre or two.

He took hold of his erection once again. Slowly, he played with himself, standing over me.

He didn't get back on the mattress.

"One of the things I like most about you is your wild spirit. I'd never ask you to change anything about yourself. You are too special. Too unapologetically you. You turn me on like you were built to torment me."

His hand moved faster.

"You walk straight through any boundary I try to put in place. Any request I make. You're a live wire. A fucking force of nature. I won't ask if you're sorry for following me because I know I'll be disappointed, both in your answer and in me asking that question."

A warning played out in my head. Something in his tone gave me pause. He'd failed to resist having sex with me but seemed to have collected himself. I didn't know what was going on or what his words meant, but I didn't like them.

I moaned, wishing I could speak.

Riordan groaned in response and fisted the quilt,

not touching me apart from with his avid, furious gaze. Abruptly, he came. Cum spilled over my belly and breasts. I squeezed around the vibrator, but it slid out of me some more.

I could hardly care, because all my focus was on the man calming his breathing to speak.

My heart hurt. This wasn't going to be good.

Riordan's gaze locked on to mine. His hair fell in his eyes. "I'm out. I can't do this. It'll end me. I can't live in constant fear for you and I won't ask you to be anything other than who you are. It wouldn't be fair. Sorry, Cassie. Goodbye."

He picked up his clothes. Turned his back to put them on. Behind the gag, I yelled at him. *No. No, please.*

With his shoulders rigid, Riordan walked away.

After a few seconds, the click of the door reached me. I roared and fought the ropes. Earlier, I'd feared being hurt, but by Manny, or a stranger. Never by Riordan. I needed him. He couldn't fucking leave me.

Minutes passed.

To save my wrists, I stopped fighting.

Only then did his words sink in. He'd asked me in his text to stay in the warehouse. It was a demand for a small degree of respect, a boundary set for my sake, not his. Or so I'd thought. I'd been wrong.

What had I done?

Riordan had left me, and it was all my fault.

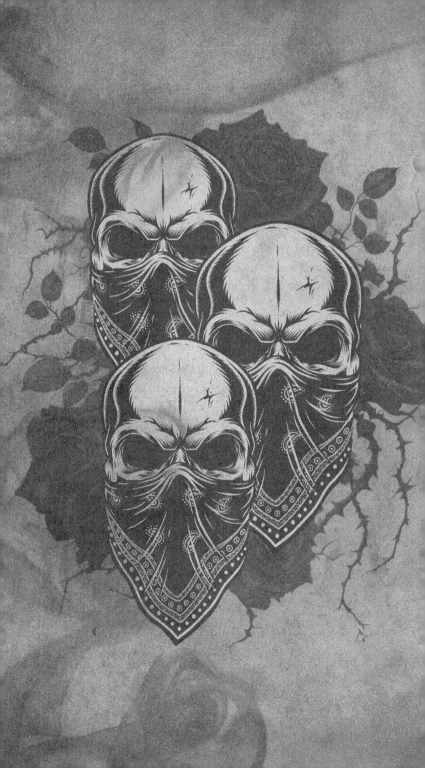

26

Riordan

Outside the door, I slid down the wall and tipped my head back. Counted to ten. Twenty. Fifty.

Started over.

I'd never acted so out of control. We'd agreed a deal. With fine print. An end date. Nowhere in there had been her *obeying* me. I had no reason to be stressed.

I'd also never leave her like that. I mean, I had, but I wouldn't do it for long.

But I'd meant what I said.

In the moment, it had been all-encompassing.

The more I breathed through my panic, the more that notion eased. Changed.

I didn't understand myself at all, but I knew what I wanted.

Taking out my phone, I paged to a website. Clicked through. Paid out my money. Then forced myself to sit and wait.

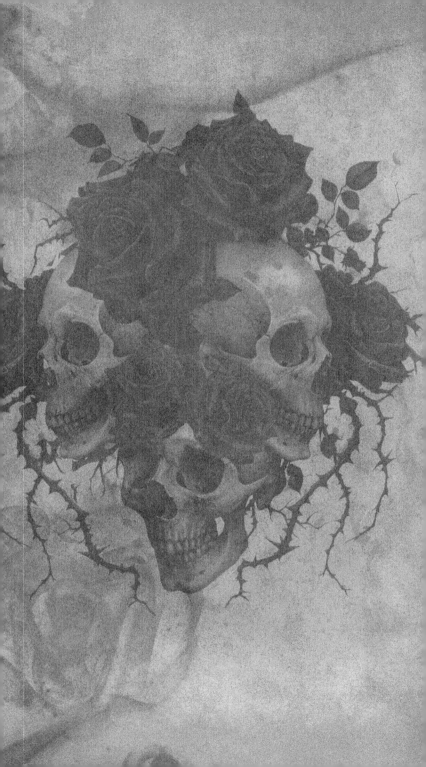

27

Cassie

Faintly, the sound of movement reached me. A person was sneaking through the apartment. Hell's goddamned bells. Riordan had sent someone to free me and told them what to expect. If they were going slow, that was through embarrassment on my behalf.

My cheeks flamed.

I closed my eyes.

Dixie, I could handle. I'd seen her naked plenty of times. Not Gen or Everly. Not while their brother's cum dried on my skin and a sex toy between my legs. My ego wouldn't take it.

Further noises came, but no blondie stuck her head into the room. Then something odd reached me—the scent of food. Spicy and delicious. God. My mouth watered around the stupid gag.

The bedroom door swung open. Riordan stepped inside.

I glared at him, my nostrils flared where I tried to project anger.

I didn't feel it.

Not at all. Only sharp, poignant relief. In the short time he'd been gone, I'd convinced myself he wouldn't talk to me again. That I'd never receive his smile or feel his touch. That our single day of being *something* was done. All the while, he'd been outside.

Okay, maybe I was a little angry.

Riordan crossed the room and reached under my head. Quick fingers released my gag, and he pulled it free then ran his thumb over my lower lip.

God help me for my unwarranted burst of lust.

"Untie me." I was proud of how my voice didn't quake.

He loosened the knots at my wrists first, then my ankles. The moment the last was done, I leapt up and grabbed a pillow then tossed it at him. Hurt and loss rushed in and shoved aside my happier feelings.

Hopping off the bed, I reached for my bag, pulling out the contents to throw them at him as well. A ball of socks. A box of hair product.

He let me, only parrying them.

Outrage filled me.

My curl comb flew at him next, loosed with a growl, and bouncing off his chest. I reached blindly for another item, my fingers sliding over something cold and metallic. The gun I'd stolen from Arran.

Riordan lowered his gaze. "Go ahead. I know you want to."

I raised it, my heart racing, palms sweating.

His focus slid down my naked body, lingering on my cum-soaked breasts. His lips parted. Cheeks reddened under the dark stubble he still hadn't shaved.

This was turning him on? My body pulsed with twin

need, and with an enraged growl, I threw the weapon. Riordan smacked it out of the air, and it clattered to the floorboards, spinning away harmlessly.

He launched at me. "You little wildcat."

I shoved him away, catching a lucky break so he stumbled. "Me? You're the one who dumped me then left me trussed up like a turkey, basted in cum."

"Maybe I should have left you longer."

"Maybe ye shouldn't have come back at all."

He rounded on me. Effortlessly, he snatched my arms behind my back and pushed me down on the mattress. Bending over my naked body, Riordan kicked my feet wider apart then rummaged at his jeans. "I see I need to fuck some more sense into you."

Lust dazzled me, and I closed my eyes, my cheek to the cool duvet. I had no clue where his head was at, but I knew we both needed this. My nipples hardened against the bed, and Riordan ran the end of his dick up and down my soaked centre. He bucked into me, shooting fire through my veins. I grounded my backside to meet his thrust.

Abruptly, his palm slapped my arse.

"Don't put yourself into unnecessary danger."

I gave up an ungodly sound. The shock and the sting of pain was nothing to the burst of utter pleasure.

"If I'm doing something alone and ask you not to follow me, don't fucking follow me."

Another crack of his palm to my cheek. This time, he punctuated the act with a punishing thrust into me. My pussy throbbed with the warning of an orgasm.

Riordan groaned. "I ought to stop. Deny you. I will

unless you tell me you learned a lesson. If not for your own sake then for mine."

I didn't reply. I couldn't.

Holding my hips, Riordan slid in and out of me. The rough fill and glide tormented my body in the best possible way. I hadn't seen a way out of the evening that could be anything good, but I'd been so wrong.

But true to his word, Riordan stopped, his fingers on the globes of my ass, and his dick buried deep inside. "I won't seek to control you, but I can't handle the thought of you following me into something dangerous. I could've fought my way out of that, if caught. But if you'd been grabbed without me even knowing you were there, I'd have lost you. How would you have felt if it was the other way around?"

Well, shite. That was different. Suddenly, I got his panic.

"At least tell me you understand."

Slowly, I nodded, my hair ruffling on the bed. "I do."

Riordan growled approval, then took off fucking me again. Every thrust hit somewhere inside that built pleasure in a slow, insistent pull. My whole body tensed up, everything winding tighter and tighter. Riordan rocketed into me then lifted my hips from the bed so there was space between my body and the mattress. Without slowing, he angled his free hand to slap me sharply between my thighs, right onto my clit.

I moaned and throbbed. Nearly collapsed from how good it felt. He repeated the action, raining three sharp slaps to my pussy like he had my backside. Each drove pleasure through my swollen flesh like nothing I'd ever felt before.

At the last, I detonated. Mindless pleasure spilled through me, my pussy pulsing around his dick. Riordan gave up a gasp and sank into me as hard as he could one final time, then he came, too.

The sensation broke me. I forgot to tell him I loved him. I couldn't speak at all. It was all too utterly, exhaustingly perfect.

A minute on, and he peeled himself off my back and picked me up. In the bathroom, he switched on the shower and placed me on my feet. Then he peered around.

"Need something?" I managed.

"Soap and towels would be good, but your curls don't like steam, so I was looking for a solution."

He'd remembered. He *cared*.

From in my toiletries bag, I found body wash and a shower cap with a cute kitty cat design. Then I scampered to the bedroom to retrieve another bag with towels. All the things Manny had arranged to be brought up for us.

In the bathroom, Riordan waited, a hand out to lead me into the shower. Warm water rained down on me, and I shivered, huddling into his body as he closed us in.

For a minute, he held me, then squeezed shower gel onto his palm and set about washing me. The soapy suds and his sure fingers cleaned my body, removing the cum from my skin and between my legs.

I reached for him so I could reciprocate, but he stopped me. Kissed me instead. Even though he was hard again, his dick pinned between us.

Everything he did, I let him.

He was leading me. Owning the kiss. Stopping us from having sex again. Something in it calmed my system, and my mind quietened.

Part of it was trust.

Part of it was fear.

When we were done, Riordan bundled us into towels then found clothes from the bags. A crew shirt for him with grey sweats, soft leggings and a hoodie for me.

As meek and docile as a lamb, I let him dress me.

"I bought food. Should still be warm."

I followed him into the living room. On the kitchen counter, a delivery bag held cartons. We sat on the floor and unpacked each, finding wooden cutlery to eat with.

I scooped up a piece of broccoli in soy sauce, spying beef in the mix with udon noodles. Damn, I was hungry. "Hate-sex builds up an appetite."

Riordan lowered his spoon. "You don't hate me. I definitely don't hate you."

"Maybe ye should. Safer than liking me."

He chuffed a laugh and tucked into his meal, devouring half before slowing to offer me some. We shared. Gave each other bites of our food.

When we were done, he watched me.

"Did I hurt you, when I...?"

He mimed the spanking I'd taken.

My body warmed. Slowly, I shook my head. "I liked it. But you're never tying me up again."

"It's the only way I can feel safe with you."

I hung my head. "I'm sorry I scared ye. Are we broken up?"

Riordan sighed and rested against the wall with one leg extended and the other knee raised. "I have no idea what we are."

Hope kindled inside me. "Ye didn't walk away, though. Not for long."

"I don't seem able. I already had one near heart attack today when I saw your face at the mayor's house. I couldn't survive another from the way my chest hurt when I left you on the bed."

My mind locked on to that sentiment. I crawled closer and rested my chin on his raised knee. "Give me another chance?"

"I don't hold all the cards here."

"Except ye do. We both know I'm already in love with ye."

Riordan's gaze flickered. Longing shone out. He closed his eyes tight and extinguished the compelling sight. "You have to stop saying that. If we're going to continue, no more saying the L-word. And we don't live together. If I ever move in with a woman, I at least expect to know about it."

Well, shite. He'd asked me not to make decisions on his behalf, and I'd done exactly that. I'd had Manny empty his car and bring up all his belongings. "It's just, we agreed to stay together. It's cold outside. This place was sitting here empty."

"I know. I get it. But we agreed a deal, and barely a day in and I'm fucked up over it."

My pulse skipped. He was going to end it. This was just his form of a gentler goodbye now the anger had left him. He was talking himself around to walking away, and I'd be without him. God, it *hurt*.

I sat back on my haunches. "Then tell me what will change that. How can I be different?"

"I don't want you different. I like you exactly how

you are. I just need—" He exhaled what looked like unhappiness. "I need you not to love me. And also not to die or be hurt. I can live with my own death wish but not yours."

Relief and heartbreak battled inside me. I gave him a tiny nod. "Do ye want to quit our deal?"

"No. I can't give you up. I don't know why I'm so messed up." He mimed his head exploding, a cute action I'd seen him do another time when overwhelmed by me.

I scrambled for a solution. "What if we slow it down? Stop your needing to worry about me constantly. I know I'm full-on."

"You're perfect."

"Clearly not."

He held my gaze. There was so much warmth in the connection, and in the eye contact I never wanted to get used to. He made me feel so much.

Where I made him feel too much.

Eventually, he inclined his head.

At last, I could breathe again. I crawled onto his body and hugged him. "I'll try harder to stay safe. But please agree to sleep over here. Don't go back to your car."

Riordan hugged me. Over my head, he eyed the tall window across the room, where rain soaked the dark night, then his focus slid to the hall where our comfortable bed waited for daylight to send us scurrying to it. "Okay."

My breathing came easier. "I'll try to fall out of love with ye faster."

His lips twitched, but the smile didn't reach his eyes.

Together, we cleaned up the food cartons and checked our phones. I had messages from my family—Lottie and

Sin were back at the Great House, thank the gods, and I scanned them fast.

> **Lottie:** Sorry for the late message, but I was so tired when we got home and slept hard. Short story: the hospital visit went fine. We had to stay another day because our first appointment was postponed. I can now confirm we are expecting a healthy baby boy. He's due in March, and his scan pictures are the cutest.

She'd attached one, and I smiled wobbly at my new nephew's black-and-white profile. A flurry of replies had congratulated them, and I added my own then read a more detailed answer about why they'd needed the appointment—some concern by Lottie's regular doctor had sent them there.

Another separate message pinged in from Lottie, just for me.

> **Lottie:** Are you okay? I know all went well with them capturing the man who threatened you, but you must be stressed.

She meant about her. I could never hide anything from her.

> **Cassie:** If you're okay, I'm okay. I can't believe we'll have another baby in the house.

The youngest was Seraphina, Jamieson and Summer's baby. She wasn't even one yet. Lottie sent further messages, my tight fear easing with her familiar and relaxed tone. Then she switched out the subject.

> **Lottie:** Sin had a message from Jamieson, asking him to inflate your tyres. Any reason why that was needed?

> **Cassie:** We had a fight. He's a jerk.

> **Lottie:** He did that to you?

I confirmed it, and she went quiet for a moment. A minute on, and a voice message from my youngest brother popped up in the family group chat.

> **Jamieson:** Cassie, I'm sorry for being an overbearing dickhole. Can we be friends again, please? I promise to behave.

The sounds of the night were behind him, but it was his contrite tone that had me snorting a laugh. I loved how Lottie had gone to bat for me, and how easily our family disputes could be solved. All she had to do was get the two arguing members to talk to each other and the problem was sorted. No one wanted to see her upset.

I sent him the middle finger and Lottie a bunch of hearts, telling her to rest up. Then I sent Jamieson one small heart to show my acceptance.

Leaning against the kitchen counter, Riordan finished up the call he'd been having. He shot me a look. "Manny said that the cops are downstairs. They asked to talk to Arran about his sister. Manny said no such person existed, and he's getting rid of them, but one guess why they came."

My lips curved in a grin. "Piggy Piers went squealing? That's just delightful. What did they know?"

"Nothing. They had a hunch based on Piers' information and a low-quality CCTV picture of two people in skeleton masks. Not enough to ID either of us." He palmed his jaw. "I'm beyond pissed off that you're in the frame for this."

Like Piers could hurt me. If Arran's pet cop didn't help, I knew someone who would.

I shrugged, unbothered. "He'd have to catch me to give me trouble, and from what Manny said, they don't even have my name."

"If that changes, if anything happens, promise me you'll tell them I did it."

"Like hell am I promising that."

"Then know that I'll do it for you."

We stared at each other, a battle of wills playing out. I was meant to be backing off and not being so in his face, but that didn't apply to this. He wasn't alone in his plan to bring the mayor down. I'd taken the first hit for him and intended to keep going.

I relented, pretending to yield by pushing up to kiss his cheek. "Want to show me what we stole?"

In the bedroom, Riordan collected his prize from the mayor's house and unrolled it on the floor. The painting was of a family tree with names and birthdates of a line of people, starting with royalty at the top and ending with the mayor at the bottom. That guy was a world-class narcissist.

"I wonder if he cried when Piers told him it was missing," I mused.

Riordan poked it with his foot. "Hope so. I want to know that he raged about it."

My grin came more easily. "I have a whole list of other stuff we can do to him. Most of the ideas are petty and anonymous, such as calling his office to leave a message about his erectile dysfunction meds, subscribing him to girlie magazines at his work address, putting his number in the city's free paper, begging for a Domme to talk dirty to him. Did Everly tell ye his landline's answerphone plays messages out loud in the house? That one will be fun to be going on all night. I'm also going to get his house keys copied a bunch of times then drop them around the city, with his address on the key fob, of course. Happy for me to go ahead with those? I won't lift a finger without your say-so."

Riordan's gaze danced. "Do it. I want the man sweating."

"If we could get hold of his phone, I'd change the ringtone to 'I have to pay pros for sex', but that means going near him and I won't do that. All the ideas on my list that involve being close to him are off the table for now." I returned my gaze to the painting. "Question is, what do we do with this?"

Riordan pursed his lips. "He can't have it back. No matter if it means the difference between me going to jail or not. He ruined lives over his precious ego. I want to take him apart in pieces, and this is the first cut."

"Then we'll go to the roof and have a bonfire. Let the cops see the flames and a rumour spread."

Riordan didn't hesitate. He rolled up the painting while I sent a voice message to Jamieson.

> **Cassie:** Are you still in Deadwater and do you have lighter fuel?

My brother's reply came in quick. I hit play.

> **Jamieson:** Course I do. Just returning to the warehouse with Shade and Arran.

> **Cassie:** Can you come up to the roof?

> **Jamieson:** Give us five. There's something we need to tell you.

I went to record another message but hesitated. There was something in Jamieson's phrasing that gave me pause. We'd known Arran for over a decade, but Shade for less. The warehouse was Arran's deal, so why had my brother named Shade first?

We waited until another message came in, Jamieson telling us to meet them now. From a fire escape in the apartment's hallway, Riordan and I climbed the metal steps to the cage at the top of the building.

Wind whipped us, the sky lightening in the east where dawn was coming in. The city was never so peaceful as in this hour. I'd spent a lot of time up here, watching the neon pink of the warehouse sign reflected in the river, or the light trails of cars in the streets spread out far beyond. It gave me a place to calm down and contemplate my life. I used to find it restful, being so high above it all.

All I felt now was a sense of foreboding. An energy in the air. Something tangible and looming.

In the centre of the space, Shade helped Everly out of another entrance. He drove her back against a brick wall that housed some kind of equipment and kissed the fuck out of her.

My brother jumped up after, passing them without a look.

Approaching us, Jamieson held out a small yellow tin. "Arran and Genevieve are coming up but needed a minute. What are we burning?"

I passed the lighter fuel to Riordan to do the honours. He unfurled the painting on a concrete block and squirted the contents over it, soaking it in even lines. The other couple on the roof drew closer, then Everly took an audible breath.

"Is that my father's family tree?" Her wide-eyed gaze shot up to Riordan. "I mean our father. You took it?"

He finished with the can and tossed it, accepting the Zippo from my brother. "If I don't tell you, you don't officially know." He paused and eyed her for a moment, the stench of the fuel rising. "Do you care?"

She paled. Huddled closer to Shade. "God, no. I hate that thing. It's why I told you about it. It was used throughout my childhood to torment me, and it was right there in front of me the night he gave me to Piers. He cares more about that twisted view of history than he ever could about us."

"Then enjoy watching it burn with me."

Riordan flicked the lighter wheel, and a spark leapt, the fuel accepting it with hunger. Instantly, a blue flame sped across the canvas, yellow flickers appearing when it began to consume and destroy.

He watched with a small, enraptured smile, not dissimilar to the one my brother wore, though for different reasons. But my attention had gone elsewhere.

Whispering something in Everly's ear, Shade wore sweats and a t-shirt, not what he'd typically be seen in after an evening in the warehouse. More like something he'd change into if his clothes had become dirty.

Or bloodstained.

My unease grew. I gestured to the enforcer. "Where have ye been this evening?"

Shade kissed Everly's temple and stepped aside. I moved with him, but his grim, satisfied expression told me all I needed to know.

My guess came out low and dark. "Ye took out Bronson?"

The enforcer pressed his lips together. "Don't give me shite about doing my job. Aye, we went back, and we got the result we needed."

"He's dead?"

My heart stuttered at his confirming nod.

"But—"

"But nothing. Your taser incident could've ended him

and left us with no answers. I took this one on my own." Dangerous control played out in his voice, and the yellow flames from the burning canvas reflected in his eyes. "It was worth the effort."

Fucking hell. I'd missed out. I'd wanted the kill so badly.

"What did he give up?" I gritted my teeth.

"Red's trafficking route was first. Arran passed that to Tyler."

First? I stood taller, the city at my back and misery in my heart. "What else?"

Shade shot a look to the main stairwell entrance where Arran emerged with Genevieve, the jewelled choker at her throat glinting in the firelight. "Tell Cassie what we got."

The gang leader closed in, and his smile was all the more savage for the words that followed. "Everything. Bronson confessed. We found our killer."

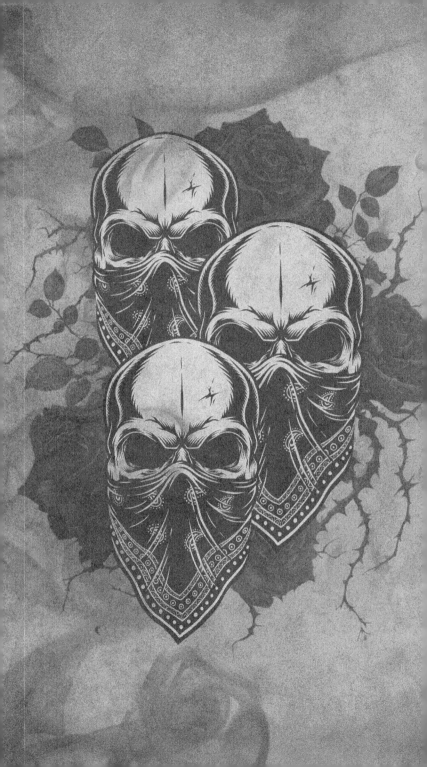

28

Riordan

My revenge haze lifted. "Bronson admitted it?"

"He did," Arran confirmed.

It had been a while since I'd seen the man dating my sister, and I jerked my gaze away as Gen kissed him way too enthusiastically for a brother to see. But her happiness had a ripple effect, a sense of lightness settling over our bonfire party on the warehouse roof.

"That's it, the killer's been caught. He can't hurt anyone else," Everly said.

"Did Bronson say why he wanted Cassie?" I asked.

Shade produced a phone from his pocket. "He said a lot at the end, they usually do. Ye can watch the recording to hear it all."

"Ye taped it?" Cassie breathed. She didn't have the same air of joy. If anything, her mood had dimmed.

Shade passed her the device, unlocked with a view of the bloodied, tied-up gangster.

My gut curdled.

"I've made a cut to give anonymously to the cops.

It contains the pertinent details but keeps us out of the frame. It doesn't show his death either. That'll be left for them to assume, or maybe think he left the country."

His death. They'd killed him. I reached for Cassie, encircling her arm. She swayed against me.

Shade continued, "Red gets it first. Then, along with the cops, it's being sent to the major news sites and some of the bigger social media warriors who've been banging their war drums around town. The news goes out in time for breakfast, so watch it now but then I need that back. I'm not keeping the burner phone or the full video as a trophy."

With trembling fingers, Cassie walked swiftly away to sit cross-legged beneath the lip of the roof ledge, her focus locked on the screen and the scene playing out. I stared after her, but Shade addressed me before I could follow.

"Strike one against the mayor. I like it." He indicated to the fire. Patches had already formed in the canvas, the thin paint layer turning to ash. "Manny said the cops were here. I take it ye were seen when ye paid him a visit."

I grimaced. "He wasn't home, but we were chased by Piers."

"We? Don't tell me ye took Cassie along."

"No, I didn't." I put meaning into the words.

Understanding lit in his gaze. "She went anyway. Fits, considering she apparently can't be apart from ye."

I rankled at the taunt.

Across the rooftop, Arran held up a hand. "Red has the video. I'm expecting his call. Eyes on me for silence."

A hush fell over us. A new tension rose in me at the thought of the drug lord seeing his second-in-command in the position Arran and Shade had put him in. At the words Bronson had said. A month ago, Red had told Arran he wasn't responsible for the murder of Cherry, but now the responsibility was in his lap. It had been his man.

Shade waited at my side.

In her huddle, Cassie continued watching the screen, a parting of her lips the only tell that what she was watching was affecting her.

I flicked my gaze back to Shade. "Cassie wanted Bronson. Ye knew that."

"He wasn't hers to take. I'll find someone else for her."

"Better, or it could be me next."

Shade blinked then laughed at my moment of levity. I'd surprised myself.

"You're a riot, Riordan."

"Call." Arran's words pulled all attention back to him. Standing alone in the centre of the roof with the sparkling city behind him, he set the phone on loudspeaker. "Red."

A long moment of silence played out, then, "Doctored?"

"I'm not dignifying that with an answer."

Red breathed audibly. "That fucking idiot. On behalf of my people, I express our regrets for Alisha. This was not done under my direction."

"You lost control of your man," Arran sneered.

"A junkie who had no hope of keeping his position. He was on the outs. It won't happen again." Red's voice hardened, as if he spoke through gritted teeth. "Is he dead?"

"He is."

"An eye for an eye. Then that's an end of it."

It should've been. Surely it was. From Red's explanation, Bronson had gone rogue and acted solo. I didn't know Red other than in passing when I'd taken a job from his gang in order to keep a roof over Gen's head. I hadn't even dealt with Bronson, so low down was the connection. But Arran's expression held nothing of peace or resolve.

His smile chilled me.

"See you around, Red." He hung up the call, my sister going straight into his arms.

Everly made her way over to where Shade and I stood. She had her hands clamped around herself, only a thin sweatshirt keeping out the chilly night. "As nice as it is to see that destroyed, the smell of smoke is making me nauseous. I'm worried about it being poisonous. Mind if we go downstairs?"

I shook my head in the negative, and she and Shade left.

Likewise, Arran guided Gen down the steps with words about talking to the crew. Jamieson had already gone, when, I didn't notice.

It left just me and Cassie on the roof.

I crossed the tarmac and settled down beside her, keeping my eyes off the screen where Bronson was fast-talking. She shivered against me.

"Listen."

She scrolled back. Pressed play.

"...I gave my life for the Four Milers. He'll see it destroyed through his own bullshit ambition. It's mine. It should be fucking mine. I proved myself over and over."

Another voice sounded. Arran's.

"You killed to provide that proof."

"Aye, and I will again."

"Who?"

"Those damn sluts." Bronson ranted on, his words becoming incoherent.

Arran's calmer tones returned. "Say their names, Bronson."

I kept my focus on Cassie's profile, not wanting to know what Shade was doing to elicit the information.

Bronson gasped, the sound wet. "The skeleton crew bitch? Alisha. She had it coming."

"And the rest?"

"Think I asked their names?"

"Then tell me where."

"The church steps, the back of a car, the empty mansion."

I swallowed. That was exactly where the others had been killed, though it was an assumption that had been made for Natasha Reid who'd been dumped from a car outside the warehouse.

"Cherry, Natasha, and Amelia," Arran said pointedly. Slowly. "You're saying you ended their lives for the purpose of taking over the Four Milers?"

Bronson made a sound, a crooked, evil chuckle that I would never forget as it chilled me to the bone. "I never had a hope, did I? That fucker is going to kill the club. It doesn't matter who I did or didn't kill."

"Confess it or deny it. This is your last chance."

Something cracked. Bronson cried out.

"Daniels' little sister would've been next. I'll promise

ye that. Aye, string me up for them all. I'll die with the Four Milers in my heart and on my tongue. In my heart," he screamed.

Cassie ended the video.

Silence fell around us. Enough light had gathered in the sky for me to pick out her pensive, distant expression. Whether it was from the loss of the kill, or his threat to her, I didn't know. But I waited it out with her, sitting side by side until she took a breath and stood.

Together, we returned downstairs, traveling in silence to the ground floor and the management office. The clubs were shut, and we found Shade on Divide's dance floor where Arran had amassed the remaining crew, dancers, sex workers, and other staff still here at the close of business.

People jostled each other, smiling. Picking up on the scent of celebration in the air.

"You'll hear it on the news over your breakfast," Arran was saying, "But I want you all to join me in saying fuck you to Bronson Lesk. He took Alisha from us. Lesk, I hope you burn in Hell. In Alisha's name, Divine and Divide will be closed for a private party tonight. You'll all get a full night's pay in exchange for raising a glass with me."

A cheer went up, relief passing over the crowd, two of the dancers hugging and sobbing.

Cassie didn't smile. She slipped up to Shade and returned the phone to his care, then led me from the nightclub and back to her apartment.

In her bedroom, she eyed my t-shirt. "Can I sleep in that?"

I stripped it. Watched with hunger as she covered herself with it. When she climbed into bed, I got in with her. Hugged her but made no move to do anything more.

And though I drifted off quickly from the night of drama and stress, I suspected the opposite would be true for her.

I woke in the late afternoon to find myself alone in bed.

"Cassie?" I called out into the quiet of the apartment.

No reply. No sound came from the bathroom or elsewhere in the spacious pad. The bedroom door was open a crack, but when I strode out in my boxer shorts to hunt through the rooms, she wasn't there.

I didn't like the silence. Missed her being near.

Worse, it sent thoughts racing through my head. Bad ones. Dark ones. Thoughts that curdled my blood.

Finding my phone, I tapped her out a message. Her reply came instantly, allowing me to take a breath.

> **Cassie:** Didn't want to wake you. I had an SOS from Dixie so came down to the brothel. Here when you're ready. Manny's around.

It settled me a small amount, but the questions didn't

stop. What if she hadn't replied? What if I couldn't find her?

I paged over to a new message, this time with Shade. That guy was into enough shady shit to earn his nickname a hundred times over. Last night, he'd smiled in my presence. It was enough to make me take the risk.

> **Riordan:** Do you have a method for tracking another person?

> **Shade:** Bodily or a vehicle?

> **Shade:** In both cases, aye, Riot, I do. Care to explain?

Cassie tracked my bike. Seemed only fair that I had a solution in return.

After a fast shower and a much-needed shave, I was dressing when a knock sounded at the door.

Shoving my feet into my boots, I answered it. Manny stood the other side, a huge bunch of flowers held out.

I snorted a laugh. "You shouldn't have."

He pressed his lips together. "They aren't from me."

"For Cassie? I'll take them for her."

Manny handed over the bouquet. "They're not for Cassie either."

I squinted at them. "Sure you're delivering them to the right place?"

"I am. By the way, you're off the clock for tonight. Arran's throwing a party. He made a point of suggesting you hang out with the crew. Get your face known a little more."

I inclined my head. I'd barely spoken to anyone since coming back, only making small talk with Lonnie and Mick who'd helped guard Cassie at her house. Lonnie had been off with me, so I had work to do in making friends. "See you down there."

He left me to the strange bouquet made up of darker-coloured flowers, berries, and structural leafy twigs. Blues, purples, greys. Not the roses you'd buy your mother. I carried them over to the kitchen and set them on the counter, discovering a card in their depths. It was addressed to me.

A strange feeling crossed my chest.

I opened the envelope and pulled it out, flipping it to read the words.

To Riordan. Did a girl ever buy you flowers?

I like being all your firsts.

Love you so much it hurts (even when I'm pretending not to) – your Cassie

Holy fuck.

I dropped to my haunches, staring in shock at the display then reading the card again.

I fucking loved that she'd done it.

She was right, no one had ever bought me fucking flowers, and no one had ever loved me like she did either. I lay back on the centre of the floor in her fancy-ass apartment and put my hand to my chest. Why did it ache so much when she did sweet things? I breathed in deeply and just let myself feel it. All the spiralling, crashing strength of Cassie's devotion.

The pale, late afternoon's light filtered over me, at odds with the urgency that burned in my veins.

Last night, I'd tried to stop my emotions. I'd felt too much, and it had fucked me up. At some point, I'd lose her, and that was more terrifying than the risk of staying with her.

A certainty settled.

I told her I wouldn't fall in love with her. Maybe that had been a lie. Whatever the rising Cassie-shaped energy in me turned into, it was my secret to keep. If she knew our being together risked my heart, she'd back away. It had been one of her conditions, meaningless for me at the time but now a problem.

I liked her. A lot. I was going to do all I could to keep her.

Including lie to her face about how I felt.

Another thump hit the door. "Riordan, open up."

That was Shade. I jumped up to answer, and he leaned on the frame, two objects in his hands. Ah. The tracker I'd asked for.

"Does Cassie know you're doing this?"

"Not yet. She put one on my bike, though."

He watched me for a beat then raised his shoulder. "Fair's fair. Safer for her if one of us can find her."

He gave me a small gun-type device. Mimed using it. "Shoot into a fleshy part of the body. Best done while asleep." On his phone, he showed me a map, centred on Deadwater, a blinking locator right over the warehouse. "This is the app to track her on. I'll send ye the link."

He zoomed in, the locator which had to be Everly,

showing a distance marker and height elevation.

I exhaled. "As easy as that."

"As easy as that." He stowed his phone. Then he paused, his mouth twisted in some dark humour. "Oh, Riot? Just so ye know, if she wants to do the same, I'll happily let her shoot ye in the arse, too."

I resisted rolling my eyes. "Good to know. By the way, is Riot my crew name?"

Not everyone had one, most noticeably Arran who people just called the boss, but the more I was around the skeleton crew, the more I picked up. Shade and Convict were crew names. I'd heard Tyler referred to as Ghost, and there were others I'd barely got my head around. Cassie's brothers had them, too.

"Let's not get excited. We'll see if it sticks." The enforcer drifted his gaze over me in a shrewd, assessing way. "I have concerns over ye and your closeness to the inner circle. Not earned but gifted by your sisters and Cassie."

"I'm working here, aren't I?"

"Because Arran decided to keep ye close and not let Red get in there first. Your loyalty is a problem."

My pulse picked up. I stood taller. "That's bullshit to suggest I'd sell out the crew. I'd never do anything to put Cassie or my sisters' safety at risk. You should know that from my actions."

I'd taken him on, not once, but twice. I'd do it again if I had to.

He prowled a step closer, no humour in his dark looks. The tattoos all over his arms and up his throat added to the menace that gave him a reputation I'd heard about long before I met the man. "Ye wouldn't hurt them, sure, but ye work for Arran and me. It's us who suffer if ye hear something and decide to give it away. It's our hard-earned position in the city that rattles when ye decide to shake the tree."

He meant the mayor. "I won't back down from my plans for my father, and I swear I'd never sell you out. Isn't that good enough? I'm a man of my word."

He tilted his head. Smiled.

Then made a tiny gesture with his fingers.

What the fuck? A skeleton-masked man rushed me and shoved me against the wall. A sack descended over my head, the black material blocking all light. At the same second, my wrists were crammed together. Secured with a zip tie.

"Get off me," I bit out.

"Don't fight it, Riot. You need this as much as we do," Shade ordered. "One little test and it'll all be over."

In darkness, I submitted to their control. I had no other choice.

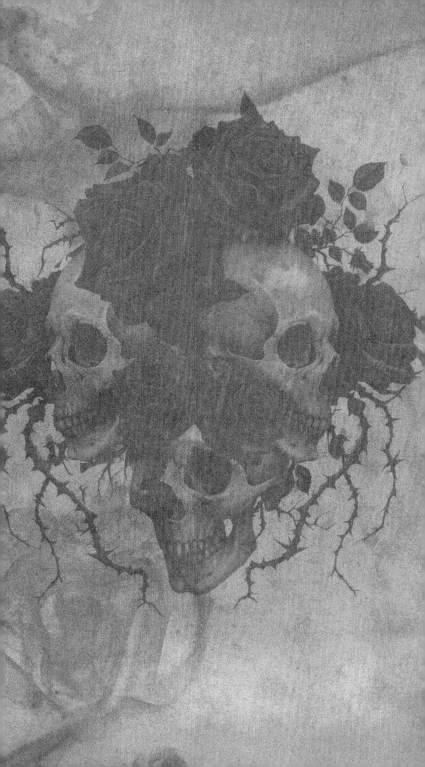

29

Cassie

At the woman approaching me, I dropped my jaw in comic appraisal then wolf whistled loudly. "Babe, ye are a fox. Check ye out in street clothes. Stu-nning. Ate and left no crumbs."

Dixie snickered a laugh and dropped into the seat opposite me in the brothel's office. Often, the dancers and sex workers who came and went from the warehouse did so with a significantly toned-down appearance. Alisha out of her wig and makeup had been barely recognisable.

That wasn't the case with Dixie. Even in a hoodie and tight jeans, her platinum hair up in a ponytail, she was the most beautiful woman I'd ever seen. Her heels gave her a few extra inches of height, but the lass was a shortie, just like me. A pocket rocket.

That wasn't why I loved her, though. She was made of salacious gossip and fun. A force of nature and my secret favourite of all the people who worked here. Way more than the skeleton-masked boys, Riordan aside.

She folded her hands in her lap. "Sorry to message like I did then take so long over getting here."

"Don't be daft. Is something wrong?"

Dixie's expression altered, her gaze uncertain. "Yes. Or maybe no. I might need a few days off."

I collected the tablet from the desk and opened the rota. "Seeing family?"

"I don't have any. I just need some time away."

"I'll schedule it in. Ye don't actually need permission, though. Ye know that, right?"

The sex workers were all self-employed. Arran's method of keeping the brothel semi-legal while ensuring the women the layers of protection they needed.

Dixie examined her nails. "It's not that that's bothering me. It's the thing I might do."

I lowered the device. "Are ye in some sort of trouble?"

"Not me. But someone else will be, if I can help it."

"I'm sorry, ye can't say something like that and not immediately follow with details. Spill it. I have never been more intrigued."

Her gaze leapt to mine, something dancing in her eyes that boosted my intrigue to sky-high proportions. She wasn't upset, as I'd started to worry she might be. She was angry. Or maybe even vengeful.

"I can't. Not yet." Quickly, she added, "And not because I don't trust you, but this is something so vital to me, I don't know how to handle it. Let alone talk to someone else about it."

On the desk, my phone vibrated once, and then a second time.

Dixie eyed it. "Do you need to get that?"

I peered at the screen and rubbed my hands together. "It's just people checking in with a few tasks I asked them to do. Take a look."

I opened it on my message screen.

> **Daria:** My boyfriend stuck fly posters all over town. This good?

She'd included a picture of a poster stuck to a wall in a rougher area of Deadwater. It had a picture of a generic black cat and MISSING – REWARD across the top. A hefty reward was offered and two phone numbers included. Beneath, with the words: PLEASE USE THE KEYWORDS 'FIND MY PUSSY' WHEN YOU CALL.

Dixie blinked. "Whose cat is missing? Oh, wait, is this to do with the revenge list you asked me about? Ohmigod, the pet isn't real, is it?"

I grinned. "Nope."

"But whoever pissed you off is going to get call after call asking them to find their pussy?" She snapped her hand to her mouth, cackling.

I giggled, too, scrolling into the next message.

> **Mick:** Got the keys from Everly. We have thirty copies and wrote out the fobs with the address on it.

I typed a reply.

> **Cassie:** Go forth and scatter.

> **Mick:** Roger that.

"That's part two underway." I showed Dixie. "There's also a couple of deliveries to the house later. The first is a glitter bomb, which has a duplicate being delivered to his office, and the second is a box of luxury baked goods."

She tilted her head. "Poisoned ones?"

"Laxatives."

Dixie gawked, then her shoulders shook as she creased up again.

I kicked my feet. "I've got a list of these to organise. This is just the start. Over the next week, he's not going to be able to answer the phone without getting enraged, and he'll sleep with one eye open because someone is going to break in. That's just at home—he'll get no rest at work either. I want all his colleagues judging him because of the calls and suspect deliveries he'll be getting. Think a parcel with 'Used Sex Toys' printed on it and something rubbery bouncing around inside."

From Everly, I knew the mayor was preparing for his next election campaign. He was considered a shoo-in, as somehow any opponents conveniently gave up their attempts, but still needed to promote his manifesto for Deadwater. He had speaking engagements. Business dinners. A conference to run.

"Remind me to never cross you. You're a baddie." Her amusement eased, her gaze distancing for a moment before it came back to me. "Is the person you're tormenting really nasty?"

"Yep. A shite human being. Are ye feeling sorry for him? Don't."

"It isn't that. I just don't want you to be hurt. I'm getting used to having you around." Her pretty gaze held mine, her thick tinted lashes making her eyes huge. "I'm not saying this to undermine you in any way, but powerful men have a habit of hurting girls like us. You're more protected than I ever could be, but one slipup, one trip out where you're alone and feeling confident."

She left the rest unsaid. It spoke volumes.

With my phone forgotten, I regarded her fully, some warning sounding in my head. "This time off ye want, will ye tell me if it's something like that? I can help. I have people. We don't have to tell Arran or Shade if you're worried about working here. I have Riordan and four brothers who'll have my back."

Her gaze gentled. "See? Protected. I love that for you. If you can help, I promise to let you know, but I think I need to do this thing alone. Now I need to get ready for work."

"Aren't ye going to Arran's party tonight?"

"I will, but I need the cash so I'll be up here before and after. You know the brothel never sleeps, even when the city is celebrating the murderer being caught. I for one am so relieved." She gave a delicate shiver and brushed her fingers over her slender throat. Then she jumped up, catching my hand to take me with her. "I'll do your makeup for you. It'll be fun. Oh, and if you can skip away from the party, too, bring your boy up and we'll get into that lesson we talked about. See if we can get him professing his undying devotion."

My cheeks flushed hot, the image of driving Riordan wild with me calling the shots too hot to handle. Together, Dixie and I left the brothel and headed down the stairs to Divine's much bigger dressing room which I knew she preferred.

"Does that happen to ye often? The undying love thing?"

"Not with anyone I'm interested in. I used to think that one day it might happen, but I couldn't date a client or a crew member, so my chances of meeting anyone are non-existent. Imagine going on a date with someone nice then telling him what I do for a living. Any sane guy would go running."

I growled. "Any man would be lucky to have ye."

"Aw, how's the weather in delulu land?"

We grinned at each other and exited the stairwell. At the ground floor central hallway, we passed Arran's office. Tyler stood in the open doorway. The bear gave a short salute to me then a polite smile to the woman at my side.

It froze on his lips, his expression shifting to something much more interesting as he took in Dixie. She regarded him then dipped her gaze and scurried past.

Outside the dressing room, Manny approached, weaving through a small crowd of dancers, all off duty with Divine and Divide being closed, but buzzing with chatter about Bronson and the fuss in the city.

When he reached us, Manny dismissed the member of his team who'd shadowed us down from the brothel and informed me he'd be my guard until the party started.

I lifted my chin to the head of security. "Have ye any idea where Riordan is? I messaged him, but he hasn't appeared. Is he on shift?"

He twisted his lips and looked away.

My intuition spiked for a second time today. "Manny, what's going on?"

"On Shade's orders, I can't tell you, and you're not to leave the building." He indicated to the end of the hall where one of his burly bouncers stood with his arms folded. At the other end of the corridor, Mick leaned on the wall, his arms folded and one casual boot kicked back, but his intention plain. I wasn't getting past any of them.

My blood ran hot. "I swear to God, if they do anything to Riordan."

"He'll be back in one piece in time for the party. That's all I can tell you, other than it's for his own good."

I exchanged a furious look with a sympathetic Dixie and snatched up my phone, angry-typing a message to Shade.

> **Cassie:** Hurt a single hair on his head and I'll slit your throat in your sleep.

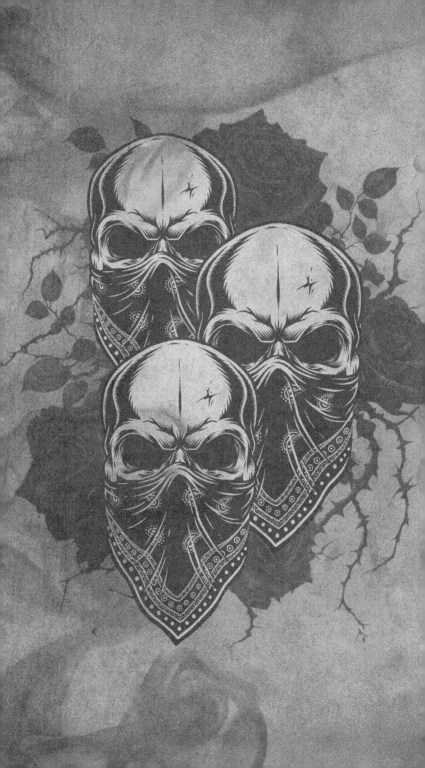

30

Riordan

The car Shade had kidnapped me in came to a rumbling halt, off-road by the sound of the gravel under the wheels. Unlike my previous experience, courtesy of Cassie, this time I was wide awake and able to move, though my hands were still constrained and my face covered.

Nor was I afraid. I knew who had me and what his intentions were.

I'd spent the car ride going from anger to something settled.

I couldn't judge the skeleton crew wanting proof of my loyalty. I'd been a member for five short weeks yet had been on the rooftop when Arran made the call to Red. I had access the other members could only dream of. They'd be fools to trust me.

Didn't mean I had to like it.

My door popped, and a cool breeze brought in the scent of autumn leaves plus something earthier. The river. The rushing water was loud enough to be heard however far back we were, which meant it was high tide.

My recurring nightmare came to the forefront of my mind. Being hunted through the city. Ending up with my back to the river, a bullet to the chest taking me down under its surface.

Mixed in with that was Tyler's musings on gang initiation rites, and Cassie's information about how Shade and Arran handled the worst of the city's offenders by ending their lives.

My thoughts were cut off by a strong arm pulling me from the car then guiding me to walk ahead of him. Two people, possibly more as I'd heard a second engine cut out.

We closed in on the sound of the river, and my shoulders stiffened. If I strayed too close to the bank and fell in, I'd die. With my hands tied up, I had no way of freeing myself.

At least in that I had a solution. Sinclair had showed me how to free myself from being taped up. I'd take a risk on zip ties breaking the same way.

Sucking in a breath, I raised my hands above my head and brought them down in a sharp motion to my raised knee.

The zip tie broke. I was free.

I wrestled with the bag over my head, holding still for fear of falling in the water and dying after all.

"For fuck's sake," one of my captors griped.

Arran. So he was here.

A hand circled my wrist, stilling me. "Hold up. I'll do it. Ye have to climb the steps anyway. I'll save your shins."

Shade, this time. He shoved my head down and undid the cord on the bag, lightly slapping my head for good measure as I came back up. I reared back, blinking in the darkness.

Arran and Shade regarded me, both wearing the same determined expression and tensed as if I was going to make a break for it.

I dragged an unimpressed look from one to the other. Fuck them, I wouldn't give them the satisfaction.

Behind me was a dilapidated wooden building. Not the riverbank after all, but obviously our destination. I jerked my head at it.

"Let's get this over with, then."

I stomped up the steps, waiting for Shade to unlock the door, then dove inside.

The wind cut out, but the rushing of water intensified. I moved through the building, following the two men across a concrete floor and through a surprisingly well-maintained interior, until the sound made sense. It was a boathouse, clearly disused for that purpose for a long time, but with a new purpose.

We rounded a wall to discover an open end to the structure, dark water flowing underneath a metal walkway, and a figure hanging from a hook over a drop.

Naked. Bloodied. Gagged but not blindfolded. He blinked, his eyes crinkling at the edges, then moaned.

My stomach roiled.

"Fucking hell." I turned away.

Shade took a fistful of my shirt and brought me back. "Talk to Arran. He has a few things to say."

I faced the leader of the skeleton crew, glad I hadn't eaten, and got my words in first. "I know this is a test of my loyalty. I know why you need it, too. I didn't join your crew because of devotion to what you do. I didn't know about this." I pointed to the hanging man. "Cassie filled me in. She'd eat this shit up for breakfast."

"Where you wouldn't." Arran relaxed in his position of watching me, understanding in his eyes. "Like it or not, you made the choice to accept my job offer. I don't know if you thought it would work as a temporary thing, or if you took it in order to keep a closer eye on Genevieve. The fact is, you had a choice. You made a decision."

Steely resolve settled over his face. "But I can't have a hanger-on. I lost two friends recently, both crew members for over a decade. Alisha and Convict were important to me for different reasons, and the fact they were both wiped off the planet showed me how vital it is for me to keep close those who give a shit about me and what I've built. As well as to push everyone else the fuck away."

Beside me, Shade folded his arms, no humour in him now.

Arran continued, "I accept my fault in their loss. It's made me fucking angry and more determined to do what I think is right. Back to you. You've impressed me in a number of ways. You're loyal. You work hard. What you did for Gen is more than most brothers would. So in view of the respect you've earned, I'm again offering you a choice. The Four Milers are going to be reeling from Bronson's confession and death, and Red is fighting for his life to rebuild. If I cut you loose, the risks of them scooping you up are small. It's a risk I'm willing to take. I'll also pay you three months' salary to give you space to find another job. Take the offer and walk away. You'll still be able to see your sisters and date Cassie, if she wants you, but you'll be an outsider and treated as such."

His proposal was too good to be true. The money meant I could find a place to live. I could have everything

I did now but freedom from life in the shadows.

Then there was the flip side of the coin.

It meant not working with Cassie. Visiting the warehouse rather than that building and the people in it being the centre of my life. I'd barely started understanding what Arran did, but a certainty formed in me. I respected it.

Slowly, I looked from him to the hanging man. "What did he do?"

Shade gave the explanation.

"His name is Leslie Kantoro. His kid rang the cops when he moved on from her to her little sister. Saved the younger one from a lifetime of being fucked up by a rapist dad and saw him locked up. Unfortunately, not for anywhere near long enough. The women are twenty-three and nineteen now, and when this piece of shite was released from prison, he applied for grandparents' rights to visit the eldest's baby girl. The prison considers him rehabilitated so the courts can't block him. His phone is filled with child abuse pictures." Shade's lip curled in disgust.

I stared at Leslie, disgusted, horrified, and with anger brewing inside me. He should never have got out of prison.

"Oh, and a trip planned to Thailand with an apartment booked for six weeks in one of the poorest areas," he added.

"What does that mean?"

He sighed. "Ye have a lot to learn. The question is whether ye want to."

He glanced over at Arran, the two of them having some kind of conversation without saying a word, then came back to me.

"You've been offered an out. A good one with respect from us both if ye take it. No hard feelings. Now let's walk through the alternative. The skeleton crew protects women. At the warehouse, with Cassie slowly trying to take over at the helm, and with people like Tyler who disrupt trafficking routes and help lost souls find freedom with us. If they want to sell their bodies for a living, we let them do so in safety. If they want to dance or clean fucking kitchens, the job is waiting. If they want out, we arrange it. Whatever the world thinks about us doesnae matter, but those who are closest to the cause should be there because they'll fight and die to defend it."

That fierce focus held me in its grip.

"There are hundreds of lasses and bairns who have been spared pain at the hands of men like Leslie and the countless others who've been washed away by Deadwater River. Ye can be part of something that makes a real difference in the world. Whether it be here or in one of the other support roles. You're already too close for comfort and still an outsider. So my question is, would ye kill a man like this to save a stranger? What about to save Cassie? Let's find out."

From the back of his jeans, Shade produced a gun.

On the hook, Leslie moaned and rocked his naked body, the chains rattling, and his shrivelled dick doing its best to creep up inside his body.

Shade offered out the weapon. Automatically, I took it from him, the same matte black model I used and the weight familiar after Struan's lesson.

The implication was clear.

Either I dispatched Leslie and helped send him to a watery grave, committing myself to the skeleton crew life, or I walked away from all but the weakest connection to it.

My mind jumped to Cassie's goals. If I managed to keep her, or if she kept me, she'd come home bloodied and exhilarated, or maybe hurt and broken over a failure. This was what she wanted—to have her own list of predators to work on. Like Shade, she'd use people to support her. It didn't have to be me.

Except all of that fell away when I considered saying no. My thoughts weren't just for Cassie's sake and my growing obsession with her, but for the want of being a part of something much bigger. Of that compelling picture Shade and Arran had painted. A brotherhood with them. A family, perhaps, with the wider crew. More than I thought possible.

Centring on the two crew members, I gave them my decision. "I always thought that being part of Deadwater's underworld was a bad thing, but now I know there are layers. What you do has more value than most could ever know. Thanks for the out, but I respectfully decline."

I closed in on Leslie, held the gun to his head, and pulled the trigger.

*S*ometime later, I slouched out of the boathouse, wired from what I'd seen, grossed out but not sickened, and with Shade tossing me another unfamiliar grin.

Blood smeared his cheek. It made me think of Cassie.

"Sorry again for faking ye out."

I stuck my middle finger up at him, earning a laugh.

Arran paced at my other side, directing me to a burning canister on the right side of the boathouse. He stripped his ruined shirt as he walked, revealing a muscular form. "If you want to kill, Riot, you'll have to earn it. If you don't, that's fine, too, but you need to know what happens on my crew whether you're in a supporting role or actively hunting. We're a family either way, and I'll get a full training programme worked out for you."

"Appreciated," I muttered.

Of course, the gun Shade gave me hadn't been loaded. Leslie had flinched then sobbed while I stared at the fucking thing and tried again, the two men watching me and cracking up.

No matter. They'd shown me how they preferred to do the work. Leslie was read a sentence and carved into pieces that the river claimed. I got to watch. Learn.

More importantly, I was a member of the skeleton crew now.

A real one. It felt fucking amazing.

In the car, Shade checked his phone and smirked, the night flying by where Arran sped us back to Deadwater, two cars of skeleton crew providing an escort.

"Cassie's informed me I'm a dead man if I hurt ye. Good thing I'm bringing ye back in one piece."

I rested my head back, lust flowing through my veins as quickly as adrenaline had. "That woman's going to be the death of me."

"Try to avoid dying on duty, aye? Messy business cleaning up after breakups."

He was joking, but annoyance rushed in on my already too-high emotional state. "We won't break up."

I meant it. Even if I had no idea how to make it happen, or the lengths I'd go to ensure it, though the tracking device, somehow still in my pocket, went some way to reassuring me.

We cruised back into Deadwater, every mile getting me more keyed up to find Cassie. To start on a plan to change her mind. One where she didn't drift out of love with me and instead only fell deeper.

The time we'd spent at the boathouse meant afternoon had changed to evening, the darkness only intensifying the scene outside the warehouse.

Cars littered the road. The blue lights of a couple of police patrol cars mixed with the neon pink of Divine's and Divide's signs, bouncing off the red-brick building and the cobblestone road. There were people everywhere, cameras and ring lights illuminating faces, snatches of their broadcasts making it through our closed windows.

"...the killer unmasked at last," one woman gushed for her internet audience.

"I have all the shocking and disturbing details," another claimed, speaking louder.

"Fucking hell." Arran spun the wheel to take us around the approach road, heading to the rear car park. "Even from the afterlife, Bronson is a pain in my ass."

From my vantage point, I took in the waiting police officers. Not moving in on the front doors of the clubs, but not leaving either. "Why the cops? If they're after Cassie, I need to know."

"I'll call Detective Dickhead and ask."

But right as we passed out of sight of the front of the building, I spied something that sent my blood pressure skyrocketing. The door opened, and three women in the club's black-and-pink uniform emerged with trays of what looked like cocktails, presumably as a gesture of goodwill to the assembled masses.

Cassie was leading the way.

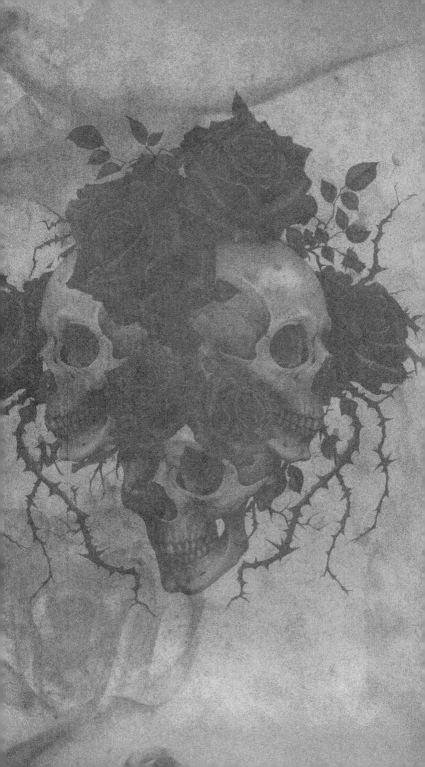

31

Cassie

"Are you sure this is a good idea?" Lara peered out from behind me, her tray of espresso martinis balanced on one hand.

Genevieve's drink of choice, caffeine fiend that she was.

I'd got a taste of them and was now hooked.

"How to make friends and influence the influencers," I quipped back. "A kind smile and a free drink will create happy thoughts about the warehouse and stop some of the bitching and the threat of further protests. I've been listening to what they're saying, and the sniping about Divine needs to end. This is our mission. Are ye ready?"

My session of getting dressed with Dixie had revealed that the protesters outside were denting business. Not good for the women who needed to earn a wage. I'd come up with a solution to fix it and enlisted Clem's help with rounds of drinks and some of her barmaids. None of us were technically working, but Lara and Moniqua had both agreed to uniform-up with me and do the circuit. Even Lonnie, my replacement guard dog after Mick was needed elsewhere, had approved the plan.

The three of us moved out and offered the cocktails with winning smiles.

A couple operating a professional-looking camera took the drinks with surprised expressions.

"Compliments of Divine's hardworking team," I told them.

I repeated the phrase to a group of ladies who were prepping to record. They cleaned out the rest of my tray.

"You work here?" one asked. She fished a metal straw out from her bag to sip the drink without ruining her makeup.

I confirmed it. "The warehouse is the best employer. We're a family."

She wrinkled her nose. "Isn't it exploitative?"

"Only when it's men at the top. When you have women running the show and helping each other, it's a whole different picture."

"Wait, there isn't a head pimp guy living off the women?"

"Nope. Not at all. Only protecting them."

Her eyebrows drifted up, and her gaze moved from me to the front of the clubs.

I hid a smile and turned around, ready to go recharge my tray and make a second loop. This was working. It was what I'd—

A pair of cops blocked my path.

I tilted my head, appraising the two big men. "Oh, hello."

Then my focus fell on the person behind them. Inch-perfect brown hair, elegantly greying at the temples. A smart casual business suit over a slim figure. The mayor of Deadwater was here, and not ten feet away from me.

I took an excited little rush of breath. Of course he'd come. Every person with any kind of audience was here to report on Bronson's confession. Trust the mayor to steal some of that limelight and spin this as his success.

His gaze locked on mine.

I popped my hip out, my tray aloft on the other hand. Used correctly, it would make a great weapon.

All of a sudden, a shoulder hit my belly and I was airborne. Strong arms clamped my legs, and wide-eyed, I dropped the tray. But no part of me was confused by the identity of my skeleton-masked captor.

Riordan stormed through the throng, bypassing the cops and ignoring all, including his father, on his quest to return to the warehouse. His heavy biker boots hit the cobblestones in thuds, and his strong fingers indented my thighs.

"Stop, right there," one of the cops called.

We didn't, and I gave them a little wave and a smile that only grew bigger at the mayor calling out an order to them.

Happiness spilled through me, and I twisted to press an excited kiss to the side of Riordan's face. "You're back. I missed ye."

Behind us, three or four skeleton crew members jogged to keep up and to block the police from following. Then we were inside and storming the corridor towards Divide's dance floor. Music pounded, and the DJ got the staff party started.

Grim-faced, Riordan dropped me down, pulling me behind him as he twisted to see the way we'd come. At the entranceway, Lonnie admitted the crew but barred the police, locking himself on the outside and presumably telling them what I already knew. They couldn't have me. Riordan had made his claim.

The door opened again, and Riordan jerked back, but it was only to let in Lara and Moniqua. They skipped past us, empty trays at their sides and neither saying a word.

Riordan's nostrils flared, and he finally looked at me. Emotion swirled in his eyes. "What the fuck were you doing outside?"

"Meeting and greeting. All those people out there were going to badmouth us. I wanted to make a better impression about female empowerment, which I'm not sure if you helped or hindered, caveman."

"The police showed up. The goddamned mayor is out there. The man we stole from and who wants you arrested." He shoved his fingers into his hair, messing it so perfectly.

I couldn't resist. Moving in on him, I brushed the strands from his eyes. "Ye are so beautiful. I can't even deal."

"And you could've been taken. Again," he roared, loud enough to combat the thudding beat from the dance floor at the end of the corridor.

I popped a hip. "I'm fast as fuck, boy. I'd like to see them try."

Riordan muttered something to himself then again snatched me up into his arms and marched down the hall. We entered the open space, a cheer going up as others noticed. I grinned, hooked on his dark energy and more than ready to see how this played out.

A vague sense of concern hovered at the edge of my awareness, but I wouldn't let it in. Riordan had asked me to be safe, and I had. Even if those cops had arrested me, nothing would have happened. Arran owned their boss. My family had a judge in our pocket, a long-term arrangement since they'd paid him off to get me out of foster care.

Shite. Maybe I should have told Riordan some of that.

On the far side of the room, the DJ worked her station, the music not stopping despite the attention of half the assembled group being on us. An escalating beat pulsed through the space. Pink neon lights swirled, the party set up to celebrate everything the warehouse did and stood for. Tonight was going to be lit.

Lifting my head again, I spotted Arran with Genevieve and Shade with Everly and gave them a wave.

Shade put his fist to his mouth, barely hiding a smirk. I narrowed my eyes.

At a high table, Riordan placed me down belly first, one big hand to my shoulders to keep me there. He wrestled with the button of my tight black uniform shorts, and my pulse quickened. Surely he wasn't going to fuck me here? I mean, I was up for trying anything, but exhibitionism wasn't his jam, was it?

He undid the shorts then yanked them down over my backside, exposing my tiny pair of black underwear and fishnet tights. One rip, and he tore straight through the tights.

With my face heating, I struggled up, needing to see his expression. Riordan pushed me right back down again. Not before I spotted something in his hand.

He pressed it to my arse cheek. "This is a fucking tracker. Seeing as I can't trust you to stay safe."

A *what*? My eyebrows furrowed, the words penetrating

before a shock hit my skin. It barely stung, but humiliation followed fast.

He'd shot a tracker under my skin like I was his pet.

In front of everyone.

I gritted my teeth. Riordan wasn't done. Tossing the gun-type device he'd used to the floor, he yanked my shorts back up and picked me up again.

Furious, I didn't make eye contact with anyone we passed.

Out of the room, I smacked my fist into his lower back, forcing him to come to a halt in the centre of the corridor. On my feet again, I whirled on him.

"I can't believe ye just did that."

"Then let the sting in your ass remind you."

I huffed in outrage, the patch of injured skin smarting. "I wasn't in danger. Lonnie was in the crowd. He was instructed to stop me from leaving the warehouse area but even he agreed to us circulating drinks through the crowd. It was low risk. Dixie and Bonnie had wandered out and spent time talking to the people outside. The vibe is happy and excited."

"The fucking police are out there."

"We own them," I yelled back. "The worst-case scenario is they'd arrest me and take me to the station to appease the mayor then quietly let me go. Two of my brothers get arrested with alarming regularity, but never have any of us been charged. We have this covered. It's a fucking game."

He backed me to the wall, his hand coming around my throat and forcing my chin to tip up. My chest rose and fell. The way he looked at me, the need and pain and hurt...

"Nothing about your safety is a game, Cassiopeia Archer. Nothing."

"What ye did—" I started.

Riordan brought his free hand to the front of my shorts, still undone from his exhibition. Holding my gaze, he drove his fingers inside to cup me between the legs. I sucked in a breath, my heart thumping, and words failed.

Every cell of my body was tuned in to the man in front of me. My furious, beautiful love.

He didn't pause at the edge of my underwear but pushed inside. I moaned, and my eyes slid closed.

"It turned you on. Driving me to the brink of insanity made you wet. I should fuck you here so anyone who passes understands how I punish you when you behave like you aren't owned."

I was so bad for wanting that. For the way my core tightened and the wave of need that drowned me and soaked his fingers. Except I had a better idea. My act of penitence. If we were lucky, we'd be right on time.

Forcing my mind to restart, I eased my hand over his, tugging it lightly out of my underwear.

"Come with me."

I led him down the hall, my shorts open and gaping around my waist. My hips swayed with each stab of my black heels to the floor. My huge boyfriend shifted his grip to the back of my neck and moved with me.

At the lift, we travelled up to the third floor. The brothel.

I shot a message to Dixie to confirm we were here, then I found our room.

Riordan followed me inside. One wall was made up

of glass, an empty room the other side providing a spill of light into our otherwise darkened one. Music played, and I smiled at Dixie's choice. 'on your knees' by Ex Habit.

Riordan folded his arms. "What's happening?"

The door opened in the other room. Dixie strutted out, bringing a man with her, Lex, another of the sex workers. In a cropped top and tiny skirt that flashed her underwear, she guided Lex to the single chair in the room and posed with her fingertips to his chest. I took the point, bringing Riordan's gaze back to me.

"Sit down. They can't see us."

"Why are they there?"

"Why do ye think?" I propelled him to the black leather sofa.

Dixie circled Lex, drawing her touch around his shoulders, but her words were for me. "I'm going to start by stating the obvious. Any guy is going to get off by someone hot touching his dick. Getting him to come is easy. Seduction is harder. It's a skill, just the same as giving a good blow job."

"You don't need to fucking seduce me," Riordan grouched.

I didn't reply, waiting for my cue from my teacher. Dixie didn't disappoint.

"Eye contact is a must. Heard of the triangle gaze? Left eye, right eye, lips. A heartbeat spent on each then eyes down and smile to yourself. It's how I used to get walk-ins to pick me above any other woman in the receiving room."

I stared at Riordan, in love with his eyes, my insides clenching again at the cruel twist to his lips. He was so pissed off with me. I had to break that.

"Assuming you've got your guy and made it to a bedroom, it's a game to keep control. You take it, then cede it at the right moment so he gets the thrill of the conquest. Order him to keep his hands to himself. Dirty talk a little if you can, meaning tell him the things you want to do to him. Then we're going to remove some clothes, enough to give him a good view and get the blood flowing to the right place. Better still, do this."

Dixie straddled Lex and whispered to him.

He smirked and stripped her cropped top, revealing her perfect, round tits in a very skimpy bra. Dixie brought his hands to them, using their joined fingers to caress her shape.

I tore my gaze away to Riordan. He wasn't watching them. Instead, he waited on me, his jaw locked and his knees wide. As if anticipating me. And making it more difficult.

Moving between his knees, I popped the first button on my cutaway waistcoat. "I know you're angry. If it helps, I'm sorry. I will make it up to ye."

"With your body."

Not a question, but I nodded anyway. "Not just that. I'll find other ways."

The second and third button opened, and I let the waistcoat slide off. Riordan's attention grazed down me to my breasts, exactly as I'd wanted.

"Touch me," I asked.

"No."

"Then I'll touch myself."

I unclipped my bra and dropped it, breathing harder at how Riordan swallowed. How a muscle in his jaw ticked.

Fresh air ghosted over my skin, and I cupped my breasts in front of his face. Level with his mouth. In my imagination, he leaned in to kiss and lick. My nipples hardened, and I moaned softly. When I squeezed them, need flickered over Riordan's features. His jeans were already tented. By his sides, his hands formed fists.

Satisfaction emboldened me along with scorching heat. I wanted to tease him some more. I wanted to take him to pieces.

"Once his hands start to wander lower, you cut him off," Dixie ordered. "Get down on the ground ready to pray, pretty girl. Give him the view down your body, knees a little wide so he's thinking about that space between them. Then hold that eye contact and undo his jeans. Carefully. We don't want any zip injuries from an overexcited dick now."

I didn't watch her and Lex. Freeing Riordan's dick took up every bit of my attention.

I was half afraid of him stopping me.

He didn't. Instead, he adjusted his position with an elbow over the back of the couch. Casual, to any onlooker, but not to me. He was locked in. So focused on me and so hard, his dick gleaming with precum.

Dixie continued, "Now you've got the goods, bestie, you give one hesitant stroke while gazing up at him like you're the sweetest most innocent thing who's never seen such a monster. So big. So impressive. All you want is that in your mouth. So let's get you there. Squeeze the base to get the blood flow to the end, then lick him like a lollipop. At the end, sink onto him, teeth covered, of course. Get him as wet as he should be getting you. Keep it slow so we don't ruin the fun too early—most guys can only last a few minutes at most—and only suck lightly. If he gets too excited, come off him, cup his balls, and draw them away from his body. Ease your thumb between them. Be very gentle here. If you want a pro tip, do this with your mouth."

I'd copied her with the first stroke, then watched for technique, Lex's dick in her hands.

Riordan swore, and I peeked up at him.

"Getting impatient?"

He clamped his jaw. I took him into my mouth. His taste flooded my hot, wet tongue.

"Fucking hell, Cassie."

I sucked. He groaned out loud.

In the adjacent room, Lex gave a low laugh, and Dixie crowed.

"What did I just hear? Fast little learner, hun. Show him you've got skills."

Riordan passed one hand over his face, but I was emboldened and even more determined. Rising on my knees, I slid my mouth up and down his dick again then sank onto him, this time remembering to add the suction, like Dixie had suggested.

Another more controlled sound of pleasure from him then warm fingers speared into my curls. He didn't try to guide me, just cupped the back of my head while I found a rhythm, getting him harder with every pass.

This was magical. I loved his taste and the thrill of the power I had over him. The slight buck of his hips he clearly tried to stop. The tightening of his body on every downwards plunge.

His breathing told me when to slow, and I toyed with his heavy balls, playing with him, and giving him space to calm down. I held his gaze and licked my lips.

"I'm close, sweet thing. You have to stop," Lex warned softly from the other room.

Dixie came off him with a wet pop. "Advanced techniques include letting him fuck down your throat to the narrowest part. It cuts off your breathing, so I don't recommend you try this as a beginner, and it's for the guy to lead anyways. A better one is to grab some lube and tease his ass. Get a toy in there if you can."

"No fucking chance," Riordan grumbled.

"But we need to cut and run," my friend continued. "Suck him good, bestie. See you on the other side."

I hardly heard her and Lex leave. All I knew was Riordan's touch when he pressed my jaw so I opened for him once more.

This time, he fed me his dick, holding my face as I took him inside. The music changed to something darker. Sultry as hell.

Without an audience, Riordan altered his attitude, too. He shifted forwards to the edge of the couch and took over the action, riding my face, though not deep enough to choke me.

Even if he wanted to.

After another few minutes, he growled and snapped his hips back then collected me from the floor to deposit me next to him on the sofa. I landed with a short exhale and automatically lifted my arse so he could remove the rest of my clothes.

Kissing my ankle, he held my gaze. "You're as beautiful as you are crazy, wild girl."

My cheeks warmed. "I did okay?"

"Let this tell you."

He tugged me to lie flat on the cushions then ducked to lay another open-mouthed kiss to my thigh. A third direct to the centre of me. I sprawled out, lost to everything except for the feel of his tongue on my most sensitive parts. Every lick and flick had me desperate, every sound he gave up brought me close to the edge.

Riordan's pleasure had wired me so tight I was filled with urgency. Bucking against his mouth and wet enough to soak his face and my thighs.

Right as I was at the precipice, he stopped.

My eyes flew open. I hadn't realised they'd closed, but I absolutely got what he was about to do.

"No, please," I begged. "Please don't stop as punishment. I was being safe. I made sure I was protected. I'm sorry I scared you."

In the dark room, Riordan loomed over me, his body forcing my legs open wide and his face all I could see. My breathing came in short stutters. I could cry for how badly I needed him to fill me. To finish me off. Whatever he said now, it was going to hurt.

With an expression resembling how I felt inside, Riordan pressed his lips to mine. Then fucked straight into me.

I moaned into his kiss. My knees fell open. My body accepted him in. He was so thick, it took several thrusts to bring him flush to my skin, no matter how wet I was. Then he rocked his hips. It hit into vital places inside me until so quickly I panted with desperate need.

"Tell me how you feel about me," Riordan gritted out.

"So fucking in love."

"Then understand the power of that is how I feel

when you do something dangerous."

He reared back and slammed into me. The action repeated. Again and again.

"Please don't be angry."

"I can't switch off caring about you. Don't make me try. Not half a day after we last had this conversation and here we are again."

"Except ye aren't threatening to leave me?"

"Not this time."

The climax which had wound up tight then been held off rushed back and broke over me. Soundlessly, I gasped and clung to him, my brain a rush of light and feeling.

My throbs seemed to never end thanks to how hard he railed me, because Riordan wasn't done. He fucked me relentlessly until I came a second time, throbbing around his dick and so well used I knew I'd be feeling it for days.

With a satisfied groan, Riordan pulled out and came over my breasts.

He collapsed down beside me, breathing as hard as I was, then drove his fingers into the mess, spreading it over my belly and down between my legs. His fingers pushed inside me.

"Dirty boy," I breathed.

"Bad girl."

His lips twitched. "Put your clothes back on over this. I want you to wear it."

If that was my punishment, I couldn't have been happier.

32

Riordan

Under my arm, Cassie preened on our way back to Divide. "First blow job experience in the bag."

My body warmed. I tipped up her face to mine and stole a kiss, smug as fuck and enjoying how she tasted of me. "Weird having Dixie and her man as part of it."

She shrugged. "Only if ye let it."

"What do I say if I see that guy again?"

"Hey, dude, nice dick?"

She cracked up. I scowled and used my pass to open the staff entrance into the nightclub's dance floor. A wall of music hit us, vibrating under my feet, and ahead, skeleton crew and staff from all parts of the warehouse lurked in dark corners or danced under the swirling lights.

Heads rose at our approach, and a few people catcalled. Cassie grinned and slid her hand down mine to lead me into the middle of the floor. We weaved through the crowd, humid from the crush of hot bodies. The thumping bass deafened me, but I didn't need to hear. I wanted to dance with her while she wore my cum and everyone else watched.

She moved against me, lithe and beautiful. To the pulse of the music, Cassie twisted in my arms, grazing her ass into my body. Fuck. We'd just had sex, but my dick was in no way done, and my blood headed south all over again. Around us, couples ground together, hands inside clothing, three people entwined in a way that had to be a full sex act, though no one else batted an eye.

I spanned Cassie's waist with my hands, sliding up her ribs. Her fingers braced mine and interlaced, creeping my touch higher to her tits. Again, she brushed over my dick, perfectly timed with the music, then dropped her head back against my chest to gaze up at me.

"I love ye," she mouthed.

Her eyes sparkled. My doomed heart squeezed. Ducking down, I kissed her, our mouths fusing and the shared energy of the dance floor driving us on until her tongue slicked over mine and she twisted back to get even closer.

The DJ mixed the track into a party tune, people throwing shapes and the beat picking up. We kept it slow. I speared my fingers into her hair, wrapping her curls around my fist to control her. Cassie's hands disappeared under my shirt.

The music quietened. I barely noticed, lost in the pleasure of Cassie's mouth.

"Do we have Riordan Jones back in the room yet? Where is he?" a call went out over the mic.

"Inside his girl," Lonnie called from somewhere behind.

It was Arran calling for me. I paused. Lifted my head.

Suited and with a skeleton bandanna around his throat, he was at the top of the room on the DJ's platform.

Arran found me, and he nodded, his gaze amused. "Since a couple of key people missed out on my announcement an hour ago, I saved one point for now. Tonight, we've mourned our lost skeleton crew member while celebrating the takedown of her killer. Burn in Hell, Bronson. Alisha dances on your grave."

Others yelled the same.

He continued, "I ask you now to join me in welcoming the newest full member. Riot, raise your hand."

I did. People slapped my back and jostled me with grins.

Cassie squeaked in happiness and hugged me hard. "Ye have a gangster name. I love it."

Arran spoke on, but the words lost out to the meaning. The feeling. I had the girl. The family. A sense of purpose I could understand and live by.

It didn't feel real. I knew too well how happiness could be stolen away.

Which gave me all the more reason to fight for what I'd found.

*H*ours later, Cassie and I snuck away, this time for good. We travelled up to her seventh-floor apartment. Showered. Fucked on the living room floor in front of the big arched window that overlooked the city. Wrapped around each other in her borrowed bed.

I lay there until dawn pierced the darkness.

We had no curtains, so the light in the room turned the blackness pale. It fell over the sleeping Cassie in a soft veil that made my heart hurt.

I'd known her barely a month. I'd been glued to her for a week. I'd fallen so carelessly I didn't notice.

What felt like obsession was something greater. I rode that edge for sure—the craving to own her, the possessive element, the constant need—but it was tinted by a desire for her to be happy.

The like I'd allowed myself to feel was giving way to more. I was falling in love.

I was so, so fucked.

Exhaling, I slowly pulled the blanket off us, revealing her body to me. She'd stolen my skeleton crew t-shirt to sleep in again, and the hem crept up her hip to reveal the line of her underwear.

Reaching out, I guided her carefully to her back.

Her head lolled, sleep keeping her in its grip. Cassie had a killer body. Slender legs, a soft belly, perfect tits.

I needed to see them.

My pulse quickened, and inch by inch, I rucked up the shirt until it was over her collarbones and her tits were mine to stare at. An idea came to me, driven by my eager dick that was awake and gunning to get into the game.

How far could I push this? Cassie slept like she did everything else—with devoted commitment. But would she stay under if I had my mouth on her? My fingers?

If I fucked her?

I knelt on the mattress and lowered my head to press a kiss to her ribs. Another to the underside of the curve of the nearest breast. I reached her nipple. Blew on it. It hardened. Unable to resist, I enclosed the taut bud in my lips and sucked. Her breathing stayed steady, so I moved to the other side, curling my tongue around her then sucking.

I snaked a hand into my boxers, giving myself a squeeze.

Loving on Cassie would drain me dry, and I'd go back for more.

With her nipples both rigid, I sat back. Drew my gaze down. I needed to know if she had become as turned on as me, but there was the small question of her underwear in the way.

Tearing it off her risked waking her, and I was having too much fun, so I climbed from the bed and padded to my jeans, finding the folded blade Arran had gifted me tonight as part of my initiation. At the bedside, I drew Cassie's legs out to give myself space between her thighs, then settled carefully back on the mattress.

My skeleton crew status meant I needed to get handy with a knife. I flicked out the blade, the vicious edge shining in the low light, then eased it under the line of Cassie's underwear at her hip. The material split silently. I did the same the other side, my breath catching as I discarded the scrap of material and the weapon and got a view of her cunt.

Just like the knife's edge gleamed, so did she. I'd made her wet while she wasn't even conscious to know it.

My quiet, "Fuck," came out on a breath, and I lowered my face to inhale her scent then touch my tongue to her centre. Her taste spilled through my mouth, fucking incredible.

I moved in and drove my tongue into her, pulling back to check her serene, angelic expression. A small line formed on her forehead, but otherwise, she stayed out of it.

I needed more. I needed a better angle.

Back on my feet, I took my time over shifting her again, this time to bring her to the edge of the mattress. Then I knelt, face on with her pussy, and carefully arranged a leg over my shoulders, the other out on the bed.

I blew on her first, testing if she'd awaken. When she didn't, I slid my tongue inside her then suckled her clit until her body tensed and her thighs tightened around me. Only then did I force myself to slow. Christ, if she could come while asleep, I needed it to be on my dick.

I still needed to play, though. Stroking my dick, I teased her, sucked and finger-fucked her to the edge then backed away. Each time, listening out for her signs to indicate when to stop.

Awake, she'd be spitting bullets at me by now. But my woman slept on, giving me all the time in the world to enjoy her.

Like with tying her up, I had all the control. It was a rush. A thrill. There was no chance of her leaving me. Of that cute face turning away, or those bright eyes dimming as she focused on me to say it had happened. She'd fallen out of love with me.

I'd rehearsed it in my head. She'd apologise. Hug me. Smile. Then take off on her next adventure. She'd destroy me, and she'd never know because I wouldn't tell her.

At last, I couldn't stand it anymore. I stood and gently shifted her then took my dick to her entrance. I was a patient man, but keeping from fucking straight into her while she frowned in her sleep and turned her head had the power to make me insane. When she stilled, I gripped my cock and glided it up and down, getting it wet. Then I inched inside.

Fucking hell. I breathed through my nose and set my palms to the bed to continue pressing in without gripping onto her tantalising flesh. Under me, her body spread out, relaxed and so damn sexy.

A series of shallow hits jerked her so her tits jogged, and I stooped to take one in my mouth as I worked in deeper. The feel of her on my tongue when I bottomed out to balls-deep inside her broke something in me.

My tolerance for keeping it slow snapped. Withdrawing my hips, I thrust into her hard. Again. She moaned low. Her head moved. Then her eyes flew open.

"What...?" Cassie reached for where I speared her open. "You're fucking me?"

"Yes, wild girl."

"Arsehole," she griped. "I would've missed out. Start again."

Elated, I barked a laugh and picked her up, keeping my dick where it needed to be. Her legs circled my waist, and her lips sought mine. Kissing, we clashed for control, and I carried her to the window and pressed her to the glass, fucking her where the whole city could see, and with broken daylight streaking across the sky.

"You belong to me," I told her. "Every part of you is mine. Whenever I want. If that's in the middle of the night, I'm taking you."

Cassie only moaned and urged me to fuck her faster.

I gripped her backside, over where I'd shot the tracker into her, and took off, so gone for her and so in need from edging us both. When she dug her nails into my shoulders and cursed me, I slowed to feel her orgasm then finally let myself come inside her so hard I saw stars. Finally allowing myself to fall.

The landing would be brutal. She told me she wouldn't be mine forever.

I had to make her realise the opposite was true.

In bed, Cassie shoved me then curled in a ball against my body and returned to sleep. Though exhausted, satisfied, I still couldn't rest.

From the bedside table where I'd left it this morning and hadn't checked it since, I took up my phone. My first action was to click on the link Shade had sent, before he'd abducted me, and checked Cassie's tracker was working. It displayed her location in bed just fine.

Then I checked through my other messages.

I had several from my sister. Genevieve swore that I ignored her texts and phone calls, and that was to some degree true. She brought questions I couldn't answer. Demands to know how I was, wanting to talk. In the past, when I'd been barely getting by, I'd never wanted to share my struggles.

Perhaps now, I'd actually message her back.

The most recent one pulled me up short.

> **Genevieve:** Thought you'd want to see this. The mayor recorded a video outside the warehouse tonight. Most of it you can ignore. He claims his excellent police force brought down Deadwater's serial killer, and that for prosecution purposes, he can't discuss further. Pretending that they have him yada,

yada. But then he says that later this week, he's going to make an announcement about his strategy for the city's gangs when he's re-elected. Right outside of our home. Fuck that guy.

I sat up against the pillows and pressed the link, setting the volume to the lowest. It was enough to hear my pompous father, smiling for the cameras, and making the announcement Gen had described. At his comment about gangs, he gestured to the warehouse. The people around him who'd gathered to listen threw worried glances.

My anger for him had simmered this evening, but now it was back.

It was on me to handle him. Like with every other aspect of my new world, I needed to work out how to get what I wanted. I'd be damned if I'd lose any part of what I'd found.

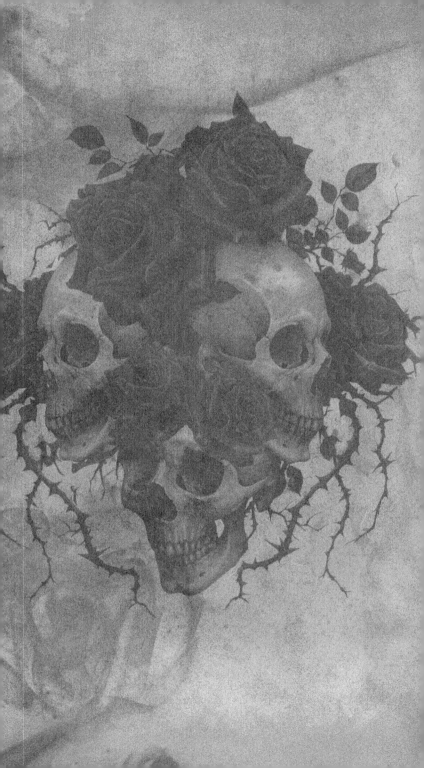

33

Cassie

A knock at the apartment door had me skipping to answer it. Riordan was at work, and I had been down in the brothel all afternoon and evening, but had been summoned upstairs by Manny telling me I needed to be in for a delivery.

I flung open the door to find the security chief in the hall with another two crew members. Between them, they hefted a big, linen-coloured sofa.

Stepping back, I made way for them. "Where did this come from?"

Manny had them set it down in the middle of the floor. It was pristine, like the wrapping had just come off it.

"I'm just the messenger."

Another crew member followed. I squinted at what he carried.

"Is that a nest of tables?"

"And a lamp." Manny retrieved the last item from the hall. "Happy with where we've put it?"

Slowly, I nodded. "Sure, but—"

"Then job done. Best get back downstairs."

He ushered the guys out. I called a quick thanks, shutting the door after them, still entirely confused.

A text message pinged my phone.

> **Riordan:** I'll be upstairs in half an hour so get ready for a cosy evening in. Clothes optional after dinner.

My heart thumped. He'd done this. Of course he had. The ceramic white-and-gold lamp, close in design to the one I had in my Great House apartment, provided a warm light over the soft couch. I set it on one of the little tables, another reserved for whatever food he was bringing home, and the last holding my laptop.

Against the red-brick walls and dark exposed steel of the apartment, his decor made it so snug. So pretty.

Riordan returned with two big bags plus his bike helmet in his hands. He stole a kiss then took the bags to the kitchen counter, the three pendant lamps highlighting him in bright detail.

"Sorry I went biking without you, little backpack. I had things to fetch."

He shucked his leathers then unpacked his rucksack, bringing out a skull.

I blinked at it. "Who's that?"

Riordan smirked then lifted it to show the barcode on the bottom. He flipped the hot tap to fill the sink, adding dish soap and setting the skull down in the water. Next from his bag he brought a box of cutlery and two wide bowls, giving it all a clean.

A tea towel followed, and he dried up then arranged the knives, forks, and spoons in the skull—damn, it was a cutlery holder—then set the bowls on the higher countertop.

Riordan unpacked the food next, two cartons of pasta landing side by side.

Mystified at the unexpected domesticity, I drifted over. "I thought ye didn't want to move in with me?"

"I'm not. Just wanted to make you more comfortable."

Damn the tightening in my chest and damn my heart for wishing he'd said the opposite.

Then I took a deep inhale, picking up more than just the meal.

Pink stained his cheeks. "What?"

"Are ye wearing aftershave?"

That almost shy smile returned. "Maybe. Do you like it?"

I knew nothing about men's perfume, but the one he'd picked out hit a place deep inside my brain and sent me dizzy with lust. "It makes me want to devour ye."

Riordan hid a smile and rifled through the rucksack for one last item. He pulled out a blanket, folded and with a ribbon around it, handed it over, then jerked his chin at the sofa. "Throw that over the back of the couch. It's to keep you warm once we've eaten and are watching TV."

My heart hurt all the more. In the past couple of days, I'd made idle comments about needing furniture but having no time to get any. We'd been busy, with endless work to do and our downtime spent all over each other or sleeping.

Aside from Riordan's secret jaunts out.

At the end of his shifts, he'd take off for an hour or two before coming home to me. Obviously, I watched him the whole time using the tracker on his bike. He'd been to Town Hall where Everly used to work and their father still did, then out to the fancy streets where the mayor lived. He was plotting something.

In time, he'd tell me. I was certain.

But until then, I was desperate to enjoy the romantic evening he'd designed.

"Put down the food," I ordered.

Two lines appeared on his forehead, but he set down the carton he'd started to open and faced me. I tossed the blanket then leapt at him, banding my arms and legs around him and holding him tight. My pulse raced.

"This is the sweetest thing anyone's ever done for me."

He chuffed and stroked my back. "It's nothing."

"It's everything. I love this. I love ye."

Emotion flared in his eyes. "Say that again."

"I love ye so much it hurts."

His smile broke my heart. Riordan needed my words like he needed air. Like I needed him.

I kissed him again. "I just need you to know what this means to me. I love the warehouse, but you've just made it into a home."

Him. Not the objects he'd bought with his hard-earned money. His presence. His biker boots beside the door. His clothes on the floor by the bed.

Riordan smiled into the kiss then carried me to the sofa. Then he put me down, dislodging my wandering hands. "Romance first, devouring later."

"But..."

"I want us to exist side by side for one evening without the entirety of it being spent fucking."

"I really like the fucking."

"I do, too."

"You're going to make me wait for it?"

"At least until after we've eaten."

He shrugged then went to fetch the food, unaware of exactly what he was doing to my heart.

Handing me a bowl of steaming pasta, Riordan indicated to my laptop. "We continuing with your telenovela? I've been wondering what Alexia's husband is up to."

Slowly, I nodded, and he set it up, cuddling up alongside me as he wolfed down the food.

It was hard to pull my attention off him in order to eat.

Riordan shovelled in big forkfuls like he'd been starved. "We've just discovered that Alexia's husband is her lover's dad, right? Eduardo had the picture on his wall which was her clue."

The next episode started with the heroine outside an office building, clipping briskly along in her sky-high heels and her fingers shaking as she approached the revolving door.

"Alexia," a shout chased her.

She twisted around.

Eduardo pursued her from his sports car. "Why did you run from me?"

"You shouldn't have followed me. I need to find out the truth."

She burst into tears, and Eduardo scooped her up into his arms. She beat him with her hands.

"Put me down. No one can see us like this."

"Why are you here? What's wrong?"

She raised her tearstained face to his. "I wish I'd never met you."

"You're breaking my heart. All I want is to keep you. I agreed to a time limit of a month in the hope that you'd fall in love with me, like I have you. Please tell me why you can't."

Alexia stilled. "No. You can't love me."

The show cut to a montage of their secret dates, their sexy evenings, their steamy messages. Eduardo tumbling into love with the beautiful Alexia. Inevitable. Laid out for us all to witness.

My fork stalled.

Riordan and I had a time limit. Ten days, we'd agreed. I'd almost forgotten. What were we on now, maybe day seven? Eight? I'd lost track.

Likewise, Riordan had stopped eating, though he was near the bottom of his bowl. His gaze slid to me. "It's your birthday at the end of the week."

Day ten. The end of our agreement. I inclined my head.

His hopeful gaze held mine. "Can I give you a present?"

"Ye just bought me furniture. A blanket." I plucked at the dark-blue fleecy material behind my head. It blew my mind. I had exactly zero idea of what things cost and how much he got paid, but I was suspicious that it must've wiped out his bank account.

"I have something else in mind."

"Okay," I breathed. I'd make Arran give him a raise.

His lips quirked in a boyish smile, and he returned

his gaze to the screen. The lamplight made him golden. I couldn't have loved him more if I tried.

Alexia finally gave her explanation to her lover. "Our time is up because my husband is coming home today. He's in there now, debriefing from his trip."

Eduardo's thick eyebrows merged. "My father works in there."

Alexia stayed quiet.

His eyes widened. "They work together? Your husband and my father?"

Deathly pale, Alexia shook her head. "They're the same person."

"That's impossible."

"It's the truth."

"It's impossible because he's married. He has a wife and two young children. They live abroad. That's why I hardly ever see him, but we video called a few days ago and he was with them."

Alexia's eyes showed her shock, and her mouth opened but no words came out. Abruptly, she fainted. Eduardo caught her.

Another man ran over. "Take your hands off my wife." His words dried up. "Son?"

The programme went to adverts, and I leapt up and took my half-eaten food to the kitchen, putting it in the fridge. Riordan's empty bowl went in the sink to be dealt with later. Then I returned to him.

Like in Alexia's startling moment of realisation, my hands shook.

As soon as I was near enough, Riordan reached for me and settled me on his lap, my knees either side of his hips. I held his face, staring into his eyes like I could see what I was suspecting. Arran's game allowed thirty days for a couple to fall in love. I'd settled on ten so I didn't risk Riordan's heart. It was too soon. Then again, I'd fallen in love at first sight.

And I still hadn't fallen out.

"What's going on behind those blue eyes?" he asked, low and sweet.

A whole lot of soul-searching over what I had to do next. Instead of voicing any of it, I kissed him. The rest of the night vanished into showing him with my body all the things I couldn't say.

The following afternoon, I sent a message to my Skeleton Girls Detective Agency group.

Everything felt...strange. Distant, almost. Like I needed to surface and draw in air.

> **Cassie:** Detective girls report in. Are you around to meet me at my old bedroom?

> **Everly:** Absolutely! On my way.

> **Genevieve:** I was beginning to think you were avoiding us. See you there.

I pocketed my phone in my playsuit, slipping on a pair of heels, and grabbed up my embroidery sample—the hobby I'd neglected. Genevieve wasn't wrong. I'd been avoiding my girls because of their brother. The night he and I had got together, I'd told them with glee, but we hadn't been alone since. I couldn't face them for fear that I was lying to them.

On the other hand, my adoration of Riordan was only getting stronger. Not burning out. Not fading. I was endlessly interested in him. That tight feeling in my chest when he came home to me, or when he did things that showed me he wanted to be around, all resolved into a feeling of rightness.

It gave me hope that this wouldn't go away. That I'd bucked the trend of my faddiness and impulsivity. I'd even booked a phone session with my therapist to help me work through my fear. I hated therapy. Every appointment had made me feel sick for days before and after, even though it helped. I'd only gone for the sake of Lottie. Now I was doing it for Riordan. And myself. I couldn't let this end.

On the cam girls' floor, I reached the room to find Genevieve already inside, staring up at the detective wall. She too clutched her sampler, half the stitches done.

I held mine up. "Ye did better than me."

Genevieve set hers alongside it so we could compare. "For something as simple as stabbing holes in cloth and tying knots in thread, this was surprisingly hard to be good at. I've never felt so rage-filled as when my stitches went off at angles and I had to start again. Even with all that effort, this was the result. It looks like something a toddler did."

I held in a laugh. "Right? That's why I only managed four. It made me want to commit murder."

"Don't you want to do that anyway?"

"More murder, I mean. Me doing hobby craft is bad for the human race."

Everly entered the room. She'd brought her sampler as well, and I tilted it up. Every stitch had been done perfectly, all the colours correct, and no loose threads.

I goggled at her. "That's immaculate. You're a witch."

Genevieve whistled. "Guess you've found your hobby then."

"Thank you, but actually, I didn't love it in the way I hoped. I've ordered us something else to try. We're learning knitting next."

I sighed in relief. "Bigger needles have to be easier, right?"

Genevieve's answer came out dry. "Or it'll put a ready-made killing tool in your hand for when we inevitably fuck it up."

Everly giggled then regarded the wall. "Are we here to take this down?"

We all turned to the map of Deadwater and the strings connecting the different locations. Like our stitches, they crisscrossed in a pattern. Alongside, we'd written out cards for the victims and a list of the suspects. So much effort had gone into this. Far more than I'd put into our craft activity, though equally, it had turned out to be of no use.

Reluctantly, I nodded. "I guess so. It's a shame, but it's not needed anymore. We can give the room back to the warehouse."

We set down our embroidery then moved in on the detective map, Everly starting on the suspects while Genevieve unpinned the string.

I reached for the first murder victim card. Cherry. Killed on the church steps. "Bronson never said why he targeted each particular woman, but I guess Cherry was easy pickings for him."

Genevieve's shoulders slumped. "I really loathe that. I hate that she worked the streets and not here where it would've been safe for her. I saw her not long before she died and I wish I could go back in time and protect her. She was so vulnerable."

I collected another. "With Amelia, I think he was stalking the mayor and happened to see her going into the dark mansion. Does that add up?"

Everly's eyes showed her sadness. "I saw Amelia outside my neighbours' house a few times. She smoked, and did so sitting on the front steps. He must have spotted her doing that and snuck in after her."

"Alisha would have been a prize for him." I plucked the next card and added it to my collection. "We still don't know who planted the note, and I guess we never will, but it was on his order."

Genevieve clucked her tongue. "Arran thinks it was done by one of the dancers. Possibly as a favour to Sydney who used to work here but defected to Red's brothel. She's the woman my father was dating, though I've no idea if he still is. Arran believes whoever left the note is too scared now to admit it, or maybe isn't even aware of what they did. He's let it drop because they caught Bronson."

That same scared person had left a note for me. Musing on that, I unstuck the last card. Natasha's. I squinted at it. She'd been a visitor to the city, here to take part in Arran's game, but turned on the warehouse and caused a scene in Divine.

My mind shifted on to the scene of her murder. There

was CCTV footage of the crime. The stolen car that squealed up to the warehouse. The body dumped out of the back.

A detail snagged my attention.

I faced my friends. "What comes to mind when ye think of Bronson? Physically, I mean."

Genevieve wrinkled her pretty nose and wound the string into a ball. "He was an addict. Opiates, I think, plus coke and weed. Probably not healthy."

"He was a big man. Heavy and muscular, even in his fifties," Everly added. She had a stack of papers, all the suspects gone and half the Deadwater map down now, plain wall remaining.

The strange sense of intuition strengthened. I held up Natasha's card. "Yet that big, cumbersome man climbed through his car to dump a body out the back. He didn't open his door, run around, and lift her free. Instead, he chose a far more difficult route, one which would take longer."

"Presumably so he wouldn't be seen," Genevieve suggested.

"Sure, but clambering over car seats? That would be hard. The engine was still in reverse gear and squealing. It doesn't make sense to do that."

All three of us swapped confused looks.

Everly spoke first. "Except he confessed. I didn't watch the video, but Connor told me how he gave up the truth. He wouldn't do that unless he was guilty. I guess he had a moment of agility and a reason to take the path he took. We'll never know, but that doesn't make it impossible."

My shoulders slumped. I dropped my gaze to the paper. "It just feels off somehow."

She gave a soft smile. "I was caught for days on the fact that he'd been tortured, and hurt people do strange things. If he was so deranged by the pain, he'd say anything to make it stop, but the fact is, he's a viable suspect, which the evidence pointed to, and he confessed. He said those words. He could've bargained his freedom in other ways. I don't think this is wrong. But more to the point, the murders have stopped. If someone else did it, they wouldn't let him take the credit. Not after all they'd done to get that attention."

Damn. She made sense. I heaved a sigh.

Genevieve bumped her shoulder into mine. "I understand. I feel it as well. I wanted to stare at this map then work it out from all the clues we'd gathered. But the fact is, the murderer has been found and he's off the streets. He can't hurt anyone ever again. It's a shame we didn't get our eureka moment, but it's better that we're all safe."

She meant me. I'd been the next target.

Maybe that's why this was still bothering me.

We continued the removal of our evidence and were almost finished when my phone buzzed. It interrupted Everly filling us in on her plans for further events at the warehouse, and I apologised, but she waved me away when I read the name on the screen.

Shade spoke without preamble. "Can ye come down to the office? I have something to share."

"Give me five." I hung up. "Shade wants to talk to me downstairs. I'm going to have to cut and run."

Genevieve nodded. "It's cool. I can't hang around either. I need to borrow my brother for a while. Our dad, I mean *my* dad, has gone AWOL again, and when I mentioned it to Riordan earlier, he said he'd come with me to the flat. Arran's busy, and it would be just me with an armed guard otherwise."

"I hope ye find him."

She sighed. "I do, too."

At the lift, Everly hugged me. "My apartment, tonight. I have knitting supplies and instructions to follow. I'll also show you my latest new video obsession."

"Which is?"

Her eyes lit. "People doing magic tricks to monkeys in zoos. I mean, I hate the poor animals being in cages, but you should see their reactions. It's adorable, and it shows just how intelligent they are." She bit her lip. "I also have some other news to share."

I stared at her. A while back, when we'd caught and mildly tortured Piers, Everly had told him she was pregnant in order for him to fully comprehend that she'd never be his bride. After, she'd taken me and Genevieve aside to say she'd been jumping the gun, but her choice of words was very telling.

My grin spread. "One friend engaged, the other about to reveal another big secret. We are living our best lives."

My family had gone nuts at the sly announcement of Arran proposing to Genevieve, done while he'd talked to the crowd before the last game. Arran had refused a bachelor party, and knowing my brothers that was a good decision, but told them they all needed to come to the wedding.

"I love weddings so much. They always make me cry." Everly took Genevieve's hand and examined the pretty, sparkling ring which matched her choker.

The apples of Genevieve's cheeks reddened, and

happiness shone from her. "I'd love your help in preparing for it. Arran wants to set a date soon. A shotgun ceremony then a big party here. It's one of the reasons I want to see my dad. Not particularly to have him attend, but so that he knows and doesn't hear it from anyone else."

Everly beamed. "I'm in."

I swung my gaze between them. "Wait, can I be as well?"

Genevieve cocked her head. "Sure, if you tell me you'll be my brother's date. He isn't sleeping in his car anymore. Is he staying with you?"

She leaned in, the question clearly very close to the surface.

The lift arrived. I hopped in.

"I'll get back to you on that. Gotta go. Love ye both."

They wore twin frowns as the door closed, and I cracked up.

On my way down to the management office, I had another text.

Riordan: Just so you know, I'm heading out with Gen this evening. In case you miss me.

Cassie: I always miss you. Even when I'm with you. Strangest feeling.

Riordan: Stop being sweet or I'll have to come and steal you away for an hour or two.

> **Cassie:** You'd prefer me to be sour?

> **Riordan:** With the shit you pull, I guess I'm into it either way.

Exiting the lift, I smiled then remembered something else I needed to say.

> **Cassie:** Just in case it happens when I'm not around, I asked my brother to talk to you about the cops situation. He's going to hunt you down.

> **Riordan:** Ominous.

> **Cassie:** He promised to be nice.

> **Riordan:** I'll take your word for it. If I never see you again, your pussy was the sweetest thing I ever tasted.

With a shiver, I stowed my phone and knocked on the office door.

Shade called me in. Alone in the space, he regarded me from across the desk. The visitor spotlight shone in my eyes, so I flipped it downward. Stupid interrogation light.

"I found out some information this evening that I think you'll find interesting."

That twinge of intuition returned. "Regarding

Bronson?"

His eyes darkened. "Piers Roache."

Shade picked up a tablet and held it out.

I took it, open on some kind of report. "What is this?"

"A secret and illegal database that exists between the owners of clubs like ours. We use it to check members against."

I scanned the details. "I've heard ye talk about this. It contains men who have hurt or abused women in other clubs, right?"

"Correct. Piers was already listed on here, and I've been monitoring it since we gave him his warning."

As part of our actions to get Piers to leave Everly alone, I'd sliced into his dick. Filmed him begging and posted it online with his name so anyone who searched on him could find it. Any potential future girlfriend. Anyone he was trying to get close to. Each time the posts got taken down, I popped them right back up again.

But the warning we'd given him was what drew fire through my blood. "We told him that if he hurt anyone else, we'd come after him."

Shade gave a dark, cruel smile that should've chilled me. It was like looking in a mirror. "Read the update."

I returned my gaze to the text. "Roache entered GGG as a guest of another member. He gave a fake name and had fake ID. Our mistake that we allowed it." I squinted at Shade. "What's GGG?"

"Girls Girls Girls. A club in Newcastle. Read on."

"He purchased time with two dancers and a private room, told them to put on a show then to fuck him. One of them noticed scabs on his dick. Club policy is no visible illness and protection is always used. The girls refused him. He got angry and struck out. One of the girls escaped. By the time security arrived, he was raping the second."

My heart pounded. I quickly scanned the lines describing how Piers had escaped, and they'd only identified him days later using video footage.

When I was done, my hands shook. "He raped a woman. He broke the terms of our agreement."

"He did."

"We should've killed him."

"Agreed. He's back in Deadwater again in a couple of days, attending some big thing the mayor is putting on. If ye want him, he's yours. We'll get him the night before the event."

"The police won't take him?"

He smiled. "It hasn't been reported. I told the club we'd handle it for good, whether by your hand or mine. The woman he attacked agreed to it and said to stick the knife where it hurts."

My certainty flared, bloodlust rising. Piers was mine, and my first kill would be worthy.

34

Riordan

My bike wheels bumped over the potholed street, and I parked outside the dilapidated Victorian crescent in North Town where my sister and I used to live. Wind cooled my hot head as I removed my helmet, and dead leaves skittered through the churchyard across the road. The place Bronson killed Cherry, though every trace had gone.

I scowled and faced the houses. The white terraced row used to be grand, positioned on a hill overlooking Deadwater River and the dockside warehouses below. Now, they were split into damp and mouldering flats.

I'd spent a decade sleeping on the sofa here and had never wanted to come back, but in the same breath, wouldn't let my sister face this alone.

Who knew what had happened to her father this time. Whether Adam Walker was on the floor in a drunken coma, or had choked on his own vomit, he went missing often, but one of these times would turn out to be the last. I hoped this wasn't it.

Two cars pulled up behind me, my sister and four skeleton crew exiting. Gen came to my side. She managed a thin smile, and together, we crossed the pavement and entered the street door.

In the narrow hall, the TV noise from the two downstairs flats battled each other. We climbed to Adam's front door.

Gen knocked. "Dad?"

No answer came.

I found my keys but stopped on the way to using them. "He's changed the locks." A shiny new cylinder graced the grimy door. "The only reason would be to keep someone out. Me, obviously."

Gen touched a long crack in the wood. "Arran said the door had been busted when he came around a while ago. Probably Dad coming home drunk and barging in. He's had it fixed. That's all."

"Did he give you a new key?"

She sighed. "No."

From behind, Lonnie said, "Need me to smash it?"

I found my skeleton key. "He'll only fly into a rage if he's in there. I'll get us inside."

Like at the mayor's house, the door opened easily under the cheap lock replacement and revealed the dark living room. My sister flipped on the light, her shoulders up as if to protect herself from what was inside.

I hid the same feeling.

I had no desire to face the man or relive the scorn and disgust he'd set loose once he realised he didn't need to play pretend with me anymore. All I wanted was to keep Gen safe.

But the room was empty.

We searched the two bedrooms and bathroom. No

sign of the man.

Back in the living room, the crew members backed off to outside, and Gen wilted against a wall.

"It's a relief not to find him... You know. He's probably slunk off with a woman. It might even be my doing."

"Why? Let me guess, he hit you up for money?"

She deflated further. "Got it in one. Not a small sum either. He asked me to tap Arran for a loan, but the reason kept changing. A holiday, a car, though God knows he's never sober enough to get behind a wheel. I told him I wasn't going to do that. He hung up on me."

"Sorry. You deserve better."

She hugged my arm in the way she used to hang off me as a kid. "We both did. I'm good, though. I have you still. And Arran now. Plus Everly and Cassie. I've actually never felt happier. If you and Cassie..."

"No fishing." I lightly shoved her.

She elbowed me harder in the ribs. "Fine. By the way, you know Arran proposed to me, right?"

I choked on a laugh. "Married to the mob boss. Congratulations."

"Dick. He'll be your brother-in-law, so you're as in it as much as I am." She grinned, too.

What a change for two kids who'd hated the gangs with a passion. I guessed we both still did, just not the skeleton crew. Somehow, that had become our life.

I pulled her in for a hug and ruffled her hair because it always annoyed her. "I noticed the ring, but it's nice to be kept in the loop."

Gen squeezed me then pushed away, smoothing the yellow strands back into place. "I know you weren't watching the last game so I wanted you to hear it from me. And Dad, for that matter."

Her father would mainly see it as an opportunity for his own gain, but I kept that to myself.

"Do you want him to give you away?"

Gen shuddered. "Hell no. I am not down for that archaic bullshit."

"Wise choice. Plus less chance of him making a fool of himself on your big day."

"If we ever find him. He was seeing a dancer who left the warehouse and joined the Four Milers. Arran said he'll keep an eye out when they next encounter Red's people."

"Is that likely to be soon?"

She slid me a glance. "Secretly, yes. He has big plans when it comes to them. I'm sure he'll fill you in now you're a member of his crew. Which I love, by the way. I had this fear of you disappearing."

"Why would I do that?"

She snorted and crossed the room to peer from the window. "You don't share the things you're upset about and have a history of sloping off to lick your wounds alone. I know why you didn't tell me about Mum, but that's an extreme example. I figured with losing your job and the fallout with Dad, I wouldn't see you for months. You'd take off, find work in another city, and rarely reply to my messages."

She had a point, and that had been my intention, though I didn't want to ghost her. I just didn't enjoy passing on stress, but a realisation hit me that I'd done exactly that with Cassie. I'd told her about my hurt over my father. I'd shared more than I ever had with anyone else.

My sister turned. "I have a question. Did you ever suspect that about Dad, before Mum told you?"

She meant the fact he wasn't related to me.

I shoved my hands into my pockets. "No. I only knew he hated me."

"I've been thinking about it a lot. If I suddenly had two kids land in my lap, I'd treat them differently than he treated us. Or you, I mean. He stayed in this flat which only had two bedrooms so you had to sleep here." She kicked the offending couch.

I hated that piece of furniture. It wasn't long enough for my frame, so sleeping there for years had been a punishment.

"He wanted me to leave," I guessed. "Why change his life for a kid who wasn't his? It would've meant putting in effort, and we both know he didn't enjoy doing that."

"But why not say? Why didn't he help you? It made me realise how small a person he is. I'm sorry I didn't call him out on it when we lived here."

I didn't need my sister pitying me. I jerked my head at the door. "Come on. We're done here. This is just him pulling a normal disappearing trick. He'll be back when he's back."

Gen sighed but nodded.

Her movement revealed the coffee table behind her. The place was never tidy, but a collection of strewn items on top of it caught my attention. A scattering of cut-up paper. Scissors. The broken shade of the overhead light had concealed it in a patch of darkness.

"What's that?"

She followed my focus and snapped on a lamp, bending over the mess to examine it. "Newspaper articles? They're of the murders. God. How macabre of him to be collecting those."

I joined her. The top sheets were of Bronson's confession. Lower ones had pictures of dark streets and crime scenes. Of the dead women. One listed the sites the women were murdered, in exactly the same way Bronson laid them out except with the addition of Alisha's hanging at the end.

My sister leafed through a stack.

My phone buzzed. I answered the call.

"Zed Alley. Fifteen minutes," a man ordered.

The line disconnected.

I stared at my phone then took a screenshot of the number and sent it to Cassie.

Riordan: This your brother?

Cassie: Friend-shaped. Have fun!

I turned back to Gen. "I need to leave. He isn't here."

She took a shocked breath and reached for something on the table. "What the hell is this?"

She picked up a knife.

A black-handled combat blade.

I recoiled. "Put it down. Why would you even pick it up?"

She squeaked and fumbled it, the weapon dropping. "I don't know. What the hell is he doing with that?"

"He bought a gun to go after a gangster. Maybe it was

backup." I knelt to examine it on the grubby carpet.

The blade gleamed with a streak of something.

"Did you nick yourself?"

She swore and showed me the side of her hand and the thin line of blood. "For fuck's sake. Must've been when I dropped it."

"Disinfect that. Now."

I enclosed the handle in the sleeve of my leather jacket and pursued her to the bathroom sink where she grabbed a bottle of disinfectant from under the counter. Gen winced at the sting but scrubbed the tiny wound.

When she was done, I placed the knife in the sink then doused it, too, scrubbing it with paper towels that I flushed after.

My sister watched me, her face pale and another paper towel clamped around her injury. "You think it could have been used. That's why you're cleaning my blood from it."

"I don't know that. But no way am I leaving a rogue knife with your fingerprints and DNA on it in this flat. If he's in trouble…"

We shared a glance that meant the rest could be left unsaid.

Then she closed her eyes and thunked her head on the peeling wallpapered wall. "Arran is going to kill me."

I blew out a breath. "I'll get rid of it. Let's go."

Outside, Gen climbed into the car and returned to the warehouse with her crew escort. I shadowed them to be sure she'd got inside safely then drove my bike to the city centre street where I'd been ordered.

Messing around with Adam's newfound interest in weaponry had cost me time, so I was late.

In a darkened street, I killed the engine and hopped off, eyeing the yellow lit alley entrance.

Zed Alley ran behind busy restaurants and city centre shops. It was wide enough for deliveries at the entrance but narrowed to a footpath between buildings. Industrial bins and piles of cardboard boxes littered the edges, and music thumped from a nearby club.

There were no people in sight.

My phone buzzed as I left my bike and paced further away from the single streetlight, my stomach tightening in anticipation. This was sketchy as fuck.

"Hello?" I said without looking at the screen.

"Riordan? It's Everly. I know you're not in the warehouse, but I was just making an announcement, and, well, I wanted you to be part of it."

I kept my voice low, a strange and ominous feeling pressing down on me. "Sorry I'm not there. Announce away."

"Connor and I are expecting a baby!"

Around her, people cheered happy sounds. Surprise caught me. One sister engaged, the other expecting.

"Congratulations," I murmured. "I already know you'll make an amazing mum."

Everly thanked me.

Ahead of me, a man in black stepped out of the shadows. A dark mask covered his face, only his eyes visible, and I went still. Gripping my helmet tighter, I peered into the gloom.

"Jamieson?"

I hadn't asked Cassie which brother wanted to see me. It made sense that it was the youngest of the men, as I knew he was in Deadwater. He'd been with Arran.

The figure took a step but shook his head. I held my ground, killing the call to stow my phone. Everly would get an apology later.

"Struan, then. Nice intimidation tactic."

It definitely wasn't Sinclair. His height would give him away. The fourth brother, I hadn't met.

In a distinctly unsettling move, the man leaned in. A snake poised to strike. It was the kind of shite Cassie would pull, but I still wasn't certain that I hadn't got here too late and come up against some chancer with a mask. God knew they were common enough in this city.

I tensed up.

The asshole uttered a growl and charged me.

Fuck. I ducked down into a fighter's stance and spun to avoid him. At the same time, I threw out my forearm. It hooked his throat. The bastard dropped down, and I landed on top of him. We tussled for control. I grappled one arm then reached for the other to restrain him, not wanting to knock him out in case this was some test.

My consideration cost me. In a heartbeat, he flipped us, then snatched my phone from the pocket of my leathers.

This was a fucking mugging?

I gave an enraged yell, but the guy danced away. Halfway down the narrower part of the alley, he whipped down the mask, revealing his face.

Fucking hell. It was Struan after all.

"Nice action. Someone taught ye well." He grinned. Waved my phone. "Cassie's gone out this evening."

"Where is she?"

"Doing something dangerous."

I sprinted to catch up. I hadn't heard her on Everly's call. Shit. "Then why the fuck are you stealing my phone?"

"Ye track her, aye? Then you'd better catch me, lover boy."

He exited into the city street. By the time I burst out after, he'd thrown himself behind the wheel of a sports car. Neon-blue under-lights made sure every person around was looking at that damn vehicle.

Struan gave me one final smirk then hit the accelerator, burning rubber as the car pulled out.

Turning, I bolted back to my bike, crammed my helmet on, and wheeled out of the alley exit before shooting off. Why would Cassie leave without telling me? Where would she go?

Why the fuck did her brother decide this was a good time for another of his goddamn lessons?

All the charitable thoughts I'd had about knowing how to shoot and fight fell away.

I was seconds behind Struan, but the slow city traffic had caught him at the lights.

Or he'd waited for me.

I weaved between a bus and a taxi, someone yelling at me from their window. The sports car's engine growled. Against a red light, Struan connected his gaze to mine in the rearview then accelerated away. I gritted my teeth and followed, running the red and missing a delivery scooter by the skin of my teeth.

I chased him through Deadwater's town centre and out past Town Hall, where Everly used to work. A police siren wailed. Neither of us heeded it. Right would take us back towards the river and the warehouse. Struan zoomed left. We wove through traffic, him going on the wrong side of the road, me keeping on his tail. Normally, I would shoot through the city with ease, but the cat-and-mouse game sent my temper into the red. I needed my phone. He had no right.

On a wide boulevard lined with student accommodation, Struan cruised on, giving me enough slack to catch up to his tail. I drew close enough to crash into him if I chose, but that would be my life forfeited, not his.

Shooting out around him, I hit the gas and zipped ahead, taking point.

Satisfaction filled me. With him stuck behind me, I was in control. I continued on until we were clear of traffic, then braked and wheeled my bike around, facing him down and blocking the road.

Struan pulled up inches away, that meaty engine rumbling. From behind the glass, he regarded me. Cocky son of a bitch.

To taunt him, I spun my back wheel, kicking up smoke while keeping to the spot. The racket my bike made reverberated off the surrounding buildings, almost masking a second police siren.

I had him. He'd asked me to chase him, and now he was caught. I raised my visor and folded my arms. For a beat, he stayed exactly where he was. Then the man gave a sarcastic wave, threw his arm over the passenger seat, reversed neatly in an arc, then sped off down a side road.

Mother.

Fucker.

I went hell for leather to catch him. The chase took us out through side streets and into an area that was more suburban. Run-down houses and broken streets.

We shot down a wide road, over and undertaking slower vehicles until we reached a junction with a graffitied shop on the corner. Only then did I realise where we'd ended up.

Four Miler territory.

A warning sounded inside me, making it through where the horns and sirens hadn't. I couldn't take that turning. I was skeleton crew. I'd be jumped. Probably find myself dead with how high tensions had become. Rumour had it there was vicious infighting going on, encouraged by Red in his search for a new second.

Struan clearly lived in some kind of grey area of invincibility as he roared past the graffiti, over the line, and blocked the end of the road.

He hit the downlights to flood the tarmac in sea blue then climbed out. "Come on, Riordan. I'm waiting."

"Give me back what you stole." I revved but stayed on the relative safety of the neutral ground.

He shrugged and leaned into the car to extract my phone. Waved it at me. "Better be quick. Cassie needs ye."

I'd fucking kill him. When this was over, and my goddamned heart got its normal rhythm back, I'd haul him to Cassie's feet and ask her permission to end her big brother.

It was then I picked up another threat.

Sirens. Multiple ones, coming in fast.

I'd been so caught up in the chase, I'd failed to pay them the right attention, but of course people had called the cops.

In nearby houses, residents peered from windows,

and in the street behind Cassie's brother, a door opened and a woman stepped out. She spotted us then froze.

Recognition ticked over in my brain. She was familiar, even with a hoodie concealing half her face. I knew her from somewhere. The warehouse, maybe.

If she worked for Divide or Divine, what the fuck was she doing out here?

Struan's asshole smile spread. He slid my phone into his back pocket and strode across the street to me.

I readied to leave. "What the hell are you doing? Get the fuck out of here or you're going to get arrested."

He finished at a run, tackling me from the bike. I fought him. Struan caught me in a headlock.

The cop cars flew down from both ends of the street and out of the junction. We were surrounded, quickly and efficiently. Doors popped and boots drummed. I struggled, but Struan tightened his grip.

"Let it happen. Learn."

My fucking idiotic brain caught up.

Cassie asked him to help me understand how he got away with being arrested. The leverage they had on the police. I'd taken the bait without a thought for anything other than her.

"Is she even in trouble?" I snarled.

"Hands where we can see them," an officer yelled.

"Nope, unless ye consider knitting needles a danger. That's what she's doing tonight with her girls."

Fucking knitting while I was out chasing her brother around like a rabid dog.

It was at that moment, as we were rushed, shoved down on the cold tarmac, I remembered something that

I should never have forgotten. The knife tucked away in my boot.

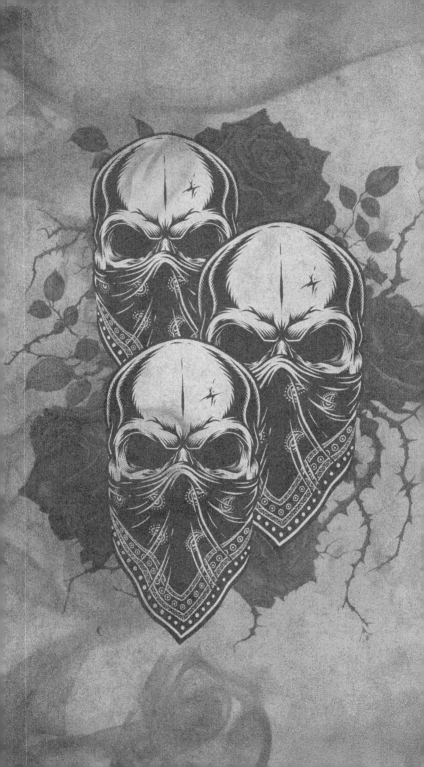

35

Riordan

At Deadwater's city centre police station, a duty cop opened the service hatch of my cell. Pacing the floor, I met his gaze.

"Ready to let me go yet?"

The man clucked his tongue. "With your rap sheet, no chance, sunshine."

"I don't have a rap sheet." I'd stayed well off the cops' radar, keeping my head down and my nose clean.

His eyes gleamed. "Don't you now?"

Something sounded in the corridor behind him. Voices. The cop glanced away, the little window remaining open.

I dropped my head back and stared at the stained ceiling. My gut was a tight ball of stress, at war with the logic of why I was here. Cassie would never throw me to the wolves. She wouldn't have arranged this, to whatever extent she'd been involved, without knowing I'd walk free.

Despite the officer's words, all I'd done was break the speed limit and cause a fuss around town. Nothing was damaged. No one had been hurt. I should get away with a slap on the wrist.

Except for the knife.

Being caught with a blade carried a minimum sentence. It could be argued that I'd been the aggressor, chasing down another man with the intention of doing him harm. From the outside point of view, that's exactly how it looked.

My hands formed fists at my sides.

What if their plan didn't work? What if I never got to hold Cassie again? To kiss her?

Another thought rushed in. I was already in deep after stealing from the mayor's house. As far as I knew, they'd only had a report of an unknown woman which they'd guessed at being skeleton crew from her mask. My name hadn't been mentioned. That might've changed.

Maybe that's what the cop had meant by the length of my rap sheet.

My palms sweated. Further voices sounded outside the cell, and I gritted my jaw.

"What took ye so long?" Struan snapped at someone unseen.

I rushed to the door and peered out.

In the stark corridor, he emerged from an opposite cell, glowering at a uniformed cop.

The officer said nothing, only jerked his thumb at the exit.

Struan passed my door and spotted me. He thumped on the thick metal. "You're next, lover boy. Hold tight."

He disappeared, and a few minutes later, with a beep of the keypad, my cell door clicked open.

The duty officer stood in the frame, his mouth twisted

in a scowl. "Seems you're free to go."

I hid the effects of my speeding pulse and exited the narrow room. No way could it be this easy. We jogged up steps and through a couple more pass-coded doors until we emerged in the brightly lit reception area.

Through the front doors, I spotted Struan with two other men. Sinclair was one, and the other was an older man with grey hair and in a suit. A solicitor, perhaps.

I twisted back to the cop who was saying something to me.

He took a clear plastic bag of my possessions and set it on a tray, then deposited it on the countertop.

My bike keys. My jacket. The knife was missing, no surprise.

I avoided his gaze as I shrugged on my leathers and pocketed my keys. It felt like at any second the narrative would flip and I'd be right back in that cell.

I needed to get out of here like I'd never needed to escape a place before.

"Thanks," I muttered then wheeled around.

From down another corridor, a man strolled, confident and smug like he owned the place, with two people who looked like plainclothes officers at his side.

The mayor of Deadwater.

I froze at the sight. In all my years in this city, I'd never been this close to my father. I'd once visited his house with the intent of challenging him, but he hadn't been home. That was the nearest I'd come.

His gaze flicked over me then away.

Heat surged in my blood. He hadn't even recognised me yet he'd dismissed my presence.

The trio stopped at the reception desk with one of the plainclothes officers leaning in to address the duty sergeant.

"Heard anything about my missing painting?" the mayor questioned.

Fuck, I hated his superior voice.

I should leave. Walk right out while I had the chance. My ideas for revenge against him were meant to start stealthily. I wasn't ready for a face-to-face attack.

Still, my mouth opened. "Hey. Nothing to say to me?"

The mayor and the other cop peered around at me.

I only had eyes for the man I unfortunately shared DNA with. I saw Everly in his features. Small details of myself.

His lip curled. "Have we met?"

"You should know exactly who I am."

He snorted like I was hilarious. "Really? Why?"

"Aren't I familiar?"

"You believe the mayor should know the name of every one of his citizens? This is what comes of extending my office hours to help the residents of the city. You give an inch and they take a mile. What is it? About to be evicted by your long-suffering landlord? Trouble with whichever gang you run with?" That narrow-eyed gaze flicked over me again. "Make an appointment and wait in line. Stay out of trouble, son."

He turned back to his companions, commenting about the amount of hands that he had to shake and complaints he had to endure.

My blood boiled at his casual use of 'son' when that was exactly who I was. But my brain finally restarted and my sense of self-preservation rushed back in.

He would know my name. The next time he saw me, I'd make him remember.

I forced myself to move and left the police station without a backwards glance.

Outside, Struan produced what was suspiciously like a genuine smile and hauled me in for a bro hug. "What was that about in there?"

I stepped back to give Sinclair a more sedate slap to the hand. "A little father-son bonding moment."

Both men balked.

Sinclair recovered first. "Your dad is the mayor of Deadwater?"

"Our sister aimed high." Struan whistled.

I couldn't summon a smile. "He's nothing to me. Or more accurately, I'm nothing to him. I intend to change that, but not in the happy families sense."

Sinclair's gaze took me to pieces. We exited the police compound, barbed wire over the gate, and took to the street. Further down the road, Jamieson stood with my bike and Struan's sports car behind. Struan jogged ahead to join him.

The huge man beside me spoke low. "If you need help in plotting the downfall of a useless parent, we've been there and done that. I know Cassie has told ye about McInver. We've also fought greater battles than him."

I lifted my head in surprise. "You'd help?"

"According to Cassie, you're practically family, in the happier sense. We look out for each other."

I halted, and Sinclair did, too.

My mind was a mix of emotions, the strongest of

which mirrored those of the night Arran and Shade had inducted me. Because of the conflict they had with the mayor, I hadn't intended to ask them for assistance. Shade only wanted me to pull the punch and not kill the man. At the time, that had felt easy. I wasn't a killer. I wanted to piss him off. Hurt him like he'd hurt my mother. *Me*. But the more I learned about the man, the less I believed he was fit to walk the planet.

The offer Sinclair made presented an opportunity I couldn't ignore.

"What if Cassie breaks up with me?" I spluttered.

Seeing her family again brought those feelings right back to the fore.

Sinclair's eyebrows formed a stern scowl. "Why would she?"

"She said her obsessions burn out. I figured I'm one of them."

She'd told me so, which was why we had a deal, but I didn't want to reveal that to her family.

Her brother's scrutiny undid me. "Her obsessions? We're talking about being crazy for a band or a book series featuring fantasy boys with magic powers. Typical fads. Not someone she loves."

I dropped his gaze. I didn't need the hope his words gave.

Sinclair's arm landed around my shoulder, and he got us underway once again with a brief slap to my back. "Good to know where ye stand, though."

"What do you mean?" I hadn't revealed anything, yet my heart thumped.

"She could do worse." He shrugged. "Take the help, Riordan. Struan and Jamieson are sticking around.

They'll be waiting on your word."

Fucking hell. He strode on ahead and left me to get back on my bike. All the while, reeling in the hope that he was right.

*W*e travelled back to the warehouse in a convoy. My mind twisted over the confiscated blade. Shade waited outside the back door, the car park almost empty apart from crew vehicles. Our game with the police had taken up most of the night.

I killed the bike's engine and stepped off the bike.

"Have fun?" Shade asked.

At last, I could see the experience with a little more perspective. Cassie hadn't lied. Not that I'd thought she had, but I'd just committed crimes that any other version of me would've been charged for. Yet I'd walked straight out of the police station.

Holy fuck.

"It was an education." Then I added, "Did Gen tell you and Arran about Adam's knife?"

He nodded. "We heard."

Sweat broke out on my brow. "The cops have it now."

He didn't flinch. "Good to know. We'll handle it."

Of course he would. The world I'd found myself in flipped everything I knew on its head.

"Congratulations on the baby," I added. It felt like days ago that Everly had included me in her call, but it had barely been a few hours.

"Thanks, uncle."

Shit. I would be. He and I were related by that child. Another, deeper connection bound me into the skeleton crew.

The door behind him opened, and a missile shot out. Cassie dove at me with a squeak of emotion, her arms and legs tucking around me. I absorbed the impact and hugged her back, all the stress of the evening shifting to something far better.

I kissed her hair. "Everything's okay."

"I had a live play-by-play from my brothers, but that did nothing to chill me out. I hated every minute of ye being in there."

"I came back to you."

She lifted her pretty face. Desire flashed in her eyes. "Aye, ye did."

God, I wanted that love to stay. I'd do anything to make it so.

Cassie kissed me. "Take me somewhere on your bike and strip me naked?"

One of her brothers made a choking sound. "Fuck's sake, Cass."

She smiled into the kiss. Kept her gaze on me while she pointed between us, saying for their benefit, "Fucking, now."

If only it could be for always.

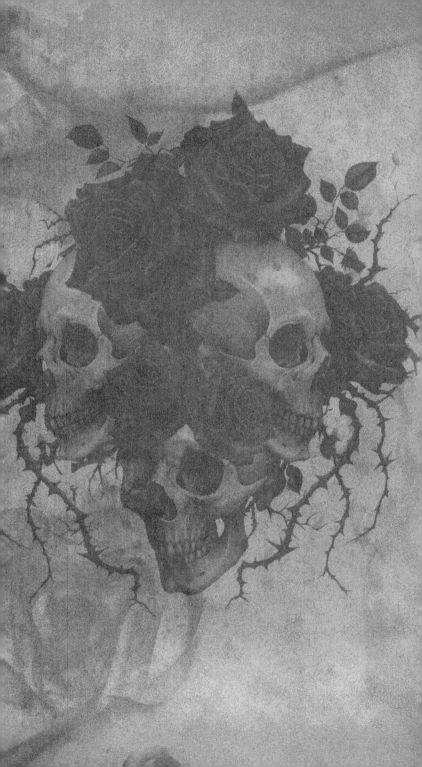

36

Cassie

Between my thighs, Riordan's engine revved, and the vibrations drove deep need into my flesh. He surprised me by allowing the trip out, encouraging me to hold tight to him in my role as his little backpack. With my arms around him and fingers grazing over his thighs, I could feel exactly how keyed up he was after his evening of fun.

Lucky me to be the recipient of all that energy.

I hugged him closer. Stroked the outline of his dick and enjoyed his shudders.

Riordan took us out of town and into empty countryside. We followed the river then climbed a dark hill, trees merging overhead to form a thick canopy and blocking out the moonlight.

At a hidden junction, Riordan bumped off the road and directed us into the forest, following what looked like an animal track. Our bright headlight lit skeletal branches that reached out to touch us, but we didn't stop. Not until the trees abruptly opened to reveal a view.

We jerked to a halt at the edge of a steep drop.

Rocks slithered from under the front wheel, trickling

down the cliff face from our grassy viewpoint. My heart hammered.

Far below us, the silvered river flowed to the sea. For a moment, Riordan stared then choked out a laugh and backed up the bike.

"Didn't realise how close I was to the edge. True in all areas of my fucking life."

He discarded his helmet then stood, taking me with him as I hadn't let go, and twisted me in his arms to remove my helmet as well. I tossed it to a nearby bush. On the chance he'd take me biking, I'd brought it downstairs when I'd tracked him coming home.

Wouldn't want him arrested twice in the same evening.

"I trust ye."

He kissed me, one hand supporting my body and the other cupping my cheek. It wasn't the gentle kiss we'd shared outside the warehouse but a rougher, need-filled claiming. He tilted up my face and devoured my mouth, showing me who was in charge now.

I drove my fingers into his hair.

Riordan groaned and broke the kiss to move us. He set me down on the saddle of his bike which rested next to a huge tree.

Then he sank to his knees. "I'm going to eat you out then fuck you over my bike. Do you like your underwear?"

I hitched up my skirt, my cheeks flushing hot. "It's the worst. Get rid of it."

He palmed my thighs and spread them, driving his thumbs up my smooth skin and taking my skirt with him the rest of the way. A kiss on my inner thigh turned into a bite, then his fingers twisted into my scrap of lace. Without pause, he shredded the offending clothing.

Cool air touched me between the legs.

I whimpered and gripped his hair, my other hand bracing me against the tree for balance.

Riordan pushed me to lie back, shaking the bike to show me it wouldn't fall, and guided my heel to the steering column. Then, with the access he needed, he kissed my clit.

"In the police station, when I was locked up, I pictured not being able to do this again. It drove me insane."

He used his thumbs to spread me then licked me, using the flat of his tongue to press down on and lap at me. At my sound of pleasure, he repeated the action then speared his tongue inside.

"I fucking love this. I fucking...love...this."

Across the wide seat, I rocked my hips, the potent pleasure already sinking me deep.

Riordan eased a finger into me, and I spasmed around his hand, my pussy dripping wet for him after the ride and the kiss. Maybe a little at the danger of the cliff edge. A second finger followed with a steady thrust in and out while he continued tasting me. I was lost to his actions and to how he knew exactly where to touch and how hard.

He didn't wait around. No toying with me or edging me. When I was close, he gave me no let-up, sensing my need and delivering into it until I cried out and came on his tongue and hand. The wild open space around us swallowed the sounds of my bliss.

I drooped on the bike, breathing hard, still wanting more.

It was too much and not enough.

"Need ye inside me," I begged.

Riordan undid his jeans and freed his cock. Gave himself a stroke while moving in on me.

His mouth met mine. "Going to fuck you over my bike now. New kink unlocked."

"I thought your kink was tying me up?"

"My only kink is you."

He thrust into me. Both of us groaned out loud in the fresh air. Holding my hips, he withdrew then buried himself deep. Like with using his mouth on me, Riordan didn't wait around. He drove into me, filling me and hitting a place deep inside that only he ever had.

The bike creaked under us at the rhythm he set. Rough from the start. Hard and fast and over and over until the coiling heat of a fresh orgasm ignited.

He knew, of course he knew. Riordan smiled and fucked me harder, the pace the same but the pressure more until I cursed his name and came for a second time.

"Good girl. My bike feels honoured to have you dripping all over its engine. Now I want a third."

Pulling out of me, he flipped me around so my boots were on the ground and the rest of me face down on the motorbike. I expected him to enter me again, filling my pussy which had barely finished throbbing from the second orgasm. Instead, his mouth took ownership of me from behind. His tongue glided up and down and in.

He knew me so well. Knew how to play and tease and torment until I was a writhing mess, gripping the saddle under me. Right as I was careening to another crash, he relented and fucked into me once more.

"Need to feel this one on my dick."

His palms moulded my cheeks. He thickened inside me while he took off like a rocket to chase what we both needed. At last, he throbbed, and that incredible sensation set me off for a third time. Silently, I spasmed on his dick, and he groaned and stilled, coming inside me with undisguised relief.

Then he draped over my back, buried deep and breathing hard.

"I love ye so much," I managed to say. Though exhaustion threatened to melt my bones, I needed him to know.

Riordan stilled and pulled me upright, withdrawing so he could turn me in his arms. Those beautiful green eyes held mine.

"I will never get over the fact you love me, Cassie. You're so beautiful. You're perfect. You should know—"

I put a finger to his lips. My hand trembled. He couldn't say he cared about me in the same way.

I couldn't explain myself either.

For a beat, he held still, as if my unspoken request weighed down on him. Then he kissed my hand and set his forehead to mine. "Let's go home."

I hoped to the gods that I could fix myself to make that a forever kind of deal.

*W*e returned to the warehouse and joined my family for a drink in Divine, the club closed to the public as it was after hours. Riordan fitted in well with them.

Struan even smiled at him once, something I never saw him do with outsiders.

Arran and a steely-faced group of skeleton crew returned a little after we did, Tyler one of the party.

The enforcer joined us. "All good with that information I gave you?"

It took me a second to work out what he meant. For over a week, I'd set my mother's story on the backburner, other matters taking over, but I nodded. "It was. Thanks for the help."

"Let me know if you need anything more."

He left us for Arran's office. Down the bar, Jamieson snorted.

"Hey, Riot, stop trying to murder Tyler with your eyes."

Riordan broke his stare with the door. "Fuck."

Struan clued in our brothers. "Cassie hugged Ty last time he was at ours. I had to disarm him or Arran would be down a crew member."

Jamieson clapped his hands to his cheeks. "Scandal. I'd throw down for that. Tyler should've known better."

I scowled in annoyance. "I can hug who I like. Mind your interfering beaks, ye bunch of cavemen."

They all laughed, including Riordan who buried his face in my hair and whispered, "Is it caveman if I wanted to grab his throat with the hand that had been inside you?"

I groaned. "That image is hot as fuck. Try to resist as I just remembered something I need to talk to him about."

I jumped up from my seat and crossed the dark floor, then paused and looked back.

From his seat, Riordan watched me. His expression had shifted to wary. Serious. Like my leaving him there was hurting him.

It did something to my heart.

His pain hurt me, too. He'd been left behind by his mother dying. By two fathers who didn't care. I hadn't realised how strong that reliance on me had become.

Hiding the shake in my fingers, I held my hand out.

Come with me. Please.

He pushed off his seat and joined me, sweeping me under his arm with a kiss to my curls like the little gesture had meant more than he could say.

And my heart ached, and ached, and ached.

At Arran's office, the door was open, only Tyler inside.

We entered, and I kept Riordan's arm tight around me.

"That contact ye gave me came up good. She gave me information on my mother's family. Cassandra Archer's father ran the Spring Hill gang, though most of the members are now serving or maybe dead. She seemed to think I still had uncles around."

Tyler scrubbed his dark-blond hair into whirls then grabbed his phone. "I know the gang by name only, and as a historical relic. They aren't on my radar as an active force. What is it you want to find out?"

I heaved in a breath. "The contact didn't know my mother was dead so couldn't tell me anything more about her life or how it ended. Maybe her family can."

"I'll see if I can scare up details for one of these uncles."

I thanked him and made for the lift.

In the apartment, we showered. Climbed into bed. Riordan hauled me to his chest, and we kissed until we slept.

It was so perfect. So sweet and loving.

A couple of hours later, at nine-thirty in the morning, my phone buzzed under my pillow, enough to wake me but not Riordan.

I left him in our bed and went to do what needed to be done.

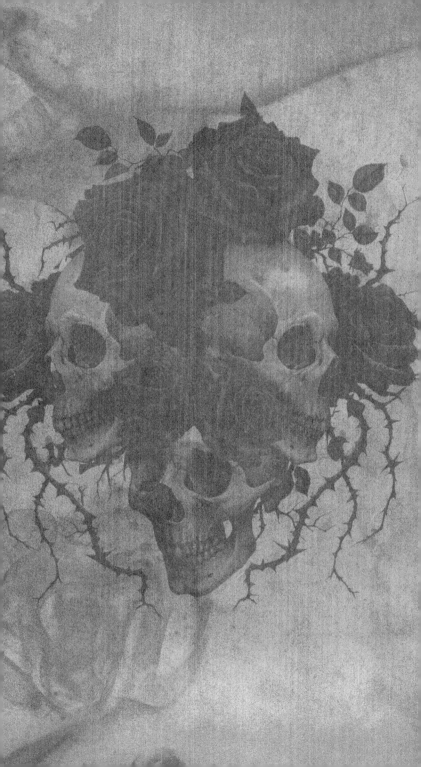

37

Cassie

The countdown of minutes until my therapist called was a ticking clock of nausea in my belly. Exiting the apartment, I summoned the lift. Couldn't hang out anywhere up here. If Riordan woke, he might overhear what I had to say. I needed to be completely unfiltered to get through the shite in my head.

On the cam girls' floor, I paused outside the room I'd previously used as a bedroom, but noises came from inside. Sexy ones which told me it was back in use.

I travelled down to the ground floor.

In the main hallway between Divine and Divide, an air of desolation clung to the warehouse. The faint scent of dry ice hung in the air along with alcohol and whatever else had been trodden underfoot and not yet mopped up by the cleaning crew.

Lara carried a box into the propped-open door of the nightclub. It seemed a little early for restocking the bars, but I gave a wave and turned in the other direction.

Arran's office door was locked, but I'd kept a key and fished it from my pocket.

The lift pinged. I peeked back to see Dixie emerge.

She yawned daintily, the back of her hand to her mouth. "What are you doing still up?"

I leaned on the doorframe. "I could say the same for ye."

She flapped a hand in the general direction of upstairs. "We had a party of international visitors, all on a different time zone, so none were ready to finish at any reasonable time. Manny just saw the last into a taxi. I am dead on my feet."

She gestured to the feet in question, encased in a pair of cute silver high-top trainers. They went with her torn leggings and slouchy off-one-shoulder jumper. Civvies again. I envied how any clothes turned stylish the minute she put them on.

Her gaze came back to me. "I'm glad I ran into you. After the lesson I gave you, something was bothering me."

She took a breath, and her gaze searched the middle ground as if she was trying to work through her thoughts. "I don't think sex always needs to be a performance. Not when the guy isn't paying. Not when he's a boyfriend. I mean, there's nothing wrong with wanting to make him feel good, but there's the loving element of it that I don't know anything about."

"The element where you just enjoy each other?"

Some of the puzzlement in her eyes lifted. "Exactly. If he cares about you, he'll be the one doing the work sometimes. And if you're happy together, then just rolling around and exploring each other would be fun, right?" She twisted her fingers. "I was thinking about something you said the other day. About a boyfriend."

"Ohemgee. Do ye want one? Can I set ye up?"

"I don't know? It's been on my mind."

"What are ye looking for?" I gave her my full focus, happy to ignore the ticking clock of the call.

"Once, I made a play for the boss. Kinda stupid of me, but I thought about why I'd done it, and it wasn't because of attraction."

I wrinkled my nose. "Arran? Gross."

"Like I said, it wasn't based on wanting him as a person. More as a bodyguard. I wouldn't mind the protection a man can offer, though maybe I want more. I like the way your boy behaves around you."

I stilled, the tone of her words worrying me. Unlocking the office, I tugged Dixie inside with me and closed the door.

"You're scared of something."

"Aren't we all?"

"If ye need a bodyguard, we'll get ye one."

"It isn't only for protection, and please don't worry— Manny is driving me home. I want more than that. Someone to care about me. To notice me, I guess. For more than just these." She pointed to her boobs. "How did you do it? You claimed Riordan before there was anything between you, right?"

My breath came in a short exhale. "I don't know if I'm the example to follow. You're right, though. I saw him and recognised what I wanted was right there in his big body. Whether I can keep him is another matter."

Her eyes rounded in outrage. "Girl, he is smitten. If he hurts you, I'll dick punch him."

My heart squeezed. "The problem is me, not him."

In a rush, the thoughts I'd prepared for my therapist

spilled out. All the obsessions I'd had. The fanatical love. The certainty that it would never end. I told Dixie it all. After a minute, I stopped myself. "I'm really sorry. I want to talk about your problems. Not mine. I've got a call with my therapist lined up to try to tackle this shite."

Dixie gave me a soft smile. "I never had any therapy, but Alisha offered it many times. She said it's the thing you need when you can't get around yourself in order to live happy."

"Aren't ye happy?"

Her smile faltered. "I try to be? Hun, I never asked for this life, but I ain't going to be good at any other so I make the most of it."

"That part about asking for it, is that something to do with your secret mission? The thing you're scared of?"

My phone rang loudly in my pocket.

I held Dixie's gaze. She moved to the door.

"Fix your head and keep your boy. We can talk another time."

She walked away before I had a chance to stop her. There was nothing left for me to do but face the music.

Dr Hillier commenced the call with the bright chirpiness of someone who'd had a good night's sleep and a tall cup of coffee. "It's been a while since we last spoke. Tell me, how have you been?"

"I'm in love," I mumbled.

She didn't hesitate. "Does the object of your affection know?"

"Yes."

"Does he or she feel the same?"

"I hope not." I winced at my own words. They used to

be true. They weren't now. "I kidnapped him."

"Cassiopeia, is he still a captive?"

I coughed an unfunny laugh. "He's fine. He's not the problem. I am. The whole time we've been together, I've been waiting for it to end."

"What do you anticipate your trigger will be in this instance?"

As always, the good doctor reached the point fast.

In all cases in the past, my obsessions would soar until an often minor event killed them dead. With the band I'd adored, it was coming face to face with them at a meet and greet Jamieson took me to when I was fourteen. *'Thanks for being a fan. We love you. Stream our new album,'* the singer had drawled, his expression bored, and his eyes red from whatever he'd snorted.

Dead to me. Instantly.

I'd quit university—a business studies degree I'd battled obsessively to get onto as my grades hadn't been that great—not because of bullying, like my family believed, but because a professor had talked to me seriously about my career options.

'You're a natural leader. You should concentrate on business management. I'll find you a mentor.'

It sank my interest like a stone.

The same thing had happened with school friends. The minute they got too close or made plans for me, I'd drop them. The interest had shifted from being mine to theirs.

I knew what my trigger would be with Riordan.

"When he tells me he loves me back." I forced the words out.

She gave an audible sigh. I was right back to being a teenager, waiting on her judgement.

"You're searching for a way to let him down as a method of controlling this," she stated.

I shook my head, not that she could see. "All I'd need to do is tell him I don't love him anymore and he'll walk away. He's expecting it."

It would hurt him. It would kill me to cause him pain.

Doctor Hillier praised my honesty then launched into a series of solutions, most of which involved calming my overexcited mind and backing off with the intensity of which I'd approached the relationship. I told her about Riordan and his father, the mayor, and how hurting him would kill me. I was an all-or-nothing kind of girl. I didn't do anything by half measures.

Finally, we got to her advice. "Ask him not to say the words that scare you. Avoid the trigger until you feel confident in handling it."

Except I so badly wanted his love. What a horrible Catch-22.

"I recently found out some things about my mother," I said in a rush. She knew how the woman was long dead. "It's stuck in my head because talking about her has made me feel like she might pop up unexpectedly."

I hadn't realised the point until I voiced it. Doctor Hillier asked for more information, and I went through meeting DeeDee and what she'd told me. It was just another item in the lists of things that could fuck me up and send me running.

Too quickly, our time was up.

The doctor gave me her parting words. "You're quick to call yourself faddy, and while it's true that you've had a history of changing interests quickly, you were young and still growing. It's normal for teenagers to change identities as often as they change clothes until they find one that fits. Consider that you hadn't yet found the right version of yourself to be."

I clutched the phone long after she'd made her goodbyes.

I'd barely begun to process my thoughts when a scraping sound came from the back corner of the office. I'd locked the door after Dixie and knew I was alone, so leapt up and searched the space.

Nothing. No hidden person behind the filing cabinet or sofa.

Then a cough sounded. It came from the other side of the wall.

Flying to the door, I fell out into the corridor, scanning the floor to work out what backed onto the office. The long wall led the way down to the lift and then the entrance to Divide. In the other direction, it rounded the central staircase then descended steps to the basement.

I sprinted into the nightclub. To the left, in a back corner, was a storeroom. I rattled the door handle. Closed and locked.

Nor was there anyone in the vast, empty space of the club.

Had I been overheard? Lara was the only person I'd seen going in here. I searched my mind for if it mattered. I'd given a ton of personal information on myself, but why would anyone else care about that?

Riordan was the only person affected by what I'd said on the phone. If he'd heard me, it could so easily have sounded bad.

Then another thought resolved. The cough had been distinctly feminine.

Relief swallowed me whole.

I made my way back upstairs and to our seventh-floor apartment. In our bed, Riordan slept on. Quietly, I undressed and climbed in beside him, my movements stirring him to haul me into his arms.

"You're cold," he muttered sleepily into my hair.

He hugged me, giving me back life where the chill of trying to fix myself had settled in.

I kissed his rough cheek. He woke enough to fit his mouth to mine and return the affection. The kisses didn't end, becoming drugging and wet. His sleepiness and my wakefulness traded off until we were both in a state of somewhere in between where everything was just us.

Riordan's hands wandered. He made a sound of approval at finding me naked, and his hand cupped me between the legs, a possessive squeeze shifting into a tease, his fingers stroking me until I moaned in need.

He flipped me over to my front and reared up behind me, kneeling between my legs. Through a sleep-soaked voice, he said, "I'm going to fuck you hard. Don't come. I'm going to first, then I'll lick you clean and make you cry out and orgasm until you beg me to stop."

He propped up my hips with a hand to my upper back to keep my head and shoulders down, then lined up his dick with my entrance. I was wet from the kissing and his touch, so he thrust inside without teasing. My lips parted over a rushed intake of breath, no feeling better in this world than when we were together like this. He filled me so good. The stretch was familiar now, and pleasure rolled through me. Every sense brightening.

With my cheek to the mattress and my arse in the air, I closed my eyes and felt every blow. Every slam into me that lit up my body. Automatically, my fingers crept up to my clit, but Riordan noticed and slapped my hand away.

"Don't come."

"No fair," I whined.

"I'll make it fair. Let me fill you up, beautiful girl. Fuck, you're so tight. You're going to make me come already."

A thrill danced over me, and I squeezed him, loving how his words faltered and turned into a groan. He never let himself go first, but I was here for it, loving the switch around and how fervently he fucked me.

When he gave a guttural shout and thrust hard into me then stilled, pulsing, I nearly came, too. Had to force myself to pant through it.

Riordan palmed my arse, stroking the globes of my cheeks while he breathed. "Keep your head down and your ass high. Tell me if you're close. I want my tongue inside you each time."

Pulling out, he kissed my spine then moved down further. His fingers slid over my soaked and sensitive flesh.

"I'm leaking out of you. Bad Cassie, making a mess."

"Clean me up, then."

I held my breath. He spread his cum up and down my pussy, dipping inside to gather more and massage it into me. I throbbed, desperation rising in a wave. He always made me feel so much. Too much. I'd never been this turned on, and every time made me only want him more.

His cum-soaked finger pressed on my rear entrance. At the same time, Riordan's tongue glided over my pussy, hot and wet and licking up the combination of us both. I moaned, and he pushed his finger into my arse.

"I intend to come inside here one day, when you're ready to try it," he warned against my flesh.

A second finger added to the first, and he stretched me, not going deep but enough to have me sweating and gripping the sheet with my fists.

All the while, he kept up his work of licking me. Until he came down to my clit and sucked hard.

My back bowed. I cried out wordlessly, heat sinking me under.

He grabbed my hip tight and glided his tongue into me, catching my fast-delivered orgasm as it took me down. Something about him playing with my arse made it another new experience, and I drowned in the pleasure of it.

When I'd finished squirming, he released me and gave a pleased chuckle.

"That was one. Now you're all dirty again with cum all down your thighs. Guess I need to start over."

He did. Multiple times until I did as he'd warned and begged him to stop.

He relented. Came back up the bed and slotted his dick into me again. My body gave a final pulse of satisfaction.

Riordan kissed my cheek, his voice low. "Tell me what I need to hear."

"I love ye. I've adored ye from first sight."

He exhaled, that familiar relief doing something happy to my heart.

"It's your birthday tomorrow night. If you're a good girl, I'll give you a present. If you're very good, I'll probably do something sappy like tell you I'm in love with you and that I'm keeping you, no matter what."

I went still. Didn't even breathe.

Then slowly I forced movement back in my limbs. I hugged him. Hard. Giving a message I couldn't say and earning a rough kiss which told me exactly how badly he'd needed my reaction.

For him, I'd change. I had to or I'd break us both.

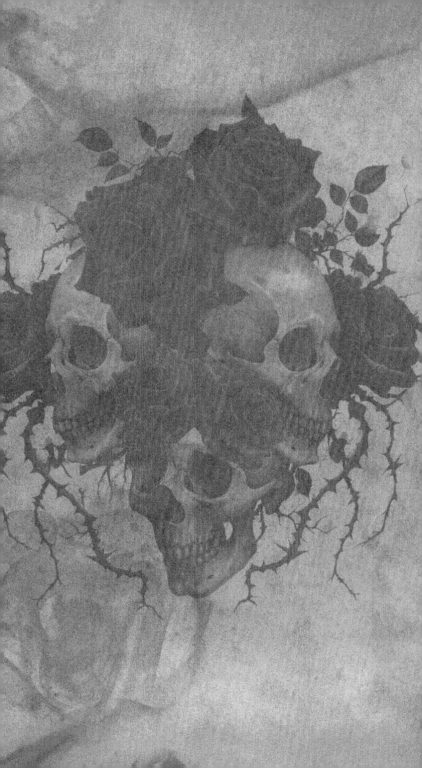

38

Cassie

*D*arkness surrounded me, the engine of Shade's car almost silent in our stakeout. Ahead, our subject stormed out of the warehouse and crossed the cobbled street, his phone to his ear and the neon-pink light illuminating one ugly scowl.

Piers Roache, ladies and gentleman. Tonight's entertainment.

Shade waited for Piers to go out of sight then pulled out in the electric vehicle. All the better for stalking our prey.

"Manny refused him entry."

I curled my lip. "Bold of him to assume he could get into our club. Do ye think he's calling the mayor?"

"Almost certainly."

"What if he comes looking for him?"

"Mayor Makepeace is deep in a three-girl show. No phones. He won't know for at least thirty minutes that his buddy is out on his arse."

Thirty minutes. Our window of opportunity.

He handed me his phone, open on a tracking screen with a green blip on the move. I hadn't known that he'd stuck Piers with a tracker until now, but I appreciated the forethought.

"Why do ye want to kill?" The enforcer kept his gaze on the street.

"Piers or in general?"

"The latter."

"I imagine the same reasons ye do."

"An impulse?"

"A bone-deep need to remove bad people from the planet."

He tapped the steering wheel. "When I was a kid, I knew there was something different about me, but it was the actions of others that brought it out. Ma had a boyfriend who put cigarettes out on my back for fun. It was terrifying and painful but also the point of my realising that I wanted to kill him and couldn't stop it. It broke or maybe released something in my head. When I take a life now, I see the pain and fear I inflict as righting wrongs of all the suffering the bastard in question caused."

I considered his words and inclined my head. "You're a check and balance of the universe. Love that. Mine's similar. There was an event that happened to me when I was six. Social workers dragged me kicking and screaming from my family. The cops had Sin on the ground so he couldn't come after me. My other brothers and my sisters-in-law were held back, and the fear on their faces was agonising. I will never forget the feeling and how it paired to the truth I was told years later that it was our father's doing. He hurt so many. It's the audacity that gets me. The arrogance."

"That was your trigger. Someone crossing the line and getting away with it," Shade observed.

I took a breath. "I want to walk in with pretty nails and cute shoes and drive fear into the hearts of people who hurt others. I want them to know what I am and realise there are consequences to the things they did. That consequence is me."

He shot me an expression of undisguised admiration. "Fuck, yeah. I need to see that in action. I was going to say it's like looking in the mirror, but I don't think I'd suit your shoes."

He took a corner, merging into traffic. Piers was still in sight further up the road. An abuser, forcing other people out of his way on his furious march down the pavement.

A bus obscured my vision, so I focused back on Shade.

For a beat, his mirror comment replayed in my mind. The enforcer had dark hair and blue eyes. He was Scottish, too.

Just like me and my brothers. McInver's kids.

I squinted at him. "Do ye know who your daddy is?"

"Aye, some deadbeat who fucked my mother then left her in the lurch. Why do ye ask?"

"Oh, no reason, other than ye could easily slot into the lineup of my family. There's a big gap between Jamieson and me, and we've often wondered if another sibling would pop up one day." I gestured between us. "The psychopath element fits, as well."

He made an off sound. "Neither of us are psychopaths. I looked the word up once. It fits those who can kill without remorse, but that's it. I see myself more as someone who has trained for the role. Where is Piers now?"

I switched my gaze to the phone. "Moving fast up

River Street. Must be in a taxi."

Shade indicated out of the street and onto an intercept course. "Next question. Who do ye want to kill?"

Gripping my seat, I told him my predator-hunter idea. How I'd get anonymous tip-offs to find my prey.

When I was done, he pursed his lips. "Your plan is too broad. You'll fuck around and waste time. Pick a specialism and you'll advance faster. Give the work of investigating reports to someone else."

I blinked. "Thanks for the career advice. I'll get myself an admin person. I guess for ye the work of sorting has been done already as they are ex-cons. How do I pick from my list?"

"Who do ye hate the most?"

I didn't even need to consider my answer. "Men in power, like my father. Okay, that was easy. I'll prioritise the wealthy."

A muscle ticked in Shade's jaw. "The men I take out are rarely rich arseholes. Even if prosecuted, those types don't go to jail. They frequent the same clubs as the judges. They have friends in the same circles."

"Ye want in on my plan. Maybe I'll let ye come along as muscle if Riordan is busy." I checked my nails, hiding a smile.

My phone buzzed. I answered the call. "Cassiopeia's house of pain. How may I hurt ye today?"

On the other end of the line, Tyler gave a snort of amusement. "Got a phone number for you. Your Uncle Patrick who's Cassandra's older brother. He runs a scaffolding company and is a minor league dealer. Fair warning, I ran a quick background check, and if you're trying to find a friendly family member, I don't think it's going to be him."

I sighed. "Lay it on me."

"His first wife accused him of domestic violence, but he got off the charge. He has two convictions for brawling at football matches and several warnings."

"A violent dealer. Awesome. Can't wait for the family reunion."

I thanked him and got off the line, staring down at the follow-up text Tyler sent with Uncle Patrick's phone number. He'd know more about his sister than most others. Maybe he even missed her and regretted what their father did. He might even know how she ended up dead.

Shade let me brood in silence while we tracked Piers' taxi.

"He's heading for the mayor's house."

I lifted my head and took in our surroundings. We'd left the tall buildings and concrete streets of central Deadwater and entered a leafy suburb.

Last time I'd come here had been in a reckless pursuit of Riordan. We'd stolen the mayor's painting then biked away into the moonlight.

My heart squeezed. We'd woken in the late afternoon with no time to linger in bed. He was heading out into the city with my brother while I had plans with Shade.

Not for a minute had I stopped thinking about him. Or what he'd said.

I hadn't messaged him, though.

At midnight, which was closing in fast, it was my birthday, and he'd threatened to say words that could operate our self-destruct. I didn't want that. I couldn't stand the thought of his face no longer fascinating me. Or his arms or his heart. Of him fading back to being just another fad I'd got over.

On my phone, I tabbed over to his tracker. Earlier, he and Struan had been at Town Hall, then another office, and a lock-up facility. My eyes widened now when his tracker pinged on the screen.

We stopped at traffic lights, and I held up my phone to Shade. "Look where Rio and Struan are."

He gave a low whistle. "Party time at the mayor's house. I'll message them to expect company."

He sent a fast text while I got a sudden burst of nerves I didn't know how to quell.

Piers would be joining them in minutes with us close behind. I had bloodlust, man lust, and both needed to go according to plan.

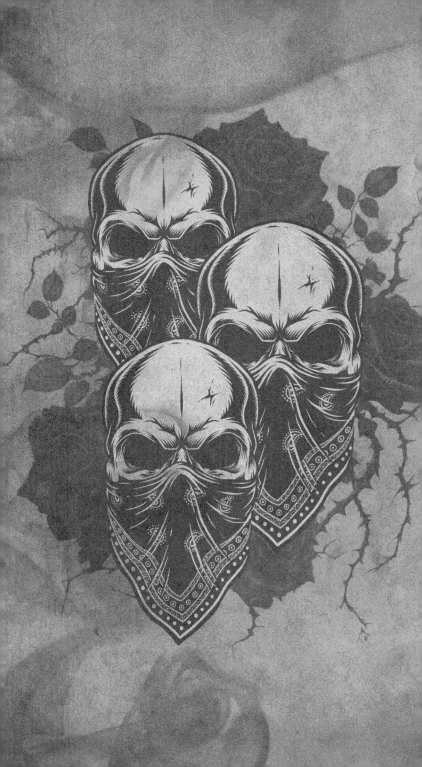

39

Riordan

With a savage-edged zombie blade held high, Struan slashed another of the mayor's suits with a satisfying rip. "So tomorrow begins his big election campaign presentation. Wonder what he'll be wearing. Not the Armani. Nor the Zegna. Wait, there's a Ralph Lauren left. Ah, shame. That one cut like butter. Nice material. Makes me almost want to own a suit."

On the opposite side of the mayor's dark bedroom, I prised open a heavy watch case and took out the first of two rows, some gaps in the lineup. A Rolex. Shiny, with a little crown symbol and a broad metal strap. I set it down on the bedside table, raised my hammer, then smashed the glass. Next, I dug into the guts with the claw end, enjoying the destruction. Small pieces of the expensive watch's mechanism went tinkling.

Throughout the course of the evening, I'd laid waste to the mayor's life. First, Struan and I trashed his Town Hall office, including stealing his laptop and throwing it in the river. Confidential files from his cabinet had been left around town, on benches and in bar bathrooms, secret budget meetings and character assassinations contained within. We'd poured cement powder into the fuel tanks of the two cars he used—those engines would never run again—and had now moved on to his home.

If he thought Cassie's set of minor tricks were disturbing, wait until he got a load of mine.

"Don't stop there." I punctuated my words with a crack to a new watch. "I want him to feel violated and scared, like Everly did when he sold her out to his business partner. Disappointed and despondent, like my mother when he told her to get an abortion. Desperate, like I was when he left me nearly homeless. I want there to be no place of safety left for him."

Struan took to a shelf of smart sweaters, cutting one right down the middle. "He'll know by now that Arran's barring him from the warehouse."

As we'd readied to leave this evening, Arran had filled us in on his part of bringing down the mayor. He knew the man was booked into the brothel and was allowing it to go ahead to give us space to play. But after, he'd inform him because of his anti-gang policy, his business was no longer welcome.

It meant a fight. From what I understood, Arran's semi-legal operations had been tolerated by the mayor because the man benefited from them. Cut off, who knew what he'd do. But the mayor had cast the first stone. This was all on him.

We continued with our tasks, destroying every personal possession and leaving them to be discovered.

Struan tossed down the last clothing item. "This is good, but we can do better. My family and I burned every stick of furniture that our father used, but that was for our peace of mind because he was already in the ground. We used the evidence we'd gathered on him to right a few wrongs. Is this helping you, Riot? What else do ye want?"

I shrugged. "That event tomorrow is a family and community seminar. A formal thing for politicians and business leaders. I'll walk up on stage while he's speaking and introduce myself as the son he never acknowledged."

"To what end? Do ye want him to give a fuck about ye?"

I considered it. "No. I want him brought down and disgraced. For all the things he's done, but more for the fact he's a bad person."

"How about killing him?"

My breathing quickened. "I considered it, but I'm not bloodthirsty like your sister."

He clucked his tongue. "She'll be happy tonight once she and Shade have taken down the business partner."

I swore softly. "I knew she'd be out with Shade but I didn't ask why."

Nor had she messaged me.

The knowledge tightened my stomach into a ball.

It was unlike Cassie to go long without needing to be in contact with me. I'd got used to her Velcro girlfriend act and had felt just as desperate myself. I needed her, too. At multiple points throughout the evening, I'd expected to see her pretty little face peering through a window, or for her to spring at me from a shadow. To have no contact at all worried me.

Struan prowled deeper into the mayor's walk-in wardrobe. "I'm just going to say this. Your revenge isn't enough. He's scum. He shouldn't be allowed to breathe for what he did to your sister. I'd end anyone who hurt mine. Think bigger. I don't want ye to regret not taking the right action when ye had the chance."

"What I'd really like is to understand the dodgy deals he's putting in place and expose them. That would be killer. Maybe even send him to prison. But I don't know shit about financial dealings."

He gave me a long-suffering look, his eyes in a slash of light from his torch. "As we speak, your girlfriend is hunting down the very person who can be persuaded to give up information. Stop being an island and ask her to help."

My sister had accused me of the same thing, and yet I'd already confided more in Cassie than any other person alive. She'd do it in a heartbeat, but it meant tying her into my crimes, again, and I'd already put her at risk with the stolen painting. Then again, she was the one doing kidnap and murder tonight. I nearly laughed at the difference in scale.

Slowly, I nodded. "I will."

"Good man. Do it now or else she might have got stab-happy already."

I took out my phone, wincing at the lack of a message from her, but texted the request, taking pains to be careful with my words.

No reply immediately came.

Struan rifled through the wardrobe. "If we think he's up to no good, maybe there's something here that can help, too."

He shone his torch into a filing cabinet, hidden in the back. I stared at it then approached and tugged on the top drawer. It was locked, but a sharp pull broke the mechanism.

Inside were stacks of paper. I leafed through then spotted something at the back. Letters. A thing of the past, because who sent handwritten letters anymore? They had to be old. I almost ignored them, but the stack slid.

The third in the pile stopped my breathing.

It was an ivory-coloured envelope, stamped and franked, and addressed to the mayor. But it was the handwriting that pulled me up short. My mother's.

I knew it instantly. She used to leave me messages to read before school. Her shiftwork at the hospital meant she either worked nights or was gone before my sister and I woke, so every day, little love messages or enthusiastic go-get-them notes waited on the breakfast table to remind us that she cared.

I'd forgotten she used to do that, but I couldn't be more certain it was in her hand. Pain rebounded inside me. I stuffed the letter into my back pocket.

From downstairs, a door creaked open.

I stilled. Struan did, too. From his pocket, he extracted his phone and unlocked it, then read something on his screen. My partner in crime gave a low chuckle.

"Piers Roache. His hunters aren't far behind. Shade gives a one-minute ETA."

My heart pounded.

Throughout the evening, I'd carried out my revenge, my acts of protest with cool execution. But knowing Cassie was here and about to go face to face with a violent man chilled me.

I found my own phone and tracked her. They were a street away, probably going slowly so they could claim their prize.

Still no text from her, despite mine being received, but I couldn't think of that now.

The rattling of keys followed, presumably as Piers dropped them to the hall table, but the rev of an engine chased it, and the bark of a radio.

My blood chilled.

We'd slipped into the house after watching the security team that patrolled the street head out on a break. The mayor still hadn't retained his own private security, which made no sense considering my recent break-in.

Carefully, I edged around the heavy curtain and gazed down. On the street, two security guards climbed from a vehicle, a second car with the same insignia pulling up behind. Fuck.

Either Piers had summoned them, or there was another reason they'd closed in.

Regardless, it meant Cassie was walking straight into a trap.

I stepped away and whispered what I'd seen to Struan. On my screen, Cassie's tracker pinged in the back garden.

"We need to help them."

In the dark, her brother's eyes gleamed. "State the outcome."

"Cassie and Shade capture Roache and get out of here unseen."

He nodded once, the noises of Piers moving through the house punctuated with a snarl of anger. He'd discovered the trashed Council Chamber. Seconds more, and the security guards could be in the building.

"Which makes us the distraction. We need to lead the boys out front away from Roache. Just realise that if we're caught, we're walking away from a pile of destruction. No matter if we persuade the police to let us go, the mayor will know exactly who did this." He cocked his head.

"Daddy dearest might get to meet his boy a day early."

I didn't care. I only needed Cassie to be safe.

I sent her a final, fast text.

> **Riordan:** We're taking care of visitors at the front.

The clock ticked over to midnight. I sucked in a breath and said what I needed to say.

> **Riordan:** I love you, wild girl. Happy birthday. Don't get caught.

There was nothing more to do but tug up our skeleton bandannas and exit the bedroom.

The light from downstairs flooded the hall. Neither of us hesitated, drumming down the stairs, heading right to the front door exactly as a door crashed open to our left, two figures startling the already wide-eyed city boy who stood dumbfounded with his phone in his hand.

Cassie's gaze met mine.

I wanted to stay. I wanted to help her, even if she and Shade had it covered.

It took until long after we'd led the security guys away that I realised how deep her silence cut me.

I'd told her I loved her.

This time, she hadn't said it back.

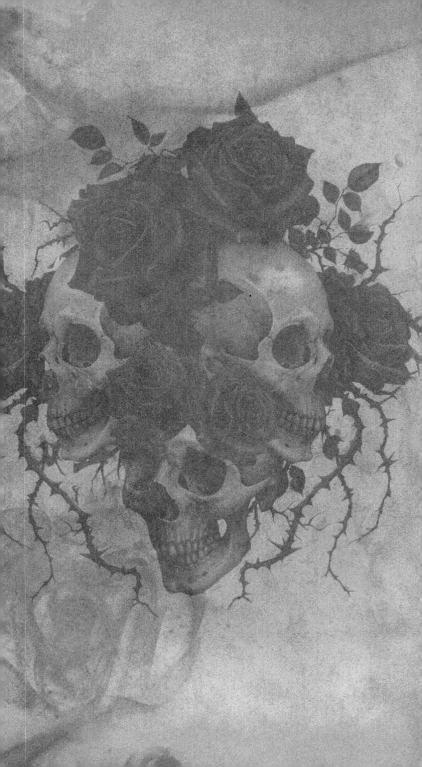

40

Cassie

Subduing Piers was disappointingly easy. He squealed like a piggie, barely shaking Shade who gripped his throat while I knocked the rapist the fuck out with a needle and a fast-acting drug.

He dropped to the floor.

I spat on his prone form.

We got out the way we came in, with Shade having kicked through the lower panels of the fence Riordan and I once climbed. The cameras that watched over the garden had likewise been smashed and left hanging. In the car, we wasted no time getting out of the fancy neighbourhood and exiting the city.

Shade had already explained that we'd finish Piers off at the boathouse, and my fingers shook in anticipation.

They also shook at the words I'd just read.

Riordan loved me.

A rush of mixed emotions threatened me, part of fear, part elation, falling into turmoil with the bloodlust.

I found my phone. Read it again. And again. And again.

Goddamn it, Rio.

To distract myself, I clicked on the number that Tyler had sent me and wrote a very short text to my uncle. Just a brief statement that I was Cassandra's daughter. He'd probably be a terrible person, but the contact was made.

The fact it was off the back of desperation was undoubtedly a bad idea.

I set my head back on the seat, trying to get myself under control. I couldn't settle. Couldn't think straight. My mind lurched to Riordan again and again.

I tried to force it elsewhere. To Lottie going to hospital but being okay, to Genevieve's engagement and Everly's pregnancy. Those were happy-ever-afters in action, and I loved it for them. I thought about Bronson, caught, the killer removed from the streets. I worried over the problem Dixie had promised to share and her obvious fear. She'd been so sweet and kind to me. I wished I'd had longer to talk more with her, but later, I'd find the time for certain.

Yet again and again, I came back to my boyfriend and imagined the words falling from his perfect mouth.

I love you.

God. I tapped over to my message thread with him. Started a reply. Deleted it. Started again.

Cassie: I'm sorry.

What was I sorry about? My carrying a burden of fear? Doubting myself? For being right? I didn't know.

I couldn't finish the text.

Killing Piers was going to be my salvation. At least in that, I knew exactly what I was doing. I'd get lost in removing him from the planet.

"What's your method?" I blurted.

Shade snuck a look at me. "For the end? I read him his rights then kill him. How fast or slow depends on my mood and the time available. Though now I come to think of it, I like them to see their dick disappear into the river before they're too far gone. Arran's the same. Ye can pick your own ritual."

He drove us on into the dark night, coming down off the hillside to follow the curve of Deadwater River. "I had a message from Struan. He and Riot want us to ask a few questions of our friend in the boot. They think the mayor is up to some shady shit but need details."

I exhaled, some of my mental capacity returning. Riordan had messaged me the same. I could do that. Torturing Piers would be worthy. He deserved nothing less than a healthy dose of pain, and Riordan deserved answers about his father.

Ahead, a car cruised into an exit off the road. Skeleton crew acting as our support. We entered the car park and climbed from our vehicles. The two crew members set a fire going in a canister then took positions of watch. Shade retrieved Piers from the car and carried him to the dilapidated wooden structure, griping about how much he weighed.

My breathing quickened again.

This was it. It felt auspicious. It felt ominous. I'd do this again and again to rapists and abusers, but I wanted my first to be marked somehow. Important.

I opened the door and let us inside.

Water rushed further on down the dark interior, and the tangy scent of the river tickled my nose. I took a deep sniff then blinked, the odour not right.

There was something else in it.

Coppery. Like blood.

My gut tightened in anticipation. That was wrong. I'd been here before, and the place was cleaned of evidence. It had to be. Shade had a process down pat.

I turned back to him. "Who was responsible for cleanup in here last time ye used the place?"

His eyebrows dove together. "Did it myself."

His expression shifted, telling me he'd picked up the same anomaly I had.

My sense of foreboding grew. Rounding to the steps, I climbed to the boat launch platform.

My boots rang on the metal walkway. My knees shook. The cold river rushed below, the open space thick with shadows.

It wasn't dark enough to hide the body.

On the edge of the gantry, in danger of sliding into the frothing waves below, a woman sprawled. Naked. Unmoving.

A red slice glistened at her throat.

Oh God, no.

In pure shock, I clasped my hands to my mouth and stumbled as recognition hit me fast.

My pulse drowned out all other sounds. My whimper, the deadly water, Shade's muttered anger, everything.

Not her. Please.

Shade grabbed my arm.

I spun around to the grim-faced enforcer, furious and with tears threatening. "Don't. Don't ye dare."

My voice cracked.

I twisted back. Put one foot in front of the other until I reached Dixie's lifeless body.

At her side, I sank down, my knees giving out at the last so I hit the metal hard. Her pretty face was tipped away from me, extending her neck to showcase the cut that had ended her.

It was the scent of her blood I'd picked up. Her loss of life as she'd bled out through the open floor.

With shaking hands, I wrenched off my jacket to cover her, and to give my friend a last shred of dignity.

"I'm so sorry." My voice quaked. "I'm so sorry."

She'd been murdered. Dumped here.

My thoughts snarled up too badly to consider what that meant for Deadwater's serial killer, only that this was how the lives of four women had ended. No, not four. Five now. My friend.

With care, I settled the jacket on her torso.

My fingers grazed her skin.

I took a short breath. "She's still warm."

From behind, Shade's footsteps thudded. He'd yelled to the crew to call for backup. Maybe for the police. I couldn't process his words.

He settled next to me. Laid two fingers on her arm.

"The killer must've just done this." I stared at him.

Shade's gaze jerked from her wrist to her face. "Wait."

Confused, I followed where his attention had gone.

Red bubbles formed at Dixie's ruined throat. Air. Her chest rose, just slightly.

Shock slammed into me.

"She isn't dead," I stammered. Then I shook Shade by

his shoulder. "She's alive. Call an ambulance. We need to get her to hospital. She isn't fucking dead."

He jumped up and moved away. Feverish for action, I collected Dixie's hand in mine. I wanted to press down on her throat to stop the bleeding, but what if I killed her with my touch?

"Listen to me, we're getting help. You're going to be okay. Do ye hear? We're going to get ye to a hospital."

I sobbed half the words.

Dixie's lips moved. The action forced another well of blood to spill down her slender neck.

I squeezed her hand, wishing I knew anything about first aid. I could make this worse. She could die just from me trying. "Don't try to speak. Save whatever ye need to tell me until later. I won't leave ye. You'll survive this. I swear."

Everything that came next passed by like a movie scene.

Piers' prone form vanished with a member of the skeleton crew, to go where, I didn't care. Others arrived. Blue lights flashed. Hurried voices came with more ringing bootsteps.

Two burly ambulance men joined me, their faces ashen as they took in my friend.

"Help her," I begged.

On their order, Shade guided me out of the way. I refused to go further than a few steps. One hooked her up to a machine while the other did something to her throat.

Dixie gave a soft, almost animal-like moan, more blood bubbling.

My heart nearly stopped. "Don't hurt her."

"I need to stabilise her breathing," the second guy said. "Can you tell me her name?"

"Dixie."

He repeated it. Talked to her as he manipulated a piece of equipment into her neck. In some quiet communication with his colleague, one retrieved a stretcher, and they moved her onto it.

Her eyes were open just a fraction, but I knew she looked for me.

"I want to go with her," I said.

"Are you family?"

"She doesn't have any family. I'm a friend." They had to let me.

"Sorry, family only. Stay and talk to the police."

Shade loomed beside me. "I'll take ye."

They loaded her into the ambulance and blue-lighted her into town. We chased them. Shade dropped me off with a promise to return after he'd handled the police.

I tracked her down to an emergency surgery ward, her bare foot uncovered by the white hospital blanket as they wheeled her into a room.

There was nothing left for me to do but wait.

41

Riordan

On foot, I circled the warehouse, noting the lack of music vibrating the air. At this time of night, the clubs should be busy, but there was no queue outside Divide. No doorman at the entrance to Divine.

Evading the security crew at the mayor's house had taken longer than expected. Struan and I had hidden for over an hour, but we'd finally managed to slip away. I'd told him to go ahead and not wait for me, needing the headspace of a long walk back. I knew for a fact Cassie hadn't messaged—I'd put my phone onto Do Not Disturb for all but her.

No text or call had come in.

I prowled the perimeter of the warehouse's grounds, delaying going inside. Some form of intuition bothered me. A doubt, or maybe a need to be alert and pay attention. Perhaps it was cowardice.

If I didn't see Cassie, she couldn't break things off with me, and I was almost certain that was coming.

Instead, I circled the building and returned to the front.

The door opened, and a woman exited. Behind her was a flurry of action. People moving.

She made a beeline for my direction, her peek up at me tentative. "Riordan?"

I didn't know her name but recognised her. She'd served drinks to the protesters with Cassie and Moniqua. She had tiny strands of something glittery in her hair, which was why I remembered her.

There was another reason. I tilted my head, trying to work out where I'd seen her previously. "Yes?"

"Cassie asked me to find you."

My wary intuition grew. "She's back?"

"She was. She's gone out again with Mr Daniels. Something's going down in the city tonight, and all the important people left. I'm not sure of the details. I'm just the messenger."

"What's the message?"

Her shoulders rose.

I didn't like this. Not at all. Why hadn't Cassie called or waited for me?

The woman held out a folded piece of paper then bobbed her head and walked away, the threads woven into her hair twinkling in the light.

A note?

Ice formed in my veins. Cassie had received one of these. Alisha, too. I wasn't the object of a killer's interest, and besides, Bronson had been taken down. What the hell was this? Not Cassie's style.

If it was even from her.

Then the memory clicked of how I knew the messenger. It was from when Struan and I had been arrested. She was the staffer with the hoodie up, slipping into enemy territory.

"Wait," I called.

She turned around.

"What were you doing in Four Miler territory?"

Her gaze shot down, and she moved to the corner of the building. "Like I said, I'm just the messenger. Read it."

I checked around to make sure I wasn't about to be rushed, then unfolded the paper.

Unlike with my mother's handwriting, I didn't know Cassie's. Couldn't be sure if the feminine hand was hers. Until I read the opening line.

Each word damned me.

Gutted me.

Riordan, sorry. It happened. I fell out of love with you.

All suspicion released from me. If it had been anything other than these specific words, I wouldn't have believed it. Yet no one could've faked this, and no weapon could've torn deeper into me and destroyed me quite so well.

My heart broke into pieces.

It shattered, and shattered, and splintered apart.

I turned my back on the warehouse and walked away.

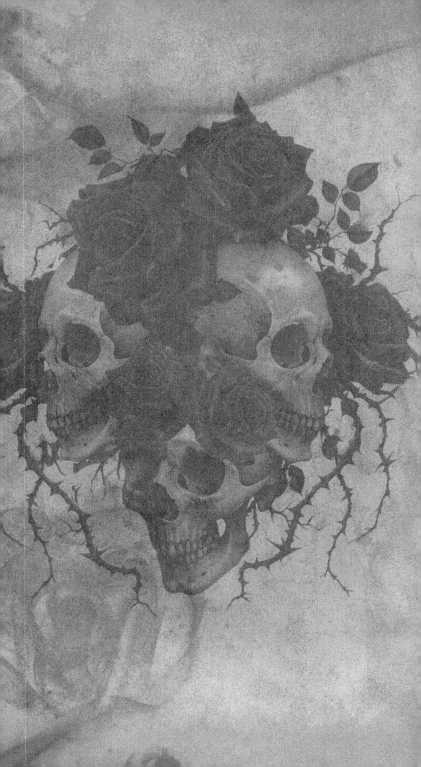

42

Cassie

Anxiety hung over me like a spectre as I paced the hospital's emergency surgery waiting room. Up and down. Up and down.

Dixie was being operated on. The hospital staff wouldn't tell us shite, but I'd found a friendly nurse who'd given me just enough information so I didn't go insane.

She'd promised to update me with any news, so long as the ward nurse wasn't around to bust her.

Dixie could die.

My helpful, sweet, bubbly friend deserved so much more from life, yet some bastard had tried to kill her.

My gut churned.

It didn't take a genius to realise it was a message.

Anger rose and rose and rose.

Footsteps sounded behind me. I spun around, sagging to see Shade. He'd had to leave to handle the crime scene but had promised to return.

"Any news?"

I shook my head, my words stuck.

"Detective Dickhead wants to talk to ye. I told him to back the fuck off, but the man is an arsehole, so don't be surprised if he shows up. He knows you're here, but that's all the fucker has been told."

He didn't need to prompt me on what to say. Chief Constable Kenney was well known to me and my family, as much as to Arran, Shade, and the skeleton crew. I knew how to talk my way around police questioning.

"Kenney will be all over this as a copycat."

Shade curled his lip, his back to the nurses' station. "He'll be jerking his stumpy dick in glee at a chance to catch the killer considering he missed out last time. If he dares talk shite about Dixie, I'll threaten to cut it off."

I stared at him.

He was right about the detective. Shade's reaction, on the other hand, didn't quite fit.

Images of the boathouse flashed before my eyes. He'd shown pain but not shock at the discovery of Dixie.

I cocked my head at the enforcer. "You're not surprised by this."

He didn't reply, his thumbs in the loopholes of his jeans and his expression sober.

Emotion rushed inside me. "Hold the fucking phone. Bronson is dead, yet Dixie's throat has been fucking slit. You said the killer, and not a copycat. Why?"

His mouth opened, but my anger took over again, dark realisations swirling.

"Ye expected another murder."

He exhaled. "I hoped not."

I exploded. "What the fuck, Shade? Is Bronson really dead?"

He shot his gaze down the corridor to where a couple slumped against each other in a row of plastic seats. At this hour, the hospital was quiet. Not empty, but enough that Shade dragged me further along and out of earshot.

"Bronson's dead, like I told ye. Don't make out that I'm a liar."

"I'm confused. Doesn't that make this a copycat?"

His nostrils flared.

No, he didn't think that.

I folded my arms, digging my nails into my flesh, waiting on his explanation.

The enforcer palmed his tattooed throat, the Scotland flag inked on the back of his hand giving me no comfort. "There was enough doubt with his confession to give us pause."

I took a shocked inhale. For a second, time stopped. I replayed his words. "You're fucking kidding me. 'Doubt' meaning he didn't do it? Ye weren't sure, and yet Arran announced the news like it was all over?"

His slight head tilt sent my blood pressure through the roof.

"What other minor details don't I know? What else did ye cut me and everyone out of?"

He didn't have a chance to answer when I was in his face again, the consequences overwhelming me. I shoved his chest.

"Do you realise what you've done? How many women were out there unprotected because of that claim? We thought it was over. We thought we were safe."

Shade snarled and backed up a step. "I did, too. It was just a hunch I couldn't shake off, and Arran felt the same.

Every woman remained protected."

My mouth fell open, and I wheeled away, unable to believe my ears. "They weren't protected. Dixie wasn't."

He swore. "No. Fuck. She shouldn't have been alone. Not going to or from work."

"But she was. Long enough for this to happen." My voice broke.

"We didn't know for certain. Both of us felt at the moment we ended his miserable life that that was it. His murder spree was finished and we'd done what we needed to do. He fucking confessed, Cass. It was after we compared notes and admitted the uncertainty. A matter of a day ago. I still believed I was making something out of nothing. Ye said I wasn't shocked when we found her, that's not true. I'm just as cut up about this as ye are."

I shoved him again. "Get out of my sight. I don't want to see ye right now. If she dies, I will never forgive the both of ye."

Shade backed up further, his features twisted in hurt and regret. Aye, he fucking should regret it.

"Don't leave here," he ordered with a stab of his finger at the floor between us.

Thank the gods, he turned and left.

I sank to the nearest seat.

All that time, the killer wasn't gone, just lying in wait and biding his time.

A hot rush of emotion swallowed me whole. That person had wanted me dead. He'd been out for blood. Riordan or Shade had been with me every time I'd left the warehouse, but the same care hadn't been taken over Dixie.

I palmed my face, more facts slamming into me.

I'd doubted Bronson's confession, too. I'd said it didn't feel right. My brain filled in all the reasons why Shade would've kept his suspicion quiet. To lure him out? Or her. I couldn't reject that possibility.

The minute I got back to the warehouse, I was reinstating the detective wall.

If Dixie survived. If she didn't... I couldn't think like that.

Alone, I stewed in my misery. An hour passed, or maybe more. Lonnie appeared in the hall but stepped out when I glowered his way.

It was only when the friendly medic returned to the nurses' station that I dragged myself up.

The older woman lifted her gaze on my approach. Then her eyes crinkled at the edges. In sympathy?

My heart thundered. "What's happened? Can ye tell me anything?"

The woman shot a look to the right to where another nurse crossed the corridor. "I'm sorry, I already told you I can't comment on a patient's care without their consent."

The second person disappeared into a room.

I swung my focus back. "Please," I whispered.

"Out of surgery," she whispered back and picked up a pen, pretending to write something on a whiteboard.

I sidled closer.

"Alive?" I barely breathed the word.

"In recovery. Come back this afternoon and you can ask to see her. She should be awake."

I sagged against the station. Awake meant the surgery must've gone well. The potential to be awake later today meant she hadn't died.

The nurse patted my hand then repeated loudly that I really should come back in visiting hours when the patient could consent to sharing information.

Weak with relief, pain, and everything in between, I stumbled back to a seat. For a long minute, I held my head in my hands and swam in the mix of happiness and horror at what my friend must've endured.

I'd avenge her. I'd hunt down whoever did this.

My phone buzzed.

I fished it out and checked the screen, then did a double take.

> **Unknown:** I heard you're searching for me. Now you have my number.

I stared, ice sliding down my spine. How eerie. Who the hell—?

"Miss Archer," a voice hailed me from the ward entrance.

Detective Dickhead sauntered my way. In a rumpled dark-coloured shirt and suit trousers, the arsehole cop looked like he'd fallen out of a club to investigate the crime. Lonnie stepped into view, but I rolled my eyes and waved him off.

"Kenney," I snipped.

"You know the drill, eyewitness."

"Not in the mood right now."

"And I wish I was still balls-deep in the pretty young thing who was on my dick when I got the call, but we can't have everything."

I exhaled irritation. "Fuck, and I can't stress this enough, all the way off."

His gaze sharpened and sank over me. "You know, I don't think I've ever seen you alone."

My phone buzzed again.

> **Unknown:** It's Cassandra, by the way. Or Ma, I guess. Is there somewhere private you can go to call me?

I scrambled back and nearly lost my footing. My pulse thumped so loud in my ears that I couldn't hear anything else Kenney said.

Ma? Cassandra... My mother?

The uncle I'd texted must've given her my details. She wasn't dead?

Reeling, freaked out, and entirely panicked, I pushed past Kenney and left the ward. Outside the doors, Lonnie stood taller but relaxed again when I snapped that I was taking a bathroom break.

A lie.

I couldn't breathe. I needed fresh air and a second to take it all in. To call back the number of the woman who gave birth to me twenty years ago. Today, I realised. It was my birthday. Fuck. No wonder she'd got in contact.

Outside the hospital's huge rotating doors, bright dawn lit a chilly autumn morning, and traffic rumbled by. I ambled into the centre of the plaza. Took a breath of mostly cigarette smoke from the cluster of elderly smokers in hospital gowns, some holding rolling IV stands.

The moment slowed.

If only my brain would settle.

I sensed the rush towards me way too late.

Material landed over my head. Someone lifted me, and tyres screeched. I was tossed onto the hard metal bed of a van without seeing who I'd had the displeasure to be kidnapped by.

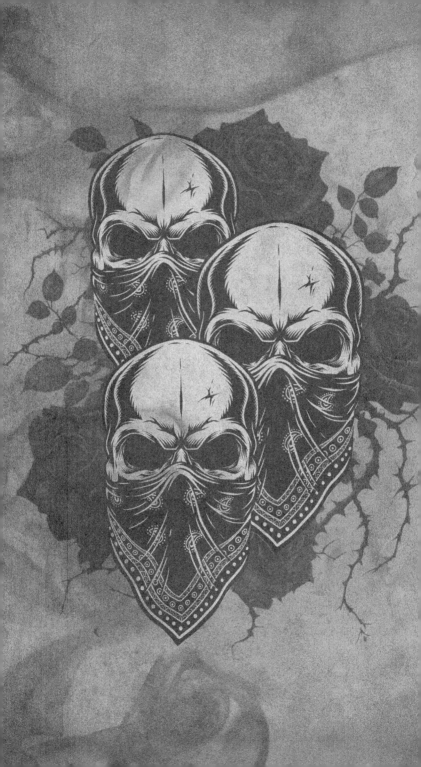

43

Riordan

The cliff's edge gave way to a sharp drop, the river far beneath me and the wind whipping through the trees overhead. A storm was coming, darkening the afternoon. I'd brought Cassie to this spot just a couple of nights ago. We'd had sex on my bike with no cares but each other. Our world had been a happy place.

Now I was making plans for changing mine entirely.

Music pounded in my ears, 'Take Me Back to Eden' by Sleep Token.

The letter in my hands crinkled under my grip.

Dear Marlon,

I hated it. No one ever referred to the mayor by his first name, except presumably those intimate with him like my mother had been. I forced myself to read on and to let it sink in.

You lied to me. You have a wife. A baby. I met them when

I came to your house, and had to lie about who I was. Your daughter is beautiful. Your wife deserves better. Do everyone a favour and don't break their hearts. I'm asking you to forget about me. I've met someone else anyway. He'll raise your child as his own, and we can all carry on in our own separate ways. Thank you for the money, I don't need it.

I don't need you anymore.

She'd signed off with a scribbled signature that spoke of high emotion when she'd penned the letter two and a half decades ago. Did she really hate him that much that she'd called those shots out of anger, or was it an attempt to push him away when she was scared of what he might do to her? I'd never know. All I could be sure of was that he'd offered in some way to support her, and maybe even to be part of my life.

It filled in a gap of information I'd had, even if it posed more questions. I'd wanted to read the fight she'd put up for me. She'd kept me, which would have been hard for any eighteen-year-old, and she'd given me a great life, even if some of it had been a lie. I didn't blame her for that.

My mind travelled over the broken pieces of my trauma.

I hated the image of her going to the mayor's house and meeting his wife. I'd gone there and met Everly in the same way, lying about who I was and backing out. History had repeated itself. He'd failed us both.

Mum said the mayor's family deserved better, but she had, too.

It fucked up my already messed-up brain all the more and brought me back again and again to my own failed relationship.

To Cassie.

Who'd dumped me without a care.

Misery crowded me from all sides, made up of the two women who'd left me.

Distantly, I recognised the trigger that had sent me running. Neither woman had told me themselves that they were going. A cop informed me and Gen about Mum. A fucking note did the job for Cassie.

A fresh wave of emotion rocked me.

Never again would she leap into my arms. Never again would I accept her slight weight and hug her to me. I was addicted to the joy she wore like a crown. To her fierce attitude and the way she needed me. I loved her taste. Her mind. Her body.

I fucking adored my wild girl and I'd lost her.

I brushed my knuckles over the crushing sensation in my chest. I'd been destroyed once in this life already and lived the impossible nightmare. An event I'd kept praying was a lie and had never truly got over.

Cassie had found a way into my ruined heart then shattered it, and I couldn't even blame her. She did what she told me she'd do. She was honest to the end. I'd brought about the end of her infatuation with me. I'd told her I loved her. I'd fallen for her, and she'd fallen right out of love, just like she'd promised.

It was me who'd broken our deal.

I was never supposed to catch feelings, but I was in so deep there was no way out.

One thing for certain was I couldn't work in the same place she existed.

I'd return to her flat and leave my skeleton crew pass in the skull on our countertop, a new failure to add to her list of lost obsessions.

Her countertop, I corrected. I didn't live there and I never had.

Exhausted, I scrubbed my eyes.

Starting over would be hard. In buying her nice things, I'd burned through my wages from Arran, barely leaving me enough to fuel up my bike and find a place to sleep that wasn't my car for the night. I didn't regret it. I wanted her to be comfortable. Happy.

Which meant getting out of her way.

After losing my last job, I'd intended to drive south and find work in another city. My lungs inflated on a heavy breath. That was what I needed to do today, so why the fuck was I sitting here, moping?

I stood on the rocky ledge, a slide of earth and pebbles clattering down into the open air.

There was one thing left to do.

Loving Cassie was going to haunt me for the rest of my life, and in the hours since I'd read her note, I'd resisted the burning need to check my phone. Her tracker was on there. I needed to delete it.

No, I needed to do something more extreme.

I needed to toss the fucking thing. Extracting my phone from my pocket, I killed the music and crushed it though the damn thing wouldn't break. Sending it flying over the cliff was the only way to free myself. I still had the link Shade had sent me to set up Cassie's tracker in the first place. Without losing access entirely, I'd reinstate it in a moment of weakness. I couldn't do that.

All I needed to do was throw.

I gritted my teeth and pulled back my hand.

Something fell to my feet, catching the breeze.

In the act of going into my pocket, I'd also drawn out Cassie's note. It fluttered over the edge of the cliff.

With a howl, I dropped to my knees and snatched it from the air, nearly losing my balance and with more rocks falling to the chasm. The drop loomed below.

I scrambled back to the base of a tree, holding the fucking thing to my chest while my heart pounded so hard I could barely breathe.

What the hell was wrong with me? Why couldn't I let this go?

I opened it again, needing the closure and to force myself to face it.

Riordan, sorry. It happened. I fell out of love with you.
You're expecting this, so it can't be a surprise.
We're split up now.
Hugs! Cassie.

Brief, to the point, damning. God, it fucking hurt.

Rain pattered down, dampening the paper like tears I'd never shed. I hadn't been able to cry when Mum died. Not when my sister sobbed herself to sleep every night and neighbours and friends dabbed at wet eyes. Mine had stayed dry.

I shoved the note and Mum's letter back into my pocket.

One day, I'd burn both when I was ready to let go.

For a long minute, I just breathed, watching the river's

swelling tide creep up the steep banks on its rush into the city.

Something churned in my gut. A sense of deep worry over Cassie, out there somewhere and vulnerable.

She had countless people who were there for her, but none of them cared as much as me. None of them loved her so fiercely as I did, with a hole in my chest and an exposed heart.

She was no one's top priority. Yet even if she didn't want me, she was still mine.

In the most secret part of my heart, another thought stirred.

Though Mum hadn't been able to tell me she was going, Cassie could. I needed to hear it from her lips.

Switching my phone back on, I called up her tracker, dismissing the countless calls and messages that crowded my screen the second I went off Do Not Disturb.

The blip pinged deep in Four Miler territory.

Fuck, what was she doing there? What the hell was Arran doing, taking her into that shitshow?

Anger broke over me, and I leapt to my feet, swiping over to my phone app as I got onto my bike and revved the engine, the sound breaking through the quiet with an anger that matched how I felt inside.

Setting out, I dialled Arran from one of the multiple missed calls from him. I'd ignored all contact since last night.

He answered immediately. "Jesus. Where are you both?"

My venom died on my tongue. I rolled off the dirt track to descend the hill back to the river road. "What do you mean 'both'?"

"You and Cassie. We're regrouping at the warehouse. I've called everyone back." To someone else, he yelled, "Got Riot on the line."

"Thank fuck for that," Scottish tones returned over my headphones, one of Cassie's brothers.

My stomach gutted out. "Cassie isn't with me. She broke up with me. I haven't seen her since last night when she was out with Shade."

Silence met my words, then my boss swore a blue streak, ending with, "Where is she?"

"Her tracker says rival fucking gang territory," I yelled and accelerated hard, banking out around a tight bend. "How the fuck did you allow it? I'm going after her."

Arran swore again. "Not without us. Get back here."

I gritted my teeth, but he was right. Alone, I was less effective. With my crew, I had a better chance. "Be there in ten," I snapped and got the hell on my way.

My bike's engine snarled as I cut through the traffic, weaving in and out of lanes on my route upriver and back into Deadwater.

Between heartbeats and raindrops, I tried to remember to breathe.

Beyond the *Welcome to Deadwater* sign, fire engines screamed past, heading up the hill to one of the suburbs. Police cars zipped into town, none troubling me.

Outside the warehouse, I screeched to a halt, leaving my bike haphazardly parked. Struan waited by the rear exit, his typically stern expression replaced by one of pain and worry. The moment I was through the door, he directed me up the steps.

"Arran's office. We're mobilising."

I seized his shoulder, jerking him to a stop. "What the fuck happened? Why isn't anyone with Cassie?"

"She skipped out on the hospital and left without being seen."

I stalled. "Why was she at the hospital? Did she get hurt?"

"Where have ye been since last night? How have ye not heard about the lass whose neck got cut open?" At my apparent horror, he amended fast, "Dixie. Not Cass. They were wrong about the killer."

Fear stunned me. Struan grasped my arm and propelled me to Arran's office. Inside, grim faces met mine. Arran, Shade, Tyler, my sisters, Sinclair, a couple of people I didn't know. Jamieson was absent.

"Tell me—" Arran started.

I cut him off. "No, you tell me why you're all here while Cassie's tracker is showing her in the Four Milers' territory." I centred on Shade. "Why the hell is she there? She was supposed to be with you."

The enforcer went perfectly still. "Four Milers? Show me."

I produced my phone and opened the tracker screen. Cassie hadn't moved, her location still the same haunting distance away.

Everyone in the room leaned in, the same horrified expression rippling over all faces.

Sinclair swore violently and stabbed at his phone, raising it to his ear. "Pick the fuck up," he ordered whoever he was calling.

Tyler and another guy made for the door, and shouts

came from outside.

I kept my gaze on the leader of the skeleton crew, the sense of panic inside me only thickening until it clogged my throat.

Arran, the grave, vicious gang owner who I'd watched kill a man, paled and reached for a drawer to pull out a gun. "As we speak, Red is holding a summit in his brothel and electing his new second-in-command. Over the past week, I've been dismantling his empire while he's at his weakest, and today, we're bringing an end to his reign."

This couldn't be good. Not for my intuition, and not from how fraught the room had become. Shade likewise weaponed up, sliding a mean-looking knife into a holster.

Arran continued, "Red and his key people are all in that basement, locked away. His drug importers, his traffickers. Anyone who wanted a chance at that top position is there, and anyone else they control is guarding the place. We only found out about it last minute and decided on rapid action." His eyes flared in anger. "Whether he murdered the women or not, he still killed my friend."

Convict, he meant. I understood the anger. The need for revenge.

"What have you done?" I breathed.

I already imagined the worst.

The words from his lips confirmed the fact. "Jamieson is torching the place."

Urgency and desperation floored me. Panic formed on other faces as they made for the door.

Sinclair lowered the phone, his eyes haunted. "He isn't answering. It means he's in the zone."

The rest was left unsaid. Cassie was in that brothel, and her brother was burning it down.

44

Unknown

Slumped in the corner of the concrete-block basement, I played dead. I was pretty close to that state anyway, so keeping my eyes as slits and my breathing slow was no effort.

For weeks, I'd been in the Four Milers' brothel, down in the rabbit-warren basement in a storeroom next to the boiler house. Beaten to within an inch of my life as Bronson's plaything, allowed to eat, heal, rest, then fucked up all over again.

Remembering the details was becoming harder, though.

My mind moved sluggishly, and different parts of my ruined body throbbed.

During my first beatdown, my leg had been shattered and my skull cracked. A few ribs, too, though they troubled me less. It was the pounding in my head that messed me up. My brain swollen, probably, and my thoughts muddied.

I'd lost track of time.

Red and his gang had lost track of me. Or didn't care

that I festered in a corner with discarded sacks and broken furniture.

In the centre of the dank, semi-underground room, the drug lord sat tall behind a desk, holding court over his meeting and oozing cruel power. Overhead, a single lamp hung from the ceiling, swaying slightly so the edge of the light cut over the group around him, then fell away.

Only minutes ago, the space had filled with people, mostly men, some I recognised, some I didn't, then the Four Milers' boss himself had strode in, locking the door behind him. In a muscle shirt, and with his dark beard trimmed close to his chin, he owned the room. Awed looks followed him.

He was a piece of shit who'd earned that reputation to be feared. Dangerous, cold, and calculating. Not stupid, though. He'd ordered out anyone without a vested interest, meaning no witnesses, but that also meant that whoever remained would be bound to him after.

Or dead.

I was in the latter category.

Trouble was, I didn't have too many fucks to give at this point. Unlike remembering the danger ahead of me and the people around, I couldn't recall my name, let alone any reasons I had for living. At least I didn't feel any pain. My body was giving up. Death would be a relief.

"Next," Red snarled.

A scrappy, rodent-faced guy who'd just pled his case scuttled back, the circle of people swallowing him.

An older man untangled his arm from the waist of a glamorous woman, *Sydney*, my mind supplied. She used to be a dancer someplace. Maybe where I worked?

My consciousness ebbed, only returning when the

man settled into his story.

"My reputation precedes me, I'm sure, but it's Adam Walker for those of you who aren't in the loop." He stuck his thumbs in his beltloops and grinned.

Red sighed. "Get on with it, Walker."

Adam tipped him a nod of acknowledgement, as if they were equals. He was drunk, I guessed, his eyes reddened.

"This is going to disappoint the rest of you, but I'm a shoo-in for Bronson's job. It's already mine, and the reason for that, Red, my boy, is that I'm an asset to you. You can't do better than this."

Those thumbs came up to point at him.

Jesus fuck, the confidence of alcohol-soaked fools. Red was going to shred him.

The boss tilted his head, no hint of amusement in his stare. "Call me boy again and I'll slice your withered balls off and give them to your girl as earrings. State your case or step down."

Adam's smile dropped. "That job is rightly mine. I'm the same age as Bronson, but not fucked up on smack. I'm what you need."

Red levelled his gaze. "Next."

A meathead security guy stepped in front of Adam who turned purple.

"No, you haven't heard me out."

Another contender moved forward. "I want to—"

Adam took a swipe at him and shoved him back, then rounded the guard to slam his hands down on Red's desk. "You'll respect me. I've earned this."

Red didn't flinch. "How?"

"I... I killed the women in Deadwater. I did it to show you what I'm capable of."

Silence fell across the room.

Red held up a finger to stall the guard who'd moved directly behind Adam. "Explain."

"Those girls who had their throats slit, it was me."

Whispers started. Sydney shifted in her place, her discomfort plain. I'd heard rumours of murders, but the information wouldn't stay still in my head long enough for me to cling to it.

Red worked his jaw. "You, whose daughter is shacked up with Daniels, killed and left bodies outside his building. By all means, give us the details. Be precise."

Adam nodded, his jowls wobbling. "The first was the prossie on the steps. She sold sex across the road from my house. It pissed me off."

"So you just...?" Red lazily mimed cutting his throat.

Adam eagerly agreed. "Yeah, and the second, that American bitch, was walking home alone, so fair game. I knew it would impress you, that's it."

The man who'd stepped up to take Adam's place interrupted with a sound of disgust. "Liar. You're stealing my thunder."

Red gave a low chuckle. "You're claiming the kills as well?"

The second guy, who could've passed for a suburban dad with a neat haircut and polished shoes, jerked his head frantically. "I did it to get this job."

Adam snorted in derision, twisting back to eyeball his girl. "Bullshit. The timelines don't match up. Bronson's job is only on the table because Daniels' crew took him out. You're full of it."

Red lifted his chin at the newcomer. "Agreed. Step the fuck down."

Suburban Dad swore but slunk away, outside of the line of the light and towards the door.

Red watched him then cut his gaze to his guard.

The huge guy didn't pursue him. Instead, he reached for the back of his jacket, pulling a gun. People gasped and shifted away in a rapid huddle.

The guard handed the weapon to Red who raised it lazily as Suburban Dad reached for the lock. He didn't see his end coming. An explosion rang out, deafening me and painting the door crimson.

The body slumped. Fearful silence held the room with all eyes on Red. He handed the gun back to the guard and returned his gaze to Adam.

"Unless anyone else here wants to claim the glory, or walk out without my permission, you were saying?"

Adam swallowed. No one else made a peep.

He lifted a shaking hand, ticking off his fingers like he was working through a mental list. "I took out the next two as warnings to Arran and his crew. The girl who lived next door to the mayor's place. Because Shade is fucking the mayor's daughter. Then Alisha was a shot closer to home. My future son-in-law deserved it because you know what he did for me? Jack shit. That's right. No job, no money. Fuck him."

My hearing faded. Alisha? Alisha was dead?

My heart ached.

It couldn't be. She was so alive. A cornerstone of the skeleton crew, even if she preferred the sidelines. Once,

I'd hoped we could be something to each other, even just friends. She was dead? Ah fuck.

Adrenaline coursed through my broken body.

If Red didn't kill Adam, I would.

Mutters grew in the crowd, and the glances towards Walker shifted to more admiring than scornful.

A slight, dark-haired woman pushed through the group. Under the bright light, she slanted a look of disdain at Adam and centred on Red. "I know exactly who the Deadwater killer is, and it's none of these nobodies."

She was familiar, but her name evaded me.

"Moniqua," Red supplied for me. "Interesting choice of evening's entertainment for a girl like you. Better suited to working on your back upstairs."

She gritted her teeth but held her ground. "Like I said, I know who the killer is. I know that they took the prostitute just because she was there when they were angry, and the mouthy American because she was trashing the city's reputation. The house-sitter lost her life because they were in a rage that they couldn't get to the intended target, and Alisha was just to piss off Daniels. As proof that I'm good to my word and know what I'm talking about, I bring collateral."

"Which is?"

Something flashed in her eyes. "My cousin once told me that you vowed to take all of Daniels' women. Sydney is here. I'll work for you, so you'll have me. I'll bring one of his barmaids, too. But there's someone more important. Someone I think you'll be happy to see."

She gestured at a man in the crowd who slid off a beanie.

Lonnie, my mind supplied. Fuck. He was skeleton

crew.

Lonnie went to the door. "Need to go into the cupboard outside. No funny business."

The guard waited on Red's word.

The gang boss's eyes gleamed in interest, and he inclined his head. "The upstairs door is still bolted. You've got thirty seconds to impress me, or my pile of bodies is going to get bigger."

The guard dragged the dead man out of the way, and Lonnie disappeared from sight, emerging moments later with a hooded body in his arms.

A scent pricked my nose. Smoke? What the hell was burning? If anyone else noticed, they didn't show it.

Lonnie placed the body at Moniqua's feet.

Moniqua untied the cloth covering its head then tugged it free. At my slumped angle, I couldn't see the reveal.

Gasps came from around the circle.

Moniqua grinned with a savagery to rival Red's. "I bring you Arran Daniels' little sister, Cassie."

Horror struck me. I knew her. We'd met several times. She wasn't really Arran's sister, but he cared about her just the same.

The woman gripping an unconscious Cassie by the hair continued, "I gift her to you on the condition you hear me out. If you like what I tell you, then give me the role of second-in-command of the Four Milers. I'm smarter and more deadly than any of these pieces of shit. I won't let you down when that job is mine."

Red stood, his fingers braced on his desk and his focus solely on the unconscious woman. He opened his mouth.

An explosion rang out. A wall collapsed inwards, a deadly slide of breezeblocks crumpling onto Red. The ceiling fell in a clatter of plaster, and the lights went out, plunging us all into darkness.

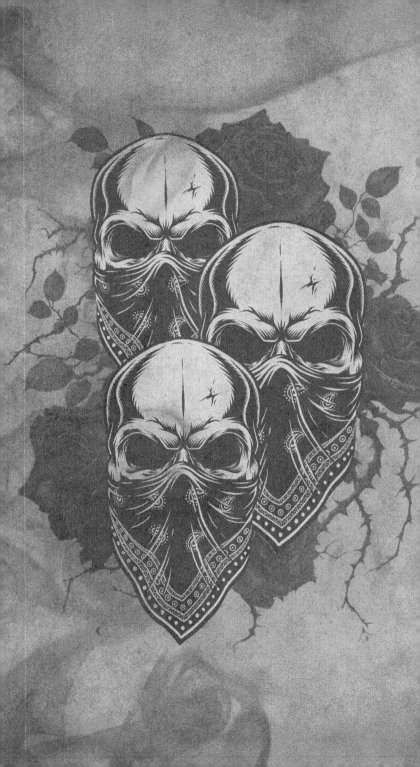

45

Riordan

Panic laced my fevered ride across the city. I paid no attention to traffic lights or speed limits, focused only on reaching the brothel and rescuing Cassie. She no longer loved me, but I'd give up my life for her if I had to.

Music played in my helmet's speakers, automatically connecting to my phone.

'Death of Peace of Mind' by Bad Omens had never been more appropriate.

Busting through a junction, I roared past a furniture showroom, red flames licking the exterior with three fire engines fighting the blaze with hoses. A Four Milers' money laundering front. Cassie had once filled me in on the way dirty money flowed in the city. Legitimate businesses fronted for the various gangs, passing huge sums of cash through the system to line the pockets of those at the top of the pile. Or to grease the palms of those with power.

A mile on, and another fire blazed, this time in a line of garages. An acrid scent filled the air, suggesting it was a drugs store. Arran really had set about destroying Red's gang.

I begged that Jamieson hadn't yet reached the brothel in his reign of arson and terror.

Behind me, engines roared and horns blared, Arran and his crew trying to keep up with me. I was faster. My need to reach Cassie was greater.

Speeding down Paignton Place took me past Moniqua's flat, all the lights on, and deep into the rival gang's territory. I hit the back alleys, thundering down a narrow lane to emerge on the street with the brothel.

Horror struck me.

The old church building burned. Yellow and orange flames flickered and lit up the early evening. I hit the kerb and half fell off my bike, my stomach gutting out, and my focus locked on to the destruction.

Smoke billowed from the windows. The open front doors revealed devastation inside. I ran up the steps but threw up my arms as the heat beat me back.

It was an inferno.

There was no way anyone could survive it.

"Pretty, isn't she?"

I twisted to see Jamieson in the shadows, leaning against the wall, and with his Zippo lighter in his hand.

He grinned, the reflected firelight on his skin making him demonic. "Easy, too. I emptied the building with smoke grenades then left each floor burning as I cleared it. The only people left are in the basement at the back. Red and his crew will be cooking nicely."

I lost it. With an anguished yell, I fell on him and threw a punch at his face, taking him down to the ground. Grappling his shoulders, I slammed his head into the pavement.

He wrestled me. "What the fuck?"

"Cassie's inside."

Jamieson's expression instantly slackened. His shock pierced another hole in me.

"Cassie is inside," I repeated.

And I was wasting time tackling her brother.

I straightened and staggered away, down the side of the building. Sirens sounded, adding to the discord of the night and the city in crisis. The emergency services hadn't reached us yet, but they weren't far behind. Neither were the skeleton crew.

I was the only hope Cassie had.

The only hope of retrieving her body, if that was all that was left.

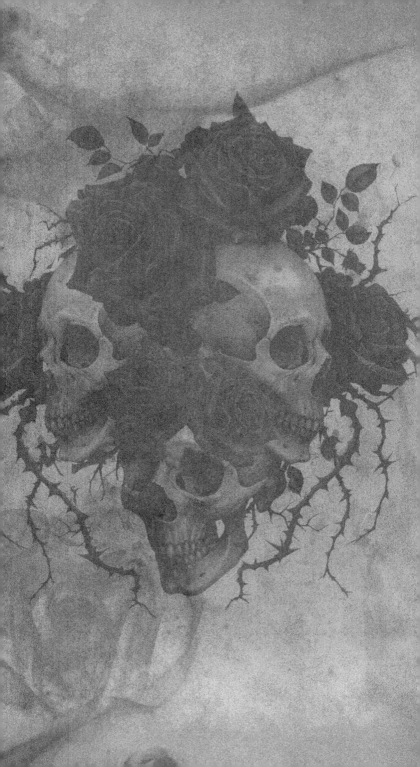

46

Cassie

In darkness, I stumbled, half walking, half being dragged by someone. My head weighed a ton, and my movements were clumsy.

The air tasted strange. I coughed. Choked. Fell to my knees.

An arm curled around my back and lifted me.

"Who are ye?" I managed.

"Friend." Pain laced his words, the voice familiar.

He supported me a few more steps, bricks or some sort of debris underfoot. The thick taste in the air grew heavier.

"Where are we going?"

"Old coal chute. You'll fit through it."

"Ye, too?"

I battled to place his voice, but my head swam again, and I lost touch with reality for another minute, only coming to when a splintering sound reached my semiconscious state. I struggled to stand, faint orange light coming through a hole in the ceiling.

It was nighttime. I'd been unconscious since... When? The hospital?

For fuck's sake. Someone had knocked me out. Kidnapped me.

"Where am I?"

The man took another swing at the wooden trapdoor, this time dislodging two short planks. It left a gap big enough for escape.

He didn't answer. "Put your foot in my hands."

I hesitated. I knew him. I knew exactly who he was. Why wouldn't my brain supply his name?

Something cracked overhead or outside, and through the hole in the trapdoor, a rain of sparks flew.

Fire. The building was burning. It was smoke infecting my lungs.

"Fucking hell, do it." He broke out in a coughing fit.

"Only if ye come with me."

"I won't fit. I can't climb either. But I can get you out." He didn't wait for a reply, grabbing me by the waist and shoving me upwards with a grunt of distress.

I grasped the edges of the broken wood and pulled myself through, boosted by the man below me. Splinters scratched my skin, but I cleared the hole and crawled to the gravel path, taking deep gasps of the night air.

Blackness overtook me, and I lay on my back on the cold ground. A whomping, beating sound grew louder, and I opened my eyes to an intense red fire scaling the old church building above me. Fear chilled me to the core. I had to get out of here. At the corner to my right, carved rock broke free of the structure and tumbled to the ground, cracking in two. In horror, I gazed up at the bell tower high above me.

Finally, my body obeyed my need to move.

I crawled to the edge of the hole. My saviour had called it a coal chute and said he wouldn't be able to get out. But the hole looked bigger now, and as I peered inside, there was no one down there.

"Hello?" I choked.

How long had I been unconscious this time? Long enough for him to get out? No answer came from below, but a bellow sounded down the track.

"Cassie!"

Riordan. My heart squeezed. I twisted around. The last thing I saw before his arms surrounded me and lifted me clear was the spire of the church tower crumbling and falling with a shower of fire and stone.

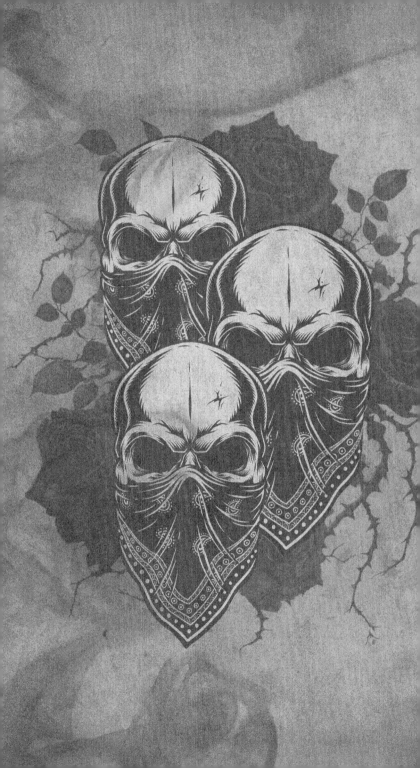

47

Riordan

Masonry from the spire landed with thuds around us, and I burst up with Cassie in my arms then sprinted down the side of the church.

Another chunk of rock narrowly missed us, and sparks chased our flight.

We emerged to a new scene at the front. When I'd left Jamieson, it was to an empty street, even the neighbours knowing better than to investigate.

Now, the flashing blue lights of police cars battled the yellow and orange flames, and a fire engine wailed, coming in hot.

A number of other vehicles blocked the road further down, Arran and Cassie's brothers leaping out with looks of shared fear.

"Get out of my crime scene," one of the cops yelled at Arran.

He ignored him, not spotting us yet, and said something urgent to Sinclair.

In my arms, Cassie stirred.

I hugged her to me, my body close to collapse from

the desperate fear of losing her. From finding her. From never wanting to let her go.

"Thank fuck." Footsteps pounded the track behind.

Jamieson swung around us, his frantic expression mirroring how I felt inside. He palmed his sister's face then swung to holler at his family, "She's here. Riot got her out."

He guided me clear of the church wall. Her brothers rushed up, Sinclair's expression crumpling then reforming as he took in the girl he considered a daughter.

The huge man reached for her.

I gave her up.

Watched as he cradled her then turned away, my arms empty, my heart even more so. I couldn't go far. I needed to stare a little longer. I needed to know she was okay, even if I wasn't the person who got to make sure of it.

I was nothing to her now, though she was everything to me.

One of the cops joined our party, and Sinclair lifted his attention from Cassie, his expression neutralising. "What the fuck do ye want, Kenney?"

Struan left the huddle and came to me. "Hurt?"

Dully, I shook my head. "I don't think so."

At least not physically. Emotionally, I'd died a hundred times today and wasn't done yet.

A rumble came from behind us, and someone screamed.

"The rest of the tower's going to go. Pull back," one of the other cops yelled.

We beat it to a safe distance, near the skeleton crew cars, Kenney coming with us.

Cassie struggled awake. "There's someone inside."

She pushed at Sin's chest. He let her down but kept an arm around her.

The tower shuddered and collapsed inwards, dust and heat reaching us even in our safer position.

The cop snorted. "If there was, they're flame-grilled and tenderised now. Better for my crime scene if I don't have to send anyone in on a rescue."

Cassie hung her head, sorrow etched into her features and her arms bracing her brother's. Then her gaze found me. Her eyes widened, and she broke away from him. I caught her in a selfish hug I had no right to claim.

"I thought I imagined ye."

"You didn't."

"Ye saved my life."

The hurt in my chest rebounded and echoed through me. I released her and shoved my hands into my pockets, forcing myself to back away. "Don't mention it."

Alone on the road, with scratches on her arms and fire in her eyes, Cassie stared at me. "What's wrong?"

Everything. Everything was wrong.

"Go back to your family."

"No. I want ye."

My very soul ached. "We broke up. I'm not yours to want anymore."

"No."

"Yes. It's over. I need to go."

Cassie's eyes filled with emotion, and she took in a rushed breath then turned and walked away.

Somehow during the course of the evening, she'd

changed her mind over what happened between us. I had no idea how she'd come to be here, but I couldn't stay and watch her take comfort from me only to break up with me for a second time when the shock wore off. It would kill me all over again.

I'd left my bike on the other side of the structure. Under the cover of the settling dust, the wailing of new emergency vehicles, and the building crowd, I'd retrieve it and get the fuck out of here.

Putting my head down, I passed her and the group. Arran called my name. Cassie was arguing with the cop. I kept going.

"Just give them to me, Kenney. I don't give a fuck who sees," she snarled.

I didn't stop.

Then a light weight slammed into me, Cassie landing on my back. I twisted in surprise, bringing an arm up to hold on to her.

Something clicked around my wrist. Silver. Metal. Handcuffs?

Cassie leapt down, her expression fierce, and her arm raised as she pointedly linked the other end to her wrist. She'd handcuffed us together. Police-issue silver bracelets.

I stared in confusion. "What are you doing?"

Cassie's bottom lip trembled, but she set her palm to my chest right over my heart and peeked up at me, her expression unlike any I'd ever seen her wear. "I love ye. Please don't break up with me. Whatever I did, I'm sorry. Just talk to me. Don't end this."

Horror and outrage crashed into my pain. "I didn't. You did. You fell out of love with me."

"What? That isn't true."

"It is." I reached for my pocket, jerking her arm with me where she'd secured us together.

I passed her the note.

Cassie took it, opening it like she'd never seen it before. Her gaze tracked the words then lifted to me. "I didn't write this."

My indignation shook. "But those words."

How could anyone else know exactly how to destroy me? I didn't finish my sentence. Couldn't.

Cassie gulped then sagged against me. I caught her.

Arran appeared at my side. He frowned at the cuffs then gestured to the crowd. "We need to leave. There are other gangs creeping up. Shit's about to go down."

In my arms, Cassie stirred. "I'm only going where Rio goes."

My boss barked a laugh. "Think we all got that, Cass. Now move it."

Together, Cassie and I jogged to my bike. There was no way I could drive with one hand behind my back, but Cassie had another solution in mind.

"Pick me up."

She wrapped her arms and legs around me and buried her head in my neck, allowing me to sit on my bike with her clamped to my front like a koala. She extended her wrist back to give me enough play to start the machine, and the engine rumbled beneath us.

For a brief moment, I buried my face in her hair, hardly daring to believe I had the right. Another rumble came as the front wall of the church disintegrated with a rain of fire.

It hid the roar of my engine as I got us on the road.

Unlike my careless, desperate drive over, I took it steady on the way back, letting myself just feel Cassie's body against mine and being careful for her sake because she was precious to me.

At the warehouse, Cassie's family and the skeleton crew arrived with us, filling the car park, with the club's neon-pink signs highlighting expressions of relief.

Cassie lifted her head from my shoulder, sighting Arran and Sinclair. "My apartment. Five minutes. I need to talk to ye all."

We went on ahead. Climbed into the lift. I held Cassie close the whole time.

Only when we were inside the front door of the apartment did I finally say the words I so desperately needed to get out.

"What if you forgot you wrote the note?"

"I didn't. It isn't mine. I don't know how someone knew to write those exact words."

I carried her to the kitchen counter and perched her on the side, standing between her knees. Then I grabbed up a first aid kit I'd stashed there and set about cleaning her wounds. I needed action. I needed to keep moving so I didn't wake up to this being a lie.

Cassie watched me, her arm shifting with mine thanks to her handcuff trick. "I told my therapist about being scared to lose ye, but there's no way she could've written that note."

"Would she have told anyone?" I wiped dirt from her cheek with damp kitchen roll. It came away grey with smoke stains.

"Surely not." Cassie took a rushed inhale. "I made

the call in Arran's office. If that isn't secure, he's a fucking idiot." She closed her eyes and dropped her forehead to my chest. "Or I am. I'm so sorry. Someone tried to break us up, and I gave them the ammo to do it."

"Who?" I wondered.

Her gaze shot back up, and her eyes filled with malice. "Your ex-ghoulfriend, Moniqua. Wait until the others get here and I'll explain what I know."

I couldn't make sense of anything. I'd lost her. Twice. Once to love and once to fire. Now I had her back, I had whiplash from the change.

Cassie's free hand cupped my cheek. With gentle pressure, she brought my face down to meet hers. Kissed my cheek softly. "I did a whole lot of soul-searching over ye because I didn't want to lose ye. My therapist told me that specific triggers were what killed my infatuations in the past, and I knew that ye saying three little words could be the end of us this time." Her gaze beseeched me. "Say it again."

"I don't want to in case it does something bad."

"Please?"

I forced the words out. "I love you. I'm so fucking in love with you it's killing me."

Cassie smiled. "I love ye, too. All that's happened is the obsession gave way to true love."

My chest ached. I asked what I had when she first told me, when I'd basked in the feeling of being adored. "Describe it."

"You're the centre of my world. As important to me as my family or maybe even more because it's different. It's like ye shifted up to their level then shot past into someplace new. I didn't know this was possible. I had no idea this feeling could be real, and I spent the day wallowing in trying to make sense of it."

My heart hurt. I notched my forehead to hers. "Don't say it if it can't be true."

"It is. I'm in love with ye, Rio. I'm never letting ye go."

I gave a strangled laugh. Shook the handcuffs.

Cassie laughed, too, then kissed me.

She tasted of ash and happiness, destruction and devotion. My world stopped and started again with that kiss. The broken pieces of my heart mended, stronger and better, fixed by my wild girl's love.

Finally, my mind accepted the change, and I cupped her ass to bring her tight against me, the act securing her wrist behind her back. I liked her in this position. I needed to tear off her clothes and see how pretty she looked chained to me.

Someone knocked at the door.

"Can I send them away?" I asked.

She sighed. "I wish, but there's too much to discuss. We're at war, and I intend to win."

48

Cassie

My brothers filed into the apartment, Shade and Everly with them. Everly hugged me carefully. Genevieve followed, and I whispered something in her ear. She nodded and disappeared with Arran.

"What did you ask for?"

I peeked up at Riordan. With my genius impulse to tie him to me, literally, we now couldn't be more than two feet apart. "I want my Skeleton Girls Detective Agency papers. We're hunting a killer again."

He frowned but circled the couch with me. We gave it up to Everly and Shade, and I sat on Riordan's lap on the floor, my brothers slumming it with us.

I patted Rio's knee, whispering among the chatter, "Good little armchair."

He put his lips next to my ear. "Stop wriggling or I'm going to be in trouble."

I ground lightly into him.

He stifled a groan. "You make me feral."

"Good, then my work here is done."

At my giggle, Jamieson shot me a look of disdain.

I scowled back. "No mean looks from ye, fire boy. Ye almost killed me tonight."

Instant shame sank over him. He hung his head. "I know. Sorry doesn't cut it."

I tutted. "Wait until Lottie finds out."

He pulled a face. "She already called when I was outside. Our next family meeting is going to go off."

Riordan hugged both arms around me. His touch and the warmth of my family being here gave me the boost I needed to own the shite I'd been through today.

Genevieve and Arran returned with the paperwork. I rifled through it, talking as I sorted. "We now know that Bronson isn't the killer of these women." I placed the victim papers out one by one.

As I spoke, Riordan took his keys from his pocket and pried at the handcuffs on my wrist.

"How do we know that?" he asked.

"Ye haven't heard about Dixie?"

He tensed up. "Don't tell me...?"

"She survived. Only just, though. She had surgery to repair her throat." My voice cracked.

Riordan kissed my cheek. "I'm so fucking sorry."

Across the circle, Genevieve shuddered. "I called the hospital this evening. Dixie woke up in the recovery ward. That's good news considering what she suffered. She won't be able to talk for a while, though."

She didn't say never. I held on to that and kept going.

"I was kidnapped from outside the hospital this afternoon. They knocked me out, and I woke in a cupboard with a bag over my head. When they came for me, I played dead, and they carried me to a cellar room and dumped me on the floor in front of Red who was holding court like a king on a throne."

I interlaced my free hand with Riordan's and held Arran's gaze. "By Moniqua and Lonnie."

Everyone reacted, swearing, or their jaws dropping in shock.

Arran stilled. "Lonnie?"

I inclined my head. "Even with my eyes mostly closed, I saw the way he watched her, like she was special to him. Which makes sense for why he betrayed ye. What they didn't know was I could hear everything being said in that room before they even took me in. Moniqua claimed she knew who the killer was."

Everly's eyes rounded. "Who did she say?"

"She didn't. The explosion went off, and half the room, including Red, was buried under a pile of bricks. I was carried out by someone else."

While Jamieson explained the timed explosive he'd used, I snuck a glance at Arran then Shade. They needed to know who helped me, but it was kinder to give them time to process it without everyone looking on.

I took a steadying breath. "There's a step before that I'm missing. Arran, how secure is your office?"

"On its own, not very. We use a noise-cancelling device in meetings."

"A what? Why didn't I know about this?"

"It's my fucking office, Cass."

"I went in there to have a private phone call. Someone listened in and used what they heard to break me and Rio up." Another factor closed in on me, pieces of a puzzle taking shape. "I think they also used that information to lure me out of the hospital. I had a text message."

My mouth dried, but I started again, focusing on Sin. "It was apparently from my birth mother, still alive, and texting me on my birthday. She asked me to call her. A minute later and I was bagged."

His big, so-familiar face softened in compassion. "I know you've always wanted answers, but the woman died a long time ago. We have her death certificate."

I dropped my head and nodded. "I know. I still believed it, though. How delusional."

He reached for my hand. Riordan kissed my hair. Arran muttered about getting my key back.

The moment passed, and I regarded the pieces of paper in front of me. "Moniqua worked out who the killer was, which means we can, too."

I wouldn't be outsmarted by that skank.

"Do you think she died in the church?" Genevieve asked.

I considered what I'd seen. "Most people were trapped. Red died for certain because he had his back to the wall that collapsed. He was buried, and the bricks blocked the door. If his henchmen and the others found another way out, they didn't take the route I did, and I didn't see anyone stumbling outside, did ye?"

Everyone shook their heads.

Shade sighed. "Kenney will recover the bodies tomorrow and give us more intel."

"We can't rule out that others survived, but I'm fucking glad you did," Arran told me.

I cocked my head at him. "Aw, look at ye, finally having

discovered emotions. Good job."

The soft expression in his eyes dissolved back into his typical scowl.

I grinned then returned my gaze to the Skeleton Girls Detective Agency papers, one arm back as Riordan continued his attempt to release us from our handcuffs. "What am I missing that she saw? The information has to be here, doesn't it?"

The person climbing through the car. The fact the killer hid their identity at every stage. That was another clue, wasn't it?

"They were recognisable," I said slowly. "Nimble enough to scramble through a car. Someone smaller? But strong enough to manhandle bodies?"

I held up our suspect list.

Shade took it from me. "We'll bring them all in. Every single one who's still alive."

I sat taller. "I love that plan. The next time I see Dixie, I want to tell her we caught her attacker."

Genevieve leaned to see the paper. "So our list is the mayor, sorry Everly, the councillors, Alisha's name should never have been on there, so I'm striking that out. Moniqua and her cousin, Don, who are both probably dead, Red, who just had a building land on him, and Bronson, and we all know what happened to him."

I curled my lip at Shade, still not over the fact that he'd killed that arsehole and I hadn't. "Is Piers still around?"

"Saved him for ye."

I brightened. "Aw, thanks. He should be questioned."

He chuffed a laugh. "If he's still able to talk."

"Also we considered Kenney, so grab the cop, and

lastly, Convict," Genevieve completed the list.

"It still could be someone else, a wild card known to Moniqua but not us," Everly mused.

She and Shade discussed it between them.

Genevieve interlaced her fingers with Arran's and squeezed his hand. He murmured something for her alone, the two of them sharing a moment.

It was comfort, because he believed Convict had died at Bronson's hands. My heart sank.

Arran's gaze settled on me. "Who pulled you out?"

I winced. There were two unpleasant conversations to be had, so it might as well be now. "I need to talk to Genevieve in private, for which ye should probably be there, and then I'll bring Shade into the conversation to answer that question. Follow me."

Along with Riordan as my quiet, constant support, and kind-of prisoner, I led them to the far side of the room, to where the city lights spread out beyond the arched, brick-lined window.

I centred on Genevieve. "I'm really sorry to tell ye this, but the conversation I overheard before Lonnie took me into the room was between Red and your father."

Her mouth rounded. "My dad was there?"

"He put himself forward as Bronson's replacement and had this whole speech where he listed the murders and claimed he was responsible."

Shock widened her eyes. Arran ran an arm around her, and Riordan muttered a quiet swearword behind me.

"Could...?" She swallowed and tried again. "Could he have been telling the truth?"

I'd already considered and dismissed the idea. "He's as

much the killer as Sin is a ballerina. He listed the murders like he was reciting it from an article. It was clearly a ploy for attention."

"That's why he had those papers in his flat," Riordan said.

Genevieve inclined her head, sorrow hanging heavy over her. "We went to try to find him, and he had newspaper clippings all over his coffee table and a knife, as well. It makes sense now. He was rehearsing so he could get a job. Stupid, stupid man. Do you think he, you know...?"

I got the end of her sentence without her saying it. She wanted to know if he'd died. I gave her a gentle smile. "I don't know for certain, but he was standing the other side of Red. I'm really sorry."

Arran kissed her forehead, and Riordan pulled her into a hug, his hand held back by the cuffs sliding to enclose mine in such a sweet move it hurt my heart.

It bolstered me for the other half of the bad news I had to give.

When Genevieve had collected herself, I gestured for Shade to join us. The enforcer strolled over, one hand to his tattooed throat.

I looked between him and Arran. "The person who pulled me out of the destroyed room was Convict."

Twin expressions of pain and emotion rippled over their faces. It socked me in the gut, too. The memory of the broken man. His certainty over his fate and all he'd still managed to do for me.

Shade recovered first. "But Bronson told us he was dead."

"He lied. It looked like he'd been through hell,

though."

"Did he talk to ye?"

"Hardly anything. I was half unconscious so I wasn't sure who he was until after."

Arran wheeled away, concealing whatever he couldn't keep inside. Genevieve went with him, and he embraced her.

He buried his face in her hair for a moment, taking comfort that I knew everyone in the room was noticing. My brothers had always said that Arran resisted emotional connections like they would scald him. I hated that I had to break this one for him.

He returned to me. "What happened after he got you out?"

"He pushed me through a hole he'd smashed through a coal chute in a narrow passageway but said he was too injured to climb out after. I think I passed out again, because the next thing I knew, Rio was calling my name."

"We don't know he's dead," Arran decided.

Shade nodded. "No body, no grieving."

I liked that. The hope, even if it was futile.

Arran's phone buzzed. He took in the screen, and his mouth fell open. His gaze came to me. "After you told me about Lonnie, I messaged the security team. Guess who just turned up downstairs?"

Shock and delight filled me. "He's alive, and he came back?"

"The dumb fuck did. Manny put him in my office with a guard but has given him no indication that we know what he did."

The absolute idiot. God, the opportunity this gave us.

I twisted to Shade. "He's mine."

The enforcer started to speak then sighed. "Fine."

"I need to fetch a weapon."

Riordan grumbled, "And I need someone to unlock us. If we're going down there, I can't protect you as well with one hand tied."

Reaching into my pocket, I pulled the key I'd taken from Kenney and unlocked the handcuffs with a clink of metal.

He gawked at me and rubbed his wrist. "I've been trying to pick that lock for the past ten minutes and you've had the key the whole time?"

I made big eyes at him. "I wanted ye to stay close. So shoot me."

With a gripe about using the cuffs on me later, he captured my face with both hands for a rough kiss that told me we had so much left to talk about, then kept with me as I collected my blade from the bedroom.

With Arran and Shade, we left the apartment, emerging from the lift to find my brothers had descended the stairs to come along for the ride. I rolled my eyes but travelled to the office. It was weird with no music pounding through the wall. Arran must've closed the clubs to secure the warehouse for an evening of lighting up the city.

Inside the office, Lonnie lounged against a wall, Mick perched on the desk.

Lonnie lifted his gaze and locked on to me. His smirk fell.

I didn't wait for the lies, reaching around him to slice my blade across the back of one knee. He went down like a fallen oak, screaming and clutching his injury.

I kicked him onto his back and placed my boot on his throat. "How did ye get out?"

"I don't know. I wasn't even there."

Leaning in, I drew a line across his face with the dull edge of my blade.

Lonnie went very still, only trembling as he clutched his ruined leg, blood blooming across his jeans and dripping to the floor.

"Do I need to repeat myself?"

"I crawled down a tunnel to the crypt and busted out a grate."

"Was anyone with ye?"

"No. There was too much smoke to see."

"Why did ye help Moniqua?"

"I didn't."

"Fucking liar. Ye betrayed Arran and everyone on your crew for that miserable cunt?" I hooked the blade under his chin.

Lonnie's terrified eyes leaked tears. "Okay. I did. She isn't a bad person. You have to believe me. All she wanted was security and a good job. I said I'd help her get it."

"Did she tell ye who the Deadwater murderer is?"

"No. I didn't even know that was part of her plan. Only that she wanted to impress Red which involved collecting you from the hospital."

Collecting? I locked my jaw. He'd knocked me out then took me into enemy territory without a second thought. "Is she the killer?"

"Of course not. She's just a girl."

Moron. "Did ye plant notes in the warehouse for me

and Alisha to find?"

His focus flew to someone behind me, Arran, I guessed. "No. You know I respected Alisha. I would never have hurt her like that."

Oh, fuck this guy. "Yet ye were willing to throw me to the wolves." I peered over my shoulder. "Anyone got any more questions?"

The lack of responses was enough.

I twisted back to Lonnie. "It's one thing ye double-crossing the skeleton crew, but it's another thing entirely crossing me. I don't forgive and I don't forget. What do ye think Red would have done with me?"

His lips worked soundlessly. He paled further.

"Ransomed me back to Arran? Sold me off? Or maybe passed me around for his gang to have a go at?"

"You'd have got out eventually," he blabbered.

Anger swarmed me. He'd happily given me over to be raped just so he could get his dick wet.

"I think different. Red was there to appoint a second-in-command. From that person, he'd need a binding gesture."

Lonnie's attempts to interrupt faded. He trembled.

"Red would have killed me," I informed him. "Which meant ye walked me straight into a death sentence. So I really need to stop fucking around."

Raising the knife, I plunged it into his chest, putting all my power behind it to pierce where it needed to go. People assumed the rib cage would protect the chest, but those suckers cracked like twigs under the right pressure. Lonnie gave an anguished scream, and I freed the blade with my boot to his torso and landed in another hit.

"Angle it deeper then slice up. Don't saw." Shade quietly guided my hand.

My next hit sank further in, delivering the killing blow.

Lonnie's howls turned to a gurgle. I wiped the blade on his shirt and stepped back, watching the life fade from him.

I couldn't let him live. Not only because of what he'd done to me, but for the fact that he was now an enemy to the skeleton crew. He'd grieve Moniqua and want revenge. Lonnie had signed his own death warrant.

When his body slumped, I breathed a sigh. "Well, that was an underwhelming first kill. He didn't even put up a fight."

"Is anyone else scared?" Shade quipped behind me.

"Ridiculously turned on," Riordan grouched.

My brothers made sounds of disgust.

I moved straight into Riordan's arms so he could hold me close, careful to keep my bloodied hand away so I didn't stain him. That didn't stop us needing each other close. I hadn't voiced my fear over my kidnap until now, but I could sense it had shaken him up, too.

To the tune of Arran arranging clear-up with Manny and bitching about my ruining his office floor, I let Riordan lead me away.

Back upstairs, Everly had brought food down from her apartment, and I washed the blood from my skin then fell on the pizza slices, suddenly ravenous.

Between bites, I thanked her. "I can't remember the last thing I ate."

"I figured. Riordan, you need to eat as well."

She indicated from her brother to the food.

A small smile curved his lips. "Best sister award goes to you, Ev."

Genevieve scrunched up a piece of paper and tossed it at him. "Hey, my dad died tonight, useless idiot that he was. You have to be nice to me."

His lips twitched. "My leather jacket still has holes in it from you stealing, I mean borrowing it. Just saying."

She growled and threw something harder. Then she closed her eyes and released a sob. Riordan hugged her and ruffled her hair. She batted him away and swiped at the tears, regaining her control as fast as she'd lost it while her brother joined me in devouring the pizza.

I liked this. I liked where I was living, and the fact my family was here. I loved Riordan and needed him to stay, right here in the centre of where his family was.

When we were finished, and everyone now knew what I'd done downstairs to the traitor, I pulled Riordan aside.

In our bedroom, I closed the door.

Backing him to the bed, I sat him down and stood between his knees, a reversal of our too-brief reunion in the kitchen. "I know I've put ye through hell, I know I'm impulsive and probably shouldn't be allowed out unsupervised, but I swear I'm all in with this. With you. Today is still my birthday—"

His green eyes crinkled at the edges. His cheeks flushed warm.

I put my finger on his lips so I could finish my words. "All I want as a gift is ye. It scared the shite out of me this evening when I thought our relationship was over. I want this, always. I don't want ye to leave ever again."

I gestured to the door and our collection of people

outside of it, then drew a line from his heart to mine.

Riordan enfolded me in his arms and kissed me. "Wouldn't leave you for anything, wild girl. I'm in love. Nothing could drag me away."

That beautiful swell of happiness rushed in me again. I prayed to the gods that was true.

Riordan drew his thumb down my cheek then set me out of the way so he could stand. He rifled through his rucksack and extracted a wrapped gift. He handed it over.

I grinned. Rattled it. The long slender box was heavy. "What is it?"

"Open it and you'll find out."

I tore off the paper and opened the box. Inside was a beautiful carved dagger with a stone in the hilt.

"Opal for your birth month."

I extracted it. Tested the edge. "It's the most beautiful present anyone's ever given me."

I threw my arms around him in a hard hug. Riordan hugged me back then carefully teased the weapon from my hand. He set it on the side table then picked me up and rolled back on the bed so I was sprawled across his body. Our kiss followed naturally, a hunger gripping me with power I could barely contain.

This, always. Me and him.

Someone knocked on the door.

"Sorry," I called, tearing my mouth from my boyfriend's. "The couple you're trying to contact are currently unavailable. Please try again in ten minutes."

"Twenty," Riordan countered.

Genevieve spoke through the wood. "Sorry, but people are leaving. I just want to make sure you're in the loop."

Reluctantly, we disentangled and returned to the living room.

Arran, Shade, and two of my brothers were at the door.

"We're heading out," Arran told us. "Riot, Cassie, you're staying here. Don't argue with me. Jamieson is, too, and Manny has the building security covered from downstairs."

They spoke in quiet voices, checking weapons and assigning their hits.

Genevieve regarded us. "While they're rounding up the suspects, we have work to do. Someone on the inside still placed those notes. Do you have both so we can compare them?"

I retrieved mine, and Riordan handed over his.

"Same handwriting. Where did you get yours?" Everly asked.

Riordan frowned. "From the bartender with glitter strands in her hair. She came out of the club and told me Cassie had left it for me."

"Lara?" Genevieve described her.

He swore. "That's her. She seemed nervous. I forgot all about it."

In all the fuss, I'd skimmed over that part, too, but I'd had my own suspicions about that woman.

Genevieve said, "Lara tried to break you up? But she's my friend. Why would she do something like that? Does that mean she left Alisha's note as well?"

Fresh anger had me clenching my jaw. "I spoke to her recently. She had me all wary over the fact she reduced her hours but moved into an expensive flat. She also brought Moniqua to me, though she claimed not to know her name. Shite. That's the connection, isn't it? The Four Milers were managing them both? Paying them off?"

The men at the door stalled, listening.

Genevieve's blonde eyebrows formed a line. "That liar. She does know Moniqua because I've talked about her in the past."

Riordan swung his gaze between us. "Which reminds me, I saw her in Four Miler territory. I barely thought anything of it, but the clues were all there."

Genevieve snarled, "At Red's meeting, did he seem surprised that Moniqua was putting herself forward for Bronson's job?"

I nodded. "Yes. He suggested she'd be better off working on her back."

She stuck out her tongue. "Pig. But it implies she wasn't already, so my point is that Moniqua isn't in that gang. Her cousin, Don, was a member, but she was making a play for it tonight. That doesn't smack of someone whose strings are being pulled by Red."

"She can't have left the notes," I said. "She didn't work here then. She had a membership to Divine, that's all. No access to the other floors."

Arran cut in, concluding what we were all no doubt thinking. "But Lara would've. I'll have Manny pick her up from her new address. Are you good to get the information out of her?"

By way of an answer, I cracked my knuckles.

A brand-new picture was forming in my mind, one where the warehouse had been infected by a ghoul and I'd even helped her. Felt sorry for her. Meanwhile, she'd taken Lonnie and Lara over to her side, assuming she was the instigator in both cases.

In the background of that, she had her eyes on Bronson's job. What had Lonnie claimed? That she wanted the security of it?

I almost, *almost* felt sorry for her.

For the fear that drove her, and for the lengths she felt she had to go for safety, all to lose her life in that fiery inferno in the church.

Behind me, Riordan swore.

I twisted, and he raised his phone to show me someone was calling him. I recognised the number ending six-one. I blinked, but it was still there.

"Holy shite," I told the room. "Moniqua's calling."

The witch wasn't dead after all.

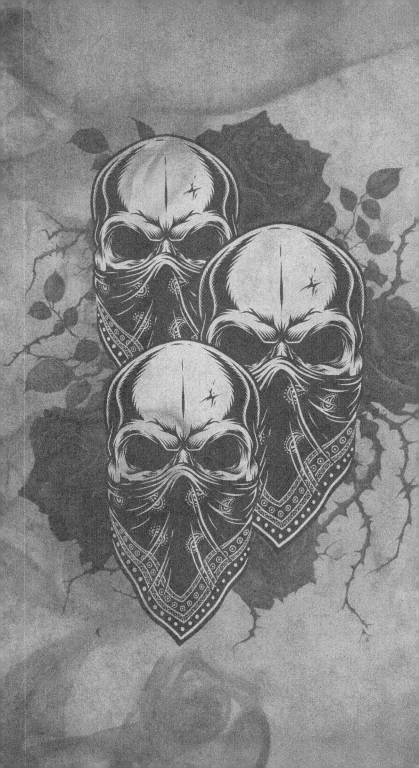

49

Riordan

A ripple of explanation sped across the room, and all gazes fell on me, heavy anticipation coming with a hush of complete silence. I swiped to answer, setting my phone to loudspeaker.

"Hello?"

A choked sob met my greeting. "Riordan? It's Moniqua. I need your help."

Fucking hell. It really was her. "With what?"

She hesitated. "You sound upset."

I curled an arm around a silent, vicious Cassie, bringing my wild girl close. Moniqua would've happily let Red kill her. She'd die for that, which meant getting to her. "I got dumped then my girlfriend was in a fire. It hasn't been the best day."

She made a sound of sympathy. "I'm so sorry Cassie died. That's tragic. Listen, you helped me so much when Don went missing. I need to tell you something. He's back."

Cassie's eyes flared.

I gripped the phone. "Your cousin's alive?"

"He is, and he's so angry. Please, I need you to come to me."

A recollection hit my mind. When I'd driven down her street on my way to the church, the lights had been on in her flat. Yet she'd been in the basement with Cassie as a prisoner. It was a small detail, but it added up.

"Why do you need help?" I breathed.

"I told you, he's in a rage. He's dangerous."

"Is Don the person who's been killing all the women in Deadwater?"

She sobbed again. "Yes. It started with your sister rejecting him. He saw Arran at her place and got so furious that he crashed his car. His friend died—that's whose remains they found. He went back to confront Gen but ended up killing the prostitute on the steps opposite your flat instead."

"He told you all this?"

She took a rushed breath. "He's coming back. I have to go. I'm so scared. Please, please, rescue me or I'm going to be next, and who knows who else. We're on an industrial estate. He had a drug deal."

She rattled off an address, then the call disconnected.

Silence filled the space. Shock, too. Because what the hell?

Cassie was first to speak. "What are we waiting for? We know who the killer is."

"She could be lying," Genevieve said.

"Okay, correction, she claims she knows who the killer is and we can torture her then decide if it's true."

Shade palmed his jaw. "Or all of it is a lie and she just wants Riot."

My girlfriend cracked her knuckles. "True or not, that piece of shite arranged to have me kidnapped. She offered me up to Red in exchange for a job. She's mine. All of ye got that? I'm going to go pick her up."

Her gaze flashed to me, feverish intent contained inside it. A challenge, too, for me to dare tell her she couldn't come.

This time, I didn't need the handcuffs.

I brushed her hair back from her eyes. "Your second kill gets to be a little more fun, but I'll grab her so she doesn't get spooked. Don't argue. You can have her after." I turned to her brothers and the skeleton crew. "We'll round her and Don up to add to the suspects haul."

Arran swapped a glance with Shade then turned to Cassie's brothers. "Sin, Struan, go with them."

I didn't argue. Cassie needed protection, and it was me Moniqua wanted, which meant arriving separately, and there was no way on Earth I was leaving Cassie unguarded.

We left Genevieve and Everly behind in the apartment with Jamieson, Shade providing a quick strategy for what I might encounter. Then there was nothing more than to kiss Cassie goodbye and take off on my bike.

It was strange riding solo over the bridge to the Scottish side of Deadwater.

The trip out to the industrial estate and suburb where Don was apparently hiding gave me an odd moment of headspace. I knew Cassie and her family were behind me, but I'd be walking into this alone.

It was past midnight and the streets empty and quiet. This part of town was far from the sirens and firelight of the burning city. Skeletal trees dotted corners, the leaves lost and scattered. I took the twisting road that led to the river, passing in and out of isolated yellow streetlights.

The houses here were workers' homes, marginally better than a slum and densely packed together. They were in clusters of narrow streets, blocked in by warehouses and with not a soul peeking out at the motorbike cruising by.

An intense feeling of discomfort settled over me, and fragments of my never-forgotten nightmare returned. The fear of being chased and ending up down by the water. All I needed now was my father to pop up and lodge a bullet in my chest to live out that horrible dream state.

I rounded the corner. Ahead, the road ended with two high-sided industrial buildings bracketing it and a scrubby wasteland beyond.

A final feature of my nightmare resolved in my mind.

When I fell under the water, I'd been clutching a little life. Something small and precious and beautiful. That was love. A part of me that hadn't existed but now burned bright because of Cassie. It was all the good and perfect things she made me feel. It was real, and I'd be damned if I was losing it.

I centred myself on the goal of bringing this reign of terror to an end and finished the trip down the road. Leaving my bike at the kerb, I eased off my helmet and scanned the scrubby ground which gave way to the riverbank.

There was nobody in sight. The main entrances to the warehouses were on the far side of both buildings, so all that was around me was the empty perimeters and the calm of the night. Only the rushing river and the distant sounds of the city made the backdrop.

A click sounded, and I spun around. A fire exit door opened at the back of the nearest warehouse. Moniqua stepped out. Relief fell over her expression, and she set her hand on her heart.

Once, I'd tried to be her friend. I hated for anyone to suffer, and she'd laid it on thick about how tough her life was with her gangster cousin and her inability to protect herself. Hindsight told me I'd been played.

Her smile appeared real, though. "I'm so glad you came. I've got something for you."

"Where's your cousin?" I called.

"In the building. He won't disturb us."

"But he's a murderer."

"Nah, not really." She returned inside, and clattering followed, then Moniqua backed out of the door wheeling a flat, metal trolley. With a body on it.

In horror, I recoiled. "Who's that?"

She turned, and the answer presented itself.

Slumped on the trolley was the mayor.

With difficulty, she wheeled him over then unceremoniously tipped him onto the road, apparently uncaring that fifty metres behind me, people slept in their houses and could look out at any moment.

Moniqua dusted her hands. "I knew you'd come. You've always been so kind and so good. It's why I brought you this present."

I stared at the body. His lolling head and pale skin. "I don't understand."

"You want him to acknowledge you, don't you? Baby, he's yours. My gift."

"Is he the murderer?"

Her smile morphed into a more frustrated expression. "Are you joking? After everything you've seen, you think this piece of shit could have done all of that?"

My gut tightened, and I dragged my gaze off my father. "I don't understand."

"God, men are such idiots."

"You said you knew who's responsible. If not Don, or the mayor, then who?"

She widened her eyes, the effect alarming. "It's me, silly. I did it. They say women aren't natural killers, but all she needs is someone to lift the bodies for her and wipe the blood from her cheek to even the playing field. I can't believe you thought he could've handled such a well-executed campaign."

She kicked the mayor's prone form.

He groaned. Unconscious then, not dead.

I scanned the wastelands beyond us and the road that led back to the houses. There was no sign of anyone else around. No indication that I had backup. Yet Cassie was listening to every word down the open line of the phone in my pocket. With any luck, one of her brothers would already be taking down Don, if he really was here. I was beginning to doubt that now, too.

For Cassie's sake, I had to make sure this was all clear.

I folded my arms. "How? Explain it to me, because you lied and told me it was your cousin."

Moniqua rolled her eyes. "Only to get you here, because I knew you couldn't resist the need to protect me. Don would've happily ruined any throats to get to the top, but he's not stealing my crown. Not after the shit he pulled. It was me in the car with him when Gen pissed him off and rejected him in favour of Arran. I barely survived his rage, and only escaped seconds before the crash. I rolled free, he toasted himself."

Then he was dead. "You're telling me that after that, you walked back up the hill and murdered Cherry?"

She flushed red. "I was having an emotional moment after losing my only family, can you blame me? A police car passed me, so I hid in the graveyard, and she...she was just there. She was kind. Her pretty smile was so wrong in the face of all that had happened, and I flipped. All that went through my head was a conversation I'd had with Don, our last, where he'd screamed about Genevieve and her new man, and how Arran Daniels' mother was killed by a single cut to her throat. Common knowledge, apparently. He said how easy it was as a killing method, and how Genevieve deserved the same. Once the idea was in my head, I couldn't get it out. He was right, too. Cherry died so sweetly. After that, I went home and found I wasn't all that traumatised by it, but I still had the problem of how to keep myself safe. I decided to do what my cousin intended. I'd get the job he coveted. Even before Bronson met his end, everyone knew Red despaired over his second-in-command. I wanted that top spot, and with Don proving he was a useless sack of shit, I decided then and there to be better than him."

"You went on a killing spree around the city." I put disbelief into my tone to keep her talking.

"I made a plan. I wanted that job. I also wanted you, so I went to Divine. I overheard Alisha say that a woman should be running the place, and it backed up my sense of doing what Don never could. So when that bitch, Natasha, started badmouthing the club and the city as a whole, I knew I had to bring her down. I had Don's stash of sedatives he'd stolen from Bronson and a boatload of anger. That tattooed enforcer guy very nearly caught me, which would be fucking hypocritical, because he drugs his victims. Don told me all about that."

She made a sound of disgust.

I needed to work this through to the end. "And after that?"

Moniqua's attitude shifted, her eyes darkening. "You made like your sister and rejected me. I followed you to the mayor's house, and I went back again. I would have killed the slut you were there to see, don't judge me because I didn't know she was also your sister, but I couldn't get in the house."

I'd led her there. Fucking hell, she would've killed Everly. "So you took your anger out on the girl next door?"

"Something like that. She was available, I still needed the practice."

"And Alisha?"

"That whore earned her fate when she slept with you."

I shook my head, the whole conversation one massive mindfuck. "I never slept with her. Why did you think that?"

Regret flickered in her eyes. "I saw the two of you go into a room together. I took a gamble and led her away with a note after finding out who she had a crush on. She really wasn't making a play for you?"

That was the night I'd started my skeleton crew job. Alisha and I had sat and talked, and the whole time I'd been thinking about Cassie who was let loose in the club. I'd worried for her safety. I'd wanted to trace my hands up her thighs to the ridiculously short skirt she'd worn.

My head pounded with the information.

"If it helps, I'm sorry about Alisha. It wasn't my finest moment, even if it felt like it at the time."

She'd strung her up from a lamppost.

She was insane.

Psychopathic, probably. She was telling me all of this like it was a conversation about the weather. Like it was logical for her to have done those things.

All of that had led her to Cassie.

"You would've killed my girlfriend."

She tilted her head, the effect unnerving. From a hidden sheath, she pulled a blade. "I would've used this to do the deed. Recognise it?"

I clamped my jaw.

"Your favourite knife."

At my complete lack of a response, her gaze turned exasperated. "Don't you remember? You admired it once when you came to my flat. It was Don's, but I quickly took over ownership when I realised it met your seal of approval."

She tapped the bladed weapon on her hip. "Lucky for me, I didn't need to waste my energy on that girl you fucked. The fire did that anyway. I mean, sorry for your loss and all that, but it's a lot neater with her out of the way. Now I get you all to myself."

Moniqua performed a little pirouette. "I can't tell you how happy I am that you're in this life, too. You were so anti-gang, but being in the skeleton crew has given you the training and experience you need to be with me. With your girlfriend and Red out of the way, we'll take over the Four Milers. The ultimate power couple. It's perfect, don't you think?"

She stepped closer and reached as if to touch my chest.

From the shadows, Cassie strode out, fury written all over her pretty, feral features. "Touch him and die, bitch."

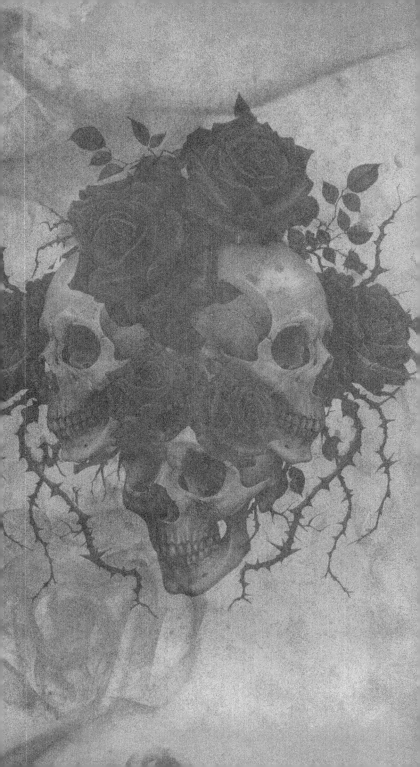

50

Cassie

I launched at Moniqua, throwing my fist into the wacko woman's face with a crack of knuckles meeting cheekbone. Moniqua screamed and whirled around, her knife arm extended.

I tossed a savage grin at Riordan to tell him I had her, no trouble.

I wanted this kill all to myself.

She slashed out at me, her snarl all the funnier from the blood oozing from her split lip, like her lipstick was melting off. Moments ago, I'd listened in to their conversation, out of sight, and texted updates to my brothers and to Arran and Shade.

I'd told Arran to stand down the hunt. We had the killer. The mayor, too.

He'd replied to say they were close by and would join us. Which meant I needed to wrap this up quickly or risk someone else stepping in on my fun.

"You're supposed to be dead," she spat.

"Yeah, well, call me the messiah, come to hand ye your arse." I roundhouse kicked her.

The knife flew from her hands and clattered from the road into scrubby undergrowth.

Moniqua started after it, but I snatched a handful of her hair and swung her around.

"Ye trampled on other women on your climb to the top. Ye killed good people. The world needs more of them, not less, ye miserable fucking cunt."

With a shove, I tackled her off the path and onto the short patch of wasteland. She swung for me, but I kicked her in the gut, leaving a muddy boot print on her wraparound dress.

"Bitch," she snapped.

"I've been called worse."

I swiped out her leg. Moniqua crumpled like a house of cards.

She stumbled down the bank that led to the river path. There was no barrier. Nothing between us and the raging river that boiled on its rush back out to sea, the tide having turned.

Shite. I didn't want her to fall in and drown. Not without me getting to her first.

Luckily, she found her balance and righted herself. "I'll kill you."

I let my crazy show. "Good luck with that."

From its sheath, I extracted my new favourite weapon. Moniqua stared at the bejewelled dagger, the pretty stone flashing in the light.

I held it up. "Like it? My boyfriend bought it as a birthday present. Oh, wait. It's not my birthday anymore. It's Halloween. Bye, ghoul."

Launching at her, I brought the blade down in an

arc, embedding it in the centre of her chest, right at the opening of her dress. She dropped to the muddy ground, her hands fluttering at the site of her injury, and her eyes so wide the whites looked obscene.

I wasn't done yet. "Ye never had anyone fight back, did ye? Cherry was a gentle soul, from what Genevieve told me. Alisha was, too. Ye either drugged or surprised Amelia and Natasha. Yet one on one with me, and you're scrabbling on the ground in your death throes."

Moniqua let out a hysterical sob. "Get it out. Get it out!"

I rolled my eyes and stood over her. "Don't make this awkward. You're dead anyway. But fuck am I letting ye take my present with ye. So just this once, I'll oblige."

Like with Lonnie, a boot to her torso freed my blade, and I examined it to make sure it wasn't damaged. On the path, Deadwater's murderer curled up around herself, shaking, bleeding, and making some fucking weird sounds.

A handful of her hair yanked her face back to me. I took my blade to her throat. "As vengeance for the four women you killed and for Dixie who survived your bullshit, I claim your life."

Confusion marred her face, but it changed to horror when I opened her throat.

Her body jerked. Blood ebbed into the mud. At last, she went still, and I breathed out then kicked her into the river.

It took her. Rushed to accept her then rolled her down deep with her curled fingers the last thing I saw as she disappeared in the turmoil.

Kneeling, I rinsed my blade of her blood.

It was done. After everything, we'd unmasked the killer and delivered justice. I could tell Dixie that I'd avenged her. I'd made sure to reference each woman so she met her end with their names in her head.

All of that because she wanted a job.

The shite people pulled to get ahead.

My brain got stuck in processing all that happened, and in a numb state, I trudged back up the short slope that had kept us out of sight, expecting to see Riordan waiting at the top. He wasn't there.

I discovered him face-on with a fresh hell.

The mayor was awake and pointing a gun directly at the man I loved.

"What the fucking Christ is going on here?" his voice boomed.

I froze, horror stealing my thoughts. The mayor had his back to me, so I sank to my haunches, keeping out of sight under the ridge of the slope. How could Moniqua not have searched him? Fucking amateur hour.

"I know you," the older man uttered.

Riordan's voice was low and sure. "You should."

"Why did you bring me here?"

He didn't know that Morgue-Minded Moniqua had been the one to capture him. In the distance, sirens sounded, and a curtain twitched in the nearest house, a side window giving them a view down to the end of the road and the wasteland. They couldn't have seen Moniqua's end, but they were witnessing everything between Riordan and the mayor. Shite. They'd called the cops. Probably recognised the high-profile man whose face was everywhere on billboards and on leaflets through doors. Or maybe scared of the gun he held.

No way was he hurting Riordan or allowing him to be arrested for the ghoul's crime.

Cursing the dead fucker for not disarming him, I scanned the area. I couldn't see either of my brothers, though one had gone on a fool's errand of finding Don, but at the far end of the road, two dark SUVs were parked up. Arran and Shade were here.

My mind raced.

Riordan said something to the mayor that I couldn't make out, but the reply was loud and clear.

He held the gun up. "Move a muscle and I'll kill you."

My boyfriend didn't flinch. "You know, I thought you'd recognised me in the past. Maybe even kept tabs on me. Piers Roache made a jibe about you not having a son you could be proud of, and I assumed you'd talked about me. I almost wanted it. But not now."

"Piers? Where is he? What have you done with him? I need him."

My phone buzzed, and I grabbed it out, reading the message under the cover of the slope.

> **Shade:** Piers is in the boot of my car. Trade?

They were watching, then. Stealthy as fuck because I couldn't see them. It was a good solution to get Riordan out of the crosshairs. Not that we'd give him up for real.

The distant sirens grew louder, and the mayor cocked his head. "Hear that? The police are coming for me. I assume this is a culmination of all the pranks you people have been pulling? My house is ruined. I have people breaking in or calling me at all hours. My workplace is a shambles. Sex toys are being brought to me by my admin team. Why? I demand answers. Rest assured you won't get away with this."

He was right. We needed the bastard dead, which would be harder to bribe our way out of if a dozen cops witnessed it as well as the nearby residents. My heart thumped, another thought piercing my panic. If they'd reported the weapon the mayor held, gun cops might arrive. Shots could be fired.

For Riordan's sake, I needed to think smarter. Quickly, I tapped out a message to Arran.

> **Cassie:** Do you still carry cash in your car?

He answered with the affirmative, and I arranged for him and Shade to meet me at the vehicles. Then I sent another to my brothers.

> **Cassie:** Sin, keep eyes on Rio. Struan, meet me up the road at Arran's car.

With a final look at Riordan, and a silent promise to return, I jogged down the riverbank to climb up out of sight,

Rounding the building, I emerged out the back of the short street that ran to the river. At this angle, I could only just see the mayor, pacing, and with his focus fully on Riordan.

Struan, Shade, and Arran waited for me.

Shade's eyes darkened. "Where's the killer?"

"I ended her. The river has her now."

"Moniqua? Ye killed her without me?"

Heh. Now he knew what it felt like. At my smug nod, he continued.

"What's your plan? Those fucking cops are coming in fast. If any are carrying, we could risk Riot's neck in the crossfire."

I shuddered. He wouldn't die. I'd take a bullet for him. "No guns. Don't rush him. So far, they're only talking. The only way the cops know this is happening is because one of the residents called it in, which means witnesses." I made move-it hands at Arran. "Give me the cash. As much as you have."

He opened the boot of his car where I knew he had a safe under the boards. "What are you going to do?"

"Un-witness them."

I faced Shade. "Carry Piers down. Arran, offer him as a trade."

Shade wrinkled his nose at his ride. "He's not looking so healthy."

I shrugged. "The mayor wants him badly. There's a reason for that. So long as he's breathing, we have to trust that it will stand."

They took off to do my bidding. With the bundles of cash in my hands, and my brother playing bodyguard, I strode out into the middle of the run-down street. The front doors opened directly onto the pavement without front gardens, and a quick glance gave up no CCTV cameras or doorbell cams. Unsurprising in a neighbourhood where few had anything worth stealing or funds free for anything not vital. I slipped down to the end house and waved the money at the living room window, trying to keep out of sight in case the mayor turned.

"Whatever ye think you saw, no ye didn't," I hissed through the glass.

Voices came from inside. A hushed argument. Then a figure appeared behind the window.

"What's the offer?"

I bit my lip to stop from smiling then peeled off a chunk of notes. "Open up and I'll tell ye."

The window slid out. I made the deal. "The mayor arrived for what looked like a drug deal or maybe a hookup with a prostitute. It went wrong. Ye saw him with a gun or maybe a knife. You're not sure. Then they all left. Keep to the truth and I'll pay again in three months. Let the cops through and that won't happen."

Across the road, another window eased open.

Quickly and quietly, I made my deal with half a dozen residents, none of them blinking at the body being carried past by Shade.

I fell in behind the skeleton crew, coming into earshot of the conversation again. Struan slipped into the shadows.

The mayor was still holding court, waving his gun and loving the sound of his own voice. "One thing I need to know is what happened to my family tree? Why take something of no value to you but great personal value to me?"

Arran and Shade strolled into view. The man stopped talking.

I slowed, needing to stay out of his sightline. But then an arm hooked me and a hand clamped over my mouth, cutting off my air completely.

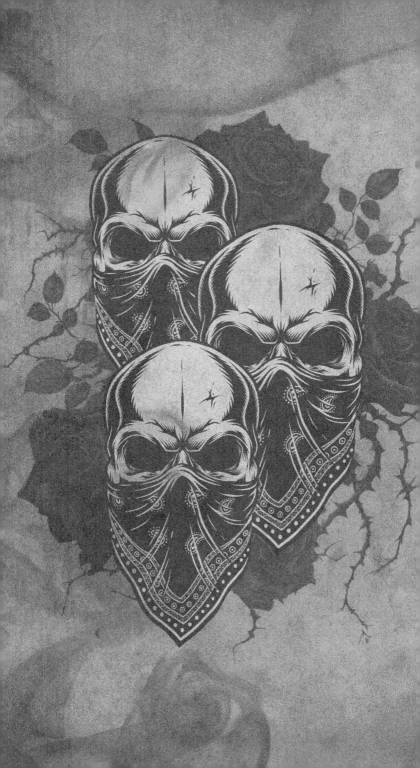

51

Riordan

Shade dumped Piers on the ground, and Mayor Makepeace's mouth fell open. I almost shared his shock. The unconscious would-be rapist's face was a mottled mess of bruises, with blood on his shirt and other suspicious stains elsewhere.

"What have you done to him? Don't you know who this man is? He's vital to Deadwater."

Shade shrugged. "After what he did to Everly, it's vital that he understands the consequences."

The mayor scowled at his ex-stepson. "When I'm elected again, I'm cleaning up the gangs, starting with yours. Piers will bring investors to the city. You don't know what you're dealing with."

"So it's money, then," I cut in.

His gaze shot back to me.

"And I dare because I've spent my life thinking about this moment. You asked a lot of questions but never waited for an answer. Abigail didn't want me to know you, and now I know why."

My father's mouth opened. "Abigail?"

Down the street, police cars arrived, the sirens silencing but the blue lights swirling over the narrow houses. From several, residents spilled, flagging them down and getting in the way.

I pushed on with my half-rehearsed speech. "I'm glad to know I'm nothing like you. It's been good having this talk because it's filled in some gaps on the type of person you are."

"You're Abigail's son?"

At last, the recognition I'd craved resolved in his eyes.

A kind of peace settled inside me. I'd missed out on having a father figure, but I'd found it in the men of the skeleton crew and in Cassie's brothers. More, I was the son of a good woman. A woman who'd raised me to be just like her—kind, caring, willing to give everything for what she believed in. My mother had gifted me all the things Cassie loved and everything I intended to keep giving back.

It turned out, I hadn't missed out on anything at all.

The mayor's aim faltered. His hand came slowly down so the gun pointed at the cracked tarmac road. "I've thought about your mother every day for years."

From my back pocket, I extracted her note and brandished it like it was a far more dangerous weapon than the one he held. "She hated you. She never thought about you, and I know that because it took a threat to her life for her to even tell me you existed. She wanted nothing to do with you after getting pregnant, and it says that right there in her own hand."

In the letter he'd kept for all these years. I hoped my words hurt.

"My mother rejected being your mistress. She called

you out on your shit and left you, and I am so fucking glad. What I need to know is why did you keep this?"

His gaze stuck to the paper. "I missed her. I couldn't throw a piece of her away."

"You wanted her back?"

"She would've stayed if not for falling pregnant. I already had one child. I couldn't have another outside of my marriage. Her mistake ruined us."

Her mistake? She'd been a teenager. As if he hadn't done that to her. It all made sense. The money he'd offered her had been to get rid of me.

I'd heard enough. "Want to know what wasn't a mistake? What I did to your painting. The family tree you left me off of burned beautifully in a fire that lit up the night. I wish you could have seen it."

The moment of poignancy left the mayor's face, and he snapped the gun back up. "You little bastard."

The word rippled off me. I smiled. "Better a bastard than a man raised by you."

He swore again, cursing me to the night, his weapon never leaving my direction.

I tilted my head. "My sister, Everly, told me a thing or two about you that made sense. You started deducting rent from her salary a few months ago. She didn't mind, but why would a man in such a high-profile job need the cash? Then there was the missing watches in your collection, the lack of a decent security crew, and the cheapo cameras you installed. I overheard Piers talk shit about you needing his cash. You're broke, aren't you?"

From his slump on the ground, Piers lifted his head. "I'll do whatever you ask if you let me go."

His abrupt splutter pulled all of our attention his way.

Piers rasped out desperate words. "He wants my connections, and we had a sweet deal planned, with my people only interested in the clean-up of the gangs because we run a coke line to executives and the gangs undercut us at every turn. I'll back out. You'll never see me again." He swung his bleary-eyed gaze to Shade. "I'll apologise to Everly."

He dealt cocaine as well as misery? This guy was a peach.

Footsteps drummed on the road. I tore my gaze to the cop Cassie called Detective Dickhead pushing through the crowd, the rest of his officers held back by a mob of residents.

"Shut the fuck up, Roache," the mayor snapped. "You were privileged to get to work with someone like me."

Piers choked on a pained laughed. "A man who can't raise his election campaign money from his own investors after years of ripping them off?"

The mayor purpled and turned to the incomer. "Chief Constable Kenney. What are you standing there for? Arrest them. I've done your work for you and found the culprit of all the crimes against me. We have the evidence we need. My testimony. Eyewitnesses." He gestured to the collection of people up the road. "Not only that. See what they've done to my business associate."

Kenney regarded the slumped body on the ground. His gaze travelled from Piers to Arran then at last to me. I couldn't read him. Tension strung me up tight.

Not for myself. I didn't care what happened to me.

If Cassie panicked and ran in, she could get hurt, and I knew my wild, impulsive love was probably considering doing exactly that.

"Riordan Jones, after your recent arrest, I was hoping not to see you again," the chief constable announced.

The mayor smiled, his eyes cold. "Previous arrest? This is the man you told me you'd found a knife on, isn't it? Like I said, I own the police and this city. Not you, Daniels," he spat at Arran. "Not your gang of thieves and murderers."

Arran ignored him, his voice low and deadly. "Careful, Kenney. First, because if you go looking for that blade, you might not find it where you left it, and second, remember what I have on you. Choose well."

For a beat, Kenney said nothing. Hope sprang in my heart. He was waiting to pick a side. Us or the mayor.

Cassie had told me about a dossier of evidence Arran had on the cop. I had to trust that invincibility would stand.

"Seems to me you have a choice, Chief Constable." I gestured to the flashing blue lights of the police cars. "Take your people and leave. Report it in as a scuffle gone wrong, but with all the parties absent by the time you arrived."

Kenney clucked his tongue. "Funny, that's exactly what the residents are arguing."

The mayor blustered, "Get your head out of your ass, man. He kidnapped me. Drugged me, too. Are you going to allow that in your city?"

I shrugged. "Walk away and leave me to this chat with my father. I'm pretty certain that after, he won't be up for the election anyway. Being broke will do that."

Kenney raised his eyebrows at me then peered at Arran. For a beat, the man hesitated then whistled a tune and strolled away.

The mayor's eyes widened, then he bared his teeth. "Stop. How dare you turn your back on me?"

Kenney didn't pause.

The mayor fumed. "Daniels, you think you've won but you'd better watch your back. You enabled your fucking enforcer to rob me of my daughter, all after I maintained a deal with you for years."

"A woman you abused. You broke our agreement. The deal's off," Arran intoned.

I cocked my head. "You don't seem to understand that you've lost. You've got no money, no daughter, you never had a son, and now, you're nothing."

The mayor gnashed his teeth then broke from his position and charged me.

I didn't try to hold back a cold smile. I needed this. I needed him to break so I could.

He threw a punch that I dodged, backing me to the river.

"The years I wasted thinking about your fucking mother are over. I would've given her anything, and all she did was throw it in my face."

Whatever cool I'd had was lost. I let my malice show. "Because you're a worthless piece of shit. A bad person who deserves to be alone."

His lip curled in cruel conviction. "If I deserve that, she deserves this. To lose her precious son."

Shock hit me. How could he not know she was dead?

The mayor of Deadwater thrust the gun at my chest.

A howl of outrage broke through the night.

Then a small figure crashed into my father. He wheeled around, his hand with the gun flailing. My heart stopped when my brain registered exactly who. Cassie clung to his back, holding tight like she was on a rodeo bull.

There was nothing in her expression but rage.

I couldn't let her risk her life. Not for revenge I'd needed and had taken. I rushed him, grasping for the weapon.

He swung around, trying to throw Cassie off, and then the mayor fell onto me and the three of us tumbled down the slope towards the water.

Everything that happened next went by in a split second. No slow motion. No time stopping so I could see it in freeze-frame details. No recognition of how this resembled my dream but deviated in key details.

All I knew was the hard hit. The desperation to protect the woman I loved.

And the explosion as the gun in the mayor's hand went off.

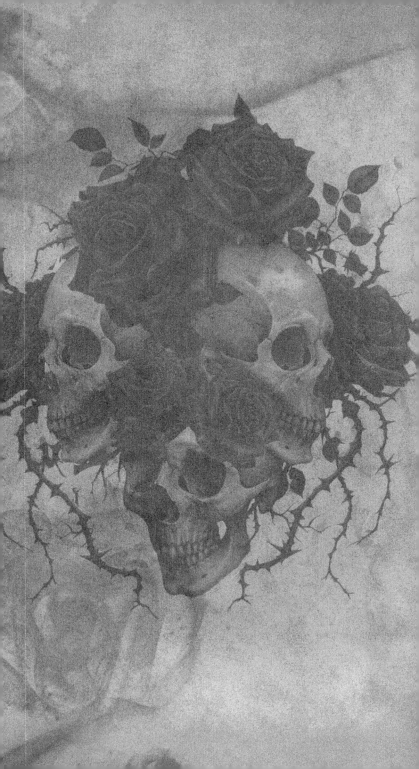

52

Cassie

The blast tore through the night. I screamed in fear and wrestled myself free from under the mayor's arm to sit astride his body.

His eyes danced, and he bucked up against me, both hands flying to my hips. "Get off me or I'll make him watch his little bitch scream as I fuck her over his corpse."

Without pause, I raised my jewelled dagger above my head and smacked it down into his chest, just as I'd done with Moniqua.

It pierced skin and bone.

Under me, the man went still, his amazed face draining of blood while red bloomed on his chest.

I loved it, how they didn't expect me. They made one quick assessment and decided I was harmless. The steel in the mayor's heart changed his tune fast.

Jumping back, I grasped the gun from his hand and threw it as hard as I could in an arc across the fast-flowing Deadwater River. It disappeared beneath the rippling surface without a sound.

Only then did I chance a look at Riordan.

My imagination threw a hundred images at me. Of his precious blood spilling. Of a deadly head wound. Of a ruined heart.

Instead, I found an intact, unbloodied man.

Riordan had been knocked on his arse, but there was no visible injury. He leapt up and ran to me, grabbing me away from the man gurgling at my feet, under the watch of Arran and Shade who'd sprinted to the edge of the slope.

Dizzy, I touched Riordan's face. "The bullet didn't hit ye?"

He palmed my cheek, his other hand gripping my waist, and his expression furious. "It grazed my shoulder and tore another fucking hole in my leather jacket. What the hell were you doing?"

I sobbed and fell against him. "I thought he'd killed ye. I was so sure. I almost couldn't check."

I'd wanted to jump the man from the moment Sin had dragged me into the shadows around the warehouse. It had taken everything in me to convince him to let me go.

Riordan gave a growl of deep emotion and enclosed me in his arms. "I thought the same about you. You reckless, beautiful, wild girl."

He kissed me, hard and with total ownership over the way we connected. I sank into the embrace, and happiness replaced my other thousand more stressful emotions.

At a gurgle from the man behind us, I reared back so I could see Riordan's face. "Look, I saved him for ye. He isn't gone yet. Finish him. Take your revenge over the man who wanted ye dead."

Just like with Moniqua, the river conditions were perfect for taking a body straight out to sea.

"There's half a dozen police officers up there."

"And twice that number of residents who will lie on my command. Kenney will go wherever we pull his strings. They can't see us now, but this arsehole tried to shoot ye. He pimped out his daughter. From what he was yelling, he wants to end the crew ye committed to. Do your thing, then we'll walk away. I promise you we'll be fine."

Riordan held my gaze for a moment, consideration in his green eyes.

Realisation struck. Riordan's revenge had already taken place. He'd shown his father exactly what he thought of him and he'd come out on top. My beautiful, warm, brave-hearted boy wasn't a killer, but that was why we made such a great team.

I pushed up on my toes and kissed his cheek. "Or I can do it for ye."

His slow nod gave me life.

Dropping to my haunches, I read the mayor the riot act. "For decades, ye schemed, hurt, and abused anyone ye pleased. Ye tried to murder my fucking boyfriend, a man who deserves only love, not a man like ye in his life. The trouble with that is there are consequences to such actions. Men in power seem to think they are above reprisals, but I'm thrilled to tell ye that isn't true."

Tugging the knife out, I slammed it in again. And again.

No one approached us. No figures were on the bank now, our friends clearly seeing we had this.

Shade would get the crime scene cleaned up. Arran would keep Kenney on our side. I'd hold up my bargain with the residents.

Blood speckled my hands on my final hit. The mayor's head thunked to the earth.

Without further ceremony, I indicated for Riordan to roll him into the water then rinsed my dagger and my fingers while Deadwater's flow carried him to a watery grave. In a few months, when he washed up on a distant coast, his absence would be paired to the police report Kenney would place where a drug deal went wrong and cost him his life.

Turning back to Riordan, I registered the look in his eyes.

My lips curved in a smile. "You're turned on."

He exhaled a laugh. "I can't help it. Your brand of crazy works for me."

Now that, I intended to exploit forever.

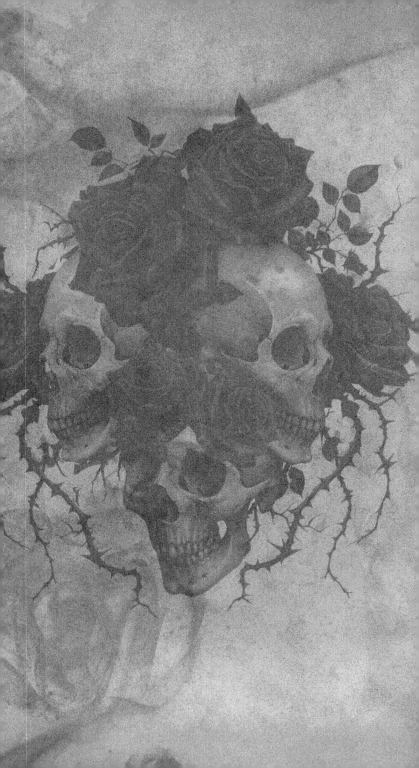

53

Cassie

My head thumped with too much information. With exhaustion, elation, and everything in between.

We left the crime scene on Rio's bike after I directed Arran to retrieve Moniqua's knife from where it had landed. I believed her, but DNA evidence of some kind would put the debate to bed forever.

Then we drove off into the night, through the arguing group of residents and cops, no one stopping us.

At the warehouse, under the neon-pink glow from the signs, a few crew members wrestled the councillors from our suspects list into the basement.

"Just let me apologise again to Everly, I mean Miss Makepeace. I swear I've been respectful to women," one blathered.

Riordan carried me past. Someone else could handle them. We deserved time alone together.

In our apartment, he locked the door and took me to the bathroom. Set me on my feet while getting the water running then reached for my kitty shower cap.

I shook my head. There was blood in my hair. I needed

it gone.

Riordan seemed to understand. He stripped me.

I slid his jacket off him, then his shirt. My stomach gutted out at the red line where the bullet grazed. It could've killed him. Just a few inches lower, and I wouldn't be able to do this anymore.

He removed his remaining clothes and drew me under the spray with him.

"Sure ye want to get this wet?" I cupped a hand over his wound.

It was the first time either of us had spoken since leaving the crime scene. Later, I'd recognise that we were in shock. Right now, all I could do was follow my instincts.

Riordan choked a low laugh. "You were in a fire, then a death match with a murderer and my father, and you're worried about me?"

He sank down, bringing me to his lap on the shower floor. Rain pattered down on us in a warm, lulling storm, and I huddled against the man I would've died for.

For a long minute, we did nothing but hold each other.

"Show me how to wash your hair. Which of these to use in which order." He gestured to the array of products I had lined up, then in steady devotion, worked through my method.

Under me, he got hard. I was wet from more than the shower.

Neither of us did anything about it, fixing each other first so we could make good our night of horrors. When we were clean, I put ointment and a bandage on his injury. He dried my hair.

For bed, I stole a shirt he'd worn a few days ago which

carried the scent of his aftershave. He took it right off me. Tugged me to straddle him. Let me own him as I rode us both to an emotional climax.

After, when my breathing regained something like a regular pattern, I snuggled Riordan, listening to his heartbeats. "I'm so in love with ye."

His chest rose and fell. "My turn to say the words. I owe you all of them. I really thought I could be near you and resist the pull. I told you I wouldn't fall in love. What gave me the right?"

I raised a shoulder. "Delusion?"

A low chuckle returned. "Entirely. Trouble was, I had already started falling from that first glimpse. You fascinated me. Not only the fact that your flawless face and incredible body are enough to bring me to my knees, and those big blue eyes see through me at every chance. But your mind does things to me I didn't know possible. How fucking smart you are. Your crazy, impulsive, and yet perfect acts. The tracker on my bike? Fucking hell. I get hard every time I think about that ballsy little number. Everything about you is hardwired to turn me on, and yet I told you I was good with a time limit." He took a short breath. "We're official, right? I didn't imagine you telling me you want it all with me?"

My lips curved. "Trust me, I am never letting ye go. You're everything I'm not. Calm, in control, hot as fuck."

He nuzzled me. "Agreed on the first one but definitely not the last, wild girl."

"I still can't get over the fact that you're real. Ye were mine from my sighting from up on the plinth in Divide, and you'll be mine forever. Just try getting away. I've still got those handcuffs."

He groaned and tipped up my face to receive his kiss. Our night went on the same. Sleeping. Giving up words of love. Having sex in between. Finally resting together when the adrenaline crashed and delivered us into exhaustion.

Late in the afternoon, showered and dressed, I rang the hospital to check up on Dixie. The ward nurse was able to give a short update that my friend must've been conscious enough to approve, but said she was refusing visitors. My heart hurt, but I'd try again tomorrow. Next, I called a meeting of the Skeleton Girls Detective Agency. Plus hangers-on.

Riordan travelled with me up to Genevieve's apartment on the top floor. "Should I be honoured to be included in your club?"

"One hundred percent."

I snagged his hand. Held it.

As badly as I wanted to see my girls, this wasn't going to be easy.

In the apartment, Rosie, Genevieve's cat, darted over and wound through my legs. I stooped to stroke her furry brown head, but my focus was on Everly.

My heart sank at her stricken expression.

Crossing to join her, I clasped my hands in front of me, wishing I could go in for a hug but not knowing if I had the right. "I'm so sorry about what happened last night. About your dad."

I'd murdered her father. No matter what kind of person he'd been, he was still her closest relative, and I'd stabbed him in the heart.

A tear slid down Everly's cheek. "I can't believe you're apologising to me. He would have killed you. He tried to kill my brother. Connor told me what happened, and I hate that my father did that."

"You're not angry with me?"

"Of course I'm not. I'm sad, but that's because of all the things he did, and what he should have been. I can live without him. My life will be better. I would have been devastated if he'd hurt you or my brother."

My voice shook. "Can I give ye a hug?"

She wound her arms around me. "I thought you'd hate me."

I gave a hiccupping laugh. "I thought you'd hate me, too."

Another pair of arms enfolded us. Genevieve's. She didn't say anything, but I suspected she felt the same way as Everly about her loss. The sadness was more for what could have been, rather than the men themselves.

We broke apart, and Genevieve guided us to the kitchen where she had coffee and pastries laid out.

Everly sent a shy smile Riordan's way. "Are you okay?"

His expression was kind. "I'm good. I need to tell you that I'll clear up the mess in your old house. It's yours now, but Cassie's brother and I trashed the place."

She tilted her head. "Ours. We'll sell it and split the profits."

He started to refuse, but she shut him down, batting back his words.

"Ours. We're both his children, and he owed you. I'm your big sister so don't argue."

I took a healthy sip of strong coffee, watching on and seeing something sweet after a world of pain. Riordan surrounded by family. Not shutting himself away but opening up.

Genevieve guided us to the sofas. She sat curled up against Arran. "So Moniqua was the murderer all along. That feels so crazy to me."

I wrinkled my nose. "Same. I gave her a job. All that time she was killing women in an attempt to prove herself and climb to the top of a gang. I'd almost respect that, if she'd targeted the right people. But fuck her. Not only that but also for wanting my boyfriend. Fricking ghoul."

Riordan hugged me close. "I didn't suspect a thing or even consider her as a suspect. Not even when I read her name on your list."

Genevieve nodded. "Honestly, same. Yet the evidence was there all along. I even saw her with the knife she said she'd used. Arran showed me a picture he took last night. She was cleaning it in her flat a few months ago, this was right when I was meeting Arran, and it feels like such a clear warning sign when I think back."

Murmurs agreed with her.

The metaphorical smoking gun.

She continued, "I was so sure Cherry's murderer was someone she knew. That it was more targeted than that."

Arran shook his head. "I thought it was a message to me."

"Same." Shade raised his eyebrows.

Riordan said, "All that time and it was a woman on a campaign of terror in order to get a fucking job."

Genevieve exhaled. "It's just so hard to believe a woman would do something like that."

Her boyfriend checked his phone. "The DNA matching results will be in soon from her weapon, but I don't think we're looking for anyone else."

I eyed him, still not entirely over the fact that he and Shade had second thoughts about Bronson but hadn't said a word.

Genevieve sat forward. "After you left last night, Manny brought Lara to us. She was already crying when we took her into the office. I didn't even have to glare and she was spilling a confession. The first note she delivered was done in ignorance. Moniqua handed it to her, and she passed it on to Alisha, then got scared after Alisha's murder. She didn't want anyone to blame her, and didn't want to lose her job, so she kept her mouth shut. After that, she was blackmailed. Moniqua wanted her to join the Four Milers, and one of their members set her up in the fancy apartment she's been living in. She was at risk of being thrown out by her mother so felt she had no choice but to obey them or be homeless."

Her gaze settled on me, her indignation clear. "That's when she slipped the note into your room."

Slowly, I nodded, working it out. Lara would have had access to the cam girls' floor. Most of the staff could move freely between the lower floors. It was one of the reasons, other than me knocking the camera out as a joke, that we hadn't been able to pinpoint who'd been there.

"Then she brought a letter to me," Riordan muttered. Our fingers intertwined, and he squeezed my hand. "I'm a fucking idiot for believing it."

I hugged his arm. "No you're not. Moniqua knew exactly what to write." To Genevieve, I asked, "Did Lara confess to listening in on my telephone call in the management office?"

My friend nodded. "She'd been tasked by Moniqua to spy on Arran and Shade whenever she could. She volunteered for extra shifts in stocking up the bars so she could hang around out of hours. She listened in on you and fed it back. Do you know what sucks? She cried as she confessed it to us and said how bad she felt. I can't believe the nerve. I thought we were friends yet she used her position here to set my brother up." She peeked at Riordan. "That's what happened, isn't it?"

He inclined his head. "I got a letter signed by Cassie telling me we were over. I thought it was real."

I thumped my head against him. "I gave her everything she needed to shred us."

Multiple gazes stuck to us. Arran's and Shade's knowing, Genevieve's and Everly's curious.

"So you two are a thing?" Genevieve finally asked.

I huffed. "Why does everyone keep doubting it? I told you all he was mine forever ago. I'm going to marry him."

The two women's eyes rounded.

Riordan squinted down at me.

"What? Ye put me on the back of your bike. That was a proposal. I consider us engaged."

Shade hummed. "Agreed. I hear that's the law."

Everly laughed softly.

I was hooked on the expression in my boyfriend's eyes. It told me he liked my words. It spoke to the need I saw in him over and over again to be claimed. To be loved and adored.

My heart thumped out of time, and I managed to shrug. "By all means ask me formally one day, but this thing is happening."

His tight hold on me was all the answer I needed. It took a solid minute before I could get back into the conversation going on around us.

"Will the cops do anything about the murderer reveal swap?" Genevieve was saying.

Arran gave a single shake of his head. "Dixie's attack didn't even make the press. Nobody knows another attempt was made, and as far as the public is concerned, the dangerous Four Miler gang was responsible, and as a result, they were annihilated. Parts of the city are still burning. All the attention has gone there and on hating the drug dealers who caused the problems."

I peered at the window where the city sparkled beyond the glass. "Then the heat is off us?"

He confirmed it, and some tight kernel of pressure in my chest eased. I hadn't been kidding when I said I loved the warehouse. I was skeleton crew now, and I'd do anything to defend my home and the people who worked here.

Everly asked the question about opening the clubs this evening.

Arran's phone rang while he was replying, and he answered the call and set it on loudspeaker. "Kenney. What do you have for me?"

The chief constable griped about the hours he'd had to work then got to the point. "We still don't have sign-off on entering the church building, though the fire is out. I'll give you a body count when I can. But that knife you turned up, Bronson's one, scored a hit for Rachel Dench with others yet to be identified. It's the hit we needed to put this to bed like where I'm heading now."

My brain joined the dots. The knife in question was the one from when I'd disarmed Moniqua. I'd told Arran to find it when we left the riverside. He must have given the blade a cover story as belonging to Bronson, rather than Moniqua, and handed it to Kenney because the cops had the DNA records of the deceased women to test against.

Rachel Dench was Alisha's real name. Fuck. Moniqua hadn't been entirely delusional.

Arran hung up the call. "Moniqua is the killer. She told the truth."

She had. And with her gone, plus the Four Milers disintegrated, calm had been restored to Deadwater. There were other gangs in the city, smaller ones who would scramble to fill the gap Red and his people had left, but right now, none had the strength to challenge us, and I didn't doubt Arran and Shade would move quickly to put them in their place.

With his arm around me, Riordan tensed up.

I peeked up at him. "Are ye okay?"

"I befriended a monster."

I released a sigh. "I gave her a job."

On the opposite couch, Genevieve shook her head. "I tried to be nice to her. We can't blame ourselves for anything we did as good people trying to be kind." She twisted to peek up at her fiancé. "If Alisha's blood was on that, she can't have cleaned it very well. Almost as if she wanted the trophy of it, you know? I meant to ask, whatever happened to the knife Riordan got caught with that could've had my DNA on it?"

Shade answered for him. "Kenney returned it to us, and we destroyed it. Unlike Moniqua, we run a tight ship."

If Moniqua had done the same, we couldn't have been sure. In her sloppiness, she'd done us a solid.

The next couple of hours, we went through all that had happened. Each death. Everything Moniqua had told us about why she'd killed the women. We said their names. We considered how different their lives would've been if they hadn't fallen victim to a deranged murderer.

We raised a toast to each, and lastly talked about helping Dixie, though Moniqua never gave a reason for hurting her.

After, Arran gave Riordan the night off, though the clubs were busier than ever, and the two of us went back to bed. We ordered in food and hid away. There was so much still to be sorted and considered, but we had answers enough to plague us.

More, we just wanted to feel the relief of being whole. Together. Safe.

While Riordan left the apartment to go collect our dinner, I quickly jumped to put in place a small plan I'd had in my mind for days, ever since he'd bought me furniture. I'd never had a boyfriend before, so I hoped he'd forgive how slow I was to reciprocate.

With glee, I made my choices and clicked through multiple websites. Then I jumped to my family chat—my brothers had all returned home, and the thread was thick with gossip and news—and made my request.

A thumbs-up from the relative in question made me grin. Riordan joining the skeleton crew had been the best event ever. I wanted to mark it as permanent.

Another thought occurred as I finished up. Quickly, I called Shade, knowing he was upstairs from a comment on the group chat with my girls.

He replied. I shot up to his apartment and borrowed what I needed.

Back in our place, Riordan was in the kitchen. He lifted an eyebrow in question. "Where did you go?"

"I had to borrow something."

Nearing, I kept it concealed behind my back.

He held my gaze, some kind of trouble in his eyes. When I reached the kitchen counter, he finally spoke. "Move in with me."

My heart seized up. "Say that again with your clothes off."

A small smile curved his lips, and Riordan stripped his shirt, revealing his hot-as-fuck muscular body. "Move in with me. I want to live with you."

"Ye mean here, right?"

The smile broadened. He undid his jeans and slid them down his legs, kicking them off. "Yes, here. It might be your place, but I wanted to do the asking."

I squeaked in happiness and dove at him, remembering my hidden device at the last second. What had Shade told me? Firm against the skin and fire.

Riordan caught me and dove in for a kiss. "Is that a yes?"

With my arms around him, I tugged up his boxers, set the tracker gun to his arse cheek, and pulled the trigger. It snapped, and he jerked, rearing back in surprise.

I held up the device, grinning as I backed away. "Aye, we live together now. And we can never lose each other again either. The tracker on your bike wasn't enough for me. You're not always on it. I can't bear the thought of ye going missing..."

My words dried up at his expression.

Furious, beautiful, *relieved*, like my love for him gave him a sense of home as much as our apartment did.

"You have no idea what you do to me." He hunted me across the room.

Down the hall. To our bedroom.

I did know. I felt it, too.

We had it to share, and we'd never lose sight of each other again.

54

Riordan

A week on, and life was in danger of returning to peaceful. The city was rebuilding, the clubs operating as normal. Arran, Shade, and Everly had held meetings with the new lead prospect for mayor, a woman named Mary Pressley who Everly used to work with. Apparently Everly had inspired her to battle her anxiety and not let it hold her back.

She was popular with voters. Leading in all the polls.

She'd also praised the warehouse and promised to advocate for the right for women to operate how they wanted to, which I guessed meant she'd taken a bribe, but either way, everyone was happy and no one missed Mayor Makepeace.

I resumed my shifts, though was spending less time on the club floors and more going out with Arran and Shade. Shade particularly wanted me to be geared up to support Cassie in her predator elimination plan. He trained me in taking down targets without being seen, and by the third attempt, told me I was a natural.

Weird way to shine, but I couldn't deny my surge of pride.

On the home front, strange things were happening. Parcels kept being delivered, all addressed to me. Gifts from Cassie. Clothes, all in my size and mostly shades of grey and black, a replacement leather jacket, a fancy sports watch that I freaking loved.

Bike helmets for us both with a comms system. We sent her borrowed one back to its owner then had fun dirty talking on rides through town.

Another notification had come in for a delivery today, not long after we'd woken.

Cassie turned off the telenovela—Alexia and her lover were now happily engaged and expecting a baby—and tugged me with her to the door, her excitement palpable. "This one is too heavy for ye alone."

We went to the lift, and I pulled her into my arms as we descended the floors. "Stop buying me things."

Her eyes sparkled with mischief. "Never."

I tried and failed to keep the smile from my face. I loved the way she loved me. Wholeheartedly. Without restraint. It spilled out into everything she did.

We slowed at the ground floor, and I put my lips to her ear. "Am I going to have to tie you to our bed for you to stop?"

"Ye can try." She led me through the corridors to the main back entrance to the warehouse, all while I pictured her constrained and naked.

Our bed was new, as well. Delivered yesterday and so heavy it had taken several crew members to help me get it upstairs. Cassie had quipped that she wanted our nest to be furnished with a mattress no one else had fucked on, but I suspected it was to gift me a bed of my own for the first time in years. I got with the programme quickly.

I also loved the way she described our home. A nest. Coming back there after a shift gave me a burst of happiness I could never have anticipated. All because of her.

At the back door, Mick stood beside a smart-looking delivery guy, checking paperwork with his forehead lined. "I wasn't told to expect this."

Cassie breezed past them. "My bad. I wanted it to be a surprise. Can ye show us what ye brought?" she asked the delivery guy.

He followed us outside. In the car park, a huge black SUV gleamed in one of the parking spaces. A chunky and masculine ride with a silver grille and darkened rear windows. Cassie made jazz hands at it.

Confused, I tilted my head. "I don't understand."

"Struan said that your ride was held together by, how did he put it, Sellotape and prayers? That sounded dangerous. I upgraded ye."

My jaw dropped. "You bought me a car?"

She beamed. "You needed something more appropriate for work. Can ye blame me?"

Beyond her, the delivery guy wore an expression of shock I imagine reflected my own.

The car was spectacular. I'd thought about how I'd support her if I needed to snatch a body and deliver it somewhere she'd asked. My ancient, knackered Rover was out of the question. Borrowing one of the skeleton crew vehicles had been my solution. This was...

"I'm speechless," I finally managed.

She peeked up at me. "In a bad way?"

At last, my muscles unlocked, and I brought her in for

a hug. "Never. You could never do anything bad. Thank you."

"Yay! Let's take it for a spin. You're already insured."

"You're a whirlwind." Still, I took the keys and helped her inside.

We drove out into the city. The damn car was a dream with every high-end feature she could've arranged in such a short space of time.

"You look so fucking beautiful perched in my passenger seat," I told her.

Cassie preened. Other than when wielding a blade, she was at her happiest when making others happy, and I loved her for it.

By unspoken agreement, I took us out of the city limits and into the countryside. While the sun set, I parked in a lane and ordered Cassie to climb in the back. With rough urgency, I tore her clothes from her and buried my face between her legs until she was screaming, then I fucked her more slowly, christening the car with the first of what would be countless fucks on its plush seats.

On our route home, we passed the edge of what had been Four Milers' territory.

Cassie took a breath. "Can we go see?"

I turned the car for a macabre tour into the ruined neighbourhood. At the church, I pulled over and idled the engine.

Cassie gazed at the cordoned-off site with big eyes. "They've cleared the rubble. I bet they've got the bodies out. Do ye think there's news on who they can identify?"

"I don't know. Arran can find out."

Horror passed through me again at the thought of

how easily it could have been her, and I unclipped her to bring her to my lap.

"I would've died without ye finding me in that lane," she said.

"I can't even think about it without my stomach turning."

"Can we go home?"

I kissed her as a way of answering to show her just how fucked up over it I still felt. Our enemies might be dead, but it would take a long time until the memories faded.

We returned to the warehouse, hunting down Arran and Genevieve.

In the management office, Arran called Kenney. "How many bodies did you pull?"

"How the fuck are you always one step ahead of me?" the chief constable griped. "We got thirteen charred lumps from the basement. No others found in the building. Forensics gave an informal identification for six, Reginald Rose, Sydney Stanley." He rattled off another three names, none of which were familiar. "Last is Adam Walker. RIP your loss and all that."

Arran hung up on him. He murmured something soft and cupped my sister's face.

Genevieve gazed up at him. "I'm glad he didn't name Convict. That still means something, doesn't it?"

"He hasn't come home."

"That doesn't mean he's one of those unidentified bodies, does it? There's still hope."

Sadness flickered in his eyes. He blinked it away in a practice I was too familiar with myself. I'd done it for years when protecting my sister from misery she didn't need to share. "I'm sorry about your dad."

"Don't do that. Don't cut me out."

Arran's eyes shuttered closed, and he touched his forehead to hers. "Okay. I'm fucking devastated. I don't want to believe it, but faith is hard to come by in this world, and he's been gone for too long."

I glanced away, tuning them out for the private moment I didn't need to share. I only tuned back in when Gen said her father's name.

"I'm okay. I expected it. I feel sad for Adam but I also know he did this to himself." My sister came to me and squeezed my arm. "I don't think I could ever forgive him for how he treated you, and with the way he was ready to join a rival gang, he could've given them the power to hurt us. Imagine if he'd succeeded and took Bronson's job. Imagine what information he could have shared on us both. This is going to sound terrible, but like Everly with her dad, I'm not sorry that he's dead, only on what we missed out on at his hands."

I felt the same. For her sake, I'd tolerated him. For my own, I'd long stopped missing the father I'd never had.

Cassie tilted her head as if suddenly working something out. "Reginald Rose, is that Red's real name?"

Arran inclined his head.

She smiled. "No wonder he shifted gears with his nickname. I wish I'd known that while he was alive."

The two of them chatted about it, and Gen led me aside.

In a low whisper, she said, "The news brings me neatly to something else I wanted to talk to you about. As you know, I don't want a formal wedding, but Everly is handling it all for us and talked me into a first-sight kind of deal at the registry office. You know, so Arran sees me in a dress and hopefully gets all teary. Will you stand at my side?"

She didn't want to be given away but instead wanted to bring me closer.

My throat clogged. "I'd love to."

Genevieve hugged me, and I scrubbed my knuckles over her hair, just to be annoying.

Then I had work to do, and during that, another sister to find.

On my request, Everly joined me in the CCTV office where I was taking my lunchbreak with Manny. Shade escorted her down then stood at the door, his expression conveying how he didn't trust her being anywhere out of his sight, but after a minute, he managed to leave her with a gruff request for us to be watchful.

My newest, older sister sat neatly with her hands in her lap. Her gaze left Manny who was on a call, and settled on me. "It's really nice for just the two of us to talk. Do you want the latest on the house?"

I shook my head in the negative. "Favourite colour?"

Everly blinked. "This week, a bold red stripe because Christmas is the next celebration I have on my mind after Arran and Genevieve's wedding. Yours?"

"Blue." Like Cassie's eyes. "Favourite movie growing up?"

A smile stole over her lips. "*The Princess Diaries*. How about yours?"

We talked until we ran out of questions. About her baby, about how we would've been friends if we'd known each other as kids. I even indulged her subtle query about if I had a big party on the horizon and would I let her do the planning.

After, I hunted down Cassie.

My emotions had been on a rollercoaster the past few days, and I needed her.

But when I entered the apartment, she was on the sofa with a stranger standing over her. A big guy with extensive tattoos down both arms.

And in his hand was a gun.

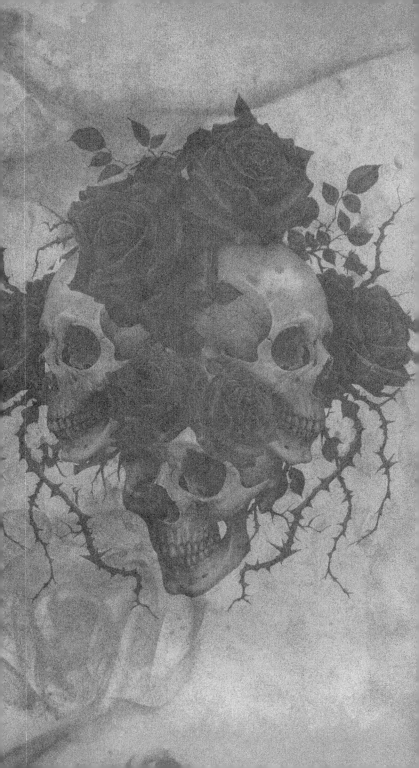

55

Cassie

The door clicked, and I leapt up to dance over and hug Riordan hello.

His embrace swallowed me, but his gaze stuck on the man holding the tattoo gun.

I gestured between them. "Rio, meet Camden, the only one of my brothers you haven't met yet. Cam, this is the boyfriend everyone's been gossiping about."

Riordan's hostile expression dropped, and he visibly relaxed. He extended a fist to bump Camden's. "How's it going?"

Camden smirked, the motion twisting the deep scar he carried down one side of his face. "I'm just going to take a second to get over the fact that one, my baby sister has a boyfriend, and two, that he stuck around even after meeting Struan. Nice to finally put a face to a name. My daughter said ye were big and scary, but I can already tell Cass runs rings around ye."

Rio hung up his leather jacket and mooched over. "Is your daughter the mini-me of Cassie?"

"Aye, Wren. They're two peas in a pod, except Wren is

a little less stabby. So far."

My boyfriend laughed and settled next to me on the sofa, and another piece of my happiness cemented in. At my home, he'd been angry at me, with good reason because kidnapping was somewhat out there in terms of courtship rituals, yet even then he'd paid attention and mapped out parts of my life. He'd remembered them. I exhaled joy made of dangerous actions and a wonderful man.

Riordan peered at Camden's setup. "What are you doing?"

"Cass wanted another tattoo. I refuse to let any of my kin get work done by another artist after the shitshow of Jamieson's last solo attempt."

Riordan's eyebrows rose. "What happened?"

"He wanted flames on his ankle and went to some fucker in Edinburgh. It took me hours to fix the piece-of-crap design he came home whining about."

I held out my arm so my brother could resume perfecting the stencil he'd created. "Camden runs his own studio and was booked up, hence why Burn went rogue. In a few days, I'm taking you to the Great House for dinner so you can experience the craziness that is my whole family in one place at once. Feel free to use that anecdote to shame Jamieson good."

Camden smirked and got busy tattooing my upper arm with the design—a skull with a plain bandanna over its lower face. It was the logo for the warehouse, and informally, for the skeleton crew. A flip of the way the crew would wear skeleton print bandannas over their faces. Arran had it, and Shade probably did, too, though he had an awful lot of skulls on his skin, so I wasn't sure.

"That is fucking fire," Riordan admired when it was done.

I nudged him. "If ye want it, too, Arran gave permission."

He blinked. "He did?"

"I asked because I wanted this for ye. I went first to show that it was okay."

Slowly, he nodded, and we swapped places so Camden could do his thing. Riordan needed this. He needed to be tied to people and place. To not be an outsider looking in. In time, he'd maybe feel secure with all we had, but even then, I'd show him every day just how important he was.

When the work was done, Camden packed up. "I'll head home. Riordan, glad to meet ye, man. Let me know if ye need any more ink. Maybe 'I love Cassie' across your chest."

I snorted. "Bet."

Riordan chuffed, and his lips curled in a smile. "Okay."

My brother and I both stared at him.

Camden wrinkled his nose. "I was joking. Life lesson. Never tattoo a lover's name on ye. It's awkward as fuck if ye break up. I refuse to do it for clients."

I pulled an incredulous expression. "Explain your wife's name on your pecs in amongst that huge sweeping pattern that covers half your skin."

Camden rolled his eyes. "I'm the artist and the exception that proves the rule."

Riordan tilted his head. "What's the pattern?"

My brother brightened. "It's this sweeping rush of lines. Her name is Breeze, and it's inspired by her."

He showed him, the two of them cooing over good

artwork. I sat back and watched, my chin on my hands and nothing but good feelings inside me.

"What could I have to represent Cass?"

"That's for ye to work out. Get a concept, and I'll turn it into a design." Camden hugged me, slapped Riordan's hand, then left us for the long drive home.

Riordan collected me in his arms and carried me to our bedroom. "Maybe a pile of bodies with a vicious woman standing on top with her arms up in celebration?" he mused, stripping me. "Or your face with a knife between your teeth?" On the mattress, he settled me in the middle, taking care not to touch my fresh, wrapped tattoo, the twin to his that I knew he'd wear with pride.

From a drawer, he produced a packet and tore it open, revealing new handcuffs. I gawked at them.

"Padded ones so they won't hurt." He clicked them around my wrists, giving me no chance to pull away as he extended my hands above my head and fastened me to a pillar on the headboard. Then he moved to my ankles, spreading my legs to tie me off to the bottom corners of the bed.

Not that long ago, this would've shown me he was angry, but not now. All I anticipated was pleasure. And my sweet, romantic boy delivered. He licked and sucked every part of me, leaving me squirming and cursing him because I couldn't grab him and take my turn.

It worked for us, though. Taking a position between my spread legs, he made me come again and again before he fucked me, then he started over, cleaning me with his tongue and showing me exactly how he cared.

Love was exhausting. Love was exhilarating. When he finally released me to fall asleep on his chest, I did so imagining all the ways I could show him how he made me feel.

*M*orning, well, afternoon, as we never got up before four p.m., I had a couple of text messages waiting on my phone.

The first was from Genevieve, finally giving me the news that Dixie was allowing visitors, and that we could go together in a couple of hours' time. The second was far less anticipated.

At long last, my uncle had messaged back.

> **Patrick:** How do I know you're for real?

I showed Riordan then hit the number to dial the man.

It rang for a while, but at last, he answered. "Yeah?"

"Ye asked how ye could be sure I'm real. I don't give a fuck about that. I'm not interested in ye or your life. What I do want to know is what happened to Cassandra. That's it."

It probably wasn't the best way to impress the man, but to my surprise, begrudgingly, Patrick started talking.

He told me a little of their childhood, and how

Cassandra had been a rebel at every stage, making their father despair.

"There's a place for lassies in our world, and it isn't trying to wheedle their way into decision-making. She had one job, and that was to get married and breed the next generation of boys." Patrick gave a mocking laugh. "She didn't even get that right in her bid for freedom if all she produced was another girl."

I ignored the jibe. "Did your father kill her?"

Patrick huffed. "No idea what you're talking about, sweetheart."

It meant he had. Poor woman.

I hung up on the relative I had no more interest in and hugged the boyfriend I wanted it all with. "If my grandfather ever gets out of jail, I'll kill him for her. She deserved better."

"I'll be right by your side as you do."

*W*e left the apartment, meeting up with Arran and Genevieve on the way out of the warehouse.

I wrinkled my nose at Arran. "I've forgiven ye for not telling me about Bronson. Just."

He pursed his lips. "I promise never to keep something like that from you again."

"Good. Does that mean I'm inner circle now, too?"

The skeleton crew's boss sighed. "Like I ever had any choice when it came to you. But yes, you're on the team."

Amused, I skipped along. "Sweet. So why do we think Bronson confessed?"

"He wanted the end to come. He knew he'd never run the Four Milers, both from what we told him and the rumbles he'd picked up from his own people. In retrospect, we should've dug deeper."

"I get it. He was the obvious culprit. Next time, we'll all be more savvy."

"Next time?" Genevieve enquired.

"Think I'm disbanding the Skeleton Girls Detective Agency? No chance. In a city like this, some other crime will need solving, and I want us there with the string and detective wall, ready to solve it."

She bumped my shoulder and grinned.

We drove out, and the closer we got to the Deadwater's hospital, the more my stomach tightened. I'd waited here for hours when Dixie had been in surgery but not been back since. She hadn't allowed it.

At last, I'd get to see the friend I'd almost lost.

Inside the huge, fifties-style building, Genevieve linked her arm through mine, and we followed brightly lit corridors to the ward Dixie was in, nerves affecting us both. In a private room, organised by the skeleton crew, a tiny figure curled up under white and blue blankets. My fingers shook as I approached.

Dixie peeked up at us, her neck thick with white bandages. Her blonde hair was ratty against the pillow and her skin almost as pale as the sheets. "You came."

Her voice was rough. To my horror, tears formed in her eyes.

I settled beside her bed and carefully picked up her hand. "We've been waiting to visit for days and days."

One of those tears spilled. "I didn't want anyone to see me like this. But I also wanted to give you the chance to quietly slide out of my DMs."

From beside me, Genevieve cooed. "Why would we ever want to do that? You're our friend."

Dixie used her free hand to wipe her cheek. "Oh, hun, you don't have to pretend. It's nice of you to come and all, but we aren't in the same world anymore. I don't have any expectations."

I tilted my head. "What are ye talking about? We're just waiting for ye to be released, but we have so many plans to help your recovery."

Genevieve nodded urgently. "The nurse said you'll be able to leave soon. If you want to go home, we've organised a nursing service to be there as much as you need them. If you want to stay at the warehouse, we'll set up a bedroom for you and have the nurses come there. Whatever you need, we'll make it happen."

Her gaze darted between us. "Am I high, or are you two just delulu? Ain't no way I can work there anymore." Her fingers ghosted over the bandage at her throat, not quite touching the white strips. "There's no way I can heal enough to come back to work. I know I'm out of a job. You're kind to offer, but I'm done."

My eyebrows merged, and Genevieve wore an equally confused expression.

Genevieve spoke first. "Of course you're coming back. We want you there. You will always have a job."

"Oh, hun, that isn't up to us. Who's going to buy a girl with a torn-up throat? I'll move on. I have to." Her gaze locked on to mine. "I heard talk that the killer was caught. Please. I need to know because my memory is shaky as hell."

I swapped a glance with Genevieve, wishing I had any kind of bedside manner so I knew how to make her feel better. Slowly, I nodded. "I'll tell ye everything, but let Genevieve brush out your hair and maybe plait it. Does that sound good?"

Dixie agreed, and in low tones, I told her about the suspicions after the capture of Bronson, the public's celebration that the killings were over and the murderer caught, then my discovery of her after her attack. I glossed over the worst of the details. If she asked, I'd fill her in, but she seemed content not to hear it. She smiled at my sworn need for vengeance. At my explanation over Moniqua being the real killer, a small frown marred her pretty brow, but she nodded all the same.

"Moniqua's dead now?"

I exhaled. "I killed her myself, and I made sure to name every woman she'd hurt as I did it. She went to her grave regretting the fact she'd ever touched a hair on your head."

Dixie cupped my hand. "Badass." She coughed, the sound wheezing. "Shit, that still hurts. I'm real sorry but I think I need more meds and they'll send me to sleep. Do you think...could you come back another day?"

My heart hurt. "I'll be back tomorrow as early as they'll let me in. I'll bring ye a nice dressing gown and some pretty pyjamas. Is there anything else you'd like?"

Dixie's eyes watered again. For over a week, our friend had lived in pain and despair. I hated how she'd assumed we'd drop her.

"Maybe something to read? I probably look like shit, so a touch of blush?"

She coughed again and moaned at the pain. I hit the button to summon the nurse, and we left her with promises to return.

At the end of the corridor, Arran waited. Behind, Riordan stalked along, both having watched over us on our visit. Dixie wanted love and had only found misery. She'd been let down by the world and had expected that everyone who cared about her would leave because she now carried a scar. I wouldn't. I'd do everything to bring my friend back.

"I'm going to offer her a job working for me," I told Genevieve. "If she doesn't want to go back to her old career, I'll give her a new one."

If Dixie accepted, my predator elimination program had its first employee, and I suspected she might enjoy the work as much as I intended to.

Back at the warehouse, Shade flagged me down. "Busy?"

"Nope. What have we got on?"

"A wee jaunt out to the boathouse."

I rubbed my hands together, needing the emotional release. "I'm happy to assist."

The enforcer grinned. "This one is all yours."

"Who?"

"Roache."

Shock stopped me in my tracks. "Piers Roache is still alive?"

"Just about. Do the man a favour and read him his rights then send him on his way, aye?"

I cackled. "Thank ye for saving him for me. This is going to be fun."

Revenge for Riordan, for Everly, and for every other person hurt by bad men was going to be served, and I was just the girl for the job.

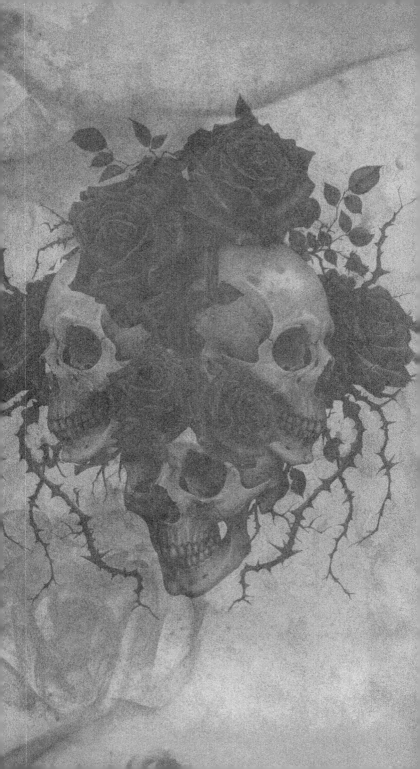

Epilogue

Dixie

Memory was a funny thing. My images of the night I was attacked were sketchy at best, mostly made of mental pictures Cassie had given me rather than anything real.

Probably a good thing, because remembering being doped up then cut by some bitch with a big-dick complex had the chance to drive me out of my tiny mind.

It...didn't sit right either. Something felt off, though I couldn't pinpoint what exactly. A shape. A figure. Harsh words I couldn't place.

Moniqua had confessed, and that was all that mattered. There was evidence on her knife, though not of me, which had settled everyone's doubt.

I'd let it settle mine, too. I had a long history of squashing bad memories, and this was just going to be crushed in the don't-think-about-it pile.

I left my follow-up appointment with the hospital's plastic surgeon and stepped into the cool corridor. Manny waited downstairs to take me home, the poor guy overprotective as hell since he'd been the last one to see me after dropping me off at home. A month had passed since I had woken up to a ruined career and certainty that my life was over. Misery passed over me, and I shook it off. Pain meds were a bitch. They'd made me depressed, and I'd kicked them to the kerb as soon as I could.

After healing enough to handle the world, I was ready to go back to the warehouse and tentatively agree to a new job.

I was trying to be happy. I'd been through worse than this.

No, I swallowed and faced facts. Everything I'd been through in the past, I'd been able to pack away in that box in my head. No one else would ever know from my outward appearance. With the deep scar across my throat and the puckered skin where it healed, I was shit out of luck in continuing that plan of delusion.

Even with surgery, it could never be completely erased. For the rest of my life, anyone who looked at me would see that first and me after. I'd made my name on being perfect. Any guy now would run a mile.

It wasn't just my clientele that I was miserable over.

I hadn't told Cassie, but I'd had a small thing for one of the skeleton crew, Arran's intercept guy who came and went from the warehouse with some regularity, and whose solid form had caught my attention and not let go. In another world, I would have maybe got brave enough to ask him out. Not now. That part of me was as dead and buried as I had almost been.

Heat pricked my eyes, but I forced away the sadness, ready to go home.

I liked the sound of Cassie's job. Got all excited over helping her track down men who deserved pain, though for more reasons than she knew.

At the end of the ward, a burly nurse assisted a tall man who was walking with an IV stand and clearly struggling. One arm was heavily bandaged, and his leg was in a cast like he'd broken it and was only just back on his feet.

I squinted at him, recognition flickering as I examined each feature. The hair that I'd remembered being a lot shorter. The snake tattoo around one wrist. It took me a moment to work out what I was seeing, and for several heartbeats, I didn't believe myself.

I was looking at a ghost.

I'd heard all of Cassie's stories about the destruction of the Four Milers' brothel. She'd nearly died in that church and would've if it hadn't been for the undercover member of the skeleton crew who'd saved her ass at the cost of his own life.

The man stared at me for a moment then continued past, his helper giving words of gentle encouragement over his slow progress. His pain was clear, even if any recognition of me wasn't.

Convict was alive, after all.

The End.

Obsessed with the skeleton crew? Reunite with Convict, Dixie, Tyler, and more in the next series of Deadwater murder mysteries. Order now.

https://www.amazon.com/dp/B0DMP2PWCD

Want to read a bonus scene with Genevieve and Arran's shotgun wedding and to discover if Shade really is related to Cassie? Go to jolievines.com/extras

(Downloading any free content from me adds you to my reader list.)

ACKNOWLEDMENTS

Dear reader,

We did it! The series is complete, and the murderer unmasked.

Did you guess right? Did your answer change throughout the series? Jump into my Facebook reader group and let me know in the spoiler thread >>> https://www.facebook.com/groups/JoliesFallHardFans

Riordan and Cassie are one happy couple, joining the other two pairings from the series. There's a series bonus epilogue where you can see all couples living out their happiness. Link at the end of the story.

Who do you want to read about next?

There's a theme of facing your fears throughout this series. Genevieve is scared of the dark so forces herself to endure it. Everly locks away her fears and lives an unhappy existence until she takes a risk on Connor. Then we get to Cassie. Everything scares her. She does it anyway. Walking the ledge. Taking on awful men. It's a lesson for all of us (though perhaps not so extreme) - do the thing that scares you if it's stopping you from reaching a goal. If it's safe and others are doing it, why aren't you? We all have something like this that we don't want to face, that we convince ourselves (or worse - allow others to convince us) we can't do. Find the support. Break down the tasks. Tell me when you hit that mark and I'll celebrate with you (from a woman who learned to drive at age 40, so I know).

Cassie's research into abusers is based on data from the commissioner of the Metropolitan police. Her figures don't include women as part of those perpetrator numbers, but those are a tiny percentage of the estimates.

One in seven men is alarming. Not that she's encouraging vigilantism, but the Cassies and Shades of the world would have their work cut out for them, even with the most conservative view of this data.

You can read more in this Guardian article which summarises some of the early findings https://www.theguardian.com/society/article/2024/jun/04/met-chief-says-millions-of-men-are-danger-to-women-and-girls-in-england-and-wales

Thank you to everyone who has taken the Body Count books to heart. I've never had a series take off so spectacularly (we hit number one in all Kindle books in the US and Canada, baby), and it's been the most wonderful experience. The interest level from readers and all across the entertainment industry has been sky high.

I have the best readers in the world! Thank you for loving my stories.

Thanks also go to Liz, my PA and friend. To Katie who drafts my newsletters and manages my social media. To my beta readers Elle, Sara, Shellie, and Lori. To narrators Zara Hampton-Brown, Shane East, Allie Rose, and Lucas Webley and the production team at Dark Star. Also to Erika for proofing things my end.

The incredible character art was created by Amanda Desilets on Instagram. Emmy Ellis edited to perfection and Lori and Patricia proofread beautifully. Cleo Moran produced the stunning interior files and graphics. Natasha created the gorgeous hot guy covers. Qamber Designs made the skull paperbacks which are chef's-kisses good. Thank you, all.

To my ARC and Street team, hugs to everyone for promoting the ass off this book!

Lastly, to N&M, my family. You both supported me in every way possible, including feeding me (Mr V) and delivering hugs (mini-V) when I needed them.

What a fabulous series this has been.

See you again in the next Deadwater murder scene.

Love, Jolie

Secret code: answer (do not look if you want to work it out!)

BROTHER'S BANE.

ALSO BY JOLIE VINES

Marry the Scot series
1) Storm the Castle
2) Love Most, Say Least
3) Hero
4) Picture This
5) Oh Baby

Wild Scots series
1) Hard Nox
2) Perfect Storm
3) Lion Heart
4) Fallen Snow
5) Stubborn Spark

Wild Mountain Scots series
1) Obsessed
2) Hunted
3) Stolen
4) Betrayed
5) Tormented

Dark Island Scots series
1) Ruin
2) Sin
3) Scar
4) Burn

McRae Bodyguards
1) Touch Her and Die
2) Save Her from Me
3) Take Her from You
4) Protect Her from Them

Body Count
1) Arran's Obsession
2) Connor's Claim
3) Riordan's Revenge

Standalones
Cocky Kilt:
a Cocky Hero Club Novel
Race You:
An Office-Based Enemies-to-Lovers Romance
Fight For Us:
a Second-Chance Military Romantic Suspense

ABOUT THE AUTHOR

JOLIE VINES is a romance author who lives in the UK with her husband and son.

Jolie loves her heroes to be one-woman guys.

Whether they are a brooding pilot (Gordain in Hero), a wrongfully imprisoned rich boy (Sebastian in Lion Heart), or a tormented twin (Max in Betrayed), they will adore their heroine until the end of time.

Her favourite pastime is wrecking emotions, then making up for it by giving her imaginary friends deep and meaningful happily ever afters.

Have you found all of Jolie's Scots?

Visit her page on Amazon
http://amazon.com/Jolie-Vines/e/B07MKS5JSC

and join her ever active Fall Hard Facebook group.

https://www.facebook.com/groups/JoliesFallHardFans

43236541R00331